W9-BLS-899

WILD EAST

Arkhangelsk
Gulf of Finland
St. Petersburg
Tallinn
ESTONIA
RUSSIAN FEDERATION
Novgorod
Riga
LATVIA
Moscow
Baltic Sea
LITHUANIA
Vitsyebsk
Orel
Vilnius
Minsk
Gdansk
BELARUS
POLAND
Babruysk
Warsaw
Poznan
Brest
Homyel
Lodz
Wroclaw
Kiev
Prague
Krakow
Kharkiv
CZECH REPUBLIC
Lviv
UKRAINE
Volgograd
SLOVAKIA
MOLDOVA
Bratislava
Budapest
Chisinau
Donetsk
Ljubljana
HUNGARY
Szeged
ROMANIA
Odesa
Rostov-na-Donu
Astrakhan
OVENIA
Pecs
Timisoara
Zagreb
Belgrade
Bucharest
CROATIA
Sarajevo
SERBIA & MONTENEGRO
Constanta
Black Sea
Grozny
BULGARIA
Varna
BOSNIA & HERZEGOVINA
Sofia
GEORGIA
Plovdiv
Tbilisi
Tirana
Skopje
MACEDONIA
ARMENIA
AZERB
Yerevan
ALBANIA
Mediterranean Sea

Norilsk
RUSSIAN FEDERATION
Yekaterinburg
Omsk
Novosibirsk
Pavlodar
Astana
KAZAKHSTAN
Aral Sea
Almaty
Nukus
Bishkek
Tashkent
KYRGYZSTAN
UZBEKISTAN
TURKMENISTAN
Samarkand
Bukhara
Dushanbe
TAJIKISTAN
Ashgabat

WILD EAST

Stories from the Last Frontier

EDITED AND WITH AN INTRODUCTION

BY **BORIS FISHMAN**

Justin, Charles & Co. Publishers
BOSTON

First edition 2003

This is a work of fiction. All characters and events portrayed in this work are either fictitious or are used fictitiously.

Library of Congress Cataloging-in-Publication Data is available.

ISBN 1-932112-15-4

Published in the United States by
Justin, Charles & Co., Publishers,
20 Park Plaza, Boston, Massachusetts 02116
www.justincharlesbooks.com

Distributed by National Book Network, Lanham, Maryland
www.nbnbooks.com

10 9 8 7 6 5 4 3 2 1

Printed in the United States of America

Contents

Acknowledgments x

Introduction by BORIS FISHMAN xi

Shylock on the Neva GARY SHTEYNGART 1

The Ambassador's Son TOM BISSELL 21

Wenceslas Square ARTHUR PHILLIPS 43

Gika WENDELL STEAVENSON 77

Spleen JOSIP NOVAKOVICH 97

Fatherland ALEKSANDAR HEMON 113

The Subjunctive Mood PAUL GREENBERG 159

The Condor MILJENKO JERGOVIĆ 181

Babylon Revisited Redux JOHN BECKMAN 187

The Bottle CHARLOTTE HOBSON 215

The English House THOMAS DE WAAL 235

Hiroshima VLADIMIR SOROKIN 255

Contributors' Notes 263

Acknowledgments

This book is a labor of love. (Truly: Its gestation coincided with the arrival of children to two of the contributors, Oscar Monroe Phillips to Arthur Phillips and Clio Tatyana Marsden to Charlotte Hobson.) It exists because a dozen very talented, successful writers, and the literary agents who represent them, always made its benefit their first consideration. My first thanks goes to them.

The idea originated with publisher Stephen Hull and editor Kim Hjelmgaard, the intrepid duo at Justin, Charles and Co. They are serious, adventurous readers, and they have a project of great promise on their hands in Justin, Charles. Their steering and counsel has been invaluable, and I am deeply grateful to them both, as well as to Carmen Mitchell and Karen Conner. Thanks to Tom Bissell for sending the project in my direction, and also for his unequivocal support and genuine friendship. His faith, thoughtfulness, and encouragement are responsible for not a little of this book's progress, as well as my own. Thanks to Wendell Steavenson, who wrote her story while on assignment in Tehran, between interviews with Iranian victims of Iraqi chemical attacks and amid preparations for war. Thanks to Tom de Waal, who found time to talk about Chechnya even as he traveled the States in support of his new book. His frantic schedule never compromised his good humor or poise. Thanks to Paul Greenberg, who, besides composing a standout contribution, has adopted this project and labored on its behalf on many fronts.

Thanks are due as well to Radhika Jones at Grand Street and Jamey Gambrell for helping Vladimir Sorokin make a long-overdue trip into English. Thanks also to Nicole Aragi, whose patience and generosity were considerable. To Jill Schoolman at Seven Stories and Archipelago Press, for mediating with Bosnia and Croatia. To Julie Barer, who helped arrange so much and is a kindred spirit. I had many conversations about post-Soviet Russian literature with Natasha Perova, the co-editor of the Glas New Russian Writing series, in Moscow, and I am extremely thankful for her counsel and efforts. Elizabeth Van Lear, of Synopsis Literary Agency, was an indispensable intermediary with several Russian authors. Alex Zucker, who is a crack Czech translator, has been a much-appreciated interlocutor, with regard to the book but also all matters Slavophile. The liaising of Thomas Hoelzl at Eggers & Landwehr in Germany was of great benefit. I appreciated greatly the advice of Howard Sidenberg, of Twisted Spoon Press, in Prague, as well.

Without the leniency and graciousness of my colleagues at *The New Yorker*, this book wouldn't have been much more than a great idea. I have never looked forward to work as I have for the past two years, and it's largely on account of the group there. David Remnick was a generous adviser throughout, and Deborah Treisman provided guidance as well. Liesl Schillinger has been an enthusiastic advocate and an inspiration. I know few people of so many talents. She brought Charlotte Hobson and Wendell Steavenson to my attention, she translated reams of German, she knows every single publication in the world in which this book deserves a review. And if the French in Paul Greenberg's story is accurate, we have Gita Daneshjoo (and Paul) to thank.

I owe more than I can convey in handsome phrases to the mentorship and friendship of Olga Litvak, Jacob Soll, Stephen Kotkin, Anthony Grafton, and Caryl Emerson.

Most importantly, I owe thanks to my loving family, which has without a complaint absolved most of my responsibilities for the past year. They are the kindest, most giving, and most patient people I know, and it is from them that I take my example.

Boris Fishman
New York City
April 2003

Introduction

Wild East is a cliché. *Stories from the Last Frontier* is not. Eastern Europe was America's last — that is, most recent — frontier for more than a decade. Before the Taliban was swept from power in Afghanistan and Saddam Hussein's regime brought down in Iraq, Eastern Europe (a term which, for the sake of brevity, I mean to include the former Soviet Union, though it is understandably inadequate for the USSR's arctic and Asian outposts) was the most recent example of a place previously inhospitable to Westerners transformed into a place restricted to none. But it's unlikely that the fall of Kabul and Baghdad will change this. Speaking crudely, the average American is an Atlanticist: for him, culture extends only as far as Europe, and exotic environs like Afghanistan and Iraq hold no lessons beyond theme-park primitivism. Perhaps expatriation is the surest confirmation of this. There are few places in the world that would induce late-twentieth- and early-twenty-first century Americans to migrate en masse, and most of them, I would venture, are in the Old World. Eastern Europe was its only corner to resist normalized contact with the West, but with the historic collapse of Communism just over a decade ago, it became the last — the latest, but also the final — frontier.

The idea of Eastern Europe as an outpost though, paradoxically, is both obsolete and uniquely timely, both an historical artifact at a museum exhibit and the headline of the morning newspaper. It's obsolete because Eastern Europe has undergone a dramatic transformation, and many of its corners betray little evidence of oppression by a totalitarian occupier, a scant fifteen years after its demise. With notable exceptions such as Belarus and the Central Asian states, its nations have, with varying degrees of success, pursued courses of democratization and economic liberalization that are as disparate as they are seemingly irrevocable. The business of statecraft — and the statecraft of business — has usurped the fluster of revolution, and the talk today is of garbage pickups instead of gulags, democratic debate instead of dissidents. The persecution of the Communist era is as deceptively distant as the lawless abandon that succeeded its downfall.

But the notion of Eastern Europe as a frontier is also timely because, for all the distinctions between the Middle East and Eastern Europe, the liberation experience of the latter offers invaluable lessons, not only for Afghanistan and Iraq, but also for the United States, as it casts its net over an increasingly recalcitrant world. The appearance, in recent years, of works of fiction and nonfiction about Eastern Europe by the authors featured in this book has created a felicitous opportunity for the men and women who conduct this nation's affairs, and they would do well to take stock of the contents here.

Perhaps it isn't a pipe dream to imagine George W. Bush's famously binary morals blurring after consulting, in this volume, "Wenceslas Square" by Arthur Phillips, a consideration of the uncertain terrain between duty and feeling in 1988 Prague, and of the futility of officialdom in times of epic change. Perhaps it's not absurd to think Donald Rumsfeld would find much of value in the limited-engagement tactics of Paul Greenberg's "The Subjunctive Mood," which takes the view that Eastern Europe reveals itself to foreigners not through grandiose pursuits of History and Truth, but through the microcosm of human relationships. Perhaps Colin Powell would be moved to rethink the mandate of our embassies abroad after perusing Tom Bissell's "The Ambassador's

Son," a hilarious chronicle of expat excess in the relentlessly forgiving atmosphere of an orphaned nation. Condoleezza Rice might adopt a less sanguine view of Russia's war in Chechnya after apprising herself of its victims in Thomas de Waal's "The English House." Dick Cheney might glean some lessons about keeping a low profile from John Beckman's "Babylon Revisited Redux," where one of Cheney's predecessors, James Danforth Quayle, decides that the post-September 11 world suffers without his diplomatic gifts and emerges from retirement for one last crack at the forces of evil. And if all else fails, John Ashcroft would be sure to find relief in Josip Novakovich's "Spleen," a tale of the ordinariness of cruelty and the salvation of love. All six, I think, would be baffled in unhelpful ways by Vladimir Sorokin's nuclear fantasy "Hiroshima," though, so perhaps that wouldn't be the best place to start.

Facetiousness aside, *Wild East* also proposes that Westerners are more thoughtful and adventurous spirits than I've allowed. Thomas de Waal ventured to Chechnya at a time when only one other Westerner resided in its capital, and has continued his tour of the Caucasus's least familiar reaches with his new book *Black Garden,* about the Azeri-Armenian conflict over the disputed enclave of Nagorno Karabakh. Tom Bissell volunteered with the Peace Corps in Uzbekistan and crisscrossed the nation while researching his travel book, *Chasing the Sea,* about the ecological catastrophe that is the Aral Sea. For good measure, he made a detour in Afghanistan at the height of the war against the Taliban there. Charlotte Hobson is the rare expat whose time abroad was spent far beyond the capital, its result one of the most lyrical and insightful works of non-fiction about post-Soviet Russia of the last decade, *Black Earth City.* Paul Greenberg owns the rare distinction of having taught seminars on management skills in Tajikistan and having produced the highest-rated news-magazine show in Bosnia, as well as programs on conflict resolution in the Caucasus and the former Yugoslavia, two places that surely needed it.

Most of the Western protagonists in their work are the antagonist kind, which is to say they are oblivious, self-absorbed, and presumptuous about the lands they have come to visit. Whether these are caricatures of the frat boys and sorority sisters the authors observed in Prague and Budapest, or, more encouragingly, amalgams of those characters and themselves, this all-too-fallible group does deserve a credit beyond the indifferent masses who remained at home. Flawed as their perceptions were, they were called by a genuine curiosity, by the idea that Eastern Europe, victim of one upheaval after another throughout the twentieth century, held out insights that life at home, largely sheltered from catastrophe by geography and the can-do ethic of democratic capitalism, did not.

I'd like to think *Wild East* also disproves the charge that expat fiction about Eastern Europe is exclusively a male enterprise. In a review in *The Nation* of six expat novels, all by men, Eliot Borenstein wrote that, "Ultimately, the post-Communist expat's story is a fundamentally male narrative of conquest, submission and coming of age. The expat experience was a perfect juncture between self-congratulatory Western machismo and the cultural anxieties of the cold war's losers and victims. One of the commonplaces of the post-Soviet media, for example, is that Russia (always represented as female) has fallen prey to Western despoilers, who ravage the country's national resources, corrupt the morals of innocent youth and turn its women into a valuable commodity for export." It's an intriguing argument, but strikes me as somewhat academic. What about, once again, Charlotte Hobson? What about Wendell Steavenson, who turned two tumultuous years in post-Soviet Georgia into the astounding *Stories I Stole,* and, here, into this book's tenderest evocation of abandonment and want in the post-Soviet era, "Gika"? What about Katherine Shonk, whose *The Red Passport,* about Russia in the 1990s, joins the sobriety of an outsider with the sympathy of a grateful guest? Perhaps most strikingly, what about Paul Greenberg's novel *Leaving Katya*? If anyone manhandles anyone – and establishes the superannuation of that verb — in that book of Russian-American love across two continents, it's Katya, the willful Russian woman who exasperates the

American Daniel. Even the literal manifestation of Borenstein's thesis — the American entrepreneur Chip indulging in that most emblematic spoil of Western triumph, prostitution, in a disoriented Lithuania in Jonathan Franzen's *The Corrections* — fails to sustain the argument: the experience, quite believably, ends up edifying him rather than reducing the women. But perhaps Borenstein would counter, equally credibly, that this is yet another wrinkle of the male fantasy. The reader of *Wild East* should judge.

Many arms have been thrown up about Eastern Europe in the last fifteen years. The region owes its peculiar inscrutability to the absurdist blend of sadness and hilarity, nobility and baseness that has characterized its course over the past half-century. Nowhere else have the lofty aspirations of social democracy been tempered so brutally by everyday cruelty. Nowhere else have brows furrowed more severely when discussing fate and politics and love, and nowhere else have they drooped more disarmingly after a carafe of vodka. Sometimes these things happened simultaneously.

Soviet attitudes toward their political system were equally complex. During the Cold War, American leaders too often made the error that now undermines George W. Bush: the error of absolutism. They considered Communism and democratic capitalism to be at diametrically opposed ends of the politico-cultural spectrum, which was true in many ways, but they rarely considered the possibility that the spectrum was circular rather than straight. In this way, Aleksandr Solzhenitsyn's protest against the Soviet regime became a sign of his attachment to American capitalism, a gross misreading of his views. So it was with countless others. Westerners have always underestimated the extent of genuine emotional investment among Soviets in the ideals of Communism, as well as the creature comforts and relative dignity its practical manifestation mostly did secure, not to mention Soviet accomplishments in science, industry, and war. Perhaps it was different in Hungary and Poland and the Czechoslovakia, countries that had their Communism mostly imposed from abroad. But in the Soviet Union, even the Jews, who truly lived the life of pariahs, departed their homeland with more ambivalence than any novel or memoir has ever conveyed.

Why is this relevant? Because this factor, coupled with resentment of American attitudes, explains the backlash engendered by political and economic reform in Eastern Europe in the last decade, all that irrevocability I asserted earlier and support of the war in Iraq by political elites notwithstanding. Because it explains that the people of Eastern Europe long for Western prosperity, but are contemptuous of the historical amnesia they think facilitates it. (Whereas the West lusts for Eastern gravitas, but resents the sluggish stride toward Western ideals that it ensures. On both sides: the ambivalence of simultaneous envy and disdain.) Because it explains the resistance of the East — the entire non-Western world, in fact — to an adoption of the West's political and cultural model and answers the West's perplexity at the intransigence it often discovers there, especially in Russia. One should be careful not to be reductive here; Russia's opposition too often owes itself to other factors, not least the wounded pride of a defeated superpower. But the essential point remains: In our tendency to project, Westerners often imagine only two alternatives, ours and theirs. This was, it hardly needs reminding, the guiding principle of Communism as practiced in the Soviet Union, and is, inexplicably, a view gaining currency in the highest circles of American government today.

Is it naïve to propose that it is the obligation of literature to remedy this mistruth, to recall how much depends on *how* rather than *what*? In America, we shudder at the idea of a literature of obligation, but I would venture this essentially Eastern tradition not only holds out something salutary for us in the West, where so often our fiction depends on beautiful human moments with no repercussions beyond the immediate, but also has proven practically unavoidable for Westerners writing about Eastern Europe. As a result, few stories in this collection flinch from the larger questions about the relations of East and West. Curiously, those that do tap into a uniquely Eastern European trend for the past decade: At a time when political revelations clutter the headlines, native Eastern European fiction writers stubbornly refrain from stories that concern their turbulent past and almost obsessively focus on individual lives, as if basking in a privacy assiduously denied them for decades.

In this way, Eastern Europe is a place of democracy and statism, world markets and government handouts, and euphoria and woe, and the stories in this collection answer its call for a literature at once of engagement and of ecstasy. They take a clear-eyed view of its pettiness, backwardness, and constraints, and an exultant view of its high-mindedness, progressiveness, and freedom. So often they consider this region as it wishes foreigners would perceive it, sometimes making fun, sometimes giving praise, always acknowledging the unsimple truth. It seems a hardly efficient means of winning over a former nemesis, of persuading Eastern Europe to drop its poses and the United States to drop its demands worldwide, but it will have to do — there's no Russian word for efficiency.

Boris Fishman
New York City
July 2003

WILD EAST

GARY SHTEYNGART

Shylock on the Neva

I awoke one day to a phone call from the painter Chartkov, a recent graduate of the Academy of Fine Arts, a lean, sallow fellow with a flaxen goatee and the overearnest expression of the Slavic intellectual — yes, we all know the kind of person I'm talking about. Bloodshot eyes? Porcupine hair? Uneven bottom teeth? Great big potato nose? Thirty-ruble sunglasses from a metro kiosk? All of it.

How did I wake up? I felt a sexual vibration in my pocket and realized I had fallen asleep with my pants on, my *mobilnik* still lodged next to that conclusive organ everyone cares so much about. "*Af*," I said to the painter Chartkov. What else can one say under these conditions, this damn modernity we all live in? May it all go to the Devil, especially these tiny Finnish phones that nuzzle in your pocket all night.

"Valentin Pavlovich," the young painter's voice trembled.

"Oh, you bitch," I said. "What time is it?"

"It's already one o'clock," the painter said, then, realizing he was taking too many liberties with me, added, "Perhaps, after all, if it's not too much of a bother, you will still come and sit once more for your portrait as we have previously arranged."

"Perhaps, perhaps," I said. "Well, why don't I wash myself first?

Isn't that how the civilized people do it, in Europe? They wash first, then they sit for a portrait?"

"Mmm, yes," said the painter. "I — You see, I honestly don't know. I've never been to Europe. Only to Lithuania, where I have an uncle."

"Lithuania," I said. "All the way to Lithuania? Such a worldly artist you must be, Chartkov." I instructed him to await my arrival patiently and then turned off the phone. Do I sound unkind? A typical New Russian? Well, let me assure the reader: I'm a very nice person, but on this particular day I was feeling a little out of sorts, a veritable crab.

The culprit was crack cocaine. On the previous night, I had the pleasure of meeting three Canadians at the Idiot Café, two boys and one girl. They had been brave (and idiotic) enough to bring a few rocks of the stuff into our drug-addled city and we adjourned quickly to my house to smoke it.

It was my first time! Bravo, Valentin Pavlovich! What was it like? Not so bad, much like going into a dark, warm room, where, at first, some pleasant things happened, a steady tingle to the nether regions, a flood of happy tears and gay sniffling, and then some very unhappy sensations, probably having to do with the miserable past we all share, the youthful beatings by parents and peers, and the constant strain of living in this Russia of ours. Yes, these are the sorts of things one babbles about the morning after he puffs on the crack pipe — "Russia, Russia, where are you flying to?" and all that Gogolian nonsense.

I retired to the parlor, and discovered that the Canadians were still there. They were sprawled out on the divans, lost beneath thick worsted blankets my manservant, Timofey, must have thrown over them. I could make out the shape of the Canadian girl — twenty-one years old, and with legs and thighs as powerful as a horse's — and hear her piercing snore. In the West, even the drug addicts are healthy and strong. I considered falling in love with the girl, just for some extra Canadian warmth in the morning. But what foreign girl would want me? They're very psychologically adept, these girls, nothing like ours, and I can't fool them with my money and good English.

So I went back to my bedroom to see my cheap, fatalistic Murka, still asleep, coughing her way through the midday slumber, her pincerlike legs folded up. Poor girl. I rescued her from some collective farm on a *biznes* trip to the provinces a few years back. She was seventeen, but already covered in pigshit and bruises. On the other hand, you should have seen how quickly she installed herself in my flat in Petersburg and fell into the role of rich, urban girlfriend — asleep most of the day, drugged out at night, weepy and sexless in between. To see Murka with a shopping basket and a charge card at the Stockmann Finnish emporium on Nevsky Prospekt, yelling brutally at some innocent shop clerk, is to understand that elusive American term "empowerment," the kind of thing the foreigners teach you at the Idiot Café. I kissed Murka tenderly, washed myself as well as I could and called for Timofey to dry me off. My manservant, a big Karelian peasant, beat me with a twig to improve my circulation and then strapped me into an Italian lamb's-wool suit jacket, the kind that makes me look ten years older than my age and fat into the bargain. Oh, what a business is fashion!

Timofey brought around the usual convoy — two Mercedes 300 M S.U.V.s and one S-class sedan, so as to form the letters M-S-M, the name of my bank, for, you see, I am something of a moneylender. As we took off for Chartkov's neighborhood, the call came through from Alyosha, my well-bribed source at the Interior Ministry, warning that a sniper was set to pick me off at the English Embankment. We took another route.

◇ ◇ ◇

Chartkov lived on the far edge of the Kolomna district. I hasten to paint a picture for the reader: the Fontanka River, windswept (even in summer), its crooked nineteenth-century skyline interrupted by a post-apocalyptic wedge of the Sovetskaya Hotel; the hotel surrounded by rows of yellowing, water-logged apartment houses;

the apartment houses, in turn, surrounded by corrugated shacks housing a bootleg-CD emporium; the ad-hoc Casino Mississippi ("America Is Far, but Mississippi Is Near"); a burned-out kiosk selling industrial-sized containers of crab salad; and the requisite Syrian-shwarma hut smelling of spilled vodka, spoiled cabbage, and a vague, free-floating inhumanity.

Chartkov shared his communal quarters with a slowly dying soldier just returned from Chechnya, the soldier's invalid mother, his two invalid children, and an invalid dog. The painter's studio was at the very rear, his front door covered with a poster of the American superband Pearl Jam. When I arrived, Chartkov was busy being thrown out of his room by a squat Armenian landlord in a filthy nylon house gown. Remember how I described Chartkov at the outset? The great big potato nose? The flaxen goatee? Well, picture the same nose now dappled with luxuriant Russian tears, the flaxen goatee moist with dread, the red-rimmed eyes working double time to produce these ample waterworks. "Philistine!" Chartkov was screaming at the landlord. "How can you throw a painter out on the street! It is we artists who have introduced Russia to the world! We who wield the brush and the pen! We gave the world Chekhov and Bulgakov and Turgenev!"

"Those were all writers!" the dying soldier screamed, peeking out of his little hole, his invalid children clutching his leg braces as he made long stabbing motions with his crutch. "What painters has Russia given the world?" he shouted. "Throw the scoundrel out, I say!"

"Yes, indeed," the landlord said. "If you walk through the Hermitage, it's all Rembrandts and Titians. Nary an Ivan in sight. Now, if you were a writer . . ."

The painter almost choked on his considerable tears. "No painters?" he cried. "What about Andrei Rublyov? What about the famous Ilya Repin?" he cried. "What about 'Barge Haulers on the Volga'?"

"Is that the one where the little doggie is in the boat and he's standing up on his hind legs?" the landlord asked, twirling his mustache thoughtfully.

Being a patriot and wanting to spare Chartkov any further embarrassment, I decided to intervene. I proceeded to ask the Armenian the amount he was owed, and was duly informed that it was eight months' rent, or U.S. $240. I called my Timofey, who ran up with three U.S. hundred-dollar bills, and then I told the landlord that no change was needed, at which point everyone in the flat gasped, crossed themselves three times, and retreated to their miserable quarters.

I was left alone with the young painter. Chartkov turned away from me, buried his face in his hands, brushed aside his tears, and sighed in a heartbreaking fashion — in other words, did everything possible to avoid thanking me for my generosity. He shuffled into his room, where an old flower-print divan from Hungary, the kind intellectual families favored during the Soviet era, proved to be the only furniture in his possession. A series of incomplete portraits of what seemed to be whores from the National Hunt strip club were scattered about the room, each girl's smile vicious and true to life.

"Here's what I've drawn thus far," he said. He showed me a full-sized sketch, my dour, opaque face staring back at me with all the bravado of a General Suvorov, my dark hair bleached to a Slavic yellow, in the background an M-S-M Bank sign in old-fashioned Cyrillic characters — I looked ready to fight the Turks at Chesme, instead of my usual daily battle with the hash pipe and the tricky zipper on my khakis. Such nonsense!

He motioned me to the divan and proceeded to apply charcoal to paper. "So you're a fan of old Ilya Repin," I said. "Is that what they teach you at the Academy these days? A little reactionary, no?"

"I'm a m-m-monarchist," Chartkov muttered, scowling for no reason.

"Now, there's a popular position for a young man these days," I said. Oh, our poor dispossessed intelligentsia. Why do we even bother to teach them literature and the plastic arts? "And who's your favorite tsar, then, young man?"

"Alexander the First. No, wait, the Second."

"The great reformer. And what kind of art are you interested in,

Mr. Painter? These days, I'm afraid, it's all showmanship, like that unfortunate Muscovite who goes around the world pretending he's a dog."

"No, I don't like him at all," Chartkov confessed. "I'm a realist. I paint what I see. Social justice for the common man, that's what I like." And he proceeded to mumble some hodgepodge of Western art theory and comfy Russian chauvinism. "Of course, it is the Jews who have brought Russia to her knees," he whispered, interrupting his work to light a nearby candle in honor of a dead Romanov.

"And do you have a lady friend?" I asked.

He betrayed his twenty-four years by blushing crimson and throwing his gaze in the four major directions, finally settling his eyes on the sketch of two whores, both provincially pretty, yet one unmistakably older than the other; one, in fact, quite old, a telltale trail of life's third set of wrinkles forming a Tigris and Euphrates on her forehead.

"A mother-daughter act," Chartkov explained. "They're from Kursk Province. A sad story." Sad, but rather typical. I will omit the particulars, except to add that both mother and daughter were graduates of some local polytechnic institute. "Very cultured people," Chartkov said. "Elizaveta Ivanovna plays the accordion and her daughter, Lyudmila Petrovna, can quote the major philosophers."

His use of their patronymics was strangely touching — I knew immediately what he wanted to do; after all, it is the only path our young Raskolnikovs can follow. "I will save them!" he said.

"Presumably it is the daughter you fancy," I said.

"Both are like family to me," said Chartkov. "When you meet them you see how they cannot live without each other. They are like Naomi and Ruth."

I chose to let this comparison stand. "My dear Chartkov," I said. "I would certainly like to make their acquaintance. You see, perhaps there is something I can do to better their position."

Chartkov examined me through his dopey thirty-ruble glasses. "I hope you do not mean to hire them," he said.

"Good heavens, no," I assured him. And then I proposed we cut short our session and have dinner with his whorish friends.

◇ ◇ ◇

On the way to the National Hunt club, Alyosha, my well-greased source at the Interior Ministry, called to warn me of a deadly Godzilla roll set to poison me at the Kimono Japanese restaurant on Bolshaya Morskaya. I changed our dinner plans in favor of the infamous Noble's Nest, by the Mariinsky Theatre, while helping Chartkov empty a small bottle of cognac in the back seat of the Mercedes, a car to which he warmed immediately. "I compare it to the troika of yore," the monarchist said without any irony, wiping his little mouth with my favorite handkerchief.

The National Hunt was all but empty at this time of day, with only four drunk officers from the Dutch Consulate passed out at a back table by the empty roulette table. Despite the lack of an audience, Elizaveta Ivanovna and her daughter, Lyudmila Petrovna, were up on the makeshift stage grinding against two poles to the sound of Pearl Jam. They looked remarkably like the sketches Chartkov had drawn. Immediately, I was reassured about the whole enterprise, about the innate talent I believed Chartkov possessed, and about my own hopes for immortality.

Mother and daughter resembled two sisters, one perhaps ten years older than the other with naked breasts pointing downward, a single crease separating them from the little tummy below. The mother was imparting to Lyudmila her theory that the pole was like a wild animal which one had to grasp with one's thighs lest it escape. The daughter, like all daughters, was shrugging her off, saying, "Mamochka, I know what I'm doing. I watch special movies when you're asleep."

"You're a dunderhead," the mother said, thrusting to the sound of the ravenous American band. "Why did I ever give birth to you?"

"Ladies!" Chartkov cried out to them. "My dear ones! Good evening to you!"

"Hi, there, little guy," mother and daughter sang in unison.

"Ladies," said Chartkov. "I would like to introduce you to Valentin Pavlovich. A very good man who only today has given three hundred dollars to my landlord."

The ladies appraised my expensive shoes and stopped writhing. They hopped down from their poles and pressed themselves against me. Quickly, the air was filled with the smell of nail polish and light exertion. "Good evening," I said, brushing my dark mane, for I tend to get a little shy around prostitutes.

"Please come home with us!" cried the daughter, massaging the posterior crease of my pants with a curious finger. "Fifty dollars per hour for both. You can do what you like, front and back, but, please, no bruises."

"Better yet, we'll go home with *you*!" the mother said. "I imagine you have a beautiful home on the embankment of the River Moika. Or one of those gorgeous Stalin buildings on Moskovsky Prospekt."

"Valentin Pavlovich runs a bank," Chartkov said, shyly but with a certain amount of pride. "He has offered to take us to a restaurant called the Noble's Nest."

"It's in the tea house of the Yusupov mansion," I said, with a pedantic air, knowing that the mansion where the loony charlatan Rasputin was poisoned would not make much of an impression on the ladies. Chartkov managed a slight, historic smile and tried to nuzzle the daughter, who favored him with a chaste kiss on the forehead.

◇ ◇ ◇

It is no secret that St. Petersburg is a backwater, lost in the shadow of our craven capital Moscow, which itself is but a Third World megalopolis teetering on the edge of extinction. And yet the Noble's Nest is one of the most divine restaurants I have ever seen — dripping with more gold plating than the dome of St. Isaac's, yes; covered with floor-to-ceiling paintings of dead nobles, to be sure. And yet, somehow, against the odds, the place carries off the excesses of the past with the dignified luster of the Winter Palace.

I knew that a fellow like Chartkov would rejoice. For people like him, educated members of a peasant nation catapulted into the most awkward sort of modernity, this restaurant is one of the two

Russias they can understand — it's either the marble and malachite of the Hermitage or a crumbling communal flat on the far edge of Kolomna.

Chartkov began weeping as soon as he saw the menu, and the whores started sniffling, too. They couldn't even name the dishes, such was their excitement and money lust, and had to refer to them by their prices — "Let's split the sixteen-dollar appetizer, and then I'll have the twenty-eight dollars and you can split the thirty-two. Is that all right, Valentin Pavlovich?"

"For God's sake, have what you wish!" I said. "Four dishes, ten dishes, what is money when you're among friends?" And to set the mood for the evening I ordered a bottle of Rothschild for U.S. $1,150.

"So, let's talk some more about your art," I said to Chartkov.

"You see," said Chartkov to his women friends. "We're talking about art now. Isn't it nice, ladies, to sit in a pretty space and talk like gentlemen about the greater subjects?" A whole range of emotions, from an innate distrust of kindness to some latent homosexuality, was playing itself out on Chartkov's red face. He pressed his palm down on my hand.

"Chartkov is doing those nice paintings for us," the mama said to me, "and we're going to use them for our Web page. We're going to have a Web page for our services, don't you know?"

"Oh, look, mama, I believe the two 'sixteen dollars' are here!" Elizaveta Ivanovna cried, as two appetizers of *pelmeni* dumplings stuffed with deer and crab arrived, both dishes covered by immense silver domes.

"We're talking about art like gentlemen," Chartkov said once more, shaking his head in disbelief.

◇ ◇ ◇

The evening progressed as expected. We drove to my apartment, taking in the sight of the city on a warm summer night — the sky lit up a false cerulean blue, the thick walls of the Peter and Paul Fortress bathed in gold floodlights, the Winter Palace moored on its embankment like a ship undulating in the twilight, the darkened hulk of St. Isaac's dome officiating over the proceedings. Here was our Petersburg — a magical set piece of ruined mansions and lunar roads traversed by Swedish tourists in low-slung, futuristic buses — and we all had to sigh in appreciation for what was lost and what remained.

Along the way, we took turns hitting the driver with birch twigs, ostensibly to improve his circulation, but in reality because it is impossible to end an evening in Russia without assaulting someone. "Now I feel as if we're in an old-fashioned hansom cab," said Chartkov, "and we're hitting the driver for going too slow. Faster, driver! Faster!"

"Please, sir," pleaded my driver, a nice Chechen fellow named Mamudov, "it is already difficult to drive on these roads, even without being whipped."

"No one has ever called me 'sir' before," Chartkov spoke in wonderment. "Opa, you scoundrel!" he screamed, flailing the driver once more.

I got the call from Alyosha, my well-placed source at the Interior Ministry, and instructed Mamudov to avoid the Troitsky Bridge, where a prospective assassin awaited my motorcade by the third of the cast-iron lamps. Why do so many people want to kill me? I'm a good man and, it should be clear by now, a patriot.

Back home it was the usual seraglio — my Murka in a half-open housecoat was dancing with herself in front of the wall-length dining-room mirror; the Canadians had fed crack cocaine to my cook, Evgeniya, and the poor woman was now running around the house screaming about some dead peasant Anton, crying black tears over her wasted fifty years. The North American culprits themselves were sprawled around the parlor listening to my collection of progressive-house records, recently airlifted out of Berlin's Prenzlauer Berg district.

As soon as they caught sight of the mother and daughter, the two Canadian boys and the one Canadian girl understood the unique sexual situation before them. Chartkov began to protest and cry against this "inhumanity," reminding the Canadians that the mother played the accordion and the daughter could quote Voltaire at will, but I quickly took him into my study and closed the door. "Let's talk about art," I said.

"What will become of my girls?" the painter asked. "My poor Elizaveta Ivanovna and Lyudmila Petrovna," Chartkov said, eying the multitude of English and German volumes that graced my bookshelves, abstruse titles such as "Cayman Island Banking Regulations," annotated, in three volumes, and the ever-popular "A Hundred and One Tax Holidays."

"Enough of this whimpering," I said. "Chartkov, do you know why I hired you to execute my painting?"

"Because you slept with my sister Grusha," Chartkov surmised correctly, "and she recommended me to you."

"Yes, initially so. But over the weeks I've come to appreciate you as, mmm, a Christ-like figure. And I use the term loosely, because our language has become as impoverished as our country and it's often hard to find the right term, even if you're willing to pay hard currency for it. See now, you alone can paint a picture of me, Chartkov, that will guarantee my immortality. The problem is, it has to be real. Not this General Suvorov nonsense. I mean, what next? Will you portray me in a tricorne hat, riding a white mare to victory? Let's be realistic. I'm a young moneylender, aging swiftly and, like all Russian *biznesmeny,* not too long for this world. Also, in case you haven't noticed, I have dark hair and a broken nose."

"But I want to make you better than you are," Chartkov said. "I want to restore Christian dignity to your battered soul and the only way to do so is . . . the only way —" I could tell his attention was occupied by the piercing Russian "*Okh, okh, okh*!" coming from the parlor, accompanied by some heartless Canadian grunting.

"That's precisely what you *don't* want to do," I said. "I'm a sinner, Chartkov, and I am not too proud to admit it. I am a sinner and as a sinner you shall paint me! Look deep into my hollowed-out eyes, try on my disposable Italian suit, smoke from my musty crack pipe, befoul my summer *kottedzh* on the Gulf of Finland, stuff yourself with my deer-and-crab *pelmeni,* whip my manservant, Timofey, until he begs for his life, wake up next to my ruined provincial girlfriend. And then, Chartkov, paint exactly what you see."

Chartkov wiped some more of his infinite tears and helped himself to a bottle of sake that I now pressed into his hand. "Will this get me drunk?" he asked shyly, examining the strange Asiatic lettering.

"Yes, but you mustn't stop drinking it even for a second. Here, it goes with this marinated-squid snack. And in return for your work, of course, I will pay you, Chartkov, pay you enough for you and your Ruth and Naomi to live a comfortable life forever. Perhaps you can even 'save them,' if that's indeed still possible."

"Eight thousand dollars!" Chartkov cried out, grasping at his fragile heart. "That's what I want!"

"Well, I would think considerably more." I was, in fact, expecting to spend at least U.S. $250,000.

"Nine thousand, then!" Chartkov cried. "And I shall paint you just as you like! With horns and a yarmulke if you so desire!"

What could I say? If only I had been a Jew there would have been no need for Chartkov's services. Our Jews are steeped in familial memory and even when they die, for instance when their Lexus S.U.V. gets blown off a bridge by a well-armed rival, they remain locked in the dreary memories of their progeny, circling over the Neva River for eternity, dreaming of their herring and onions. I, on the other hand, had no progeny, no memory, and really very little chance of surviving this country of ours for more than a few more months.

Why deceive myself like the rest of my New Russian compatriots? My wealth notwithstanding, Chartkov's was the only eternity I could afford.

"Well put, Chartkov," I said. "So we are in agreement. And now let us not keep our company waiting. I shall send Timofey out to fetch an accordion. That way the beautiful Elizaveta Ivanovna can entertain us with her other talents."

"God bless you, Valentin Pavlovich!" cried Chartkov, pressing my hand to his cheek.

◇ ◇ ◇

The next afternoon I woke up with the usual tinnitus in my left ear, a series of duck flares going off in my peripheral vision. The crack-cocaine pipe — the "glass dick," as the Canadians had called it — stared at me accusingly through its single eye. My pillow was covered with alcoholic slobber and what looked like little crack mites dancing their urban-American dance. Meanwhile, coiled up next to me, my Murka was making tragic whistling sounds in her sleep, shielding herself from phantom childhood punches with one upraised skinny arm.

It was a fine moment to be a St. Petersburg gentleman. I called Timofey on the *mobilnik* and he came ambling in from the next room, already dressed in his morning frock. "Did you deliver the painter Chartkov to his digs?" I asked of him.

"Yes, *batyushka,*" said Timofey. "And a great one he was, that painter. Soused, like a real *alkash,* and easy with his fists, like my dear dead Papa. I had to carry him up to his flat, and once I laid him out on the divan he started hitting me with his belt. Then we had to get on our knees and pray for a good half hour. He kept shouting 'Christ has risen!' and I had to reply 'Verily, he has risen!' Such people I do not understand, sir."

"The ways of artists are beyond us, Timofey," I said. "And did you give him nine thousand dollars in ninety consecutive bills of a hundred dollars each?"

"That I did, *batyushka,*" said Timofey. "The painter then took off all his clothes and touched himself in many places with the American currency, while whispering *batyushka's* name most reverently. I was so scared, sir, that I spent half the night in the alehouse."

"You're a good manservant, Timofey," I said. "Now go tend to our Canadian friends while I spend the day frolicking about."

I meant what I said about frolicking. Being a modern moneylender is not a difficult occupation. Armed with computers and bookkeepers and hand grenades, I find the work pretty much takes care of itself. My most pressing duty is showing up at the *biznesmenski* buffet at the T Club every Thursday and glowering across the swank airport-lounge décor at my nearest competitors, the ones that keep trying to blow me off the Troitsky Bridge.

On this warm summer day, the Neva River playful and zippy, a panorama of gray swells and treacherous seagulls, I walked over the bridges to the Peter and Paul Fortress. But unless one gets very excited about third-rate Baroque fortifications, there's really nothing to see, so instead I followed a group of young schoolchildren. In their own way, the children were sublime: destitute in their lousy Polish denim and Chinese high-tops, scarred with acne and low self-esteem, members of the world's first de-industrialized nation but still imbued with our old cultural deference, a Petersburg child's mythical respect for Dutch pediments and Doric porticoes. I watched them fall silent as the tour guide intoned about an occupant of the fortress's ramshackle prison, a revolutionary who once wiped away his tears with Dostoyevsky's handkerchief, or some other such luminary.

Can it really be true, as the sociological surveys tell us, that only five years hence these tender shoots will forsake their cultural patrimony to become the next generation of bandits and streetwalkers? To test this theory, I looked into the face of the prettiest girl, a dark little Tatar-cheeked beauty with a pink, runny nose and flashed her my standard Will-you-sell-your-body-for-Deutschemarks? smile. She looked down at the monstrous Third World clodhoppers on her feet. Not yet, her black eyes told me.

Saddened by our children's plight, I doubled back over the Palace Bridge and pushed through the long line of sweaty provincial tourists at the Hermitage, shouting all the while about some obscure Moneylender's Privilege (*droit du dollar*?). I wangled a self-invented Patriot's Discount out of the babushkas at the box office by pretending I was a veteran of the latest Chechen campaign, then ran straight up to the fourth floor, where they keep all the early-twentieth-century French paintings.

I stood before Picasso's portrait of the "Absinthe Drinker" and marvelled at the drunk Parisian woman staring back at me. How many Soviet years have we wasted here on the fourth floor of the Hermitage, looking at these portraits of Frenchmen reading *Le Journal,* pretending that somehow we were still in Europe. In our musty felt boots we stood, staring at Pissarro's impressions of the "Boulevard Montmartre on a Sunny Afternoon" and then, out the window, at our own dirt-caked General Staff building, its pale semi-circular sweep forming the amphitheatre of Palace Square. If we squinted our eyes, or, better yet, took another nip out of our hip flasks, we could well imagine that the General Staff's delicate arch was somehow a portal onto the Place de la Concorde itself, its statue of six Romanesque horses harnessed to Glory's chariot really an Air France jetliner ready to sail into the sky.

And, let me ask you, For what all that suffering? For what all those dreams of freedom and release? Ten years later, here we were, a hundred and fifty million Eastern *Untermenschen* collectively trying to fix a rusted Volga sedan by the side of the road.

You know, it was best not to think about it.

So I returned my gaze to Picasso's absinthe drinker and this time discovered a previously elusive truth. The drunk Parisian had not been staring at me all those years, as I had romantically, egotistically supposed, but solely at the blue bottle of absinthe, her face radiating as much slyness as despair, a careful contemplation of the heavy poison before her. I do not know a great deal about Western art theory, but it seemed possible to me that this woman, this absinthe drinker, had what the American louts at the Idiot Café called "agency."

Cheered on by my deductions, I sneaked a mouthful of crack cocaine in the men's room, then sailed out of the Hermitage, through the arch of the General Staff building, and out into the hubbub of Nevsky Prospekt. I wanted very much to buy a warm Pepsi for eight rubles, just like the common people drink, and a piece of meat on a skewer. But, as I approached a food stand manned by a fierce *babushka* wearing what appeared to be a used sock on her head, my *mobilnik* vibrated with a text message from my friend Alyosha at the Interior Ministry: "Beware the meat skewers of Nevsky."

◇ ◇ ◇

The next few weeks were manna. I drank, I smoked, I wrestled with warm-bodied Canadians. I came down with an awful itch in that conclusive place we all talk about, but what can you do? And then I got a call from the painter Chartkov. "Patron!" he cried. "Your likeness is almost ready!"

I had not expected such haste. "But we haven't even had another sitting," I said.

"Your physiognomy is imprinted on my brain," Chartkov said. "How can a moment pass when I do not think of my savior? Please, let me stand you for a drink at Club 69, and then we'll examine what I call 'Portrait of the Raven-Haired Moneylender; or, Shylock on the Neva.' I know you'll be pleased with me, sir."

I agreed to an immediate viewing, and summoned Timofey to fetch the cars. Could it be? My mortality giving way to an oily doppelgänger's everlasting life?

Anyone who can afford the three-dollar cover charge — in other words, the richest one per cent of our city — shows up at Club 69 at some point during the weekend. This is without doubt the most normal place in Russia, no low-level thugs in leather parkas, no skinheads in swastika T-shirts and jackboots, just friendly gay guys and the rich housewives who love them. It brings to mind that popular phrase bandied about at the Idiot Café: "civil society."

Chartkov showed up, wearing a colorful sweatshirt several sizes too big and imprinted with the logo of the Halifax Nautical Yacht Club. He'd grown plumper in the last few weeks and shaved off his flaxen goatee to reveal a little hard-boiled egg of a chin. "Looking good, Mr. Painter," I said.

"Feeling good," he said. "Hi, Zhora." He waved to a slinky boy behind the bar filling a bucket with grenadine. "How's life, cucumber?"

"Zhora's going to Thailand with a rich Swede," Chartkov said to me. "Let's go upstairs," he added, "and I'll buy you a hundred and fifty grams of vodka. Oh, how we'll celebrate!"

We sat beneath a statue of Adonis and watched a submarine captain trying to sell his young crew to a German tour group. The seventeen-year-old boys, sporting heroic cosmonaut faces and hairless scrotums, were awkwardly trying to cover their nakedness, while their drunken captain barked at them to let go of their precious goods and "shake them around like a wet dog." I suppose civil society has its limits, too.

"Look what I bought today at Stockmann," Chartkov shouted. "It's a Finnish hair dryer. It has three settings. And look at the color! *Orange*! I'm going to do a lot of work with orange now. And also lime. These are the colors of the future. Is there an electrical outlet here? This machine not only blow-dries your hair; it sculpts it."

"What about your lady friends?" I said. "Lyudmila the philosopher and her mother with the accordion. Weren't you going to save them?"

"You know," Chartkov said, handing me a vodka from a passing tray, "you can't really save somebody until they want to save themselves. In the past few weeks I've been peeking around the English bookstore on the Fontanka. There's this one volume on how to deal with people, 'Hand Me My Cheese!,' or something of the sort, that has made a great impression on me. The problem with the modern Russian is that he is not . . . Ah, what's that word? He is not 'proactive' enough."

"Also, he is frequently drunk," I added, raising my glass. "That's another problem. Well, here's to us modern Russians. May God save us all!"

"God won't save us until we save ourselves," cautioned the former monarchist. "We've got a lot of work to do in this country. We've got to start by looking seriously at our 'core competencies' —"

I grabbed Chartkov by the shoulders. "Enough," I said. "Let's go to your house."

Chartkov blanched. "Please, sir," he said. "I am not a pederast. I merely come to Club 69 for the atmosphere."

"The painting!" I said. "I must see it at once."

"Very well," Chartkov said. "But I paid three dollars a head for the entrance fee, so together it is six —"

"Look here, painter," I said. "If your rendering is as good as I think it is, I'll give you another nine thousand U.S. dollars on the spot!"

"We must hurry then!" Chartkov cried.

◆ ◆ ◆

The hallway of Chartkov's communal flat was littered with paint cans and spent bottles of Crimean port wine. "I bought the whole floor of the building for seven thousand U.S. dollars from that awful Armenian," Chartkov explained, "and the first thing I did was throw the dying soldier and his whole invalid family out on the street. That'll teach them to blacken the name of the Russian painter, may the Devil take them all! When this place is finished, I want to create a multimedia studio. I met this French guy at Club 69, and together we're going to offer painting seminars and a hatha-yoga clinic —"

"Just please hurry!" I cried as we raced through the long communal hallway.

The painter opened the door to his old room.

The first thing I saw was my own jutting lower lip, the one that had given me the nickname Flounder in Pioneer camp; then my eagle nose bent at several junctures from years of schoolyard beatings and domestic scrapes; then my hazy dark eyes, two dim ovals set way back into my skull; then my arms thick and corded, bulging with implied violence, one raised to strike my manservant, another hovering over my lap to protect myself from life's intimate dangers.

My skin was yellow and black in places, my forehead crossed by a monumental green vein. I was caught off center, staring joylessly into an empty corner of the canvas, where the painter had added his own initials.

He had me, Chartkov. He had done well, the poor idiot. There were some excesses, to be sure: I was sporting a pair of Hasidic side curls, while a copy of the "Protocols of the Elders of Zion" floated incongruously in the background, a ten-ruble note sticking out in the form of a bookmark. There was no point in telling Chartkov that I was, in fact, not a Judaist; rather, a mixture of Greek and some kind of Siberian mega-Mongol. If he was inspired to paint me in this manner, so be it.

"Here's what you must do, Chartkov," I said.

"What is it?" said the painter. "Should I put on some Pearl Jam? Fetch my patron some tea?"

"Just add a little detail," I said. "Paint a *mobilnik* pressed to my ear."

"Of course," the painter said. "It will be done first thing in the morning! Oh, but now my mind is filled with questions of an embarrassing nature —"

"Timofey will bring you another nine thousand U.S. dollars," I said.

Chartkov threw his arms around me and wept convulsively. His body felt thin and reedy compared with my own. I smelled American herbal shampoo on him, along with the stench of stale Parliaments. "If you wish," he whispered in my ear, "you may also take me from the back."

◇ ◇ ◇

I woke up the next morning to the familiar cellular vibrations in my pocket. Alyosha, at the Interior Ministry, was warning me of a prospective assassination on Leninsky Prospekt. The day had come. I kissed sleeping Murka goodbye, leaving her the number of a colleague who would treat her no worse than I had. I climbed past the Canadians in the parlor and ordered my driver to set off for the southern suburbs.

I had spent my entire adolescence on Leninsky Prospekt. A wide Soviet boulevard filled with nineteen-seventies apartment blocks that might as well have landed from the Andromeda galaxy — long, cumbersome rows of flats, a grayish, intergalactic color, flanked by ten-story towers on which the words "Glory to socialist labor!" and "Life wins out over death!" used to lord over us in fantastic block letters.

As soon as I got out of the car, my phone rang once more. A strangled sound emerged from the earpiece. On the far edge of the Kolomna district, in the studio of the painter Chartkov, my immortal double was calling out to me. He was singing a childhood song in a boy's sweet voice, breathless with Leningrad asthma:

Let it always be sunny,
Let there always be Mommy,
Let there always be blue skies,
Let there always be me.

I breathed in the real and imagined smells of Leninsky Prospekt, the factory coal fumes, the Arctic frost, the black exhaust of my mother's cardboard cigarettes. Two figures emerged from behind a burned-out milk stand and approached me. I stood there waiting for them, my hands protectively cupping myself but my jacket open and my tie askew. I did not say a word to them. What was there to say? I heard them clicking their rounds into place, but my gaze fell elsewhere. I was mesmerized, as always, by the orange-yellow aurora of pollution hanging over the horizon of the contrived city, that juncture where snow banks and apartment towers meet to form nothing.

TOM BISSELL

The Ambassador's Son

I liked the Capital because you could always find something to do there. Booze, women, dancing — you name it. As for the rest of the country, the guidebook writers could have the place. They didn't even have *toilets* outside the Capital. Please realize I require very little as a human being: bread, water, flush toilet. Something about living on the cusp of the millennium and still shitting over a hole calls into question the entire concept of historical progress.

I'll tell you a little about the country. It was one of the old Soviet republics where you started drinking at ten, started *really* drinking at fifteen, and dropped dead of it around fifty. The kind of place that was so corrupt that you had to bribe yourself to get out of bed in the morning. This wasn't one of the European former Soviet republics; this was one of the Central Asian republics you've never heard of. As for the culture, I'll say this: its combo of Soviet paranoia and Muslim xenophobia made red wine and fish look like peanut butter and jelly in comparison.

You didn't see a whole lot of tourists hanging out in the Capital, needless to say, but there were a few Americans around. (There are always a few Americans around.) First, you had the Professional Expatriates at the Embassy. Their ranks were filled with a lot of uptight stuffed shirts, stuffed blouses, stuffed heads. Most of them couldn't stray a block from embassy row without their cell phones, chauffeured cars, and *International Herald Tribunes*. Second, you had your Do-Gooders. These people, God bless 'em, needed a serious fucking clue. Each fall I'd see a new group of hatchlings turn up in the Capital, their first day in-country, snappily dressed, taking pictures with disposable cameras for Mom and Dad back home in Iowa and Nebraska and Michigan. Then they'd get shipped out to the villages. Three months later I'd see them back in the Capital shopping for Snickers bars and deodorant, crazed and dandruff-ridden. Finally, you had your Sharks, men and women whose in-country presence consisted solely of pocketing ducats. This wasn't as evil as you might think, not even by folk-singer standards. After all, the more money the Sharks made, the more the country made (usually, in a perfect world), and then everyone was happy. Sometimes Sharks were Do-Gooders who'd stayed but got wise; sometimes they were Professional Expats who'd had their fill of Embassy politics; and sometimes they were twenty-four-year-old ephebes with liberal arts degrees pulling down seventy-five grand a year — tax free — serving as "consultants" for Pricewaterhouse Coopers or Boeing or British-American Tobacco. As for me, I had an in-country sinecure but didn't consider myself one of the Sharks. Although I was around the Embassy a lot no one would have mistaken me for a Professional Expat. A Do-Gooder, then? Hardly.

I was the ambassador's son.

◊ ◊ ◊

A dilemma: What do you do when you're sunk to the hilt in the lovely, splayed spasm chasm of bent-over Olga, who to your utter, surprised delight is finger-diddling the lipsticky and raven-haired Svetlana, when suddenly you hear your mother coming down the stairs? Did I mention that these stairs and the darkened basement they lead to are found in a home belonging to the United States Embassy? Did I mention you live in this palace, which supplies for you a chauffeur named Sergei and an idiotically generous stipend? Finally, and most significantly, did I mention you're two caterpillar-lengths away from an orgasm of Vesuvian proportions?

When the lights came on two things struck me. The first was that Olga had an American flag tattooed on her porky left rump-cheek. The other was the difficulty of the choice I suddenly faced. The light switch was found halfway down the staircase, so I knew I had a second or two to pull on my pants and do at least a modicum of damage control. But Svetlana was spread-eagled on a large purple leather couch, bent-over Olga was before her on her knees, and I was screwing Olga from behind — this is not an easy situation from which to extricate oneself. In all honesty, I was too close to destroying Pompeii even to have considered stopping. I suppose it would be fairly easy to second-guess my judgment but I'd never screwed two girls at once. My only defense is that you do not ask Columbus to turn around when the guy in the basket starts screaming "Land ho!"

How long my mother watched before I heard her outraged gasp I'm unsure. I should point out that I love my mother. She'd stuck with my dad through his long, often dreary embassy-to-embassy career. ("A diplomat lives the life of a dog," Jefferson said, and he was in fucking *Paris.*) First, until it blew up, we were in Beirut, where Dad was a staffer; then we spent a tense decade in the Soviet Union, where Dad was an ambassador's aide; then to Dad's first real gig as American Ambassador to Afghanistan, which was about as much fun as you'd think; and then to our reward, the Capital. My mother was a woman who made an effort to learn the language of every country she traveled to. She shopped in the bazaars shoulder-to-shoulder with the locals. She *cared.* And this is what she had to see: an orgasmic Sveta hooting *"Da, da!"* and slapping the couch cushions with her hands, Olga's finger rubbing her blood-swollen clit with the blurry speed of a hummingbird, and me, her son, ejaculating with enough torque to cross my eyes. When I was done — this process took a bit longer than I would have liked — I had no choice but to turn to her.

Mom was no shrinking violet. She'd been in bullet-peppered cars in Beirut, she'd had a rotten cabbage pitched in her face in Kabul, and by the time we locked pupils she'd composed herself. She wore a fuzzy white bathrobe with the American Embassy insignia embossed smartly into the breast. Her hair was flattened and color-drained to the shade of gray found only in black-and-white movies. Her eyes were dry and unforgiving. "Oh," she said, except it was more of a sigh. "Oh, *Alec.*"

By now Olga and Sveta knew the score. They were huddled naked against each other, whispering in Russian. I draped a nearby blanket along the three of us, and we sat there, the girls looking at the floor and me looking at the girls while my mother shook her head. I didn't care about Olga and Sveta, really. They were Russian strumpets I'd picked up in a nightclub. They didn't care about me, either. All they wanted was a chance at the Alec Tuscadero Visa Application Program.

"Mom," I said, vaguely remembering my mother's oath after my urine showed simultaneous traces of cocaine, marijuana, and opium that it would be the Last Time she'd forgive me. She made that quite clear — it would be the Last Time, as opposed to the last time. You still have seven or eight "last times" left once you get that first one, but once you're given a Last Time, it's serious. (The drug test was on the request of the Embassy's regional security officer, a doughy guy called — not to his face — Genghis Ron.)

"Alec," she said again, closing her eyes, her face hardening.

I figured I had one chance to fix all this, to say the right thing. (Before I tell you what fell out of my mouth I feel it's germane to point out that I'd spent the better part of the evening smoking Afghan poppy seeds that Sveta had seemed really surprised to find in her purse.) I put my arms around the girls, hugged them to me and said, "Two chicks at *once,* Mom."

In a flash of fuzzy, hazy white my mother vanished from the staircase. The next thing I knew my ear was twisting between her sharp fingers. She pulled me to my feet, my pants still around my ankles, and dragged me trippingly across the room. At the stairs I turned and saw Olga and Sveta on the floor, on their backs, kicking into their pirated American blue jeans.

◆ ◆ ◆

The Hotel Ta-Ta was a nice place. Built by Indian investors — anything built by Soviet architects had a tendency to fall apart — it relieved you of three hundred dollars a night for the privilege of stepping into its marble lobby and sleeping on its crisp, laundered sheets. I could afford it; I could have afforded twice that much.

The next morning, ten steps past the hotel fountain, I saw Sergei, my chauffeur, sitting on the hood of a gleaming, freshly washed white Toyota Land Cruiser, reading the Capital's Russian-language newspaper. The night before he'd helped me haul all my shit into the suite.

"Sergei," I called, waving. *"Zdravstvuite! Kak dela?"*

"A, prekrasno, Alec," he said, just about extinguishing our shared vocabulary. (I knew roughly enough Russian to fill the backs of two postcards.) Sergei folded his newspaper into a small square and held it pinned under his arm as he opened my door for me.

I fell into the Embassy-supplied Land Cruiser's back seat and rubbed my hangover-tenderized temples. Seconds later Sergei was weaving through the traffic on Rashidov Avenue like an out-of-control darning needle.

"Sergei," I said. "Café, *pozhaluista.*"

In the rear-view mirror his vodka-reddened eyes flicked onto mine. *"Amerikanskoe Café, da?"*

"Da," I said, leaning forward. "Sergei. My father. *Moi* . . . um, *otets?"*

"Da," Sergei said with a solitary nod.

"Where is he? Uh, *gde moi otets?* Do you know?" I knew Ambassador Tuscadero was in Kiev at a human-rights conference sponsored by all the former Soviet Republics. That morning on CNN International, though, I'd seen that a bomb threat had ended the conference three days ahead of time. Was he home, did he call, had my mother debriefed him?

"I no know," Sergei said with the typical shrug that followed all his heroic efforts at English. "My father, I no know where is he." He looked at me again in the mirror. *"Khorosho, Alec?"*

Still, after several months, I was pleased to see the fruits of Sergei's and my daily five-minute English lessons. *"Khorosho, Sergei.* Great. To the café. Me want coffee now chop chop."

"Chop chop," Sergei said, shifting, and I sat back and watched the Capital's weird, oppressive architecture fill the spotless square of my window, then, after a moment, slide soundlessly away. I dozed off for a few blocks and woke to the sound of Sergei beeping his horn at a big-bottomed Tatar girl wearing black stretch pants and a tight white T-shirt. She was standing on the corner of the trendiest street in town, the street on which one found the New World Café. Sergei turned around, grinning, showing me his mouthful of substitute gold teeth. "Alec," he said, grinning. "Beeg tits, nice ahs, *a?*"

"Da," I said. "Good. Big tits. Nice ass."

"Beeg tits, nice ahs," he said, his hands up like scales, weighing the desirability of each description. He jerked the steering wheel over, slid into a space three hairs bigger than the Land Cruiser, turned and gave me a big thumbs up. "Beeg tits, nice ahs, I love America!"

◆ ◆ ◆

The New World Café was the Capital's one reliably American hangout. Inside was a woman I recognized as Genghis Ron's secretary and who was thus my arch-enemy, a pair of guys in bran-colored suits who worked for the Capital's American Chamber of Commerce, and the smiling Korean triplet waitresses, daughters of the New World's owner. I paid for my customary four cups of coffee, my cold hamburger, my roll that was as hard as a piece of chipped-off foundation, and sat down at a table alone.

I was bored. Days in the Capital were the worst. Usually I holed up in my bedroom, listening to *Let It Bleed* on my headphones, sometimes putting in an appearance at my job to make a few ceremonial bribes. I don't know if I had one friend in the Capital I'd ever seen while the sun was up. I was puzzling over the unbelievability of that when he walked in.

Of all the young American Do-Gooders I'd seen dragging their crushed aspirations behind them, gushing stale idealism the way a slashed tire gushes air, I don't know why I felt any urge to pal around with this one. Maybe it was my hangover, or my remorse at how I'd treated my mother. Maybe it was guilt: so many times I'd seen the Professional Expats dick around with the Do-Gooders in the New World. One of the poor, glassy-eyed kids would stumble in, looking to hear some English after going without for weeks, deluding himself into thinking that just because we all knew which sport the San Diego Chargers played we were also friends when we saw each other. The Expats would ignore them, then start talking extra-loud about their satellite televisions. Even though I thought the Do-Gooders were crazy, this stuff made me wince. Only country music singers deserved *that* kind of torment.

The Do-Gooder stood in the café's doorway, his eyes moving in their sockets like a couple of caged hamsters, his fists furiously clenching and unclenching. His blond hair was butched on the sides and slightly longer and tousled on top (a haircut he'd probably given himself). In his hand was a cache of official-seeming white papers. He hopefully scanned from table to table — looking for someone I already knew was not there — and by the time his gaze fell on me his face was crushed, long and pliant.

He ambled over to the cash register, ordered in bad Russian (all three triplets spoke English), and turned to face the café holding a paper cup of Fanta and a grease-spotted boat of warmed-up french fries. That was when I stood, pulled out a chair from my flimsy plastic table, and invited him to join me.

He considered me with a sort of queasy smile, then looked over his own shoulder, like a complete nimrod, to make sure I was talking to him. "Yeah," I said. "*You.*"

He shook his head in a surprised, flattered way, marched up to me, set his order on the table and extended his hand. "Hey, thanks," he said. "I'm Ryan."

"Howyadoin'," I said, briefly shaking with him. His grip was lackluster, his hand moist. "Alec."

"Yeah," he said. "I know. The ambassador's son, right?"

"That's right," I said. We looked at each other and smiled. We sat down. After a few moments Ryan quietly ate a french fry and picked at a silvery psoriatic scab on his forehead. I finished what was left of my third cup of coffee.

"So," I said after a minute of silence, "who were you looking for?"

Ryan looked at me with a french fry peeking out his mouth, his chin swarmed with small red stars of acne. "Huh?"

"When you came in here. You were looking for someone."

"Oh. Yeah." He briefly looked into his lap. "Someone was going to meet me here. She said if she wasn't around when I got here she wasn't coming. I wasn't really expecting to see her." He bit the tip off a fry. "I'm leaving the country tomorrow."

"Vacation?" I asked.

"No," he said. "For good. Forever."

I didn't say anything. Ryan didn't either. Instead he straightened the edges of what I now knew were his dismissal papers.

I looked at him. "Which organization are you with?"

He stared at the papers and didn't answer me. I asked him again. He looked up, startled, and rubbed his eyes. "God, I'm sorry. I just . . . I can't think. CARA. I'm with CARA."

I nodded. CARA: The Central Asian Relief Agency. Missionaries were illegal anywhere in the country, and CARA was one of the first groups to figure out that since volunteers could be invited by the Capital as engineers and nurses and teachers, why not start a relief agency that sent *Christian* engineers, nurses, and teachers? So you can imagine what it was like for the locals: you sent your kids off to their English lesson only to have them come back blabbing about King Solomon and John of Patmos. My dad got more official complaints about CARA than he did about any other American agency. The Capital wanted them gone.

"So you were a missionary," I said.

To his credit, he immediately fessed up: "I guess so. I mean, I tried to be. It's hard."

This I believed. Though the country surrounding the capital was nominally Muslim, everyone — including the non-Russians — drank vodka, smoked cigarettes, and engaged in a good deal of illicit hairy-donut-spearing. "Well," I said to Ryan, "I'll give you guys credit for having gargantuan balls."

"For what?"

"For trying to convert a bunch of Muslims to Christianity when they're not even interested in being Muslims."

"Oh," he said. "Thanks." He sat there holding a half-eaten french fry, staring again at his dismissal papers. That was when I noticed the wedding ring — a simple, dimmed gold band.

I looked him in the eye. "You married?"

He nodded, frowning.

"Is she here or back home?"

He cleared from his throat what sounded like a fist-sized wad of phlegm. "Home," he said with difficulty.

"It'll be good to see her again, I bet."

He smiled a little, lifted his hand off the dismissal papers, delicately slid his ring from his finger and dropped it into his glass of Fanta. With a soft *plunk* it struck the cup's bottom, leaving a trail of chemically reactive bubbles popping at the soda's orange surface.

I looked at the bubbles. "Your marriage could be better, I take that to mean."

He ran a hand into his hair, plowing it back from his forehead and revealing a thinning window's peak and a bright red sore at the hairline. "Yeah."

Things began clicking into place. "This person you were meeting, this 'she' — are you porking this girl?"

Some affirmative sound grunted out of him.

"And your wife found out."

He shook his head back and forth.

I leaned back in my chair, having heard about CARA's method of dealing with indiscreet adulteries, premarital dalliances, and other generally evil living: outright dismissal, no trial, no appeal. Just because I'd heard about this punishment didn't mean I believed they actually enforced it. In a weird way I was impressed.

From a pragmatic standpoint, though, enforcing rules like that was no way to run an overseas operation, since eventually everyone figures out that fucking is one of the only things that improves the farther you get from America. “CARA found out,” I said.

Hands still clenching his hair, he nodded.

“Well, Ryan,” I said, “that’s a tough one.”

He looked up at me with sudden dry-eyed conviction. “I’m a sinner, and a fornicator. My forgiveness lies in the hands of God.”

“That’s one way of looking at it.”

“It’s what they told me. I just left their office.”

“Who told you?”

“The director of CARA. Mr. Vandewiele.”

I burst out laughing. “Let me tell you something about your Mr. Vandewiele. First of all, he’s a major-league, drinks-his-own-aftershave drunk. Second of all, the guy’s embezzled half of CARA’s dough into a private state-side account.” This was such common knowledge around Embassy-folk it seemed weird everyone else didn’t know it, too. “Man,” I said, shaking my head, “it’s one thing for them to boot you out, but I can’t believe they let that hypocritical old lizard call you a degenerate before they did it.”

Ryan folded his arms and leaned back in his chair. “You think CARA’s staff knows what he’s doing?”

“Of course they do. The SNB” — the new KGB —“has got their offices bugged. The American Embassy gets all the transcripts hand-delivered. All in the New World Order’s spirit of cooperation.”

Ryan looked away.

I said, “You don’t seem very surprised.”

“In the past nine months,” Ryan said, “I’ve repeatedly had to go to the bathroom in a hole. Horse has been a dietary staple. I’ve been stoned, mugged twice, and harassed by the SNB. I’d never tasted alcohol in my life before I came here, but I managed to spend an entire week drunk. I’ve been in three fistfights, two of them with children. I cheated on my wife twenty-seven times, nearly lost my faith in God, and in the meantime successfully managed to evangelize only ten people.”

"That's not too bad. Only two less than Jesus."

"So if you tell me that Mr. Vandewiele is a drunkard and an embezzler, then no, I'm not surprised. Not anymore. I am beyond surprise as an experience or an emotion." He blinked, his eyes the veiny, cloudy red of boiled shrimp. "All I want now is to go home. That's it."

"Where's home?"

"New Jersey. That's where my wife and my divinity school are."

"What possessed you to leave New Jersey for here?"

Ryan pushed away his boat of french fries. "I have no idea." He looked at me, a fist up to his mouth. "How about you? Where are you from?"

I shrugged. "Nowhere, everywhere."

"Where'd you go to college?"

"College of Life."

He stared at me, puzzled, then nodded sharply and looked away. He chewed at his thumbnail, his right leg bouncing under the table. How he'd made it through nine months of life outside the Capital I had no idea.

I clapped him on the shoulder and said, "Hey, there. Cheer up. When's your flight leave?"

"Tomorrow afternoon." This said like it was two thousand years away.

"Okay. Perfect. I've got it. Tonight we're going to a restaurant that isn't a certifiable shit-hole. Then we're going to a dance club to watch Russian breasts bounce up and down. And then it's back to the Hotel Ta-Ta for your first good night's sleep in months. Now how does that sound?"

His eyes widened. "The Ta-Ta?"

I showed him the palms of my hands. "Relax. It's my treat. All of it."

"I don't know . . ." he said with a new, almost streetwise wariness about him.

"Yes you do know. Where are you staying now?"

"The Hotel Chorsu."

"The Chorsu!"

"Look, Alec," he said, standing, "thanks for the offer, but I have to go and —"

I grabbed his rayon sleeve and eased him back down. "Listen to me. You've lived like a goddamn animal for, what, *months,* right? Don't you deserve one night, one measly night of splendor? How much does CARA pay you guys, anyway?"

He told me.

"No, seriously," I said. When he didn't answer I realized he wasn't joking. I continued, delicately: "I think you *need* this, Ryan."

He looked away, shaking his head. Suddenly he coughed out a disbelieving laugh, turned to me and said, "Why are you doing this?"

"Because I'm a hell of a good guy. Why do you think?"

He looked around the café. "It all sounds nice," he said, "it does. I just . . . I don't think I could repay you."

"Nonsense. I've got more money than ten popes."

"I . . . I don't know." With his finger he fished his wedding ring from his cup of Fanta, wiped it off on his shirt and pocketed it. He bit his lip, the pink draining to white where tooth met skin, and then he nodded, nodded *hard,* to himself. "All right. What the heck. Let's do it. Except for that club part. I don't know if that's my speed, exactly. Despite everything I just told you, Alec, I'm still, you know" — his nose scrunched up — "a *Christian.*"

I smiled and stirred the contents of a sugar packet into my last cup of coffee. "Golly, Ryan. You don't say?"

◇ ◇ ◇

We walked out of the café to see a violent struggle going on in the back seat of the Land Cruiser, but I realized it was only Sergei fooling around with the Tatar girl. My heart sank a little, seeing something my father often said once again proved true: every beautiful girl in the Capital was either for sale or willing to negotiate. Sergei was always dropping my name to get girls, promising them one-way tickets to California if only they'd blow him, fuck him, grab his slab. It would be easy to get all judgmental on Sergei, but the guy had had an awful life. His family was exiled to the Capital after Stalin killed his father, grandfather, and three of his brothers. Now he was just a measly percentage point in the Capital's shrinking Russian population. He could have used my name to get down the pants of every girl from the Capital to Islamabad for all I cared.

"That's my truck there," I told Ryan as we approached the Toyota. "I'll break this up and we can split."

Before I could, though, the Tatar girl fell out of the Toyota with her shirt on inside-out and backwards, wiping her chin. I figured for Ryan this would trigger a rectitudinous meltdown, and turned to him and started to say something. Ryan just stared at the girl as she reached around and fixed her twisted bra strap. When she finished he looked over at me and said, "Let's go."

◇ ◇ ◇

I soon realized that Having Fun was a pretty dainty concept to withstand all the weight I was piling on for Ryan's sake. (There isn't even a word for "fun" in Russian — how's *that* for revealing?) As much as I tried, he wouldn't cheer up. In his hotel room, Sergei and I were laughing and kicking roach corpses at each other while Ryan packed up his gear. In a lull we looked over to see Ryan sitting cross-legged on the floor, his face plunged into his hands. Sergei hoisted Ryan up, took him into his sausagy arms the way only a Russian male can, removed a flask of vodka from his breast pocket and tenderly proffered it. The stuff Sergei drank belonged in a medicine cabinet, but Ryan tipped the flask and dumped it down his gullet. He nodded in thanks, took a bleary-eyed steadying sidestep, and returned it to Sergei, who peered into its shadowy opening in astonishment. I took advantage of the moment to cry out, "To the Ta-Ta!"

And now he and Sergei were drinking in the Ta-Ta's restaurant like they'd fought Napoleon together. We'd had our four-course dinner, half a dozen appetizers, drinks, everything. Inviting Sergei may have been a mistake. The guy had the alcohol-intake capacity of the Strength of Ten Men, and surprisingly Ryan wasn't faring too badly against him, getting down one drink to Sergei's every three. The restaurant was large and spare, its decor severe, its atmospheric lighting like that of a fish tank. The tab we'd started at the beginning of the evening was creeping into territory so astronomical that waiters and cooks and waitresses were all huddling around the restaurant's bar, peering at the tab and then, hands to breasts, looking over at us.

I was drinking Black Label. Ryan and Sergei were chasing tequila shots with bad Turkish beer. Between Sergei's long Russian toasts I listened to Ryan dissect his troubled heart. He was young — my age — and had been married for two years. It seemed that Ryan's wife ("A good woman," he kept saying, "a good woman") tended to interact with his whammer a little as though it were made of poison ivy. The wife's father was CARA's stateside accountant, which made Vandewiele's improprieties even more vexing. I asked why he was here alone, and he explained they were prepared to evangelize together until his wife failed her physical. "She's a little overweight," Ryan said quietly. But he still wanted to do it, and she wanted him to do it, too.

"She sounds like a wacko," I said.

Sergei took delighted, sleepy-faced note of this word. *"Vacko,"* he said, chuckling thickly.

"She's not a wacko," Ryan protested, softly shaking his head. He closed his eyes, his face dark with resignation. "You don't understand."

"Vacko," Sergei said again, nodding off.

Unbidden came Ryan's tales of Christian persecution. Thrown rocks, SNB wiretaps, outright assaults. None of it was Saint Paul on the Appian Way or anything, but scarring enough for a Divinity School grad from New Jersey, I'd imagine.

Finally we arrived at the shores of his unfaithfulness. By the standards I was familiar with, the story was tame. Moist things developed between him and another CARA volunteer named Angela, Ryan flushing as he described how their trysts became progressively more "wicked." I pressed for details but, sadly, received none. Now he was afraid of who he'd become. He had desires now, cravings and doubts, and felt adrift on a sea of whims and decidedly un-Christian stimuli.

"Sounds like you've become a human being," I said.

A hollow smile spread on Ryan's face. "I belong to the world."

This sounded promising to me. "Now you're talking straight, Ryan. You're goddamn right you do!"

"'Because you do not belong to the world,'" Ryan said, *"'I have chosen you.'"*

I frowned. "What the hell was that?"

"That," Ryan said, "was Jesus talking to his disciples."

"My opinion on Jesus," I said, "is that he was probably a nice guy who wound up in the wrong place at the wrong time." I raised my hand, ordering another round.

Ryan rubbed his face and said, "Wonderful. Can I go to my room and sleep now?"

I felt frustration spread its wings in my chest. I suddenly wanted to reach across the table and slap him, grab him by his boyish hair and remind him that, unlike some of us, he had a life to go back to. I was within moments of throwing silverware when a skullful of soothing perfume wafted into my nostrils and I felt a hand fall lightly on my shoulder.

I turned to see a tall Russian woman in a short, tight black dress standing next to me. She was one of those Capital women you only saw in places like the Ta-Ta or in pricey clubs. Her wrists were ringed with onyx bracelets, her earrings were stylish black hoops, her hair was an enormous black vortex, a spray-hardened shell. "Comrade Tuscadero," she said, smiling. Her lipstick was either black or a deep, sooty red.

"Zdraste," I said, seeing Ryan's jaw drop open like a chain-snapped portcullis. Sergei had passed out.

Her hand rose from my shoulder and fluttered around stylishly. "Oh, no, no, no, zis Russian greeting is unnezessary," she said in accented, flawless English. Her lips pouted. "You don't remember me, Alec?"

Had I screwed this woman? I didn't think so. If I had I would have run around spray-painting it on the sidewalks. "I — I'm not sure," I said.

"How embarrassing for me," she said with a loud, solitary laugh. "I am Lena, acqvaintance of your friend Trenton. Ve met at party, two months ago, I sink."

Trent was a Shark who worked for Boeing, the kind of guy you wound up doing cocaine with if you were around him for longer than five minutes. I remembered the party — at least, I remembered *arriving* at the party. "Oh, yeah. Trent's party."

She laughed again. "You are a terrible liar, Alec." She extended her hand. I took it and she yanked me up from my chair. "You vill make up to me viz a dance at ze Dutch Club."

The Dutch Club was a mobster-haunted hive across town, a place where, I knew, Ryan didn't have a chance. I looked over at him, eyebrows raised in apology. "Well," I said, glad to be rid of his sadsack bullshit.

"Yeah," he said, nodding, standing up, wobbling a little. "Thanks for everything, Alec. Maybe, you know, I'll see you again some time."

"No, no, vait, vait," Lena said, stepping between us. "Your friend" — she put a black-fingernailed hand on Ryan's acne-splotched cheek — "von't be coming to ze Dutch Club viz us?"

"I've got a flight tomorrow," Ryan said, swallowing.

Lena nuzzled up against him — they were the same height — and put a hand on Ryan's left hip, her fingernails raking across his blue jeans. "Alec," she said, looking over at me, "vhat is your silly friend's name?"

"Ryan," I said.

"Vhy is your friend Ryan such an idiot?"

"Maybe you should ask him."

Her face moved toward his, stopping when her black lips brushed against the cracked fissures of his. "Vhy von't you come to ze Dutch Club, idiot? Come dance viz me, fuck your stupid flight."

Ryan looked at me for help, his face a twitchy, nervous white orb. I said nothing.

Lena stepped away from Ryan and looped her arm through mine. We started to walk away, Lena's rump swaying so broadly it smacked me on the hip with every other step. "Wait!" Ryan called. We turned. With a guilty-looking smile Ryan was behind us, dragging Sergei, one of the table's chairs upended behind them.

◇ ◇ ◇

Underneath the Dutch Club's neon sign were the words AMERICAN DANCE CLUB in English, and even though it was probably the hippest place in the Capital, it fell a little short of this. For one thing, you don't find many Kalashnikov-toting security guards in American dance clubs, and usually the hookers don't outnumber the patrons, a mathematical goof tricky enough to send that Malthus guy home thinking. The rest of the formula — seizure-inducing lights, manufactured smoke, music so loud it felt as if something were laying eggs in your eardrum — they had down cold.

We deposited Sergei in the back of the Land Cruiser and stumbled up to the Dutch Club's entrance. I was drunker than I thought, and by this point Ryan was having trouble finishing his sentences. Already I could tell Lena and I were not going to happen, at least not tonight. I'd taken it upon myself to drive, and Lena spent the trip across town sitting in Ryan's lap, sticking her tongue down his throat and fishing her hand into his pants. Ryan fought back with a weird mixture of total surrender followed by violent rebuff. When he pushed her away Lena would laugh — throaty, loud, off-putting — and continue undeterred. The Dutch Club guard manning the velvet rope recognized me and waved us inside, past the surly line that spanned two blocks.

Once we were in, Lena got behind Ryan and shoved him out onto the dance floor the way a bully might push a kid into a school bathroom for a beating. The dance floor was not too crowded and Lena hit its scarred vinyl planks atwirl, then lapsed into some incredibly intricate serpentine rumba that had her wrapping herself around Ryan, who I was starting to see was *way* out of his fucking league. I was tempted to get him out of here but stopped myself when I saw the look on his face. He stood in the floor's precise center, grinning, clapping out of time, bobbing like a cork, while Lena vamped all around him. Soon the floor filled up with fat, tieless, Nike-wearing mafiosos and their teenage whores in sheer black stockings and fake pearls. Lena and Ryan disappeared in the tangle. He had one night left, I thought. It might as well be a good one.

I waded through the ocean of whores to the bar, ordered a drink, and struck up a conversation with a fey young girl named Tanya. The next thing I knew I was getting blown in a corner of the Dutch Club's women's bathroom while a bevy of women crowded around the mirror to reapply their makeup. It wasn't very good — Tanya kept nicking me with her teeth — and the fact that I wasn't yet sure if she was a whore or not made it a little hard to concentrate. Paying for sex is just about the biggest turn-off I can imagine. Well, that, and shitting in a hole. Tanya must have sensed my distance because she wrapped her lips around me even tighter and squeezed my balls with her free hand about twice as hard as was necessary. Two people were fucking in one of the stalls next to us. Outside the bathroom techno-bass pounded in Kong-summoning booms. I closed my eyes and imagined Lena blowing me instead. It seemed unbelievable that I wouldn't remember her, especially if she was at Trent's party. I'd screwed some mutty German girl at Trent's party, hadn't I? I suddenly remembered free-basing, together with Trent, a thimble full of coke that filled my head with glassy winter air and then stumbling into a bedroom with her. And wasn't it a little fucking odd — this I thought with sudden, startling clarity — that Lena was a friend of Trent's, since everyone pretty much knew that Trent was as gay as a picnic basket?

My eyes opened. I glanced down to see a puzzled Tanya shaking my non-tumescent dick. She looked up at me with a shy, wet-lipped smile and said in heart-breaking English, "Me no good, Meester Alec?" *Oh, Ryan,* I thought, *oh, buddy,* zipped up, gave Tanya ten dollars American, and strode out to find him.

It didn't take long. They were still on the dance floor, grinding and making out like two teenagers, Ryan's hands clutching the globes of Lena's ass. There was no other way to do it: I walked up to them, peeled them apart, and then pushed Lena away hard on her breastless chest. She tumbled back and sat down on the floor, looking up at me open-mouthed and muss-headed, her lipstick smeared all over her face and one of her strappy black shoes hanging from her big toe. "You stay the fuck away," I shouted, then grabbed Ryan by the arm.

I got across the dance floor before he figured out what was happening. When we reached the edge he turned to go back, his face a twist of angry, drunken spite. "What the hell, Alec!" he said, trying to pull away. "Just what the hell!" His arms were flailing, his eyes half-closed.

"Come on," I said, "we're leaving. Fun's over."

"I want that girl," he said, looking back at Lena. She was still sitting on the floor, watching us, lights flashing across her black dress.

"No you don't," I said, giving him a good hard yank on his arm. "Come on, Christian. Time to go."

A low blow, maybe, but it worked. He stopped struggling and looked back at her briefly. When he turned to me, some shiny sense of belated recognition was sparkling in his eyes. "Why don't I want her, Alec?"

"Let's go, Ryan." Even though he'd figured it out, I couldn't bear telling him. I just couldn't.

Now he grabbed me, both his hands digging into my white button-down shirt. "Why *don't* I, Alec?"

"Look," I said, as one song gave way to another, indistinguishable song, "we've got to go. All right?"

What happened next is kind of hard to describe. Something caught my attention — I don't remember what — and at the same time Ryan wildly swung his arm back to wrestle it free from mine. He'd caught me off guard and so his arm went flying without any resistance. The song had ended, the floor was clearing, and walking right behind Ryan was a squat, crooked-nosed gangster.

Ryan's elbow caught him in the face, breaking his sunglasses and from the look of it doing some serious damage to the guy's eye. He swore, bent over, cupping his eye, and when he looked up at us it was as if his eyeball had been injected with a syringeful of blood. He started saying something in Russian — too quickly for me to understand — and then a flat-topped goon in a squarish suit had Ryan in a headlock. Ryan didn't fight, didn't do anything — he only kind of hung there, like a Puritan in the stocks. It was left to me to punch the guy, and when I hit him, I guess the force was with me. I mean, I killed him, though I didn't find that out until a lot later. All I remember is this satisfying feeling of something hard going splat under my knuckle — this was his nose — and he let go of Ryan as if I'd said the magic words.

That we made it out of the club was a miracle. That we made it to the Toyota was a miracle. And that no one shot us as we were peeling out was a miracle. But I realized the miracle quiver was empty when minutes later I looked in the rearview mirror and saw two Mercedes-Benzes on our tail and rapidly closing the distance. There was a cellular phone in the glove box, which I had to scream at Ryan twelve times to get for me — he was gone, he'd lost it — but finally he did. He said, *"Here! Here! Take it!"* and covered his face with his hands. That was the last thing I heard the poor kid say: *"Here! Here! Take it!"* Pretty shitty last words, I think. Anyway, I called the Embassy switchboard, shouted into the phone what was happening, where we were, that I was driving there as fast as I could. Sergei woke up in the back seat and said something to me. I heard a pop, and then another. Suddenly I couldn't steer worth shit; they'd shot out the Land Cruiser's tires. The next thing I remember is picking glass from my hair. I'd flipped the Toyota, apparently, trying to turn too fast on too few tires, and we went tumbling through the front window of an *apteka,* a pharmacy.

I didn't have a scratch on me. Not a single fucking mark. And I hadn't even been wearing my seat belt. The Toyota was upside-down, all its windows shattered. A lot of the broken glass from the *apteka*'s big windows had splashed inside the Toyota, too, so my only problem was all the glass in my hair. Relieved, happy, I started picking the shit out piece by piece. When I looked over at Ryan I stopped. There's some debate whether or not he was dead by then. All I can tell you is that if he wasn't dead he was going to be soon: a massive, nasty shard of glass had pierced his throat, severing his right carotid artery. His eyes were open and there wasn't much blood yet, so it was very tempting to start talking to him because he didn't look that bad. I mean, there was a huge piece of glass sticking out of his throat, but, you know, nothing *too* bad. I tried to get out of the car but couldn't, and so I sat there next to Ryan, looking into his eyes, while somewhere behind us tires bit into cement and car doors slammed.

They pulled Ryan out first. The instant they moved his body blood started squirting. Sergei and I were next. Sergei's nose looked like a smashed ketchup bottle, and he was bawling — too drunk, I think, to understand what was happening. They dragged us into the middle of the deserted street and pushed us to our knees. I'll never get over how empty the streets were. It wasn't even that late yet — eleven, maybe midnight. I saw Ryan's body, face-down, next to an open manhole, the guy he'd hit with his elbow standing with one foot on Ryan's neck. He kicked Ryan in the ribs a few times — his hand still cupped over his eye — then pulled out a small handgun and shot Ryan twice in the head. Again, there was no blood, and Ryan's body didn't even seem to register that it had been shot. It was like the guy had blanks in his gun. Maybe I've seen too many movies, but it was strange. They pushed his body into the manhole. I don't remember hearing a splash.

They shot Sergei next. This happened so quickly I'm sad we never got to say anything to each other, to look at each other one last time. One moment we're kneeling there side-by-side, the next a pop explodes next to my ear and Sergei flops face-first onto the pavement. Why they waited to do me, I don't know, but the guy who shot Ryan and the guy who shot Sergei had an impromptu conference while the third and fourth guy held my arms behind my back. I've been told it was because they knew who I was, but I doubt it. Why, then, would they have executed Sergei? You don't fuck with the Embassy and every gangster knew it.

Anyway, it doesn't matter. Genghis Ron and a fleet of Embassy security vehicles pulled up half a minute later. The mobsters gave up without a fight, probably since they knew they had the receipt on every judge in the Capital. Back at the Embassy Genghis Ron read me the riot act. The next day I was on a plane back to Washington, where I spent a week eating room service and sleeping with a medium-attractive Congressional page I picked up on the Mall and not answering the phone in my hotel room, which rang every seventeen seconds. Back in the Capital, my father was a dervish of spin, working the hush-up gears like a seasoned apparatchik. Not that it mattered. A BBC reporter (a young lady, it retrospectively occurs to me, I probably shouldn't have jilted) broke the story and . . . well, there's no need for me to go on. You know the rest.

I do feel awful that my dad lost his job. None of it was *his* fault. I feel awful for Ryan's family, too, which is a big part of the reason my lawyer wanted me to tell *my* side of the story — to demonstrate that their wrongful-death suit is, in his words, "misguided." It's my hope that I've done so.

As for the man I killed, there might be some trouble. I doubt anything much will come of it — I *was* the ambassador's son, after all — but I'm being arraigned, if you can believe that, in the Capital next month. As slight as the chance may be, my lawyer says, I have to prepare myself for the fact that I might yet see the interior of a Capital prison cell. *Prepare* myself, the guy says. Gee, if you put it that way, I suppose I can *prepare* myself. Why I hired an American lawyer I have no idea. I'm told, though, that some of the cells have flush toilets. I'll have to look into that.

ARTHUR PHILLIPS

Wenceslas Square

1. 1986. Ottawa, Canada. Tyler Vanalden, a young U.S. political officer on his first diplomatic posting, waits alone in an expensive restaurant where he is supposed to dine with his father, visiting from Cape Cod. His father is unsurprisingly late. After more than an hour, drinking Cokes, Tyler orders a bottle of Bordeaux and, slowly at first, drinks the entire thing, feeling a little sorry for himself as his father neither comes nor calls nor answers at his hotel, predictable, predictable. Tyler is drunk, but not too visibly, when he decides he can't afford much in this place, so orders only a dessert, eats it very slowly, ready to blame his father should he develop diabetes or alcoholism from the meal. He shakes his head, pays the check, and goes home to the answering machine message from his jaunty, microscopically apologetic father. The End.

Except that sitting at the bar with his back to Tyler's table, studying Tyler in the mirror behind the bottles, was an unremarkable employee of the Soviet embassy in Ottawa, one of a team assigned to keep a discreet eye on U.S. diplomatic personnel, from the lowest to the highest, and note when any of them behaved oddly. He had been in the bar quite coincidentally to see if a particular secretary to the deputy chief of the U.S. mission came in that evening for a lonely martini or three, a habit she had been indulging with some regularity the past two months. She never came that night, but the Soviet recognized Vanalden from the pictures he kept on a bulletin board over his desk. Later that evening he filed a brief report: Third Secretary Van Alder dines alone eccentrically, visibly frustrated, drinks alone, departs intoxicated, emotional. Vanalden's cyrillicized name entered a computerized Soviet filing system, which would track the young diplomat wherever his job carried him for the rest of his career, as long as there was a KGB to gaze at him and sympathize with his frustrations.

2. From 1947 to the end of 1989, when Soviet Communism evaporated from Central and Eastern Europe, the CIA spent most of its mental and physical energy battling it. American pragmatists in this long twilight duel saw themselves as temporary players in an eternal task of secret guardianship, peering into the murk, straining to contain the hydra's heads, imagining how the beast might slither out from behind its walls. In the hearts of secret idealists, though, hopes sparked that the monster might sustain secret or public defeats, might perhaps be turned back here and there, or even, in some impossible future, somehow be destroyed — an improbable ending which, even if it came true, could only be apocalyptic.

Was Tyler Vanalden an idealist or a pragmatist? The CIA's Personnel Office had hoped to answer that and other questions by submitting the untested Vanalden to a début posting as chillingly unexciting as the U.S. embassy in Ottawa. Personnel was also trying to gauge the boy's staying power. Would he, posing as a low-level diplomat while attempting to recruit low-level foreigners to spy for the U.S., succumb to boredom-induced burn-out? He wouldn't be the first over-excited young officer to leave the service when he saw firsthand that late-1980's espionage lacked James Bondian dash and generally felt like incremental fidgeting with illusory gains, a game of arthritic cat and limping mouse.

Personnel also judged that Tyler Vanalden was at higher-than-usual risk for boredom and drift since he was a legacy case, the latest in a long line of Vanaldens who had spied for the United States, often in periods of high drama. Tyler's first taste of espionage had come when he was a boy of seven and, at his father's request, had accidentally overthrown a football into some hedges behind the Eiffel Tower, where his father then had to go look for it and a hollowed-out Zippo lighter. That same father had missed Tyler's birth, as he was on a Florida beach preparing Cuban guerrillas for their coming reconquest of their betrayed homeland. Missing births was a duty-dictated tradition in the family. Tyler's grand-father had missed Tyler's father's birth (1930–The London Naval Disarmament Conference) and his Aunt Jenny's (1938–Sudetenland crisis).

In 1986, Personnel sent its appraisal of its newest Vanalden upstairs, and down floated a Guiding Directive: *Plant the royal acorn in desert sand. Does it blossom or rot or does it guard the sacred wisdom deep inside it?* That settled that: off to Ottawa for young Tyler.

Where he did just fine, it was decided after two years. He kept his cool and his ambition, and played his small part in the successful recruitments of a Bulgarian filing clerk and a Hungarian translator, among others.

Therefore, in October of 1988, Tyler Vanalden received his second foreign posting, his first in the Communist bloc. He was dispatched to Prague, Czechoslovakia, posing as a third secretary in his second post, and not long after the faux-diplomat's arrival was made public, a flagged file, describing him as a "likely alcoholic eccentric, probable depressive loner, possible malcontent materialist" turned up at the Soviet Embassy just a few blocks away. A copy was shared with the Czech Intelligence Service.

3. Eight weeks after his arrival, Tyler was standing at the cramped and decaying bar-café he visited for an hour or so after work most days, where he could practice a little Czech, even very occasionally strike up innocuous conversation with a brave or curious local, usually a student or artist or a worker with a portable chess set. It was a Friday. The room was filling up and growing noisy with talk and music. He had a second drink and re-read the letter from his mother on Cape Cod where they had just put down the aging family Labrador. Tyler read the letter again, recalled poor old Vic. He practiced Czech by eavesdropping. He heard a little boy tell his mother, "Weather changes when the weatherman on television tells it to." He turned around, leaned backwards against the bar, read the letter again, and nearly shed a tear for the death of Vic, who had slept next to Tyler's empty bed for a month after Tyler left for college. Tyler looked up. Across the room, a beautiful young woman with short blond hair was staring at him. She held his eye for a moment, then turned away, bit her lip, lit a cigarette with a shaking hand.

"What made you suspicious?" his supervisor, Ed Marshall, asked Tyler nine hours later in a dawn meeting back at the Embassy. "You're a good-looking guy. It could have been real."

"No. She looked a lot like a girl I went out with in college. When I first saw her, I really thought it was her for a second. There's a picture of us in the yearbook, kissing at a hockey game, and the little tattoo on her neck, you could see it in the picture, but not its shape. It was a heart."

"And your new friend, this —" Ed examined his notes — "this Jarmila, has a tattoo on her neck?"

"And the same haircut. But her tattoo's a flower. My guess is they guessed from the blotchy picture."

"The sweet scent of nostalgia," said Ed Marshall. "The stimulant effect of coincidence."

"You look as sad as I feel," said the girl in not-bad English, twenty uncertain minutes after he first saw her. "Will you join me for a drink?"

Closer, of course, she didn't really look much like Kim Wilsey — Tyler's happy, wholesome, psych-major girlfriend for a few months of his senior year at Colby until, in a baffling and uncharacteristic rage, she had dumped him for being "emotionally unavailable, artificial, perfect, untouchable, impenetrable, affectless." But the Czech looked similar enough to attract him (he really did find the type powerfully appealing, almost hypnotizing) and to remind him of Kim, or at least of his effort trying and failing to prove her accusations wrong. The Czech girl ran the tips of her fingers over her tattoo and said she was embarrassed by her poor English.

She had been crying. "You are from U.S.A.? What is it like there? We are told some very strange things about U.S.A.," she said with a sad, ironic smile, the clever child of worn-out, brutal, formulaic Communism, not believing the propaganda for an instant and signaling that disbelief discreetly and sweetly. She would like to visit the U.S.A. someday, but this is surely not possible, because . . . she trails off. She is sad. Does the handsome diplomat Tyler know what it is like to be sad, to feel hopeless? She thinks from his sensitive eyes that he might. "Yes, I have known this," he says in slightly poorer Czech than he can actually speak. "I would like to help you, if I can," he offers, just a sad young man attracted to a sad young woman, hoping to win her trust and affection. Her boyfriend has beaten her, she whispers, after refusing, for another drink or two, to say what was troubling her so. Tyler looks duly horrified (though he nearly laughs at this excessive, almost Baroque ornamentation). "I would like," she whispers so low that Tyler has to lean close and place his ear next to her lips, "to escape from Czechoslovakia somehow, and from Igor . . ." She pours wine for them both.

"How much did you drink?" asked Marshall.

"Enough to be convincing."

"At which point, conversation led to . . ."

At which point, the apparently drunk Vanalden, to help her believe she had picked the right target, spoke of how much he missed his home, how much he hated the diplomatic service (a tradition in his family he was forced to carry on), how she should not, really, think too much of the U.S.A., because, let's face it, the country was a mess, our politics were a joke, we're barely even a proper democracy, blah, blah, blah — a horny and disgruntled diplomat letting off steam, trying to hold the attention of the gorgeous maiden-in-distress fate had provided in a burst of daffy generosity — then, for good measure, a bit of credibility-enhancing truth, though a little untruthfully slurred and maudlin: "You are the most beautiful girl I think I have ever seen in my whole life," muttered in clumsy Czech.

"Nice," said Ed Marshall, not looking up from his note taking. "Was that true, by the way?"

"No. She's cute, nothing special," Tyler lied unnecessarily, even as he wondered why. Later, he told himself it was a tiny self-medicated dose of necessary privacy, a small, soluble grain of the adventure to keep for himself, knowing as he did that everything after would all have to be shared: reported and discussed and analyzed and filed.

After almost two hours, a significant silence sat between them until she said, "Do you want to kiss me?" He said, "More than anything I've ever wanted ever." She placed her soft lips on his, just long enough for him to taste a drop of her wine . . . she pulled back hastily. "Oh, dear God, what time it is?" She wrenched her head to look at the clock behind her on the stained brown and white wall, and executed a flawless Cinderella: "I'm so late, he will know, he will ask me, oh, Tyler, don't forget me, please, you are so good, and I so much need something good . . ." A flustered gathering of her things, a momentary hand on his cheek, and out the door she ran in tearful panic.

"And you boiled with desire," said Marshall.

"That's right. And felt conspicuous. And got stuck with the tab."

"So you feel she owes you. And she's in danger. And you want her. The trifecta. But you have no way to reach her, so all you can do is boil with desire."

Next, Tyler looked successively stunned, confused, embarrassed, defensive in the face of suspicious Czech bar patrons. Hot, claustrophobic, he paid the bill, dropping far too many crowns on the table, stumbled outside and slumped on a bench, held his head in his hands for a good ten minutes. He staggered around in the appropriate mist almost at random, kicking things, gazing up at the half moon and once, just once, even saying audibly, "God DAMN it" before apparently coming to his senses, looking around in embarrassment and sprinting all the way to his apartment.

There he had a glass of water and called Marshall on the secure line, set up this meeting for first thing the next morning. "One other thing. I took the liberty of being even a hair more tormented, a real idiot romantic. In the heat of my departure, I left my briefcase at the bar. Nothing of value, unclassified profiles of Politburo members, letter from my mom. But still, shows real discipline problems."

"Very nice," said Marshall. "Very."

"Thank you."

"So. How do we proceed?"

That afternoon, a second meeting with a larger team was held in a secure room at the Embassy. She would surface again, no question, and when she did, Tyler would churn with contradictions. Angry, but worried about her. Relieved she is okay, but his pride injured that she ran off. Infatuated, cautious. When alcohol entered the scene, he would slowly repeat that he hated his job, especially working for (here a vote was taken by the committee) David Kelsey, Tyler the Diplomat's nominal boss, who was conveniently on vacation at the time and could not be consulted, but who, Ed Marshall decided, put Tyler down whenever he could, stuck him with menial tasks, never took his opinions seriously. "Better to be a grumbling vengeance-seeker," said Marshall, "than to be in a position where they feel they have to blackmail you. That way, you won't have to . . . it won't come to . . . Say, Michael, what are the surveillance options?" Marshall asked an electronics specialist.

Every night for a week, Tyler returned to drink at the Wounded Bear. But now he spoke to no one. Accepted no challenges to a game of portable chess. Practiced his improving Czech on no one. Just sat and stared at his drink, looked up every time the door squeaked. Seven nights, giving up later each night, dribbling smaller and smaller tips behind him.

Night eight, December fourteenth, 1988, she appears, very late, after Tyler has apparently drunk quite a bit, alone in the noisy crowd. "Oh, thank God," she murmurs as she slides next to him. "I hoped, Tyler, but I did not dare to dream . . ." He pulls away from her. She apologizes. He pouts. She tries to explain why she cannot explain. He doesn't care, what does it matter to him? Do not be like that, please. Then how should I be? If only you knew what Igor was like, you would not be cruel to me, I thought you were different. Yeah, well, maybe I'm not different. Oh, please do not hate me, I could not stand this. Who said anything about hate — I barely know you. I see, so this is how you are . . . She stands and leaves again. This time, though, he swears aloud, drops money on the table, runs after her. He reaches her outside on the cobbled street, the snow just starting to turn heavy, he grabs her arm, turns her towards him, her tears mingle with melting snow flakes on her cheeks, he tries to kiss her. "Have you gone mad?" she hisses in terror, pulls away. "We must not be seen together . . ." and she glides over the snow into an alley, a single dim light barely dispersing the shadows around trash barrels and rats and the stinging reek of urine. He has her tightly now. "My God, you are such a handsome," she whispers, still crying, still nervous. "We can meet, in my friend's apartment," she says between kisses. "Where is it?" he gasps. "I'll meet you there now." "I want you terribly," she says. The moon is full, the snow and mist make postcards and old movies of everything; Prague effortlessly scatters its infallible magic all around them. "But," she says. "But?" "But, Igor . . ." Igor is cruel, a weasel, a wolf of a man, he terrifies her, she thinks he is having her watched, perhaps even right now . . . if only she could think how to be free of him . . . "I'll kill him," boasts engorged Tyler Vanalden. "I have diplomatic immunity!" "Oh, dear heaven, God, no. He is powerful, he works for . . ."

"Of course he does," said Marshall the next morning. "Bless his heart."

Weasel Igor worked for some vague division of the secret police. Jarmila certainly didn't know its name or where it was, only that Igor's job was to find out secrets about foreigners working in Czechoslovakia. And she simply could not think of how to escape his violent and lustful embrace, described in increasing, moist detail. He would never let her go, never, he would kill her before seeing her with another. She pulled Tyler deeper into the dark alley, kissed him again, allowed him to feel her shape pressed against him. She would go anywhere with Tyler, if only she knew she was free and safe. His kiss makes her bold: she will meet him, enough of fear! She whispers an address and a time next Monday night, her friend's apartment, for God's sake be discreet going there. "I have an idea," she says, "but I am afraid to ask you." "Ask me anything, anything at all," he says. "If you could bring me something to show Igor, nothing really of value, I don't care what it is, a box of paper clips with your Ambassador's name on them, then maybe I am thinking I can make Igor think I am useful. I will not tell him about you, of course . . . I am so frightened of him." She trembled. She kissed him. And, in the intoxication of his kiss, she apologized, told him not to take her seriously, she was wrong to ask anything of him, begged him not to take any risks for her, she would think of another solution. "Until Monday," she sobbed, and off she ran, looking all around in fear.

4. The conference the next morning was a little heated; the real diplomats complained at their required presence, muttered about childish games and low-margin gambles. "Jumping through fire for the promise of peanuts, Ed," said the Ambassador. "Possibly," replied Marshall politely, but proceeded according to his own logic. "So who is this traitor Tyler Vanalden?" Marshall asked Tyler and the team. Tyler, they decided, is eager to please her, but still wary of doing any real harm, more out of habit than principle. And so he has photocopied the personal information page from David Kelsey's file, nothing much more than you could find in a Washington, DC, phone book, but plainly stamped CONFIDENTIAL. This first stolen document was prepared. How Vanalden had procured it was determined. His attitude to his lover for Monday was debated and decided. Bits of pivotal dialogue were drafted and rehearsed. "Are we finished now?" asked the Ambassador, standing to go. "Tyler," asked Marshall, apparently as an after-thought when everyone else had left, "have you thought through the possibility that . . ."

"This is for you," said Tyler, panting, nervous, pushing the searing envelope into her hands when she opened the door of her friend's apartment.

"No, I told you I do not want it!" she cried, letting the poisonous thing fall. "I do not care, I do not want to see it. It does not matter. Only you matter." And she pulled Tyler Vanalden onto an old mattress on the floor of the bare, unnecessarily underheated room, where, to the audible accompaniment of a cassette of Beatles songs in Czech and the inaudible accompaniment of hidden video cameras, Tyler displayed a wide range of emotional turmoil having passable sex with Jarmila Hrbek of the Czech Intelligence Service.

"Oh, my brave boy!" she exulted an hour later over the document that she saw at once was perfectly worthless, but which was her novice traitor's tentative first step. While she did feel a thrill that she could actually do this (inspire men to treachery), she was also slightly insulted that he didn't price her affections any higher: a Form 12-c Dept. of State Personnel File Cover Page? It was like bringing a few wilted daisies.

"Oh, my brave boy!" She had examined the paper only after a display of loving unwillingness — vowing to make him take it back, she would find another way — and only when he made clear how proud he was of having stolen it for her. "How did you get such thing?" she cooed. She pulled the rough blanket around them both, and lit another candle after melting its base directly onto the splotchy, splintered planks of the uneven floor. She flipped the cassette; "Hey Jude" warbled in Czech again.

"No. Take it back," she said on second thought. "I want only you."

"No. If it can help you, then it *is* me."

Tyler performed for her, a lover with a full heart, eager to make her laugh and proud of him in just the right amounts. He reenacted his heist: under a million watchful eyes, he had pretended to Xerox the crossword puzzle from the *Herald Tribune* but copied the hated Kelsey's file instead. She clapped her hands and stared at him in wonder and love, then her face suddenly wrinkled with worry. "How do I use this now with Igor?" she asked, not having thought through her scheme at all, just a simple girl in way over her head. "What do I do now?" And Tyler took manly control of her fears, rehearsed her (his sister was an actress, he said). Until three in the morning Tyler the traitorous diplomat (a figment) coached his endangered lover (a figment) on her approaching performance (a figment), advised her on how best to present herself to her abusive boyfriend (a figment), helped her craft a story of a different girl (the figmentary friend who owned the real apartment) who had an American diplomat lover, and who had given Jarmila the worthless document she was pretending — in order to strengthen the figmentary ego of a figmentary traitor — was valuable. Tyler pretended to teach her drama by guttering candlelight, pretended to swagger with false bravery as he imitated some brutish boyfriend whom he was creating as much as she, knowing that if he said Igor spoke with a growl, then from now on he did. Tyler was very happy: the candle did gutter in the cold apartment, the mattress did smell of her perfume, the Old Town Square did glow gold outside the window. That there were other realities shrouding this one did not mean this one wasn't there. "You really are so very beautiful," he said, "like nothing I've ever seen. You're spectacular."

"And now we are up and running," said Marshall. "She'll ask, you'll provide. Not in a straight line, but catch as catch can. You'll get better at it, produce more impressive results. Igor is going to get more specific and demanding before he'll consider freeing her, a date we can rely on him to postpone indefinitely. And now and again you'll stumble. They have to get addicted to you, just like they're trying to get you addicted to her. Now, how you feeling about all this, Ty?" The answer mattered: Ed Marshall knew better than most that operations like this one had expiration dates, and that those dates were dictated by pre-existing tolerances and thresholds carved into the psyche of the agent in the field. Marshall was, after all, the co-author of Training Paper 5588, based on years of agency experience, entitled "Better than the Real Thing: Blurring and other Emotional Asymptotes to the Managed Love Affair."

"I'm watching from six miles up," responded Tyler, believing it himself.

Marshall's ad hoc team in the Embassy kept control of Operation Brief Encounter for a few more weeks. And into the middle of January, (after a Christmas lag, when Igor took Jarmila away for eighteen days and Tyler publicly moped and appeared to drink to excess), the new lovers met, each with their own mating dances of precaution, each pretending to hide from someone on the other's behalf. Poor Jarmila, hounded and tragic, behaved erratically, caught in a storm of emotions, torn by her love for Tyler and her fear of Igor and her shame of what Tyler was willing to do on her behalf: she would miss dates, then appear unannounced, weeping madly. Treacherous Tyler, too, swung wildly. His clenched-jaw bravado would evaporate into hot remorse the day after he had excitedly given her some new, more valuable document. Late at night, lying in her arms, shaking with cold and fear and shame, he would whisper, "What am I doing? This is all wrong . . ." and Jarmila would have to steady him: "No, my darling darling, sweet boy. You are saving me. Every time you are saving me a little more. They will let me leave the country with you, soon, I am sure of it. Just a little longer . . ." and she would stroke his hair as he choked on tears then whispered hoarsely: "Whatever he wants, I'll get it for you."

All of this Tyler understood and duly filed in his well-written reports. But once, she was waiting for him at the apartment, sobbing and drinking. She had a black eye. The sight of it so enraged Tyler that he punched a wall, breaking his wrist.

As he is having it bandaged later that night by an Embassy nurse ("I slipped on the ice," he sheepishly told her, the same lie he'd used in his report, embarrassed by the truth), he replays the moments leading up to impact over and over again in his mind's eye, trying to understand them, even as the Czech Intelligence Service's actual videotape of the incident is replaying, with the sound off, over and over again in a darkened office on a suburban street.

Rewind: he entered the room, her face was turned away from the candle. She turned to greet him and he was stunned. He approached her, touched her face gently, even touched the bruise itself, could not believe what he was seeing. He turned away, words were spoken, and his fist struck the wall (narrowly missing a pin microphone, producing an explosive, super-human sound effect on the video when played at volume) . . . Rewind . . .

The nurse asks him to rotate the wrist to his right, and he recalls gently touching Jarmila's eye, showing the appropriate horrified concern tinged with anger, though in fact he was invisibly amused and just curious to see how the Czechs had achieved the effect: make-up was too risky, so a sub-cutaneous dye? A temporary tattoo? Henna? When he saw and felt that the bruise was real, saw her flinch from his touch, he turned away to gather his thoughts, even as he displayed appropriate anger and said something appropriate, and as he was deciding how he was supposed to react, he was also trying to understand why he was so upset, though he realized it a split-second later: they had really punched her. He was heading to the wall by then (he recalls as the nurse tightens the bandage) and was wondering: what the hell kind of organization was the Czech Service anyhow? They wouldn't have gone this far in the CIA, and it was suddenly as if she was someone's prisoner, not of Igor but of an organization that would do that to her just to squeeze stolen secrets from him, a band of thugs from whom she needed to be saved even as she was pretending she needed to be saved from Igor. He was powerless to save her in either case. He knew that a display of ostensible rage was needed even as he was in fact enraged. He watches the nurse pin the wrapping around his throbbing wrist. He remembers that he thought to himself, "I suppose I would punch the wall in frustration," even as he remembers seeing, with some surprise, his fist already approaching the wall, and he remembers thinking, "I should pull this punch so

I don't hurt myself," but by then his fist had been seized by the fist it was portraying and they had punched the wall together, with the strength of the latter. His wrist popped with a nasty sound and he saw a light behind his eyes, several shredded copies of the candle's flickering cone. Smiling, bantering, he accepts the proffered pain-killers and icing instructions from the nurse.

She rewinds the video, recalls his face as he approached her, touched her injury. An unforgettable look in his eye, sadness and anger and disappointed plans for the night ahead: he is like a child, lusts and rages and muddled loyalties, and she is helping him grow into a man, a man who will do anything she asks. She knows she (they) will have to be more careful with him now, as she watches the green, infrared fist hit the black void again and again. She will have to be careful not to push him too far or too fast; this sort of devotion must be replanted even as it is depleted or it will be spent too soon. And there is something more, she sees now, replaying his entrance into the apartment, recalling his heart-broken, twisted face. He is more than what Management and the Steering Committee have seen in him: he is not just a lustful fool, "a boy of the fraternity," and he would not have responded this way, with this devotion (and extraordinary intelligence payoff) to just some semi-trained prostitute coughed up by the Intelligence Service. No, he is responding to something quite specific only to be found in a professional, only to be found, she knows now, in her. She carries and can control some element that is triggering him to grow and to bind to her (to them). And she understands now that he is feeling for her (violence aside) what women usually feel for men, a devotion men are not usually capable of. This boy has a unique ability to give himself to something or someone, an ability that would only express itself when he met precisely the right object of devotion: her. She rewinds the tape again.

5. "I really like this one," Johnny 1950 said to Jarmila as he entered one morning, drawing from his briefcase the video cassette of one of her recent evenings with Source Prep-school. Someone had labeled the Betamax cassette "February 1, 1989.

Four-and-a-half stars!!" "It is excellent work," he continued. "You do excellent work for the Party, Comrade." He was a creepy little bald man, and she had gagged when he maneuvered to direct the video surveillance of her trysts. He was called Johnny 1950 because in 1950, when he was eleven and a farm-boy in Canada, his Canadian Communist parents decided that what was happening in post-war Eastern Europe was the coming of the world proletariat democratic paradise, the end of history, and they were not going to sit on their six acres in Alberta and let it pass them by. They sold all their belongings and were three of a very, very small number of people who emigrated to Czechoslovakia when most Czechs were pulling their hair out trying to emigrate somewhere like Alberta. Miserable young Johnny McDougal the backwards immigrant easily learned Czech, which, for the rest of his life, he spoke with only a trace of an unplaceable accent from somewhere that no longer existed. A smart boy, in high school he already had work teaching English in a variety of capacities, perfecting the accents of Czech trade officials, diplomats, and spies, teaching them all small-town Canadian slang from 1950. His obvious value to the Intelligence Service was noted when he was still in the Agricultural College, and he had been comfortably employed by them in Prague since 1966. He was single and increasingly odd. He was ugly and lonely. He repeatedly fell hopelessly in love with unattainably beautiful women, all of whom, whether he consciously knew it or not, had some access to or knowledge of the West. They scorned him or treated him like a goofy, odd uncle, or patted his bald head as if he were their mangy pet. He did not mind, fell asleep imagining showing them Canada, because the scent of the West just wafted from them like a rare perfume, enchanting the man who as a boy had been torn from his home for his parents' ideology. He would have done anything for Jarmila.

6. Six days of demonstrations against the Communist government took everyone by surprise, but the force with which the Czechs dealt with it surprised no one in the U.S. embassy who understood the permanent nature of Communism. The arrests of

800, including the dissident playwright Havel, proved that this bear was here to stay. At the same time, Marshall decided that the value of Brief Encounter was proven and should now be managed as a piece of the Big Picture. Feeding false information to the Czechs had positive value, perhaps now more than ever when cracks in the Soviet Bloc were widening, so an Operational Guidance Group was established in the U.S. The forged documents, the chronology of hand-offs, the scripts, the course of the love affair, and Tyler Vanalden's personality would all be managed by the Group back in Langley, Virginia. The Group would determine (with Marshall's input) when Tyler should hold back, when he would be too frightened to continue, when he would hint that something big might be available soon, when to pout and demand renewed evidence of her love, when to turn giddy and promise her a house in Miami Beach, when to produce.

With an Authorizing Directive from upstairs (*Let the human heart in all of its mysterious runnels guide us*), the Group set to work, staffed with Czech culture experts, psychologists specializing in the emotional terrain of romance and treachery, an in-house playwright, forgers, counter-intelligence strategists, game theorists, and two mid-level managers, one of whom had for the last three years been a paid agent of the KGB, copying whatever came across his desk that might be of interest and cash value to the men who operated him out of the Soviet Embassy and met him at bowling alleys throughout the Virginia suburbs.

This authentic traitor, Michael Bortz, estimated that warning the KGB that one of their Czech ally's operations had been spotted from its very start and was now being played against them should be worth 20–25,000 dollars. After only three meetings of the Group, he steeled himself to betray Brief Encounter (preparing himself for the painful and repellent stomach ailments that would inevitably follow), left work on February 17, stopped for gas, and used a pay-phone to call his wife. Misdialing by one digit, he reached a man instead:

"Meest-ah Chow's catering, how help you?"

"Catering? I'm dialing the Bortz residence."

"Seem rike long num-bah, sah."

"That's easy for you to say, jackass." Bortz hung up, called his wife, told her he was going bowling and would be home late.

The final price was 12,500 dollars, as Bortz did not have Vanalden's name, but could only speak generally of something in Prague between a Czech girl and a CIA officer under diplomatic cover. The Soviets discussed the matter in Washington, then Moscow, then Prague. It did not take long for the KGB to identify the operation, and to learn that the false information the Czechs had received had already led to the arrest and near-execution of a loyal Romanian intelligence officer, implicated as a Western spy by Vanalden's disclosures. Clearly the Czechs should be notified that they were being lied to. But there was a problem: it would be unacceptable to end the operation with any suddenness, since the Americans would immediately begin looking for leaks, putting Bortz at unnecessary risk. Other solutions were discussed, including more or less staging the girl's death, thus ending the farce and confusing the Americans who had so arrogantly assumed she was a plant.

In the end, they told the head of the Czech service that Source Prep-school was contaminated and any information gained from him was to be considered 100% unreliable. However, under no circumstances was the female agent to be told anything which would affect her performance. In six to eight months' time, the Czechs should consider pulling back, but no sooner. In the meantime, say nothing which would cause the agent to have any "difficulties playing the role to which she was accustomed."

7. Jarmila found the persistence of the riots a little baffling, considering the presence of unyielding security forces and tough sentences. True, there were no executions, but the playwright Havel and others were certainly going to a rough prison for a very long time. She sat at her desk and watched videos of the last day of the riots, tried to identify familiar faces, made notes, wondered what drove these people, grew distracted by her own concerns.

Something was wrong. The Steering Committee for Source Prep-school was being reshuffled and the caliber of its new members was noticeably shabbier. Why was she being treated like this? She deserved respect and promotion. She'd bleached her hair for this. She'd gotten a stupid tattoo for this. She'd even convinced vile little Johnny 1950 to punch her in the eye (twice, since he'd been so feeble on the first swing and she had to call him a pathetic little faggot before he put any force behind it). And, obviously, she'd sacrificed in other ways, even if Prep-school was not an ugly man. She had to sit through meetings where videos of them having sex were analyzed for potentially valuable conversation. Johnny 1950 took the videos home with him, for God's sake. And yet the Steering Committee (responsible for planning Igor stories, her moods, her requests for information, her attitudes, even her wardrobe) was now chaired by Johnny 1950 himself, and of course the meetings dragged on and on as he leered and dreamt of being Tyler Vanalden and could not control the stupid contributions of the second-rate team now in charge of her life — the U.S.A. attitudes expert who spoke no English, the playwright who mooned like a little girl over Havel stories, the pimply kid who operated the video camera and had a weakness for unnecessary close-ups. And, honestly, by now they had more than enough video to start blackmailing Prep-school rather than prolonging the love affair, but Johnny 1950 kept the camera teams in place for every session. He imperiously proclaimed he was Chair and the time was not yet ripe for blackmail.

Was the changeover what she wanted? she asked herself. Would that be a relief to her personally? Would the information be better, more regular (she corrected herself) if they got on with things and made the painful but relieving shift to blackmail? What if Prep-school, learning the harsh truth, choking on his shame and potential disgrace and embarrassment, killed himself for love of her? He did love her — that was clear, even if "her" was a distorted version of herself. Of course, it wasn't that far from her real self (it wasn't as if she'd never been scared in her life, or needed a man's help), so Prep-school's mad, all-consuming love was really for her. She had inspired a love and devotion that led the American to trample all other priorities, and yet was unquenchable, even three months on. His will flagged from time to time, just as the Steering Committee had foreseen, but that just provided her a chance to demonstrate how quickly her words and kiss restored him to his better self. (Yes, *her* words, *her* kiss, no matter what the playwright had sketched out for the evening.) And this callow boy, this little diplomat was not without his appeal. He was weak, but brave when she asked him to be. He had been selected by Management for some reason, but still . . . still, he betrayed his country for her, not for Management or Johnny 1950. He threw tantrums, wept with shame, questioned everything, hid nothing. For her. He came to her with pure desire, a feeling so strong in him that it dissolved everything it touched, and not without pain, but with a searing pain that was fascinating to watch. The scenes! She had once thought he might even hit her: on the cold winter's coldest night they sat on the floor, crowding a small heater, drinking hot wine, listening to the British pop cassettes he had given her. He shouted: she had made him a liar and a criminal and a traitor and she didn't care about him and even as he was destroying himself for her, betraying everyone and everything, she risked nothing and — and she didn't even have to reply. She merely had to tremble a bit, sniffle only slightly, and he fell backwards into the one chair and looked at her in horror and pain, the shame of hurting her was too much for him to bear, even if it was all he had desired an instant before. He looked stricken, sickened, as he pulled his hair. "Please forgive me," he stammered. "You're the one at risk here. Oh, God, please forgive me, please . . ." And Jarmila said not a word, moved not at all, just let one more tear fall. Why do more, after all? He would project more easily onto a blank screen. Sure enough now he was promising to be better, he'll prove he's worthy, he's on his knees hugging her legs, sobbing that he will do more for her, save her no matter the cost, take her to the U.S. or anywhere else. And then he was kissing her with a hunger he sometimes showed after such scenes, and in the freezing apartment (unnecessary, but dictated by age-old protocol as good for Americans' sense of self-sacrifice), he made love to her with a passion marbled with anger. What a thing she had built: he had come to her a mess, a boy with no internal balance. And now he was a man who functioned according to her will. Without her he would fly off into smoke.

8. The Spring of miracles. While Communism crumbled in Hungary and Poland, the Czech Communists held on against the crowds of protesters, and Tyler Vanalden had the strangest sensation as he read each unimaginable dispatch from these other countries: he prayed the democratic virus would be contained. Irrepressibly, he hoped that Czechoslovakia would become an ever more restrictive dictatorship, lock every border, throttle every free voice. Otherwise it would come to an end, this thing he did for his country, he reminded himself. He walked amidst the thousands protesting on May Day and tried to figure out how things could end well if the government started instituting reforms as the Hungarians had. What if Czechs were allowed to emigrate freely? Then her story about Igor would no longer hold water, she could just leave. Which, of course, as a Communist agent, she wouldn't want to do. She'd be trapped in their story, and he couldn't see how to end it with them still sleeping together. If things kept up like this, soon he would have to say, "Come with me to the West." And she would stare at him dumbly, unable to speak. If only the Czechs would crack down on these marches once and for all! Then he and she could go back to the simple story line where they were forced to meet, indefinitely and always at the same fever pitch, and nothing would ever have to change. But only two weeks later, the Czechs had already paroled the damn hero-playwright, letting him out early when, obviously, now was the time to show some spine and not give in to mere kids and Bohemian bohemians.

Spring turned to summer and they were meeting about every two weeks, both sides careful not to be too available. He helped her when her stories about Igor sounded feeble; he would change the subject, or sound more guilty or angry or worried than her lame offerings dictated. They certainly didn't seem to have much of a creative staff on their side, besides just beating her up, so he pitched in. As for his part, he didn't need to fake much, just the shame about handing over whatever documents the Group had prepared, just the stumbling, getting a detail or two wrong but the gist right, talking about something hot coming around the bend. The rest of it was a pleasure. To think constantly about their next meeting, to beg her to meet him, to make love to her — none of this required an MFA in the dramatic arts. Of course, he knew that when he looked directly at her, he was not seeing her; of course, everything visible was a lie. But still, he told himself (though he had no reason to include the notion in reports) that if one looked at her as if at a photographic negative, one could easily develop the reversed print in one's own mind.

9. The Group received a Directive in July, apparently telling them to slow down a bit: *Let them play like sweet children, with the innocence of children, but also with their guile.* Marshall, accepting the need to vary the rhythms of the drama they were creating, nevertheless worried about his man in the field. To ask a young man to engage in this sort of intimate intrigue, to ask him to play with the most basic of human impulses, to help him keep straight his truest, deepest feelings and the distorted simulacra of those same feelings — this was asking a great deal, as anyone would know who read the transcripts of thirty years of post-operation agent interviews in Training Paper 5588's moving Appendix B: "Stuck in the Honey — Emotional Risks in Our Agents' Own Words." And now, Ed had to tell Tyler that weeks were going to pass in which Tyler was simply to "carry on," without making any obvious progress, without handing over any tangible lies, just pretending to want her while resisting her efforts to force things. "Director's trying to stoke their hunger, Ty. We want them to focus their desires, really boil for something specific, then we can pass them a zinger. Look, I'm sorry, I really am. I know this isn't easy. But a walk's as good as a hit. Think of these coming weeks as a chance to deepen your character in her eyes. Everything you help her see will strengthen their faith in you. Jesus, Ty, look at your face. Are you still up for this?"

When he left Ed's office, his heart was thumping: he had won himself at least four perfect meetings with her in which there was to be no talk of work. He was worried only that her people might not let her come out to play.

He invited her for a picnic in the countryside.

Her Steering Committee was divided. No video or audio team could hide near the picnic, argued Jiri from eavesdropping. There was no question of wiring her, considering she and Prep-school were likely to become intimate. Johnny 1950 left it up to Jarmila, who couldn't see how she could say no.

They ate in a wooded grove, not far from a stream, a lover's scene from the Bohemian countryside under any regime: Communists, democrats, Hapsburgs, Czech kings. Tyler fed her grapes. He made her laugh with a story of how he had snuck out of Prague to meet her. She started to say she was nervous about Igor, but he merely put his finger on her lips. "Not now," he said. "No Igor today. This is ours." After lunch he slept soundly with his head on her lap and she stroked his hair. She debated whether to broach work again. When he woke he described his parents' house on Cape Cod, and Vic the Labrador he'd loved and lost. After a long silence he said, "You know, I would do anything for you. Just ask. You have more power over me than, than any blackmailer."

"What a strange thing to say," she said quietly.

"Just an expression," he said. "But now that I think about it, I don't think I would respond to blackmail. For you, though, I'd jump through fire." He had been thinking just how to say this for some time now, to make it sound like the natural conversation of an unsuspecting traitorous diplomat. If her service was thinking about making the shift, using the pictures of him they must certainly have had by now, he wanted her to argue against it and for a continuation of the love affair instead. "I love you," he threw in for good measure. "I'd kill myself if anything came between us."

At the Steering Committee's disorganized meeting on the first of August, Johnny 1950 asked the Committee if, considering how little information Source Prep-school had provided in the preceding weeks, they thought the time had come to squeeze him, to tell him he had better start coughing up or the news of his betrayals and some compelling video would be sent to his Ambassador. Jarmila argued that this would be a mistake, she just had a feeling. Actually, she had two, but she didn't mention to the Committee that she'd rather, by a long shot, spend evenings with a slavishly devoted lover than have some moron from Manipulation pretend to be Igor and run the blackmail while she took a dull holiday on the Black Sea. "Be patient with him," she told the Committee. "I know him. Come up with a convincing threat to me instead. Put me in danger and ask for something specific. Prep-school will produce. I know he will."

And they did. And he did. Marshall was satisfied, as was the Group, which received an Approbatory Directive for its good work: *There is in every season a moment when the birds sing in unison and the heart is glad.*

The Czech government denounced the betrayals of Communism in Hungary and Poland, and arrested another few hundred protesters. Vanalden had the recurring feeling he was living the happiest days of his life.

10. That joy continued through his next four highly productive meetings with Jarmila and even into the first protests of November. The police were brutal on the seventeenth and there were rumors of martyrs; it looked as if the Communists were going to hold on no matter the cost. But Civic Forum marched again on the nineteenth. From the twentieth to the twenty-third, the protests were constant and direct: they demanded an end to Communist rule, nothing less, no euphemisms or half–measures. The twenty-fourth saw 300,000 protesters.

The Politburo resigned.

He could not find her anywhere. It was beyond belief. It was inconceivable, the secret pipe dream that the giddiest idealists in the West would have once been embarrassed to discuss. It took him hours to push through the crowds of jubilant Czechs and reach the friend's apartment, but it was empty. He could not find her anywhere. He had no way to find her if she didn't want to be found. He walked slowly among the crowds, the music, the dancing and singing, the art, the photographers and journalists, the loopy rumors that Havel would be sworn in as President. It could not possibly be happening; he could not possibly be seeing this, this most glorious moment of twentieth-century history, the sudden glowing apparition of pure and visible human spirit and heroism.

He was useless here, of course. The real diplomats' assessments and reports, even the reports of mere journalists without access to secrets, were of more value now than the classified speculations of the spies. Everything that mattered was happening in the open, on these streets where he walked and smiled at the kids and handed out high-fives and posed for pictures arm-in-arm with old women and poets.

What if he never found her? If the Communists really fell, so would she, and disintegrate in her descent, shedding her name and looks and papers and addresses and every flake of identity, landing where? Moscow? Pyongyang?

He was at a loss. He returned to the embassy and tried to write an Assessment, as if his assessments mattered to anyone now, as if his assessments determined events and did not merely guess at their hidden nature. He drafted a cable to Washington, which read: "This will all blow over. Communism is eternal. There is nothing to be done but get back to the business of Containment and observation. Now, of all times, we must refocus our efforts at subterfuge." He shredded it without sending and pushed his way home to sleep.

11. Ed Marshall, a laughing idealist, was also a perpetually striving pragmatist. Not wasting time to celebrate the momentary or permanent victory of justice, he set off to take advantage of his temporary position. Receiving an Authorizing Directive from Langley (*Build your bridges of smoke, cross them if you can, carry back across on your shoulders those who would drink of your well.*), he arranged to meet with the head of the Czech Intelligence Service, telling no one in his embassy. Standing under a bridge crossing the black Vltava, Marshall implied to this troubled spymaster that since the game was up, and whatever happened next was going to be a whole new world, now would be a good time to begin realigning the secret webbing that girdled any secure world order. Perhaps as a sign of good faith, these two men could close up the last chapter of history right here, under this bridge, next to the broken bottles and vomit. Marshall seemed to wave NATO and most-favored-nation status and billions in private investment around in the murky light: "But, if, for example, there were agents in place right now, the later discovery of whom might foster suspicion rather than the trust necessary between two free democracies and friends . . ." Marshall, generously taking the first step, revealed that the CIA had long ago recruited a particular Czech nuclear physicist (now safely dying of throat cancer). The head of the Czech service apologetically told Ed Marshall that, regrettably, he had a spy in the U.S. embassy named Tyler Vanalden.

Marshall sat at his desk a few hours later, trying to think through what was happening, not in the marches and the Velvet Revolution (yesterday's news), but what was going to happen tomorrow, whether the new government's secret service would be an ally or an adversary. He was puzzled. Why would the Czechs choose to give away Vanalden, who was strongly productive, rather than someone old or worn-out? Two days later, Marshall had his answer: a month earlier the IRS had found lumpy, indigestible discrepancies in Michael Bortz's tax returns, and an investigation, conducted without Bortz's knowledge, soon revealed he had thirteen separate savings accounts.

12. She could not convincingly avoid him, considering what was happening on the streets. Now more than ever, the story demanded that she be near him, excitedly discussing History's unimaginable, beautiful blossom and their future here or elsewhere. What's more, practically, if the government actually fell, well, maybe she would need his help for real. And, of course, if it didn't, there would be no reason to throw away this source or her career prematurely. Maybe there was a way to keep everything just the same: the work, the cold bedroom, the drama, the nights with the dedicated lover. She contacted him.

They walked, side by side, December third, as 150,000 protested the Communists' last-ditch effort to allow only a minority Opposition presence in a new government. They did not hold hands. They pretended to smile at what they saw. Neither of them spoke. Tyler the Traitor should have been delighted: it's over, she's free, he did his dirty bit for her without hurting anyone or getting caught and now it's past. Jarmila the Oppressed should have been delighted: her country was free, her future was her own.

Instead they walked in silence, arms crossed. Neither of them had reported this meeting to their planners, as her Office was in disarray (some people had already headed off to Moscow, others to the West) and his own embassy was busy reporting on overt events and expanding contact with the heroes of the Civic Forum.

"The world might look very different now," he managed to mutter as all around them the people of Czechoslovakia screamed that the world was going to look very different now. She nodded silently.

If, in character, he told her now she could come with him to the West, escape Igor and their shameful past, but she said no (as she certainly would), then he would be forced to ask her why not and she would be forced to admit she had been lying to him all along, and their time together would end. Or, he could tell her he knew she was a spy for a Communist spy service and now in the new world unfolding all around them, she would be in danger of arrest and retribution, so she should come to the U.S., be his pet defector, and they could be together. Of course, that would mean admitting to her that he had been lying to her since the beginning, that there was no Tyler the Traitor, that there was nothing about him that she actually knew. And, of course, that revelation would also mean his first act of actual treachery; it was impossible. So he imagined staying in character instead, telling her that his people had recently discovered he was betraying them for her, had shown him pictures of them and had told him she was a spy, not at all a maiden in distress, and that she had been using him, had tricked him into betraying his country for a lie, an illusion of love. His eyes flashed with tears at this horror, and he had to remind himself that actually none of that was true. But what would she say if he tried that story? Might that convince her to run off with him, now that she might actually be in danger, now that these crowds of gleeful democrats would probably start hunting for their oppressors, which surely included her? Perhaps he could claim he had been caught and offered a deal: if she returned to the U.S. with him, his government would not imprison him. In other words, she could save him now, a neat inversion of their original story. But what if she was tougher than that? Of course she was: look how she had spent the past months. If he tried that, she would just stick it out, buy time until she could escape him and this new republic forming itself out of the mist, run off to Moscow, somewhere far out of reach. So he kept silent.

She watched him. Something was not right here. According to all logic, he should have been happy to see the changes underway. He should have been offering her a way out with him. This should mean the end of his spying for her, this should mean the end of Igor's control over her. Why was he silent? Why didn't he realize that if there was no more Communism, no more Igor, then there was no more need to pass secrets and there would be no more meetings unless he said something? For that matter, why wasn't he telling her to come away with him to Cape Cod, to a wedding on his parents' lawn, frolics with some new Labrador? She saw clearly: he was a liar, that was why. He felt no slavish love for her, he had done what he had done out of lust and weakness and then lazy momentum and fear of being blackmailed and nothing else.

He was precisely what the playwrights and the planners on the Steering Committees had always said he was — someone perfect for their needs: a depressive, a weakling, lonely and vulnerable, randy and shallow, unprincipled and uninterested. In other words, he was an ordinary man, taking what he could get, an overheated dog talking love when necessary and not for a moment longer. She felt foolish: she had thought she controlled him but she had only traded sex for secrets, done what any Service-trained stripper could have done. She was disposable. Even so, did this egotist really fear she would want to come away with him? Had she painted herself as needy as all that? How embarrassing now, in daylight.

She had no real feeling for him (or for the "him" he had shown her, which, he had to admit, wasn't that appealing). That was clear. If any part of her had felt something real in this little farce of theirs, she would say so now, would playfully offer something, would make it up as she went along, would say she'd just this morning stabbed Igor in the head, would leave her now completely irrelevant job behind her and skip off with him as the new world figured itself out around them. True, she hadn't seen the best of him, she was judging from false evidence, but surely she had seen something under that stuff, surely she had been having fun, too? Surely, also, he had been the very opposite of "emotionally unavailable, artificial, perfect, untouchable, impenetrable, affectless." And that's what they all wanted, wasn't it?

Complete silence, except for the throng of cheering, pot-banging Czechs who washed into them. He moved to their left. She moved to their right. The crowd swelled, and they both kept walking, not even looking up to be sure they'd lost sight of each other.

13. The speedy secret investigation that followed from the IRS discovery, and the subsequent CIA interrogation of a sobbing, farting Bortz revealed much of what Bortz had betrayed over the years, including Operation Brief Encounter. In response to this news, a Guiding Directive floated downstairs: *Build castles* *on castles on clouds and place frilly flags in their highest towers! Sing louder!* And so, before his arrest, and in exchange for vague promises of leniency at his trial, Bortz delivered a final flurry of reports to his Soviet handlers, including one put together by the Operational Guidance Group at the request of Ed Marshall: Jarmila Hrbek had been a CIA agent all along: when Vanalden gave her false information, she had knowingly passed it on, and, when she was out of her bosses' view, she had delivered Czech secrets to Vanalden. This happened in the countryside, on picnics.

Well, it was better than nothing, Marshall figured. It would throw the remaining Czechs into chaos. But that was a small comfort, when you admitted you had just spent months accomplishing exactly nothing. The poor kid. Marshall put off telling Tyler, but it had to happen eventually. He looked over old reports Tyler had duly submitted, carefully abiding by every rule. After every encounter with her, he had checked off the boxes indicating which intimate acts had been performed, had even filled out the blank lines next to "Other." He had even taken an injury, breaking his wrist falling on the ice outside her place. Now what could Marshall tell him? What had it all been for, this strange game the kid had played like a pro? Nothing, maybe the girl would get arrested, maybe the Czech Secret Service would fall apart, and that might be a help to the new democratic government, however long that lasted before the fascists or refreshed Communists inevitably made their play. This was small beer, if it was beer at all. He called Tyler in, told him he had been doing a stellar job. Marshall himself was putting Tyler up for an Intelligence Medal. Everyone was enormously, you know . . . "The self-sacrifice, the commitment, exemplary. And probably a real, tangible help in bringing down Communism in these historic times, during this complicated endgame. The down side, though, ah, Ty, is a little more complex. It would appear that, possibly, they knew about you, about us, from a pretty early time, ah, actually likely." Marshall couldn't mention Bortz, couldn't mention that in fact the Czechs had known about Tyler from as early as the second or third pass, that they kept it going for their own reasons, which Marshall himself couldn't quite figure. Tyler looked wrecked.

Tyler knew he should be depressed; his life and work for months had been a travesty. He was a videotaped joke. Yet he felt some growing sensation of happiness, the cause of which he couldn't place, until he realized there was a question he wanted to ask but did not dare ask aloud: why had the Czechs kept it going if they knew it was garbage? Because she had wanted to. She must have argued for it, for him, propped up the whole shabby structure with justifications, just to see him. Every time she met him had been a victory for the two of them, snatched from a dubious Czech service.

"Now cheer up, Ty. We got a lot out of this nevertheless. We twisted the knot one more time, just recently, I can't say more, but it might throw them for a loop. Which would make all your work valuable, retroactively. Now the thing is, we still have to play out our little endgame drama here, keep our cards close . . ." In other words, Tyler the Traitorous State Department Employee (as revealed by the head of Czech Intelligence) had to be "called back to DC for consultations," where, unfortunately, he had to be "fired" and live for a few months under a vague and unfulfilled threat of prosecution. Of course, as far as the CIA was concerned, promotions and new opportunities were coming, but diplomatic cover was over. "How we proceed we'll figure out later, but you have to be on a plane, looking worried and under discreet guard, in a little under three hours."

14. "Sit down," said Johnny 1950. She had come in to see if there was an Office at all today, the day the Communist President swore in an Opposition Government and then resigned. The few people still in the Office were visibly worried; nobody knew if they were going to be the Secret Service of the new Republic or a pile of corpses shot for their work on behalf of the late People's Republic. "There is some news," said Johnny. "I told you to sit down." He was such a turd, this little man. All bossy and official now, of all times, probably thought his background would protect him. He could claim he was a Canadian, she supposed. No, if she was going to hang, she was going to take the smarmy dwarf with her. "News?" she said, unconcerned.

"About two weeks ago, Management gave up Source Prep-school to the Americans. To try to win their blessed favor." She was confused, then realized Tyler was going to jail now, and wondered if and how she could save him — a sentimental, girlish thought that offended her even as it occurred to her. Because did this change anything? she asked herself. Not at all: on that last sickening walk, Tyler had said nothing to her, had not even tried to keep her. Let him rot in jail. Half-men like that deserve nothing less. She nodded, said nothing, turned back to her desk.

"Wait. Don't ask me any questions yet," said Johnny. "It gets worse. Management also has known, for months and months, probably from day one, something he didn't tell us, so you wouldn't make any mistakes." He examined her beautiful face as he told her that they had been holding a losing hand, that everything she had done on Prep-school had been meaningless, a waste from minute one, that she and all of them had been fucked, beaten. Prep-school was CIA from the very first pass, and she had never noticed. Her sacrifices had been worthless, Johnny repeated twice more for good measure, trying to soften her up. "Wait," he said, with a mix of pity and vengeance and pride at knowing more than anyone else, "it gets worse." And she laughed out loud. This one was so beautiful; she made Johnny's heart shake in its cage. "Yes, worse: a report has come in from our old friends, perhaps ex-friends, to the East, a report that I happened to see, since we're a little short-handed right now, and Management is giving this report serious consideration: that you have known since day one that Prep-school was CIA. Wait, don't talk. It's better if you don't say a word just yet. This report also says you have been sending things the other direction, working for the Americans the whole time. On a dozen country picnics with Prep-school. Don't speak. At first, Management was going to have you arrested, but we actually don't have anyone who does that sort of thing for us right now. We are in a vacuum. Listen and think: if you did this, no one is sure if that's good or bad. If you did this, no one knows what to do about it. Maybe you're a traitor to the Czech people. But maybe you're a hero of the Revolution. Don't speak."

She wasn't listening very hard. She had been Tyler's little joke, whoever Tyler was. He had even sent her this nasty little valentine as a farewell.

Johnny's tone softened: "Don't worry, Jarmila. I can handle this for us. I know how these people think. I grew up among these people, you know. You and I, we can help each other." When Johnny 1950 smiled, he looked like a reptile she had kept in a glass box when she was a little girl, feeding it live bugs, frightening her sisters.

15. Personnel approved Tyler's quick, unsolicited proposal, agreeing that the venture would place him near potential sources, and that the role fit his real personality and official history excellently. Approval came from upstairs: *Is not liberty charming when she allows us to be ever more vigilant on her behalf?* The Financing Office determined his operational budget and how to fund his new company secretly.

And so, in May, 1990, four months after he had been bundled out of Prague, he returned, a vaguely disgraced but unindicted ex-diplomat running his own business, hawking to the new democracy an expertise they were sure to need. He sat in his hotel room and watched a documentary on Czech TV. It had been made in April by a once-banned filmmaker and was written and produced by a J. McDougal. "The Revolution's Hidden Heroes" profiled those extraordinary souls who had secretly helped the democratic cause from the inside. She looked good on television, even better as a brunette.

The president of Vanalden Communications paid five hundred dollars to attend a meet-and-greet in the banquet room of the Palace Hotel. He arrived two hours early, examined the seating arrangement and discreetly changed it. Returning later to the crowded room, alongside representatives of a dozen other political consulting firms, he drank cocktails and chatted with an assortment of Civic Forum candidates running in the first free Czech elections since 1946. Over and over he outlined to the novice politicians his firm's services, the role of a political consultant in a modern campaign. He shared the sample advice he had overheard the real consultants offer: The moment you are elected is the start of your re-election campaign. Let the voters know you embody the Velvet Revolution while your opponent would return to the past. Be photographed with Havel as often as possible.

Dinner was served. He took his time going to the seat he had usurped.

"You look like someone I once knew," he said to the parliamentary candidate seated to his left, handing her his business card.

"I have that kind of face," she said, smiling.

"I saw you on television. You sacrificed terribly for the Revolution."

She laughed: "You can't begin to imagine."

"You know, I think I could be of great help to you in your campaign."

"I'd have to consult with my fiancé," she said, gesturing to the suddenly despondent bald man who, far away down the long table, had just recognized Vanalden. "But I doubt he'll protest. Tell me about yourself."

WENDELL STEAVENSON

Gika

One autumn day in Tbilisi, Georgia, where I lived, I was standing on my balcony, which overlooked the street. It was early evening, the light was faded and warm, and a breeze was blowing the blue out of the sky in preparation for dusk. Esma, my neighbor, was leaning out of the window, her generous bosom hefted over the sill, her habitual stupefaction radiating from a pair of large, vacant eyes. The tomato-widow on the far corner of the street sat in her shapeless black dress in front of a bucket of tomatoes (half sold, half hopeful). Sandro leaned on the doorjamb of the Manhattan Bar across the street in the vain expectation of early customers.

The group of street children who operated along my block — the gang of four, I had nicknamed them — was lurking on the narrow sidewalk below. It consisted of a girl, who had fat arms and a plain, ruddy face, and the three boys she directed. I had seen them many times before, working the corner where Vashlovani met Perovskaya, where the confluence of bars and restaurants produced the greatest number of potential wallets. The girl was sullen, the two pre-pubescent boys surly and blank, with dilated pupils and glued-open eyes. The little one was much smaller. He was dirty, dressed in a pair of old trousers cut into ragged shorts that hung below his knees, and a torn T-shirt. He wore a pair of black rubber village shoes and no socks. His body was strong and lithe, he lived close to the ground, and when he ran (which was often; he ran wherever he had to go), he ran fast with unself-conscious energy. He was my favorite, and I had begun to look out for him on my way home at night. When the four of them ran up to me to clutch at my hem and plead for cash, I always put a small coin into the hand of the little boy. His face sold well; it was too young. His eyelashes were long, his cheeks smeared with street grime.

He never looked up at me, his entreaty was cold and dull, and his gaze went past my shoulder. I liked to think there was just enough pride left in him to stop him meeting my eye. He knew his business well. He rubbed his nose as if he were ill, he beseeched in several languages, *"Bitte,* Pleeze, *Pazhalsta, Sivplay,"* his clothes were rags, his knees were bare. Sometimes, when I had no coins, I would reach into my pocket for a mulchy one-lari note. His eyes never left my hands as I searched through a pocket. He would hop impatiently, and when a corner of the note appeared, his hand would dart out, fluid as a fish, to snatch it from my fingertips, and he'd scamper away on his toes.

On this afternoon, he was walking down the street with a bucket of water, concentrating his frame against its weight. Then, across the street, from the confusion of the opposite courtyard — tumbledown, rotted balconies and standpipes, heaps of scratched gravel, lines of washing, an outside stove burning with pungent *shashlyk* — came a medium-sized yellow dog. It was chasing a pigeon like a ball. The bird was injured and rolled along the ground, furiously flapping a single wing. It batted the pigeon with its paw and encircled it with its jaws, but then suddenly thought of something different, wagged its jowls, and rolled the bird further down the street.

The commotion interrupted the slow drip of the afternoon and caught everyone's attention. The boy saw it too. He dropped the bucket, which landed on the ground with a leaden thud and sputtered, and burst toward the dog. His legs scrabbled, his elbows pumped the air, he rushed at the dog, shouting and waving him off. He stood in front of the pigeon to protect it, and the dog looked up, worried and upset by this intervention. It stepped back in deference to the boy, and hung its head. The boy scooped up the pigeon in the crook of his arm and raced off down the street. The dog crouched low with its tail curled under its body, ashamed, and walked away. The street was quiet again — the entire drama had lasted barely a minute.

I was left leaning against the wrought-iron balustrade of the balcony, half-wondering if I had seen it at all. "Stupid boy!" said Esma, "running about like a hooligan." Esma, according to Venera, the building's matriarch, was too lazy to pick up her baby at night when it cried. She was a simple, bored girl. Sometimes, she would sit on her balcony for hours, tearing leaves from her dried-out plants and watching them flutter to the ground below. Sandro had already disappeared inside the shadowed doorway of the bar. The tomato widow hadn't moved (for weeks, it seemed). Her head was slumped gently against her chest. Perhaps, I thought irreverently, she was dead. Who to tell about the boy's heroics? How he knew in an instant the injustice of size, threat, violence and bullies.

◇ ◇ ◇

"Hello," I told him the following evening as he rushed over. "What is your name?" He had never recognized me (though I liked to think of myself as his best customer), never looked up at my face, watched only for the coin I might produce.

He was undeterred. "Pleeze, give me money."

"I want you to tell me your name."

"Pleeze give me money," he repeated, his voice scratching a soft whine. How many times a night did he say those words? I took a two-lari note out of my pocket. This was a jackpot indeed. He moved toward it like lightning. I moved faster and held the note above his head where he couldn't reach it.

"Tell me what your name is and I will give you two lari," I told him, firm and unsentimental.

He took his eyes off the note for a second and looked me full in the face. There was a moment of hesitation, and then he understood that the game had changed. He smiled at me, revealing for the first time a row of grubby milk teeth. I raised an eyebrow back in contest.

"GIKA!" he shouted and grabbed the two-lari note, flourished it in the air with triumph, and raced away to show it to the sullen girl.

◇ ◇ ◇

The next time I saw him, I held up a one-lari note.

"How old are you?" I asked.

"SEVEN!" said Gika, grabbing the money and scattering dust around the corner.

"What is your sister's name?"

"NO SISTER!" One lari and Gika ran off together.

◇ ◇ ◇

"So who is that girl?" I asked, pointing toward the figure slouching on the corner.

"Her name is Maka," said Gika and stopped for a thoughtful millisecond. I put a lari into his hand and he dashed away.

◇ ◇ ◇

In this way I discovered that his mother was dead and that he was a refugee from Abkhazia. He said he came from the seaside but that he didn't remember it. "I remember the bombs," he said, "and we had to walk a long way." Abkhazia was once part of Georgia and was known as the Riviera of the Soviet Union, where subtropical hills fell into pebble beaches and so many blue Natashas came south in the summer to play with the Georgian boys. When the Soviet Union broke up, there was a nasty ethnic war, which the Georgians lost. Half of Abkhazia was Georgian, and the Georgians fled when the Abkhaz took Sukhumi, the new capital. Now

Abkhazia was only a besieged, shuttered place — listless, empty, full of ruins.

I also discovered that Gika had an unclear relationship with his father that did not include the knowledge of his whereabouts ("He's in Tbilisi," Gika had shrugged), that sometimes a woman came to give him clothes, that he slept on the floor (I couldn't pry where; off the street, his life was his own), that Maka had an older brother he did not like, and that he usually ate at the back of the Ovatio restaurant because Nena liked him — "She doesn't like anyone else," he had said with a touch of pride — and as long as he didn't bring other people, he could eat left-over soup.

◇ ◇ ◇

During the day, I would see Gika on the street and wave. He would wave back.

"Maka doesn't let you wash the cars?" I asked him once on a late October night with a great fat moon above. The two other boys were wiping down a red Grand Jeep Cherokee. (Everyone in Tbilisi knew that car. That was Dato Abashidze's car.)

"Maka can get ten lari, but people only give me five," he said morosely, looking down at the road. "They give me five because I'm only a child."

"Ah, so it's begging for you until your baby teeth fall out!"

"They won't fall out! If I don't eat apples, they won't fall out," Gika insisted.

Maka emerged from some doorway, saw him talking to me, and snapped her fingers.

"Get up the other end of the street," she shouted, "Don't stand around here doing nothing."

Gika did not seem menaced by her, but she was his authority. He obeyed slowly, casting a nonchalant look up and down the street, as if he hadn't heard her. Her hips were buckled under the weight of standing up; she was tired and red-rimmed. There was a small sore at the corner of her inflamed bottom lip. She shifted weight from one leg to another, the antipathy of fatigue driving from her a final declaration of displeasure. "Gika, you're a fuck. Waste of time," she told him without interest and turned back, leaning against her doorjamb, predatory, proprietary.

◇ ◇ ◇

"You know they make fifty lari a day begging," Kakha told me once. We were walking along Perovskaya toward Andropov's Ears, great loops of concrete from which the apparatchiks used to watch parades. A crowd of dark girls with burnt faces and hair tied with bits of rag and colored ribbon had come up to snatch at our clothes, their fingers deft tiny tentacles. These street children were younger than Maka and her boys; a five-year-old carried a baby on her hip. They answered to adults loitering in apartment building entryways, underneath arches, behind low walls. When we kicked and flailed at the scratching girls to drive them away, they ran off in a scrum of dirty, colored calico toward a woman who took the baby from the five-year-old and began to hector the brood.

"It's a business, organized, gypsies." Kakha was unsympathetic. Kakha was a lawyer. He spoke perfect English. He had studied at Stanford for two years. "They send their grandmothers out in old clothes to stand in the underpasses with their hands out. Fifty lari a day —" His mobile phone rang and he broke off to answer it.

◇ ◇ ◇

Soon it snowed, not much, but wet and cold. Tbilisi put on its thick coats, hacked firewood from the trees along the highways, and stocked balconies with jerry cans of kerosene. One night I found Gika shoeless, padding through the snow with raw naked feet, begging. I noticed that one of his front teeth had fallen out after all.

"Where are your shoes?" I asked him as we walked into my doorway, out of the wind. The grand old art-nouveau entrance hall was filthy, full of trash and stink from passersby. It was sometimes lit by two twenty-watt bulbs, which were so dim it was possible to look directly at the wriggle of glowing filament. During the winter, though, the power was out most of the time. Gika and I shivered in the dark.

He didn't answer me.

"You'll get sick if you don't wear shoes, and then you won't be able to work," I told him. "Don't your feet hurt already? That's the first sign of sickness. Then it will get worse and you won't be able to run in the street. And if it gets very bad your feet will turn black and a doctor will have to cut them off."

"No, he won't."

"Did Maka tell you to take your shoes off?" I asked him.

"I get more money without shoes," Gika said flatly. There was something different to his voice, changed from the innocent summer whine. His face was white with cold, his lips and feet were blue.

"Well, if she had half a brain, she would tell you to keep your feet warm, or they'll fall off. Very difficult to walk without feet." He fiddled with the ragged woolen ends of his sleeves and didn't say anything. He seemed to be debating whether to ask me for money.

"Where are the other boys? What happened to Igor and Edik?"

I hadn't seen the other two boys lately. Or perhaps they were around, perhaps they had merely dissipated into a broken doorway and become part of the hardscrabble scenery.

I looked at my watch. It was midnight, January, frost on the streets, snow on the hills.

"Why don't you come upstairs and I'll make you a cup of tea and you can get your feet warm?" I said. I don't know why I offered. Perhaps it would have been impossible not to.

"How much will you give me?" he said. So we weren't friends after all! Now I was irritated with my generosity.

"You're a charity case, Gika. This is how it works. I give you something and you say thank you. So if I give you tea, you say 'Thank you for the tea' and not, 'How much money will I give you.'"

"I need money." Gika was sour. His face was tensed and screwed up against the glare of the headlamps coming from the cars that occasionally drove past.

"I need money," Gika repeated, stamping his blue feet.

"I'll talk to Maka," I said, annoyed at the whole charade, annoyed that, somewhere, there was a Minister sitting in front of a centrally-heated radiator looking over the architectural plans for his new dacha.

I walked around the corner to look for Maka. She was almost a woman now, beyond the innocent beg. She sat in her disused doorway next to the Mexican Restaurant and held her hand out when men went by. I'd seen her try and catch their eye. She'd glance up at them aslant, with a look she had fashioned as allure but which came out as desperation. Her lipstick was smudged, her frame was heavy, her face thick-skinned, as if it were permanently bruised. The smeared cosmetics — a patch of shiny pink on each cheek, a ring of purple eye shadow — only brought out her village roots. She was a lump of painted earth sitting on a lump of concrete.

I found her folding a small bottle of vodka into the interior layers between sweater and singlet and nylon rain jacket and woolen coat. "Gika's feet are frozen. He needs to go inside for a couple of hours," I told her. She returned a look of malice. I reached into the pocket of my fleece jacket and gave her the half pack of cigarettes I had there.

"Give me twenty lari," she demanded in a voice that was even, dull and lifeless.

Resigned, I took out a ten-lari note. "You can have this," I told her flatly. She took it without looking at me, waving me away, turning her head toward a man walking by in an expensive cashmere overcoat.

Gika was still standing in my entryway when I returned. "I've given Maka some money for you. So you can come upstairs and warm up your feet." Gika shrugged his little shoulders at the big world. Time was money. But as I walked up the stairs with my torch playing a weak beam, he followed me.

I unlocked my door and pushed him a little ahead of me into the hallway. It was pitch black, as there was no electricity, and the streetlight, which I had hooked up to an illegal second line, was also off. I lit a match and carried it as far as a group of three candles on the table in the living room. "Go and light the other ones," I told Gika, handing him a box of matches and pointing in the direction of the other candles, scattered on the mantelpiece and the side tables. "I'll turn the gas fire on and the room will warm up."

He stood in front of the gas heater with his hands out, his scratched palms facing upward. His face remained covered with a wrap of scarf. He had on a wool hat that was pulled down over his ears. As his feet began to defrost, they dripped puddles of melted street slime onto the floor.

I made the tea and set two mugs in front of us.

"You can sit down, you know."

He sat down.

"So where do you sleep? I don't want to ask. But you can't sleep outside in this weather."

"In the Iveria sometimes," Gika answered, his hands wrapped around the mug of tea.

"You have people you stay with there?"

"There are a couple of empty rooms that they keep for foreigners in the summer, and I can climb over the balconies. I know how to get in."

◇ ◇ ◇

The Iveria had been a grand, high-rise Intourist hotel once. Now it was full of refugees from Abkhazia. They divided their balconies into narrow rooms with plastic sheeting and flyboard, strung up washing and television aerials, cooked on electric coils sunk into pottery slabs. I had been there once, to see a family that my friend Zaliko knew. He had brought them through the mountains after they'd fled Abkhazia at the end of the war. He'd found them huddled under a tree in the snow, sitting by their grandmother, who was already dead from the cold and the climb. There were five of them in one room now. The old twin beds were still there, mattresses tucked between them, as well as two chairs and a low veneer table that must have once been used for room service coffee. "The husband can't find work — I help them from time to time," Zaliko had told me, and I had silently stood and looked, accepting a cup of tea that the wife made in an electric kettle in the bathroom. "They used to have a farm," Zaliko said. "He doesn't know how to do anything else — I tried to get him work as a driver, but he doesn't speak any English and the foreign organizations want someone with their own car who speaks English —."

◇ ◇ ◇

The color was returning to Gika's thin cheeks, and he was beginning to shiver. "I'll make a bath," I said. "Do you want a bath? That'll warm you up properly." Gika regarded me suspiciously, but when the water began to run (open the gas canister, light the gas heater, click, click, whoosh of blue flame), he went inside the bathroom. I could hear the odd splash and drip of water against water, its slap against porcelain. Perhaps he was playing? He ran like an imp, but always in a direction, with a purpose. He was without insouciance. This was not a child and not an adult. He had neither the dependence and uncertainty of a shy child nor the easy, tearaway rampage of a confident one. He reacted to things without thinking about them. He had no sense of perspective or of the peripheral world beyond Perovskaya. He had a present and a pair of cold feet, Maka and her henchmen, and that simple phrase, "Pleeze, give me money."

◇ ◇ ◇

He emerged, half wet, half dressed, with several towels wrapped around him.

"More tea?" I offered. He nodded and sat back in front of the fire. He seemed to have lost his concave hunch, and as he flapped and swung his feet in front of the radial red of the gas heater, he began to relax and talk. Strange Gika sentences; he sounded like a bird, part squawk and part child, part gang thug, random, staccato bursts of information, gossip and tough talk.

"From the Iveria on the 17th floor you can see the whole city. You can't see anything here," he glanced around the room. "Plus it's a noisy place you live in. And it's not good — many people know you live here alone. Last week there was blood all over Dato Abashidze's car. He said he hit a goat on the road. We washed it off. Did you know that the same people who own the Nali own the Manhattan Bar? And there's a man who comes down from Moscow and watches to see they don't steal any money. There was a big fight about the Mexican Restaurant; the supermarket next door wanted to buy it, but then someone else wanted to buy the supermarket. The same man who shot his partner at the Saburtalo casino. Have you been there? They've got a car outside you can win. Sandro says Moscow is much colder than here, but Abkhazia is the warmest place in the world and it never snows there.

Why don't you have any husband?"

Gika stopped for breath and drank his tea.

"I don't have any husband because nobody ever asked me to marry them except for a Pole on a train once."

"Why did he ask you on the train?"

"I think he was a bit drunk."

"What's a Pole?"

"A person from Poland."

"Oh."

There was a pause.

"Where's your radio?"

"On the bookshelf." I went over to the radio and turned it on.

"I want to listen to Ricky Martin."

"Ricky Martin?"

"I saw his name written on a wall. I never heard him. Is he American?"

"So you can read?"

"Of course I can read. Maka taught me."

I poured myself a whisky. Gika was unwinding, suddenly my responsibility, too smart a survivor, apparently at ease in my flat, his cowlick drying by the gas heater and a string of questions in his mouth.

"How many do you smoke?" Gika asked.

"Too many."

"In one day, how many?"

"Twenty," I lied.

"Twenty," Gika calculated. "Kent?" he fingered my pack.

"Whatever they have. Sometimes Marlboro, if I can find them."

"I know a man who sells Marlboro to the women who sell cigarettes on the street. I can get some for you. He's not a bad man."

"Thanks."

"That's no problem for me. Your radio is bad," he commented, looking it over. "It's small."

"It's a radio," I told him bluntly.

"It's not loud enough."

"The batteries are low. I forgot to buy new batteries."

"Have you got television?"

"I have a television, but no *electricity.*"

Gika was unperturbed. "You can get electricity from the Santa Fe bar."

"I asked the guy already. He wants me to give him $700."

"$700, that's not much."

"Not for you, street millionaire. How much do you make in a day, anyway?"

"About fifty lari."

"Not such a bad business."

"Not so bad. It's better than selling those stupid roses."

"But at least selling roses is honest work," I told him. "Begging is just taking people's money for nothing."

"But they give it to me," said Gika logically.

"Only because they feel sorry for you. Do you want them to feel sorry for you?"

"I don't care," replied Gika easily enough. He looked around himself, considering his surroundings.

"Can I sleep here?" he asked, suddenly plaintive; now that he wanted something, his tone was different. "It's late now and there won't be many people on the street." He looked up at me and blinked.

"And how much will you pay me?" I asked him, and he had the grace to laugh at that.

I found him an old, long-sleeved T-shirt and extra blankets. I told him to leave the electric fire plugged in, and if he was lucky, it would come to life in the morning. He came in behind me and took off his clothes (down to a pair of muddy underpants), put on the T-shirt and clambered into bed, so that he was just a small lump under three quilts and a heavy blanket.

"You'll be OK," I told him, and left him with a candle.

◇ ◇ ◇

Gika slept late the next morning, heavily, wriggling slightly through his dream world, fluttering his eyelashes as if he knew I was watching him and he wished to perform his very best impression of an adorable, lost thing. On the chair was a nest of his grimy rags. I peered at them, thought about burning them.

He woke up at noon and came into the kitchen in his muddy underpants and my T-shirt (which came down to his knees) and his bare feet.

"And you have three rooms all by yourself?"

"Yes."

"And you don't have any children?"

"No."

"Where are your parents?"

"In another country."

"In Russia?"

"No, somewhere else."

"In Kakheti?"

"No, across the sea."

"Oh."

◇ ◇ ◇

Gika evidently felt quite at home and opened the cupboard to help himself to some bread.

"My mother is in heaven," he said, sitting down at the table and tearing apart the loaf. "That's what Nena says. And I believe her. Maka says she is only dead and there is no heaven. Maka used to know her before we came to Tbilisi and Maka says she was quite old, about thirty-two, and had brown hair and lived next to the sea. Maka says she sold ice cream in the summer, six flavors, as well as chocolate."

"And your father? Does Maka know your father?"

"I don't know. I can't find him. I asked Maka but she doesn't know. She says he was a bad man and never came to Tbilisi and maybe he's dead, but no one ever saw him." His mouth was full of bread and he stopped to swallow it. "I want to go back to Abkhazia," he said thoughtfully, still chewing, "and I can live in the house where I lived with my mother. It will be warm there."

The only thing I had in the house was pasta, so I boiled some. Gika wandered around picking up the objects strewn about, examining them and putting them down again.

"Come and eat," I told him, and he obediently came into the kitchen and sat down and began to dig into the spaghetti with two fists and ten clawing fingers.

"It's like hair! What is this?" He was tangling it around his thumb, dangling long strands in the air and making no effort to eat it.

"Eat it. It tastes good. It's got tomatoes on it. You can use the fork to eat it, just pretend the fork's a comb." Gika regarded the fork with skepticism, testing the tines with his index finger.

◇ ◇ ◇

There was suddenly banging on the back door. Venera was shouting from the other side: "Are you at home?" I opened the door. Venera stood there, wrapped in her bedding and wearing two pairs of woolen stockings. "It's so cold! My dear, please, some kerosene? Have you some small jug of kerosene?"

Venera was a tireless borrower. My telephone was her telephone and whether it was kerosene or a bit of garlic or an extra blanket or some coffee or a couple of cigarettes or a few balls of naphthalene or three eggs, she wanted them and I gave them to her. Venera was a loud old witch, unlike the rest of her family, who were silent and mean. She was not closely related to them. She might have been an aunt; I could never quite gather. My apartment was merely an extension of hers. She banged on my door, drank my tea, complained about her headaches.

"You have your foreign medicines. Your very good pills. Please, just give me one because my head is swollen like a watermelon and I can hardly breathe with the pressure of it!"

My medicine cabinet (diminishing as my reputation as a free pharmacist spread) was her medicine cabinet. I was down to half a packet of indigestion tablets and twelve Valium, which I was hoarding in case winter turned brutal and hibernation became necessary.

I would of course have given her kerosene if I had any, but she had already borrowed my last liter.

"Venera, you've had the last of it. You know I don't even use kerosene any more since the kerosene heater died."

"It's so cold!" repeated Venera, sitting down. "Maybe you have just one glass of wine — for warmth?" And then she noticed Gika.

"Ah, I see you already have a guest," she told me as I poured her a glass of sweet red wine, thick as blood. "Where is he from?" She regarded Gika with hostile curiosity because he was using up the hospitality I could have been lavishing on her.

"I found him on the street."

"You want to be careful with these stray children. They'll steal things from you," said Venera as if Gika couldn't hear her. "They're not angels at all. He'll make a copy of your key and the next thing you know, a whole gang has cleared you out." She leaned down and pinched his cheek with a fierce kind of maternalism. "He's a dirty thieving bastard child, there's no doubt, but he's a skinny wretch! He should be eating something nutritious, not that macaroni, and you never have any soup or porridge!"

This was a constant reproach. My fridge could never properly be her fridge because it was always missing vital ingredients. And since the fridge stood on our communal balcony, outside the back door of the kitchen, she kept a daily inventory.

"All you ever eat is macaroni and whisky," she said. "It's no food for a growing boy." She rose with her bulk and shuffled the two meters from my kitchen table across the balcony to her kitchen table to fetch a saucepan of *kasha*. "This is much better," she said, taking a jar of honey from my cupboard and pouring a generous spoonful into the *kasha* for Gika.

Gika looked at Venera suspiciously. "Eat, you idiot!" she told him, "I haven't poisoned it." And she sat down again, exhausted by her efforts, and plumped one of her meaty forearms on the table. "I don't know why I bother. The idiot is probably happier eating stray cats." Gika gave her a mean look with slanted eyes and began to shovel the *kasha* into his mouth, pointing each giant spoonful throatward. Venera felt herself momentarily vindicated and threw the glass of red wine into her mouth.

"Have you seen the Janelidzes' new satellite dish?" Venera was obsessed with the family downstairs, who were so rich that they had bribed someone to join their electricity line to the Metro — an almost permanent supply. "Merab Janelidze has stuck it on his balcony. He says it will receive programs from the BBC!" Venera shuffled me out of the kitchen to have a look. Indeed, across the courtyard, tied to the Janelidzes' balcony with wire, was an enormous satellite dish. "What does he think he's going to do with that? Talk to Mars? And never an invitation! Merab Janelidze never invites anyone to share his bright electricity — he won't even let you use his telephone! No sense of neighborliness at all. I remember when his mother was alive, nothing was too much trouble. We'd share things back and forth — she was always forgetting to take their washing in when it rained! Now they've got a washing machine and a drier. They never even bother to talk to us. And he's having a big fight with the council about putting a new gas pipe down the street . . ."

The satellite dish was indeed vast. Venera was indeed verbose. I made two or three appropriate comments: "Yes it's a giant, no they've never said hello to me either, God knows how much they paid for that electricity line," extricated myself and went back inside.

Gika was gone. The bowl of *kasha* was finished. I checked the important things; TV, radio, key in my pocket. Everything was still in its place — except for a pile of change I kept on the windowsill.

Gika hadn't been so foolish as to leave that behind. I went to the balcony to look out at the street, but there was only the tomato widow sitting on her fossilized stoop. Vashlovani was empty.

◇ ◇ ◇

Several times that month I asked Maka where Gika was, but she wouldn't tell me, or she didn't know, or she didn't like me. I didn't want to give her money, she didn't want to talk to me. I thought he must have sidled up to some family in the Iveria or changed his patch; in any case, there was no sign of him on Perovskaya, and when the weather turned warmer, I forgot to look out for him.

◇ ◇ ◇

I had two more reminders of Gika. The first came two days after Gika had disappeared. I was sitting in the second bedroom one night, reading with my torch, when I noticed dust motes jumping around in the light beam. I watched them carefully, moving like bromide atoms, randomly zooming up and down. I found an ivory-handled magnifying glass and held it up to the cone of light. Gika had left behind his fleas.

◇ ◇ ◇

The second came in the spring, when the hills were green and there was blossom and tiny new leaves on the trees. My friend Lela and I were getting our hair cut, and she was reading the newspaper for me.

"Nothing's happening," she complained. "It's all about the pipeline. More port redevelopment in Poti — oh — Dato Evgenidze's giving a concert next week, we should go."

"There must be something. Read me the scandal about the Minister."

"Which Minister?"

"I don't know, but there's always some scandal."

"No, there's only Sharadze shouting about the government taking out the ethnicity clause in the passports. He's finally given up demonstrating about the McDonald's opening next to the statue of Rustaveli."

"Is he cutting off too much? What do you think?" I was trying to look at myself in the mirror through strands of wet hair.

"No, I think it looks alright." Lela wasn't even looking at me, she was concentrating on the newspaper.

"Here's something —" And she read, translating for me:

"A boy aged eight, who had been missing for two weeks from Tbilisi, has finally turned up in Sukhumi. He was found sleeping on the beach, close to the Russian compound, and has been handed over to the Red Cross. 'He is well,' said Nikolai Turshin, a spokesman for the Red Cross in Abkhazia. 'He seemed to be tired and hungry from the journey but otherwise his condition is not bad.'"

The boy, a refugee from Abkhazia, was reported missing by a relative. He had told the Red Cross that he had traveled from Tbilisi to Abkhazia on foot, catching lifts with sympathetic drivers and sleeping on people's verandas. When he had reached the Enguri bridge, the cease-fire line that has divided Georgia and Abkhazia since the end of the war in 1994, he attached himself to an elderly woman going back to her small farm in Gali. The woman was known to the soldiers guarding the bridge, and the boy pretended to be her grandson.

"'They said they wanted to see where their house was,' said Turshin, of the Red Cross. 'The boy would be returned to Tbilisi on the next UN convoy,' he added. An Abkhaz reporter asked the boy if he liked Abkhazia and he replied that he liked the sea and the beach very much, but that he was disappointed not to find ice cream."

"That's all there is," said Lela, turning over the pages of the paper to check. "That's a good story for you."

I knew the Enguri bridge well. It was an ordinary concrete bridge, a suspended no-man's-land above the Enguri river. There was a Georgian checkpoint on one end of the bridge, and an Abkhaz-Russian checkpoint on the other. The soldiers stood next to their concrete breezeblock huts and low sandbag walls, their rifles slung over their shoulders, cadging cigarettes from the very occasional car that passed through, waving armored UN patrols around the barriers and not very effectively inspecting documents. (I had once been admitted to the "Republic of Abkhazia" with a library card.) The traffic across the bridge was mostly limited to old women in black, walking on foot, cowed and slow.

I thought about a small Georgian boy walking along the empty M27 highway toward Gali, and then to Sukhumi on the coast. Gali was a vacuum of control; bands of Georgian partisans, mines, drunken Abkhaz militia firing bullets into the air, bandits selling scrap metal across the cease-fire line, Russian peacekeepers sandbagged at checkpoints.

Gali was a wild rose overgrowing a derelict house, an abandoned cow chewing wild barley, an old man carrying a sack of hazelnuts in the summer heat. It was a deserted paradise: unharvested, the plums ripened and festered on the hot trees, smashed down through the branches when the wind blew, and bled on the ground. The apricots were pregnant, cherries swollen red, burst clumps of boysenberries and crimson cornels, grapes that hung purple over abandoned balconies. Standing still behind the branches laden with fruit were the gray-brick skeletons of houses that had been burned and stripped.

And beyond Gali were the minefields that stretched either side of the road beneath feral tracts of waving wheat and grass. After the minefields there were the two bridges that the Georgians had blown up when they were retreating from Sukhumi — blasted concrete collapsed into gullies, twisted metal. And then the checkpoints on the outskirts of Sukhumi itself, Abkhaz militia and cement anti-tank barricades like giant hurdles. Perhaps an NGO car gave him a lift, maybe a local car; it couldn't have been an armored UN convoy — they were under orders never to stop. By the time he saw the big blue sea stretched out in front of him he must have been exhausted, tired of the untrusting, unknowing fear of a journey: Who to ask? What to answer?

I tried to follow up on the story through the Red Cross, but there were three separate departments to navigate, and twice as many desk officers, and everyone was always out to lunch, and a week had gone by before I had finally found someone to talk to.

"The boy, yes," said the male voice, uninterested. "He was returned to Tbilisi a week ago. I am sorry I can't make any further comment." He didn't have a telephone number for the relatives. "Most of these refugee families don't have a telephone," he added.

When I went to Sukhumi in October for the Abkhaz presidential election, I tried to make inquiries at the Red Cross office, but there had been several personnel changes in the intervening months. Somewhere in the static of the telephone and the overlapping beige casework folders, between a frigid Tbilisi winter and a tropical Abkhazian spring, the boy who might have been Gika, at least in my imagination, was lost.

JOSIP NOVAKOVICH

Spleen

When I found out that a Bosnian family had moved into our neighborhood, just across from my place, I was thrilled. I had left Bosnia seven years before, and I hardly ever saw anybody from there, at first deliberately, because the circumstances under which I left were not pleasant, and then out of habit.

To me it didn't matter now whether the neighbors were Muslims, Croats, or Serbs; the main thing was that they were Bosnian, that they spoke the language I loved and hadn't heard in a long time. But when I learned that a Croatian family from Bugojno, my hometown, had moved in next door, I was especially delighted.

Maybe it was the timing. Perhaps I could have already gone back home, but I was wary because Bugojno was in the part of Bosnia controlled by Serbs. NATO supervision had made it possible to go back, and probably nothing bad would happen to me if I did, but I couldn't imagine sleeping there at night, without streetlights; I would think of masked thugs coming in, and then, inevitably, I would recall that night.

◇ ◇ ◇

When the news came that the Serb army was advancing on our town, many people gathered their things in a hurry and fled, but I didn't think the army would bother me. If they were targeting people on ethnic grounds, I thought I was safe, as I was half Serb, half Croat. Then, one night, somebody knocked on the door, and shouted, Open up! Police.

I looked through the door and saw two men with masks over their heads.

I went to the kitchen, took a sharp, mid-sized knife, put it up my sleeve and waited while they tore down the door. I hid in a closet. The two thugs went through the house, overturning the tables and smashing the china. They shouted for me to come out. One walked into the basement, and the other opened the toilet. At that moment, I snuck out of the closet and tiptoed toward the front door. But he saw me and knocked me to the floor. The knife slid out of my sleeve and made a dull sound on the parquet, but it was drowned out by the crashing of the plates he had knocked down when he lunged for me. He tore off my clothes. I could hear his partner smashing jars of jam and pickled peppers downstairs. Then the noise stopped. Probably he had found the wine bottles.

The thug pinned me to the floor. When I tried to throw him off, he whacked my head against the boards. I felt dizzy, as though my brain had come apart in my skull and was now loose and wobbling.

He slid a little lower and sat on my thighs. Help me get it hard, he said.

I don't want to.

You must. Here, take it into your hand.

I did. It's awkward like this, I said. Can I sit up?

Sure, no problem.

I sat up sideways, felt around the floor behind me for the knife, grasped its handle, and without hesitation plunged it into him. I wanted to get him in the middle of his abdomen, but I missed and struck somewhere on the left side. It didn't go deep.

He shrieked and didn't react when I shrugged him off and ran outside. I ran into the hills, naked in the cold November night. I turned blue and nearly froze. I didn't know where to hide, except in the Benedictine monastery on top of the hill. I broke into the chapel in the middle of matins, five in the morning now, still dark. The poor men crossed themselves, hid their faces, and prayed in Latin. I especially liked one word: *misericordia*. Finally one of them said, Brothers, don't be silly. Help her! He took off his brown habit, covered me with it, and stood there in his striped shirt and long johns.

The monks gave me hot water and coffee, and when I stopped shivering, I decided to leave. I told them what had happened and advised them to run away as well. The one who had spoken up for me drove me west, to Mostar. He wanted to hold hands with me while he was driving. What was the harm, I thought? This fifty-year-old man, holding hands. He didn't ask for anything else. I think he just loved being close to a woman.

In Mostar, I stole a bicycle, and rode it all the way into Croatia, to Metkovic. It wasn't hard, since the road mostly goes downhill. And in Croatia, I appealed to Caritas, the aid group, which helped get me to the States.

I've always been a homebody. I never had wanderlust. The only thing I enjoyed about travel as a kid was the homecoming. I'd rush to the side of the train as it crested the hill before my hometown, and seeing the church steeples and the minaret and the old castle rising from behind it made me happy. So it's miraculous to me that I have traveled halfway across the world and become an American.

The bank where I work is a nice place. Next door, there's a restaurant, Dubrovnik. I don't eat there, but knowing this tiny bit of homeland is just next door comforts me. I did go in recently with another bank teller, a Polish woman named Maria. We walked upstairs to the restaurant and entered a tobacco cloud. The customers suspended somewhere in the stinging smoke made me think of angels nesting in a cloud. I could barely make out their silhouettes, blowing smoke from their cigarettes, feeding their blue cloud, as if they would all fall to earth the moment it vanished. But of course there were no angels here; most of the people were recent immigrants from Herzegovina and Croatia, and some had participated in the war.

The chicken *paprikash* was soft and juicy, tasting of green and orange peppers.

Have you met the new Bosnian family next door? Maria said.

No. I had no idea that anybody had moved in.

They are having a barbecue next Saturday. They invited me, said I can bring anyone I want. Want to come?

Maria wiped her shiny lips and cheeks with a napkin and said, The men are quite handsome.

Her napkin turned red.

◇ ◇ ◇

My new neighbors' backyard was shrouded in smoke from the barbecue. I enjoyed the smell of the coal. Grilling is one staple of American culture we from the Balkans quickly adapt to, although we use our own meats, like the spicy *chevapi*.

The boom-box on the windowsill played folk music, the kind that used to bore and irritate me, but now made me feel at home. You know, accordion, bass, and a wailing voice.

The bald host wore a green outfit as though he were in a hospital, and when I asked him whether he was a doctor, he said, I work at Mercy Hospital as an X-ray technician.

That's a good job, isn't it? How many hours a week counts as full-time?

Twenty-four.

So you have lots of free time. Nice.

It could be nicer. I studied to be a doctor in Sarajevo, did very well, but wasn't very wise: I participated in a protest against Tito, had to go to prison, and couldn't go back to the university afterward. I had no choice but to emigrate.

Have you met my nephew yet? He pointed to a man who was facing away from us. The man turned around, balding like his uncle, with a wide bony face, and teeth unusually white for someone from our parts. They were also spaced far apart — maybe that's what saved them.

He looked familiar, but the more I looked at him, the more I was certain I was mistaken. Many people from my native region evoke that feeling of familiarity though I have never met them. In my hometown, they'd all be strangers to me, but the familiar kind of stranger, and I decided the nephew was this kind of person.

He came over and asked where I was from and what I did, the kind of questions you would expect from an American, not someone from our native region.

He got excited when I told him I worked for a bank. I need to buy a house, he said. Can you get me a mortgage? What's the best rate you can offer?

That depends on your credit rating.

Credit rating?! Phew. How would I have any? But I have refugee status, and a Lutheran church backing me. And I just got a job, as an electrician.

You must be smart then. A dumb electrician would be dangerous.

You're right about that. But maybe I am a dumb but brave electrician.

Have you ever gotten shocked?

Of course, who hasn't. Even you have, probably.

True.

The bank, he said. Isn't it boring to work there?

Not in the least. There are many Croats and Slovenes. But no Bosnians.

So it must be boring!

It's always interesting with our people — they're still our people, to my mind. One day a man paid for a house entirely in cash. He opened a brown suitcase — it was full of ten–dollar bills. Nothing but ten–dollar bills.

'Why don't you write a check?' I asked him.

'Can't trust checks,' he said.

'And why only ten–dollar bills?'

'Can't trust hundred dollars bills,' he said. 'Too many Italians here. They print fake bills. Ten dollars best.'

He was an old Croatian car dealer. The motto of his dealership was, "Honest Cars for Honest Cash." You wouldn't imagine that someone stuck in the cash economy could become rich, but that man did. He brought half a million dollars just like that. I wonder how he walked in the street, alone, with all that cash.

Dragan laughed. Our people are such hopeless hicks! We are all peasants. He had kept inching closer and closer, and I had kept moving away from him, and in this way we kept circling the yard. I was keenly aware of it, but he wasn't, apparently, or didn't mind. Perhaps I had adopted the American concept of personal space, usually defined as an arm's length, which helps make sure nobody can touch or hit you without your having a chance to get out of the way. It's also just far enough to protect from bad breath. I like this Anglo-Saxon personal space, but naturally, a recent arrival from Bosnia wouldn't understand it, would find it cold and standoffish.

But after a while it occurred to me that he was not so much after a house and a mortgage as after me.

In the meanwhile, his uncle was telling Bosnian jokes to some woman, who rewarded him with her booming laughter.

Then we ate *chevapi*. I looked forward to it, but the meat was too dry. In their eagerness to talk, our hosts forgot the meat. Actually, because we didn't have refrigerators in the Balkans, we always overgrilled in order to be sure all the bacteria had been killed. It was in America that, for the first time, I saw people eating bloody meat, calling it rare and medium rare. With us, there was only one way: well-done.

I drank the red wine Dragan offered — it was spectacular, deep red and purple *Grgich*. It tasted of plums. Both he and I relaxed, and he showed off his repertoire of Bosnian jokes. I found many funny then, but strangely I can't remember any now.

Anyway, I agreed to go out with this man, Dragan, for no serious reason other than that I loved speaking Bosnian. We met in the neighborhood beer hall. Cleveland has many ethnic neighborhoods, and this was the German contribution.

You know, he said, my uncle is a funny cat. At night, he sometimes dresses like a doctor and pretends to be one, and visits patients in the clinic, even offering them new diagnoses and advising them to undergo surgery; he loves to advise heart patients to get transplants. He was caught impersonating a doctor and fired, but then, there was such a shortage of nurses and medical technicians that they let him come back. He suffers on the job because he imagines he knows much more than his superiors. He is so absorbed in his status struggle that he neglects other aspects of his life. He lent his life savings to a friend from Bosnia, 40,000 dollars, without a security note, just on the man's honor. The friend disappeared, and that was that for his life savings. What an idiot!

How can you speak so badly of him? He takes care of you.

I am not speaking badly of him. Everybody knows what he's done. It's funny.

Mostly sad. He lost so much money. And he pretends to be what he isn't. Does that run in the family?

What do you mean? Reckless generosity? Well . . .

No, pretending.

I don't pretend anything.

I did not say you did. I simply wonder whether what he's doing is a family trait.

Is that how you talk for fun?

Yes, I continue a theme, a thread. He's your uncle.

And so? What are you getting at? (He stood up.)

My God, I thought you had a sense of humor.

Yes, I did once.

OK, mellow out. Have a beer.

Good idea. Two Guinnesses please, he asked the waitress, and turned his head. The waitress wore a short skirt and black stockings that rose only a few inches above her knees, so there was a stretch of thigh between the hem of the skirt and the stocking.

Good body, I said.

Guinness has lots of body.

She has a good body.

You noticed?

I noticed you noticing.

Oh, here we go again. You are testing me or something?

No.

I noticed her style. I don't know whether she has a good body, but the style —

Sexy?

I forgot how difficult our women can be. Now I feel right at home.

Same goes for our men. I do feel at home. That's the point, I wanted to feel like I was home.

And that's why you agreed to come out with me?

Yes.

It doesn't matter what I am like, the main thing is I'm from over there?

It matters what people are like.

The beer was foamy and cool, and left a creamy edge on his lips, but he didn't wipe it off, and talked like that, with the foam on his upper lip.

The second round of ale went to my head. American bars are dark. We kissed in that darkness under the spell of the dark ale, or under the excuse of it. He tasted of unfiltered cigarettes, and I liked that; it reminded me of home. I had kissed a few Americans, and nonsmoking immigrants, who, before the kiss, regularly chewed mints, so their mouths were cool, slightly antiseptic. And afterward, they would always go to the bathroom, no doubt to floss and brush their teeth. But this was a European kiss, old–style, with a nicotine bite to it, and an undercurrent of hot peppers — he must have had *feferonki* somewhere. The kiss was an old sensation, momentarily replacing the longing for home; I closed my eyes and floated into a smoky space where Turkish coffee was poured from *djezve,* leaving heavy dregs on the bottom from which old peasant women read fortunes. After drinking a cup, you'd have a few coffee grains left in your mouth to chew on and chase around your mouth with your tongue, and that is what the kiss now felt like, a grainy chase. He kissed my neck, his five o'clock shadow rasping me like sandpaper, but I liked that feeling of rawness.

We were so impatient when we got home that we didn't even fully undress. I still had my skirt on, and he had his shirt and tie, though everything else had come off. I pulled him to me by the red tie, and the tightening collar, together with all the exertion, made his face go red. Blue veins sprung out on his forehead, shifting shape and altering their course, like the overflowing tributaries of a river urgently seeking the shortest way to sea.

I wondered why this man trusted me to pull the tie. I felt a sudden impulse to strangle him, inexplicable, but tempting. Instead, I let go and loosened it. He panted with his mouth open, baring his teeth, and again he kissed my neck, and bit it, perhaps playfully, but hard enough that a wave of fright shot through my blood. I bit his ear. We kept biting each other, as though we were two wolves, steadying each other in the grip of our teeth. Our lust seeped down to our bones, and came from our bones, and flesh was in the way. The bones of our love made us sharp, not dreamy and sleepy, as I used to feel during lovemaking, not floating in the delicacy of sensation, but aggressively alert. It was as though we wanted to destroy each other — it was the kind of feeling you have when your life is suspended in mid-air, when you are jumping off a cliff into a deep azure bay, or when you hit a bump while skiing downhill.

There was an extraordinary undercurrent of hatred in our sex, and it shocked me. I was shuddering in the premonition of an orgasm, I thought at first, but no, it was from the fright. He let go of my neck, and his tie tickled my stomach and breasts as he rocked back and forth. I was nearly strangling him again, holding on to his tie like a friar to the church bell while he was smashing his pubic bone into mine in rhythm to the bell. Love and lust aren't synonyms, as everybody knows, and hate and lust aren't antonyms, I learned. Love is safe, and in that sense, antithetical to the abandon and collapse of an intense orgasm. Hatred helps along that delicious sensation of ruin and self-destruction.

I slid my hands under his shirt, and touched his stomach. It twitched like the flank of a horse when bitten by a horsefly. His skin was smooth and soft. That surprised me because his neck hair stuck out of the collar of his shirt. When my hands roamed further, he grabbed them and brought them back. That tickles, he said.

So? Tickling is good. You can tickle me, if you like.

I touched him again, and he twitched and lost his erection. That was just as well; we had been at it for several hours, and we sighed with relief, perhaps contemplating for the first time the unsettling nature of our collision.

Even after he was gone, I sat in amazement at what had taken place and the animosity which hung in the air like the fallout of a war of different body vapors, his sweat and my sweat, his garlicky, mine olivey, his sugary, mine salty.

After he was gone, I wondered why he had kept his shirt on, and thinking this I fell asleep. I woke up, certain I had had an enlightening dream, like that biochemist who had a vision of a snake eating its own tail, which became the solution for the circular structure of benzene or whatever it was. In my dream, Dragan appeared in a black T-shirt. Why don't you take it off, I asked him?

I can't.

I will make love to you only if you take it off.

I'd rather not.

So I undressed and teased him, and when he took off his T-shirt, I saw a brown scar on his left side, under the ribs, in the area of the spleen. The scar paled, then blushed, then turned an angry red. Drops of blood slid out of it and slipped down his flank. Give me back my shirt! he yelled. I had thrown it behind the bed. I don't know where it is, I said.

Find it! He said. Blood was gushing now.

When I decided to take mercy and hand him his shirt, he fell to the floor in an oily red puddle. There was so much blood now that the furniture floated, and my bed turned into a sinking boat. I shrieked, and woke up to its echo, from the attic and the basement; the house was full with the ring of my shriek.

I went to the bathroom. The floor was dry. My gums weren't bleeding. My eyes weren't bloodshot.

We were supposed to meet again the following evening after work. I dreaded it. I would not answer the door. I would turn all the lights off and pretend I wasn't there. As eight o'clock approached the next day, I became terrified that he wouldn't come, that he would know I had figured him out.

Suddenly, three police cars squealed to a stop in front of the house next door, their lights flashing. Ha, I thought, they got him. Once they walked him out in handcuffs, I would run out and tell them what I had to add. I put on my Nikes, remembering that Nike comes from the Greek for "Victoria," the woman who wins. Soon the cops escorted the familiar bald silhouette, which wore green. It was the poor pretend-doctor. The nephew appeared on the doorstep and smoked a cigarette. Why didn't he talk to the cops, why wasn't he upset? Maybe he liked it this way, maybe he was even the one who turned his uncle in, to have more space to himself. Now he wouldn't need to buy a house. But what did I know what had happened there? I went back to the kitchen and made a cappuccino, letting it hiss and spit like an angry cat.

Soon the doorbell rang. I let him in. This time he wasn't formal; he wore a black T-shirt, just like in my dream. He brought red carnations and a bottle of merlot. I turned on the music, Mahler's Fifth. Some of the funeral chords in Mahler's music give me chills, so this was masochistic of me, in all the redness and blackness, to have these jarring notes in minor keys.

You like that music? he asked.

Love it.

Why not play some real folk music?

Later. This is good for a slow start.

We have been anything but slow and we are way past a start.

I've never heard a man complaining about getting to bed too quickly.

I'm not complaining. But then, maybe I could if you let others sleep with you so quickly. How many were there before me?

Oh, there's been no one special. (I was trying to sound nonchalant, but it was true. There had been no one.) That poor uncle of yours. Why did they take him?

How do you know?

I am a good neighbor; I look out the window.

My uncle is totally insane. He went around the kidney ward, injecting morphine into the patients. He kept repeating, There's too much pain in the world, too much pain.

He's right about that. That's kind of charming.

It would be if the drugs weren't an additional stress on the kidneys. If he'd done it in the orthopedic ward, maybe nobody would have complained, but he almost killed some of those people! It's shameful.

But he meant well, and probably the patients were in pain, and felt better afterward. Maybe he knows better about it all than we or the cops do. I think it's touching.

He chuckled. That gave me the creeps. Or maybe it was a particularly well-placed dissonance in Mahler. As though he sensed the chill in my spine, he repeated, You sure you like that music?

He slouched in his chair and smiled. He didn't look dangerous, but almost amiable, low-key, not like an alpha dog, but a beta, sitting by the fireplace with his tail curled under his legs.

He massaged his chest through the T-shirt, slowly, sensually. It seemed strange to me that a man would caress himself like that — it was surprising and slightly erotic.

Out of nervousness, I drank half the bottle, and soon we were kissing on my bed. I grew excited, partly because there was a forbidden quality to it: I had forbidden myself, and now I was transgressing. I had of course planned to get to bed and check for his scar, but I had wanted to keep my cool and avoid being aroused, but here I was, trembling.

I had a kitchen knife under the pillow, just in case. But maybe a man should have his last wish, without knowing it is his last, to make love. I didn't mind; in a way, I almost wanted him to become aggressive and dangerous.

As we kissed, I slid my hand under his T-shirt and touched his navel.

He pushed my hand away, and said, I'm ticklish.

Yes, I know you said that, but you don't mind being touched elsewhere.

Only my feet and my stomach are ticklish.

I touched his neck and tried to slide my hands further down, but his T-shirt was too tight.

What are you trying to do? He asked. You like collar bones?

Collar bones are my weakness. Why won't you take off your shirt?

Out of vanity. I don't want you to see how my stomach sags.

Now that you've told me that, what's there to hide? I know what to expect. Let's fully undress. Isn't it funny, we haven't been naked yet. We've screwed the living daylights out of each other, but we haven't seen each other naked.

All right, but turn off the light then.

I thought about it. I wanted the light to examine him. But I could do it in the dark, with my fingers. I turned off the overhead light.

Good, that will be romantic, I said. I'll light the candles then.

I took out half a dozen candles and lit them.

He pulled off the T-shirt, his red underwear, and his soccer-style socks, which almost reached his knees. He was in good shape for his age. He had lied: his stomach didn't sag. There were candles in every corner of the room and a tiny crack of light coming from the bathroom, but it wasn't enough to make out his scar. So as he lay down, I put my hand on his flank. He shrank, and his stomach twitched.

Just let go, I said.

All right, I guess you know a technique.

I felt all around, touched his ribs, below them, and I could not believe my fingers. There was no scar. Could my dreams have been wrong? It was horrible to think I'd found that man, that he was under my fingertips, but suddenly it was more horrible to think that this wasn't him, that he was still out there somewhere. How would I find him? Why did I want to find him? Why didn't I feel relief now? I should have been overjoyed to be with a man who made love so vigorously. I could have a boyfriend, maybe even a new family. That wouldn't have been outlandish at my age.

◇ ◇ ◇

I was in such a state of shock that I pulled away. I can't do it, I said.

Why not?

Bad thoughts have crossed my mind and won't go away.

What are your bad thoughts?

And I told him, in detail, about the attempted rape, and how I fled. Except I didn't tell him about the knife and the wound. I said I knocked the guy down with a candelabra.

That's admirable, that you had so much courage to do that, he said. But why would you think of that now?

Why admirable? What choice did I have?

Do you know what happened to the guy?

No, and I don't think I want to know. Do you?

Why would I? What a question!

I have no idea.

What, did you think I knew something about this?

I didn't answer. I decided not to worry. (I could continue to; I was tempted — the thought flashed in my mind that if this wasn't the first man, perhaps it was the second, the one who went to the basement to drink wine. Dragan certainly liked wine. Then again, what's so unusual about that? Oh, no, I decided, this had to stop somewhere.) We drank more merlot; he'd brought two bottles, it turned out, and had kept one in his briefcase.

Let's shower together, I said. Maybe we'll make love, maybe not, but let's shower.

He agreed and followed me. I soaped up both our bodies, and, covered in foam and hot water, we washed, our hair dripping, eyes stinging from soap, gasping from exhaustion and the lack of air in the steamy cubicle, suspended in a smoky cloud of our own. He tried to grasp me, and I reached for him, but we slipped from each other's grip. The evasiveness of our bodies undermined my balance, and I sensed the exquisite illusion of falling through a cloud.

ALEKSANDAR HEMON

Fatherland

Kiev
August 1991

Meantime we will express our darker purposes. Chicago, London, Amsterdam, Vienna, Warsaw, whence I took a cheap train to Ukraine. I boarded my train, found the couchette waiting for me, enveloped in thick veils of smoke and an obscure cologne called Antarctica: I watched the man in the bed across splashing a few palmfuls out of a gelid-blue bottle before the train left the station. He unbuttoned his shirt, as if stripping for me, slowly divulging his sooty tapestry only to stop an inch above his navel. The discomfort I felt then I am inclined to see now as a sense of momentousness — doubtless a rearview interpretation. The man lit a cigarette, eagerly opened a booklet with a chesty damsel in sexy distress on the cover, with a title that I — the uncertain, occasional speaker of an obsolescent Ukrainian dialect — decoded as *The King of Midnight.*

The King of Midnight offered me a sip now and then from a smudgy bottle. Having quickly slurped his way to the bottom, he threw himself on his bed with such force that an earthquake suddenly took place in my dream: the earth cracked open, swallowing swarms of citizens; roads whiplashed, throwing cars around like matchboxes; buildings collapsed flat. As the train crawled through Poland, I crept through a series of nightmares — all sequels to the earthquake one and involving a WalMart and the Sears Tower, plus mice, midgets, brooms, and other Freudian gewgaws. The final one was staged on the Soviet border: a mob of shabbily uniformed men with humongous flat hats waited in a shower of sallow, gnat-infested light; they stepped into the shadows and then onto the train. They alternately looked into the King of Midnight's passport and into his woozy face, as if comparing them until they matched. They flipped through my American passport, determinedly not impressed with the plentiful freedoms it implied, let alone the rich collection of visas collected on my existentialist peregrinations. They still let me in, albeit with a humbling frown, conveying that they could stop me, indeed vanish me, had they only wished to. But they wished other, more profitable things, so they practically threw my passport at me. I went to have breakfast in the dining car.

◇ ◇ ◇

The dining car is a generous description of a few tables adorned with tablecloths that looked like a canvas of the local Jackson Pollockovich. A painfully bored attendant was reading the papers, his body telling — *begging* — the tired traveler to go away and never come back. Two men were sitting at one of the tables, their foreheads occasionally touching above the full ashtray in the table's geographic center. They argued over something, downing a glass of vodka (which, for a moment or two, I hoped was water) between florid bursts of rhetorical affection. From what I could understand, the focal point of their argument was one Evgenij, whose distinguishing feature was that he was simultaneously a filthy bastard and the kindest man alive. You could never know with Evgenij, who would stick a knife between your eyes, but who would also give you the undershirt off his back if you asked him: they agreed and kissed and downed a glass of vodka, and then another one. It struck me then — and I still have an ocean-shaped bruise where it struck me — that there was no reason whatever to talk about me, that I was extraneous to almost all of the conversation taking place in this world at any given time. And I envied Evgenij, the kindest living son of a bitch.

◆ ◆ ◆

I went back into the couchette. I fell asleep again and woke up only after the train entered Kiev with a poignant decrescendo. The King of Midnight sat up with a grunt, clawed at his chest for a minute, then hawked and mindfully spat into one of the empty bottles.

◆ ◆ ◆

Humid evening heat; the streets covered with a dark, oily placenta. A man named Igor was waiting for me, holding a sign with my name on it. He was blond, blue-eyed, sinewy as a marathon runner, cautiously clever — painted with many colors, as they say. I present that as a fact, while it was barely a somnolent impression at the time. I got off the train, stepping on top of a steam cloud (though the train was not a steam train — what we have here is a remake of Karenina getting off the train to be welcomed by Karenin and his banal big ears), walking slowly toward the station building as the arriving women kissed the waiting men. I got into Igor's car, which reeked of vomit and pine. A man named Vladek silently sat in the back seat, inhabiting a magnanimous smile. We glided through the streets of Kiev, entering light from darkness, darkness from light. I could not speak, as I was tired and dazed. I managed to understand whatever Igor was saying in his guttural Ukrainian, but what he was saying I do not remember. I do remember occasionally looking back at Vladek, to check if he still existed, and he grinning with the demented enthusiasm of full-fledged existence, flexing his eyebrows and winking at me, as if we had already become fellow conspirators in an obscure plot.

◆ ◆ ◆

Everything in the building was exceptionally orderly, hall carpets stretching straight, walls white like Christmas snow. Igor told me that the place was a Party school, normally, but that they were permitted to use it for the summer.

He opened the door of a room, I walked in reluctantly, Vladek dropped my suitcases, and winked the final wink. My roommate-to-be was frisking a pillow, bare-chested, wearing only shorts with an anchor pattern. "I am Jozef," he said, and offered his hand, still warm from patting the pillow. "Jozef Pronek." Allow me to introduce myself: I am Victor Plavchuk. Nominally I came here for the sake of connecting with my roots, but really was looking for something to do until I figured out what to do. Now allow me to invoke Jozef's slouched shoulders, his square chin, and his eyes: almond, dark, and a mile deep. This is how I remember it now — the excitement is ex post facto — but it was much different then: thus is his cheek a map of days outworn. We stared at each other for an embarrassed moment, waiting for Igor to say something and pull us out of the mud of silence. Then there is a confusing blank: what we did or said after Igor left, I do not remember.

◇ ◇ ◇

When I woke up the next morning, Jozef was still in bed, hence I pretended to sleep, so as to eschew the awkwardness of waking in a room with a stranger. I heard him straightening up in his bed, scratching (his chest? his thighs?) with such unfaltering vigor that I suspected masturbation for a moment. Then he rummaged through his stuff, closing the door, then leaving — his steps echoing in the hallway. I got up with a heavy steel ball in my belly — the regular morning meaninglessness of everything, when all the uses of this world seem weary, stale, flat, and unprofitable. I unpacked my stuff, hung up my shirts next to my roommate's. The color of his shirts was predominantly Eastern European bleak, and the sneakers at the bottom of the closet were well worn, so I was self-conscious putting my attire next to his: my sandals, my sneakers, my shoes, and a lavish collection of khakis and colorful shorts in need of ironing. For an instant, I could not remember why I had them all: the arbitrariness of those choices appeared abruptly transparent, and all the other choices I had ever made seemed absurd. I liked (and still do) the smell of his clothes — the musty smell of a lived life.

◇ ◇ ◇

When my roommate walked back in, I was sitting on the bed with my head in my hands, looking at my toenails in dire need of truncation.

"Good morning," he said earnestly, which forced me into replying.

"How are you?" he asked. I was pretty tired.

"You want one coffee?" he asked. "Bosnian." Sure, I said.

"You Americans always say sure," he said. I didn't see the point of arguing, so I said sure, and he chortled.

My name was Victor. "I know," he said. He put a little pot with a long handle on the table between our beds. He dipped what seemed to be two razors attached to a wire, with a button between them, in the pot, then plugged the bare ends of the wire into a socket. I calmly realized that he was risking his life, along with my mental welfare, by doing that.

"I know this from army." You were in the army? Whose army?

"Yugoslav. We must go. It was many years ago, when I was eighteen." How old are you now?

"Twenty-four," he said.

He had a rotund nose, which seemed swollen, and thick meaty lips, which he kept open. He had the darkest eyes I have ever seen, like two perfect marbles. We sipped coffee, too bitter and biting — I furtively abandoned it. The birds just outside the window warbled, and someone in the room above ours was apparently tap-dancing. He was from Sarajevo, Yugoslavia. He used to have a band and write for papers. His father was Ukrainian, just like mine, though his was born in Bosnia. He came to Ukraine to see his grandfather's fatherland, but he also wanted to be away for a little while from "crazy things" in Yugoslavia. He had this idea they (who were they?) put things in your head and that you have to make it empty. I had stomach cramps and needed to go to the bathroom.

"We must go and eat breakfast," he said. "I wait for you."

Sure.

It was while spending time in Eastern Europe that I learned to appreciate unremarkable things, and the cafeteria I entered, following Jozef, occasionally bumping into him (our steps had not yet synchronized), was spectacularly unremarkable. The light in it was gray; a window wall looked out at a parking lot, which had no cars other than a gigantic black Volga, like a beached walrus. On one of the walls there were men leaning forward with fiery eyes and mountainous muscles bulging under their work uniforms. The women in folk uniforms facing them off hugged tall stalks of wheat that used to be golden and now were merely washed-yellow. There was a long line of people sliding their screeching trays down a rail, toward the food. Some of them were foreigners, recognizable in their clean, crumpled clothes, glancing around, trying to figure out where they might be. We took our trays and they were sticky, still wet in the corners, reeking of socialist grease.

I piled different sorts of blebby pierogi and a cup of limpid tea on my tray. The young woman in front of us, with arms that were bones coated with skin — Jozef introduced her as Vivian — put on her tray one pierogi, which looked like a severed, ashen ear. I lost my appetite instantly. I sat across from Jozef, and he munched his pierogi while I sipped the absolutely tasteless tea.

"What are you doing?" he asked me, looking straight into my eyes.

"I am drinking my tea," I said, suddenly perplexed as to what it was that I really might be doing.

"No, in your life."

"Oh," I said. "In my life." My life. Ripeness is all, and I ain't got it. "I am writing a Ph.D. thesis."

"I see. What are you studying?" Let it be made clear, I did not want to have that conversation. I did not want it to be known that I was not doing what I claimed I was doing.

"Shakespeare," I said.

"What about Shakespeare?" He was an unrelenting bastard,

looking straight at me all along. Look away, you knave, look at the men with fiery eyes, look at Vivian nibbling her pierogi, preparing herself for a bout of bulimia. "What is called your thesis?"

I must have blushed. I sat there facing a Jozef from a crumbling country, up to my neck in fucking Kiev. I said: "Queer Lear." I was about to say: "The Collapse and Transformation of Performative Masculinity in King Lear," but Jozef said:

"My little horse he thinks it is queer, that there is no house near."

"Not quite queer in that sense," I said. It occurred to me that what I was doing was *inapplicable,* that I could spend days explaining it to Jozef to no avail, under the forlorn mural, the world's fresh ornament. I used the opportunity to change the subject. "You like Robert Frost?"

"I was reading him on faculty," he said. "I am also studying litrch — litrchoo — I am studying books."

It was as he was fumbling the word *literature* that I befriended him. It was painful for me too to utter that word, and I grinned in warm understanding, wanting to hug him like a stack of wheat. Even now, when I teach, when I am forced to utter the word "literature," I have a strange sensation — my nipples tickle, my eyes well up with tears.

◆ ◆ ◆

There was a time, I freely confess, when I thought it noble not to know where one was heading. I thought that being lost meant being in mid-chapters of one's own Bildungsroman, but then I became very lonesome climbing up the steep, craggy cliff of self-knowledge. I kept reading and thinking, and thinking and reading, and drinking, in order to figure out what life was all about, and whose fault it all was, before I even started living. Then I went to graduate school. I learned that desire was important, in a class populated by lonely, insecure searchers who sought people like themselves in literature written centuries ago. (The teacher's claim to academic fame was entitled "Karaoke and (Re) Presentation.") My father once asked me what I desired in life, and I was happy he used the word *desired,* for by that time I considered myself an expert on the matter. My father was the kind of man who fixed old chairs and obsolete magneto-phones, thereby restoring the original order — no search, just restoration. Anyway, I followed the path of desire, but it led me nowhere, and I roamed and wandered, and became a typical American young existential tourist — Jack Kerouac was my travel agent. And for reasons I could not fully understand at that time, I had a terrifying feeling that sitting in front of Jozef, answering questions he had no right to ask, I had reached the terminus.

"You want to eat that?" Jozef asked, and pointed at the remains of my sorry breakfast.

"No," I said.

"Can I eat that?"

"Sure."

He grabbed a pierogi and devoured it.

"Always is sure," he said.

"Sure," I said, and laughed, with a gurgle of pleasure, for we had already acquired an inside joke. He stood up with the tray and said: "See you later, alligator." I resisted an urge to follow him, studying instead the differently shaped grease blotches on the table, and their relation to the straight lines that ran across the table — the configuration all made sense then, as if it had been a coded message. I looked at Vivian. "Hi," she said, in a whispery voice, and nodded as if to confirm that she really meant it.

Vivian was a graduate student too, but in Slavic languages — she spoke five of them, including Ukrainian. She was in school in Madison. She told me there were other Americans here, and pointed vaguely toward the undiminished food line. There was Will, who was a tennis player, he was from Somewhere, California. And there was Andrea, who was from Chicago. And there were Mike and Basil, who never had breakfast. Vivian would punctuate the end of every sentence with a nod, and an occasional tucking of her hair behind her ear, on which a fence of rings stretched across her earlobe. I could not see her eyes, because she kept looking down at her plate. She had a shirt with a sunflower pattern, with a wide, open collar, which exposed her chicken chest and the slight curves of her breasts. She told me that this place was *okay,* that she spent a lot of time in the library here, that we were all going to take a train to Lvov tomorrow, early in the morning, and stay in Lvov for a couple of days. I complained about not being informed about it, allowing for some good old-fashioned solidarity of Americans in a hostile foreign country, then took off, having made up my mind to spend the rest of the day sleeping. Good night, lady, good night, sweet lady, good night, good night.

◇ ◇ ◇

We all got up at the crack of dawn — Jozef had shaken me out of my weighty slumber — picked nocturnal crud out of our eyes, then crawled into a bus stinking of harsh cigarettes and machine oil. The bus took us to the train station, down the same desolate streets that I had roamed yesterday, which created a profound sense of moving in circles, even if there was a wobbly morning worker here and there. A statue of Lenin or a socialist hero ambushed us from behind every corner, invariably leaning forward, implying a future. I wanted to point out those things to Jozef, who was a few seats away from me, too far for conversation, close enough to be aware of me.

The train station was swarming with citizens dragging their overstuffed bags and underfed children, anticipating torturous departures. There is a history in all men's lives, figuring the natures of the times deceased. Pensive and ponderous I was indeed, squeezed in the middle of an alien rabble — a fog of garlicky sweat and exhaustion wafting about us. "Look on us, we are like salt going out of hand," Jozef said. I envisioned identical grains of salt, slipping out of God's furrowy palm. It was humbling, to say the least.

The train was much too salty: the Soviet masses everywhere, wearing the expression of routine despair: women with bulky bundles huddled on the floor; stertorous men prostrate up on the luggage racks; the sweat, the yeast, the ubiquitous onionness; the fading maps of the Soviet lands on the walls; the discolored photos of distant lakes; the clattering and clanking and cranking; the complete, absolute absence of the very possibility of comfort. I thought that if another revolution were ever to break out in the USSR, it would start on a train or some other public transportation vehicle — the spark would come from two sweaty asses rubbing. I survived the prerevolutionary grappling only because I followed Jozef, who cheerfully moved through the crowd, the sea of bodies splitting open before him. We found some standing space in the compartment populated solely by our schoolmates — the only ones I recognized were Vivian and Vladek.

There was Father Petro — whom Jozef called Father Petrol — a young, spindly, pimply Canadian priest, who kept touching his left tit as he spoke. I could easily see a future in which Father Petrol's parish, somewhere deep in the Canadian Western provinces, was in a community-tearing upheaval after Father Petrol had been caught innocently fondling a gentle boy. There was Tolya, a teenager from Toronto or some such place. She used every chance to press her melons against Jozef, who endured the assaults with a bemused, avuncular expression. Vladek, the man with a "Komsomol face" (Jozef) — wide-open eyes, freckles, and an impish lock on his forehead — kept hugging Tolya, trying to pull her away from Pronek, sharing his bottomless vodka flask with her and anyone interested, including myself. Priggish and prudish though I may have appeared, I had a few hefty gulps that scorched my throat and earned me approval from the mob and a smile from Jozef. There was Andrea, the Chicago woman, with whom I avoided eye contact, for I did not want to detect any common acquaintances, and she played along. Like all tourists, we wanted to believe that we were alone among the natives. Jozef kept glancing at her, and his upper lip teetered on the verge of a seductive smile. There was Vivian, sitting in the corner, refusing drinks, and, incredibly, trying to read, which she eventually abandoned for talking to Father Petrol about — as far as I could discern — martyrs and saints. In the next compartment — I peeked in, hoping against hope that there would be seating — there was Will, with two other guys who looked American in their flannel shirts and an assortment of traveler's gadgets: backpacks rife with pockets, pouches pendant on their necks, digital wristwatches with an excess of useful little screens.

Needless to say, windows could not be opened, and within a couple of hours moisture painted pretty sparkling pictures on the panes; the walls were sticky; my skin was itchy and I kept gasping for air. The train was speeding through a misty forest, through an army of parallel trees visually echoing the tranceful clatter. Then the train slowed to a stop in the middle of a ravine. In total silence, the trees around the ravine loomed over a couple of brawny does grazing.

"It is beautiful," Jozef said.

"Yeah," I said.

"How can you kill them? I don't understand." Jozef said.

"I don't either," I said.

The does looked up at us as if aware we were talking about them. Jozef said nothing, but raised his hand slowly and waved at them. One of them made a little step forward, as if trying to see us better — I swear to God the does knew we were watching them, they did see him waving at them. It seemed like a natural, ordinary gesture, just a simple motion of the hand. I did not dare do it, because I realized Vivian was looking at me, and I was embarrassed. The train moved on, the clatter accelerated, and the does turned their butts toward us and galloped away. Jozef and I stood wordless for an hour or so, our backs pressed against the damp coldness of the pane. I often recall that moment (the moist morning mist, the collective clamminess; the mirth of Jozef's body, etc.), and I am forced to own up to the fact that I had never had — and then lost it again — what Jozef had: the ability to respond and speak to the world. Then it was Lvov, and we disembarked from the train together, stepping into a nipping, eager air. We inhaled deeply, simultaneously, as if holding hands. What country, friends, was this?

◇ ◇ ◇

It was in Lvov that Will the Tennis Player fully entered my field of vision. He stood in front of the glum Lvov train station, with his arms akimbo, giving assured direction to the random somnolent sojourner. He had piercing blue eyes, sinewy tennis arms — his right asymmetrically thicker than his left — and the squat, sturdy body of a Ukrainian peasant, no doubt the sludge from his ancestors' genetic pool. Quickly did I succumb to his wise leadership — he led me and Vivian and Vladek and Tolya and the others toward a bus identical to the one that transported us in Kiev. I took a window seat, and looked out, when Jozef slumped his body next to me. In front of us, Vladek was telling a lame joke in lamentable English to Vivian, who managed to produce a gracious giggle.

I woke up in front of a morose building, with my cheek pressed against the promontory bone of Jozef's shoulder. Will informed us — he always seemed to know where we were and why — that was the student dorm that would provide lodging while we were in Lvov. The students coming in and out retracted their heads between their shoulders, their chins poking their chests, their mood clearly surly. I could tell that the showers in the dorm did not work.

Jozef and I shared a room, which was, to put it mildly, ascetic: bare walls (although my memory keeps stretching on its toes to hang up a Lenin picture); steel-frame beds with thin, sunken mattresses; a wobbly chair and a wobblier desk, which sported two symmetrical nails on the insides of its rear legs, a student-torture contraption.

Will burst into our room, asked us — me, in fact, for Jozef ignored him — if everything was all right. It was, I said. Will announced that he was trying to find out if we could have better accommodations, and stormed away.

"Who is this?" Jozef said. "I don't like him."

"He's okay," I said. "He just wants to help."

"Maybe," Jozef said, and then just as abruptly walked out. I did not want to be abandoned in this dreadful place, but I could not just follow him. So I was alone, sitting on a bed that reacted with a screech to the minutest muscle contraction, staring at an empty wall that called for a Lenin. I pressed my hands with my knees, until they were numb, distilled almost to jelly with the act of fear.

I thought of the day when my father took me to a baseball game, after years of my pleading and weeks of my mother's lobbying. He loathed baseball — hitting a ball with a stick for no discernible reason, producing mind-numbing, indulgent boredom, that was how he saw it. He had informed me that there would be no hot dogs or soda for me, but I was still giddy with excitement. We sat in the Wrigley Field bleachers, and I had my baseball mitt (a present from my mom), which had spent long months closeted. I was convinced that I would catch a ball, that it was my day, when everything would come perfectly together. My father refused to stand up for the national anthem, because he was still Ukrainian, as if "The Star-Spangled Banner" wounded his Ukrainianness. He made me stand up, he wanted me to appreciate America, for I was born here. During the game, he was bored out of his mind, and he kept looking anxiously at his watch. It did not happen, I caught nothing. We left in the sixth inning, and I hated my father for being a fucking foreigner: displaced, cheap, and always angry.

Whereupon Jozef walked in with a handsome bottle of vodka, unscrewed the cap, and said: "You want drink?"

"Hell, yeah," I said, and took a throat-parching gulp.

"Do you like baseball, Jozef?" I asked him.

"It's stupid," he said. "You kick ball with stick, it is nothing."

"Yeah, I know." I told him the sad story of the eternal misunderstanding between my father and baseball. Jozef listened to me not with the mandatory we-have-all-been-there interest, but with a detached, patient involvement, leaning slightly, and kindly, toward me. Now I realize that it could have been because he was trying to decode my English words, which still does not diminish my belief that he understood me better than anybody, precisely because he could go beyond my vapid words. He told me how his dad used to punish him: he would sentence him to twenty-five belt lashes for a transgression (going through the pockets of his father's suits, or stealing) and determine the time of the execution — normally, Jozef said, after the evening cartoons. He spoke in his broken English, with articles missing, with subject, verb, and object hopelessly scrambled — yet I understood him perfectly, clearly visualizing the sequence of punishment. There was no screaming or yelling, no random disorderly violence — so much unlike my father, who would rip off kitchen cabinet doors and slam them against the walls. After the cartoons, they would go into the bedroom, and the lashing would take place, red butt cheeks and all — I am loath to confess that I envied him for having had those moments.

"Fathers," Jozef said. "They are strange."

Then we talked about our mothers, and their domestic sufferings. Jozef remembered how he had always hoped that his mother would come into the bedroom and stop the lashing, but she never did. I told him how my mother would throw things out of the kitchen cabinets onto the floor, smash the plates, fling pot lids at my father like Frisbees, and they would bounce off him. We talked about women, our first loves — a topic that required some embellishing and enlarging on my part. We talked about our childhoods, the friends that we had had and were now gone — except Jozef's were not gone, they were all in Sarajevo. The silly adventures in school: snorting Kool-Aid in order to sneeze in the biology class (Jozef), smoking pot in the tenth grade, and then being high and afraid to climb down the rope in the PE class (me). The trite acts of rebellion which seemed revolutionary in our adolescence: saying "Fuck you, bitch!" to a nun (me); throwing a wet sponge at a Tito picture (Jozef). We compared Chicago and Sarajevo, how lovingly ugly they were, and how unlovingly parochial. Our mouths went dry, vodka diluted our blood and rushed to our heads. I was so drunk and excited at dawn that I wanted to hug him, but did not want him to think that I was strange. When we finally went to bed at dawn, I lay with my eyes open, watching the sunlight crawl across the wall above Jozef's bed, discovering stains shaped like Pacific islands, my heart throttling in my chest. I could still hear

Jozef whispering, telling me the funny story about the loss of his virginity. His breath kept tickling my earlobes, even as he was tossing in bed, and the soft nurse would not come and stroke my curls.

◇ ◇ ◇

Oh, Lvov, with your old downtrodden monuments of comfortably bourgeois times; your Mittel-European ornaments on the facades, barely visible through the thick filth of progress; your squares with nameless statues of obscure poets and heroes! Did I fail to mention I had never been in Ukraine before? All I knew I heard from my father, who had left a long time ago. Jozef and I wandered the streets of the old town and were sickened by the geometrical landscapes of the new town — to him all of it had familiar Eastern European shapes; to me it all seemed like a dream dreamt by another dream. Somewhere there — but where I knew not — was the Lvov my father had grown up in and had since left, and, bad son that I was, I had little interest in seeking it out.

Jozef needed to have coffee in the morning, so he was on a quest; we found an Armenian coffee shop, where we drank the muddy liquid, not unlike Jozef's Bosnian coffee. I am an herbal-tea man, so having had coffee that you could spread on a slice of bread, I was jittery and warbly, could not stop talking. Everything had to be told, and fast. I talked about my father, about his being born in Lvov. I talked about all the things he had never told me, things I found out eavesdropping on my mother's furious rants when they fought. I told him that my father had been a member of a secret Ukrainian organization — very secret indeed. They prepared for a war of liberation, and hated Russians, Poles, and Jews. And then in World War II, he was an eighteen-year-old fighter with Bandera partisans, fighting Bolsheviks and avoiding fighting Germans. Bandera himself was imprisoned by the Germans and then was shot by the KGB after the war and . . . "I know," Jozef said. Anyway, my father and his fellow fighters hid in the woods around Lvov, here and there robbing a truck of supplies, paying a high price in lives. They drank water from poisoned wells, ate cattle corpses found in villages burnt by the Germans or the Bolsheviks, then died of animal diseases, boils exploding all over their faces. Man's life was as cheap as beast's. The few surviving fighters slipped into the disorder and carnage of the German defeat, and ended up happily imprisoned in the Allies' POW camps. My father had been a student of music — he was a baritone — so he sang in those camps: old Ukrainian ballads, Italian arias, and prewar Paris chansons that had somehow reached Lvov. He went to England, lived in Liverpool, worked on the docks, then he was off to Canada, where he ran the memberless Ukrainian-Canadian Opera Society and sang at weddings and funerals — mainly funerals. Then he went to Chicago, where he conceived my miserable self.

My father rendered his pre-American days in disconnected details: how during wartime they all shared cigarettes when they had them, and smoked lint from their pockets when they didn't; how he was the handsomest, most sonorous singer in Lvov; how the POWs wept when he sang "Ukraine Hasn't Died Yet"; how he and his best friend embraced in the snow, warming each other up with their breaths, until his best friend's breathing ceased; how he had sung opera only once, in Kitchener, Canada, in the role of Wotan, terribly miscast in a local production of *Die Walküre*. Sometimes, at home, he would break out into the Magic Fire Song, which always scared the crap out of me.

Boy, was I on a roll, I kept babbling — it is very possible that Jozef did not understand most of my prolix monologue. As a matter of fact, out of the blue sky, so I was a little irked, he said:

"You know, Bandera, when he was young, he wanted to be strong, to not feel pain. So he put his finger in door and then close door so he can see how long can he feel pain. He has did that every day."

What could I say? I said: "That's crazy."

Anyway, after the demise of the Opera Society, my father drove a truck — my mother told me once that one of the things he had transported was foreigners across the border. He drove his truck to the US and he met my mother in Chicago. My mother was a South Side Irish girl, nineteen at the time. He knocked her up, possibly deliberately, in order to get American citizenship (my mother screamed out that secret in the middle of one of their more destructive fights). In any case, he married her, maybe for his sense of manly duty, maybe for the passport — I did doubt it had been love, for love was hard to come across in my father's words and deeds. He was, I attested, an unaccommodated man.

"It's like American novel," Jozef said.

"Yeah," I said.

But that could be because my older brother, born a few months after they had got married, was killed in Vietnam ("Vietnam — big war," Jozef said). I remembered him as this remote uniformed presence, someone who had thrown a baseball at me not trying to hit me in the nose. Here on my desk (Please, take a look!) I have a picture of him in his uniform, smiling, with a baseball mitt, yawning like a carnivorous plant, on his left hand. My brother was blown to pieces by a land mine. Years later, we received a visit from his army buddy, who was now peddling booze money in exchange for the true story, and who in pathologically gory detail described my brother's death: spilled guts still throbbing in the dirt, ungodly howling, a Charlie sniper shooting off his knees, etc. My mom blamed my dad for her son's death, she blamed all his fallacious army stories, all that sleeping-in-the-woods bullshit that deluded my brother into thinking that the army built a man's character — it kills the body, she wailed, screw the character, my son's body is gone. My father thought that every man needed character — that a life that produced pain built your character the way that door built Bandera's. So my brother's absence, the paint of his death on the walls of our home, *that* had built my character. My father, nunckle motherfucker, never talked about it, just went to the Chicago Avenue church, sang in the choir, his jaw eternally clenched. My brother was killed a week before he was to be discharged. He was twenty-three, his name was Roman.

"Very interesting," Jozef said. "Roman means novel in my language."

"Oh, fuck you," I said, and that was the first time I got mad at him. But it didn't last long: we sat on the bus next to each other again, in silence, and I was just about to tell him I was sorry when

I realized he was asleep, the wanton boy, his head on my shoulder, his saliva dribbling on my sleeve out of the corner of his mouth, my hand levitating above his nape, a touch away from his gentle neck.

◆ ◆ ◆

Returning to Kiev a couple of days later was like coming home: the smell of socialist grease and vinegar was as familiar as my mother's kitchen; in the humble room, a pair of silk socks I had taken off upon my arrival waited crumpled under my bed. Jozef dropped his bag, leapt out of his shoes, and threw himself on the bed, its steel edge leaving a scar on the wall. I did the same thing, but a little more cautiously. We stretched on our respective beds, staring at the ceiling, in silence, as unspecified words were choking me — I wanted to talk, because silence seemed to be undoing our friendship.

"This is microphone," Jozef said, and pointed at the fire alarm on the ceiling with frightening certainty. "Maybe also camera."

It made sense, of course, we were in the Soviet Union, in a Party school dorm — if there had been only one camera in Kiev, it would have been here. I started recalling all the things I might have done under the fire-alarm gaze: shaking my naked booty; singing aloud while dancing in my underwear; lying on Jozef's bed, sniffing his pillow; investigating his suitcase and touching his things. I imagined the man who was watching me: a bored, mustached man, with a stainful tie; his armpits crusty with perspiration; playing chess with his ulcer-tormented comrade; not paying attention to the flickering screens, until they sense the motion of a funky American on one of them. Then they would ho-ho-ho and ha-ha-ha, and they would call the fatherly officer, who would come in, impeccable and humorless. He would not care that I put on Jozef's shirts, still in the groove. He would loathe my weakness — as my father had when he caught me masturbating once — and order them to keep the camera on and bring him the tape every day.

The camera annoyed me terribly, for your sense of sovereign self, of the completeness of your body, entirely depends on the illusion that no one can see inside you, that the only people you ever allowed to enter you would be the people you loved and knew well.

Jozef, on the other hand, was waving at the camera and saying: "Hello, comrades. My name is Jozef Pronek and I am spy."

"Don't say that," I said. "Just don't."

"And this is my friend Victor, also spy. He is American and he works for CIA."

"Don't say that."

"Please come and arrest him. He was bad. I tell you everything what I know about him."

"Stop it," I yelled. "Stop it."

So he did — yet another awkward silence — but then he got up and left the room, leaving me alone with the buzzing camera over my head.

◇ ◇ ◇

The camera incident notwithstanding, the days upon our return from Lvov were wholesome. We would wake up, my beloved roommate and I, into a blissfully sunny morning. The memory of the view from our room contains an implausible sheet of snow, covering the parking lot below and the tips of the trees on its edge, straight as pencils (beyond which, I learned, was Babi Yar), solely because the summer sunlight was so bounteous that it washed everything white. Jozef was one of those people who are happy in the morning: he started his day humming a song that was a sound track for his dreams (I recognized "Something Stupid" and "Nowhere Man," for example); then he sauntered in his underwear, gabbing steadily. It was in the morning that he told me about his numerous girlfriends; about his crush on Andrea (which, he freely admitted, provoked serious erections); about his band (Blind Jozef Pronek and Dead Souls) and his best friend, the rhythm guitar in the band; about his ancestors (a granduncle shot by Stalin; another who worked for the Austrian railroad; another an orchestra conductor in Czechoslovakia, a long time ago); about his family (parents, aunts, uncles, hard to follow).

I remember my brother doing pushups bare-chested on the floor next to my bed. His panting, yelping, and chest-slapping woke me up. Sometimes, I woke up scared, and my brother comforted me, stroking my hair, smiling. Then he did stomach crunches — it seemed to me that he was going through hurtful convulsions, but nothing could harm my brother's morning joy. I am exactly the opposite: I had long ago — but wherefore I know not — lost all my mirth. Hence I passively absorbed Jozef's cheerfulness, never quite responding, often wanting him to shut up, for I realized that he would talk to an armoire with the same morning enthusiasm. I wanted to be alone, but you couldn't be alone with Jozef — he brought buckets of cold world into your life and poured it over your head and you gasped for air.

We would head toward breakfast, down the stairs in synchronized steps, his hand on my shoulder, lodged gently on my collarbone. Seldom would we be alone at the table — all of a sudden he had an army of friends — which forced me into reticence or, worse, into nonsensical utterances, all sounding like pretentious misquotations: "Everybody knows someone dead"; "Words are grown so false that I am loath to prove reason with them." Jozef would indulge in dalliance and glance-exchange with Andrea ("You had nice dreams?"), which would always make me recall his erection; he would tease Father Petrol ("You dreamed pretty women?"), which would make Father Petrol's pimples sinfully purple; he would greet the Polish teenage twin brothers, who had been following Father Petrol like a double dose of temptation ("You switched names last night?"); he would provoke Vladek, asking him what kind of information he provided to the KGB ("Tell them I am spy"); he would make a crass remark to Vivian, whom he didn't seem to like because she was a vegetarian ("I have sausage for you"); he would even address Will, reading the *International Herald Tribune* he brought with him ("What are news?"); and he would embarrass Tolya and me, suggesting that we could "make love" after breakfast. We all revolved around the axis of Jozef's morning mirth, and the revolution could make you nauseated.

After breakfast, we were expected to go to classes and expand our knowledge of Ukrainian history and culture. I usually skipped the Ukrainian language classes, but I went to the Ukrainian history class, much with the same interest that would make me gawp at a train wreck, but also because Jozef was in the class. We would sit high in the amphitheater, almost at eye level with the solemn pictures of Marx, Engels, and Lenin, looking down at Vivian's emaciated back as she took notes, looking at Will's persistently raised hand, and at a puny Toronto professor who had written a thousand-page book on Ukrainian history. I made intermittent notes, chiefly out of graduate school habit, while Jozef frantically drew herds of butterflies and demented rectangles. I was raised with my father's version of Ukrainian history in which frequent and regular defeats were in fact triumphs of martyrdom; in which feeble intellectuals and hesitant politicians misled the common man and betrayed the hero; in which pogroms were merely self-defense; in which Ukrainians preserved Orthodox Christianity from Poles and Communists. "Empty story, yes?" Jozef said. He liked the empty story about the Cossacks throwing mud at their elected chief as part of the inauguration ritual. He thought that everybody should do it, and add some shit to the mud too. Once, as the Ukrainian SS division was being wiped out by the Red Army in its first and only battle, our knees touched, and a little furry animal of troubling pleasure moved for the first time in my belly, but I quickly smothered it with the soft pillow of denial.

In the evenings, we would go out, stroll by the Dnepro, while the greatest fleet of mosquitoes ever assembled attacked us, wave upon wave, some of them resembling small storks — it was hard not to think of Chernobyl, and evolution taking a different turn in these parts. We would embark upon a quest for beer, up and down Andriivski Uzhvis, usually ending up in an Armenian restaurant, frequented by all the other foreigners in Kiev. Once the entire school crowd went to the restaurant and ordered a whole piglet — Jozef's royal idea. He delightfully gnawed on the bones, greasing up and licking his fingers, daring everyone to try the brain, and no one dared except Andrea. (Vivian paled at the far end of the table.) I retch at the very thought of eating pig's brain, but they put the decadent morsels into each other's mouths with delight. Strange is the taste of desire.

We would go back to the dorm and drink in someone's room, cheerfully exchanging funny anecdotes, talking over each other, though I cannot remember what about. Jozef would disappear to make out with Andrea, and I would be stuck with a ranting-in-Russian Vladek, whose idea of fun was to drink vodka out of a vase; with Father Petrol, who would pontificate (mainly to the twins) about the spirituality of beekeeping; with Vivian, who was somehow always sitting next to me, trying to commence a quiet conversation about bad food or the water shortage in the dorm. I would depart only when I was sure that Jozef was not in our room with Andrea, quietly humping in the darkness, while a moonbeam sneaked into the room and tickled his bare dolphin-like back.

◇ ◇ ◇

One day, all the Americans in the school were summoned to Igor's office. I cannot say that the possibility of a summary execution of the imperialist enemy did not cross my mind, but I went nonetheless. There were six of us: there was Will, with his flaxen hair, half-open mouth, and undergrowth of blond hair on his tight forearms — he in fact came with a tennis racket in his hand. There was Mike, whom I hadn't ever talked to, from Schenectady, with a large Slavic head and an itch in his crotch, to which he responded by constantly touching his penile area ("You play tennis?" he asked Will). There was Vivian the Vegetarian, with her translucent skin and knobby joints. There was Andrea, with her rangy Chicago prettiness, freckles and all ("You're from Chicago too?" I asked her. "Yup," she said, and that's all the conversation we had). There was Basil from Baltimore, with thin-rimmed spectacles, positioned at a studied equidistance from anyone, and a stack of money neatly held together by a silver clip — he was a banker ("I am a banker," he said). And there was me, a graduate student, mired in the middle of a project called "Queer Lear."

Thus, in streaming bad English, spoke Igor: the American president George Bush was coming to Kiev for a goodwill visit. The people of Ukraine wished to welcome and accommodate the American president, because the people of Ukraine had a lot of respect for the American president, and they wanted to develop friendship with the American people, and so on in a portentous voice. He said we were needed, since we could speak Ukrainian and English, to be on hand as interpreters. "Sure," Will said instantly. "I'll be proud to serve my country," Basil said. "Bush is a prick," Andrea said. "No way I'm gonna do it." Then Vivian and Mike agreed, and it was up to me. The way I remember it, which is most certainly inaccurate, is that they all turned toward me, in slow motion, tilted their heads slightly — it took me a few long moments to decide. I am one of those people who is always a little embarrassed to stand up and turn toward the flag at a baseball game, though I always do it, my father's invisible hand pushing me. And I never thought that my brother's death was quite worth it. But it was different now: there were these people in a foreign country and I knew them — we were a "we." I was tired of confusing, unrelenting perceptions and feelings. I wanted to go to a familiar place. I said: "Okay," and avoided Andrea's gaze.

A bus was supposed to pick us up Thursday. We would be accompanied by a person from the consulate. Igor thanked us very much and told us how important it was that our school could be part of the historic visit. Igor had no shoes on, just snow-white socks, except for a red blot on his left foot, suggesting that his big toe was painfully bleeding.

◊ ◊ ◊

But there were throats to be cut and work to be done: we boarded a humble bus, with smudges on the window panes probably predating Brezhnev. And in that decrepit ark we sailed together with other unnamed Americans, collected around Kiev, who all sat in the front seats. We were heading to the airport, we were told by a red-haired young woman in a neon-blue suit. She was from the consulate, her name was Roberta, and she said she was delighted to see us, but then she instantly forgot us, firmly focused on the Kiev streets ridden with potholes and her goals — say, a position in the Moscow embassy and an affair with a good-looking CIA man. I liked the way she raked her fluffy hair with her carmine claws.

I sat next to Vivian, attracted by her scent of coconut sweat and her radiant skin — she gripped the handlebar on the seat in front of us and I could see her velvet veins bulging. I could also hear her breathing, her tresses' ends dithering from her breath. Her bare legs brandished a bruise here and there, amid goose bumps. It terrified me to see how fragile she was. I believe that Vivian was aware of my gaze, for she looked straight ahead, only occasionally smiling, exposing her gums reluctantly.

But then Will threw his tennis body onto the seat in front of us, and said: "Roberta said we might get to see the president."

"Wow," Vivian said.

We arrived at the airport, at a back lot, with no one around except a square-shouldered man in a dark suit, a cubical jaw, dark sunglasses, a gadget in his ear, his hands lethal weapons — exactly how I had imagined a presidential bodyguard. I get a kick out of meeting someone who is a cliché embodied. It produces a pleasant feeling of a world completed, of everything arranging itself without any of my involvement, yet not veering out of control. And a diminished Vivian was reflected in his sunglasses. He ushered us into a waiting room, told us to wait in a voice that sounded synthesized, and then vanished.

There we sat waiting.

We were killing time, choking every little minute with the muscly hands of mortifying ennui. There was absolutely nothing in the room: no pictures on the walls, no magazines, no paper or pencils, no crass inscriptions on the chairs, not even dead flies in the light bowls. I exchanged irrelevant information with Vivian: our favorite Dunkin' Donut (same: Boston Kreme); our favorite TV show (*Hogan's Heroes*); our favorite Beatles song ("Yesterday," "Nowhere Man"); our favorite salad dressing (she had none, I couldn't think of any). We agreed on almost everything, and that cheered Vivian up. But I must confess — and if you are out there somewhere, Vivian, reading this woeful narrative, find it in your heart to forgive me — I lied about everything, agreeing with her only because that was much easier than professing the flimsy beliefs I had never firmly held, and it was nice to see her smiling.

We turned to silence, and time simmered until it evaporated. They took us back to the school, but they told us that the president would speak at Babi Yar that evening and that we might be needed again. 'Tis the time's plague, when madmen lead the blind.

◇ ◇ ◇

The Babi Yar ravine was full of people, swarming against the green background of trees. They grew out of pits that once upon a time had been filled up with human flesh, which had on me a disturbing effect of feeling unjustly alive. President Bush walked on stage, in the long dumb strides of a man whose path had always been secure — around him a suite of tough motherfuckers bulging with concealed weapons and willingness to give their lives for the president. We were close to the stage, over which the monument loomed — I could not make out what it was: a cramped lump cast in black bronze. We — Will, Mike, Basil, and Vivian, and I — watched him appear before the Ukrainian crowd that followed his every move, like a dog watching a mouse, with detached amazement: it was now in front of them that he became real. His bland, beady eyes scanned the crowd for a loyal face — a habit from back home, where voters grew like weeds. He looked at his watch, said something to a man carrying a clipboard, all efficient and chunky. The man nodded, so the president approached the microphone. The microphone screeched, then the president's voice cracked in the speakers. He touched the microphone head with his lips, receiving a jolt from it. He tried to adjust the unwieldy microphone, as if choking a snake, speaking all along. His voice then came from a tape recorder deep down inside him, plugged into the electric current of his soul. Nobody was translating.

"Abraham Lincoln once said: We cannot escape history . . ." he said somberly, still wrangling the microphone. Under the stage, there were men in uniforms, squatting, leaning on their rifles. Their heads brushed against the wooden beams. They had striped sailor-shirts under the uniform, which meant they were from the KGB. They smoked and seemed absolutely oblivious to what was happening right above them.

"Today we stand at Babi Yar and wrestle with awful truth." He pronounced Yar as Year. The men under the stage were laughing about something, one of them shaking his head in some kind of disbelief.

"And we make solemn vows," the president went on, his voice getting deeper, the microphone making a *wheeee* sound. I spotted Jozef in the crowd, his face beaming out of the crowd's grayness, standing close to the stage, with his hands in his pockets, Andrea next to him.

"We vow this sort of murder will never happen again."

The KGB men under the stage simultaneously dropped their cigarettes and stepped on the butts, still squatting, as if they were dancing *hopak*.

"We vow never to let forces of bigotry and hatred assert themselves without opposition."

I realized that President Bush reminded me of one Myron, who would eat earthworms for a quarter when we were kids: he would put a couple of earthworms between two pieces of bread and bite through. You could sometimes see their ends wiggling between the slices, while he chewed their heads. With his quarters he would buy some booze — Colt 45 or Cobra or something.

"And we vow that whenever our devotion to principle wanes [the microphone suddenly went silent] when good men and women refuse to defend virtue [silence] each child shot [*wheeee,* silence, *wheeee*] none of me will ever forget. None of us will ever forget."

The setting sun peeked through the treetops and blinded Bush, who squinted for a moment, a fiery patch on his face. Jozef whispered something into Andrea's ear and she started giggling, with her hand on her mouth. The people standing behind the president on the stage were uneasy. The men under the stage were on their backs now, looking up at the stage ceiling, their AK-47s laid next to them. Vivian silently moved next to me — the coconut aroma perished from her sweat. The chunky guy with the clipboard shook up the microphone, as if it all were a matter of its stubbornness, and then gave up.

"May God bless you all [. . . . . *wheeeeeumph* . . . .] the memories of Babi Yar."

And then Bush came off the stage and after a sequence of microevents that I cannot recall — you must imagine my shock — Jozef was standing in front of Bush, behind the moat of the bodyguards' menacing presence, his face extraordinarily beautiful, as if an angelic beam of light were cast on his face. Jozef was looking at him with a grin combined with a frown — which I can recognize in retrospect as his recognition that the moment was marvelously absurd. Bush must've seen something else, perhaps his divine face, perhaps someone who would make his presidential self look better on a photo (and the cameras were snapping), someone who looked Slavic and exotic, yet intelligible — the whole evil empire contracted in one photogenic brow of woe. So he asked Jozef, looking at the fat man, expecting him to interpret:

"What is your name, young fellow?"

"Jozef Pronek," Jozef answered, while the fat man was mouthing a translation of the question, spit burping in the corners of his lips.

"This place is holy ground. May God bless your country, son."

"It is not my country," Jozef said.

"Yes, it is," Bush said, and patted Jozef on his shoulder. "You bet your life it is. It is as yours as you make it."

"But I am from Bosnia . . ."

"It's all one big family, your country is. If there is misunderstanding, you oughtta work it out." Bush nodded, heartily agreeing with himself. Jozef stood still, his body taut and his smile lingering on his face, bedazzled by the uncanniness.

I knew then that I was in love with Jozef. I wanted Bush to embrace him, to press his cheek against Jozef, to appreciate him, maybe kiss him. I wanted to be Bush at that moment and face Jozef armed with desire. But Bush took off, his body exuding his contentment with his ability to connect with everyone. Would I were a rock — I stood there trembling with throbs of want, watching Jozef, with the sun behind his back. I replay this scene like a tape, rewinding it, slowing it down, trying to pin down the moment when our comradeship slipped into desire — the transition is evanescent, like the moment when the sun's rays change their angle, the light becomes a hairbreadth softer, and the world slides with nary a blink from summer into fall.

"Isn't that your roommate?" Will asked.

"Yes," I said. "Yes."

Jozef saw me then, waved at me, and shrugged, as if it all were an accident, rather than destiny. Oh, smite flat the thick rotundity of the world so we may never be apart.

◆ ◆ ◆

Naturally, I stayed away from Jozef thereafter. That same night, I succumbed to Vivian's persistent, quiet presence, invited her to my room — as Jozef was off carousing somewhere — where we made out in my bed. She pressed her lips against mine and sucked them, I let my hands wander across her ribs and breasts, and tried to push my tongue into her mouth. It was a cumbersome protocoitus: I kept banging my knees against the steel edges of the bed, she — my slim Ophelia — kept slipping between the bed and the wall. In the end, we never managed to get to the penetration point, though there was some heavy, nervous petting. Need I say that I was distracted by Jozef's absent presence, that I could smell his clothes, and that, as I was trying to approach the lovemaking process from a different angle, my leg slipped off the bed and I stepped on his shoe? The part that I enjoyed, however, was the talk after our hapless semi-intercourse had been abandoned, under the pretense of everything being too soon. We were facing each other, inhaling each other's breath, whispering about the times when we were kids, when joys were simple and bountiful. She told me, her hand softly on my hip, how she had been so little as a kid that she could hang on a kitchen cabinet door and swing herself, back and forth. I remembered how my brother would swing me between his legs, then swing me somehow above his head and put me on his back. I did not want to fuck Vivian, I just wanted to hold her and talk to her. Even as she talked, I kept imagining Jozef in his bed, in his shorts, absentmindedly curling the hair around his nipples. Ah, get thee to a nunnery!

I spent a lot of time with Vivian henceforth: we were, for all intents and purposes, having a relationship. We would go to classes together, and sit next to each other — Jozef way above, behind my back, beyond my gaze. We would ask each other: "What do you wanna do tonight?" and respond: "I don't know, what do you wanna do?" It was always the same thing; we would go for a walk, then to the Armenian restaurant, then to Vivian's room — her roommate, one Jennifer from Winnipeg, was sleeping with Vladek somewhere else — where we made out a little, inching toward the ever remote penetration (Vivian was not ready yet, still afraid of the pain, though she was not, she said, a virgin), then exchange our memories. We had progressed to high adolescence, when I had taken up drugs, and she had taken up vegetables. Sometimes, she would decide to stay in her room and read about Ukrainian history, or translate some lousy Ukrainian poem, and I would play tennis with Will. He would easily crush me, generously suggesting exercises that would improve my regrettable footwork. Or we would play doubles: Will and me versus Mike and Basil. Will demanded an elaborate high-five after every win, though I never had anything to do with it. Then we would play poker, drinking infernal vodka. Will seemed to know everything about the current baseball season and we discussed it enveloped in the air of elite expertise, conscious that nobody in that damn country knew or cared about it. They also liked to talk about women: they wanted to know about Vivian's fucking habits (I could tell them little), while they seemed to possess information about Andrea (Mike claimed she liked to suck uncircumcised dick) and Jennifer of Winnipeg (she paid Vladek per fuck) and Father Petrol (who was caught jacking off in the bathroom). I was disgusted, of course, but on the other hand, their idiotic discourse was familiar and comfortable — it was my summer camp all over again.

I would go back to my room, feeling guilty, as if I had betrayed not only Vivian, but Jozef as well. He would sometimes be awake when I came in drunk, and we would engage in small talk. He told me about his little adventures in Kiev: in the post office, a man had whispered to him about the Stalin days, when people used to disappear, but you could buy sausage in stores; he had had some kvass and it was so horrible that he was happy he had tried it, because he could now tell everyone about it; Andrea had bought a Red Army officer's hat from a guy, who was also selling night-vision goggles — he was thinking about getting the goggles tomorrow. It was all laughter and amiability, but I felt as if we had broken up and were only friends now, desire banished from our land, even if it had never settled there.

Wide awake, I would stare at the ceiling camera, wishing I could get my paws on those tapes and watch Jozef waking up in the morning, his skin soft, with crease imprints, the fossils of slumber, on his bare shoulders; or see him making out with Andrea. I would close my eyes, and my mind would wander with my hand across his chest, down his abdomen. I would stop it on the underwear border, forcing myself to think about Vivian — you have to understand that I had never been attracted to a man before. It frightened me, and it was hard sometimes to discern between fear and arousal: the darkness throbbed around me, in harmony with my heart.

Occasionally, I would feel a compulsion to confess to Vivian: to tell her that being with her was only out of need for something safe and familiar; to tell her that I could not stop — and God knew I tried — thinking about my foreign roommate, even as she touched me and breathed into my face. But instead of confessing, I lectured her about my thesis and the homosocial relations in *King Lear*; and how the collapse of Lear's society was rendered by the emasculation in it; and how Lear's being alone with Cordelia before she dies was when he went beyond his masculinity, entering a different identity. I babbled and babbled, understanding along the way that I understood very little. Incredibly, she found it interesting: she swore in faith 'twas passing strange, 'twas wondrous pitiful. But what she actually said, I shall not recall before the next lifetime.

Jozef, naturally, suspected nothing: he cheerfully walked around half naked, was convinced that our new distance was due to our respective new girlfriends. I assumed this fake voice of male solidarity — the voice, I suspected, often heard in army barracks and trenches before nightly masturbation sessions — as we shared petty treasures, trinkets glittering only to easily arousable men: a vivid description of Vivian's nipples; a joke about Andrea's orgasmic yelps; the standard fantasies about having more than one woman in bed, and so on.

I remember the time when my father had been fired from his work as a security guard, spending a lot of time at home, mainly drinking, telling disconnected Bandera-times stories, and ripping cabinet doors off. But occasionally, he would be in a somber mood, slouching on the sofa in the dark living room, blinds rolled down, watching a daytime talk show with the sound off. I was sixteen or so, prone to avoiding my father's proximity as much as I could, but he seemed so helpless and aching at the time that I would just join him and watch TV in complete silence. I could never muster the audacity to prompt him to talk, and he never wanted to talk. We could hear Mother trudging through the apartment, but she was as shut off as the talk show. Once, as some shoddy porn stars were being interviewed, my father said, slowly, as if he had been thinking about it for a while, that he had some porn tapes and that we could watch them together sometime. I retched — I swear to God — it was so unthinkable to me. So I said: "No, are you fucking crazy?" and stormed out of the room. Yet, despite the nausea I still feel, that seemed to be the last time my father had wanted to give me anything and I had declined it. Men have died — worms have eaten them — but not for love.

The days after Babi Yar were days of torment. I spent a lot of time with people who ultimately made me feel frightfully lonely. More and more often, I roamed the streets of Kiev alone, collecting random particles of someone else's life: a throng of wizened carnations, sold by a decrepit *baba;* a woman tottering under the weight of bag clusters in her hands; a naked mannequin in the dust-infested window of an empty store; a boy waiting with his father in front of a kvass kiosk, pale, a chenille of greenish snot stretching over his lips to his chin; the gnarly bars on the post office windows, eaten by rust; the ashtray brimming with cigarettes, lipstick moons on their ochre filters, in front of a post office teller named Oksana, who provided me with a phone line to Chicago.

My mother picked up the phone. I could hear the echo of my voice, and she was confused by the delay, so our words kept running into one another:

"Mom, how are . . ."

"Victor, how . . ."

". . . you?"

". . . are you?"

"I'm good, . . ."

"Are you . . ."

". . . Mom."

" . . okay?"

"How . . ."

"Is everything . . ."

". . . is Dad?"

". . . okay?"

"Everything . . ."

"He . . ."

". . . is okay."

". . . is okay."

"Great."

"He is only . . ."

"Is he . . ."

". . . a little weak."

". . . okay?"

"Hello?"

"Okay?"

He was sick, I understood in spite of the echoes. High blood pressure, my mother said. He wasn't eating, couldn't digest food, my mother didn't say why, and I knew he wouldn't see the doctor, claiming he was fine, meaning he was tough. But I didn't want it clarified, I wanted to pretend that it was all so distant, many echoes away, because I could not deal with it. I finished the conversation with love that was to be shared by my mother with my father, an unlikely event. This was mid-August 1991.

◇ ◇ ◇

I went down the stairs, still hung over, vaguely afraid of breaking my ankle and tumbling down the stairs only to have my neck snapped. As I was sinking into the hall, I saw Natalyka, the cleaning woman who would often walk into our room and admonish us for the mess; I saw Natalyka sitting despondently, watching TV, her head on the blubber-padded shoulder of another cleaning woman. Her log-thick legs were crossed at her swollen ankles. She kept her hands in the pockets of her formerly blue jacket, as if despair were a marble in her pocket. No one had ever watched TV in the hall, let alone this early — it was breakfast time. There was a crowd of people, whose faces had wandered through my hazy stay in this building, whose faces were now richly made up with dread and desolation.

August 19, 1991, will always have Natalyka's sorrowful face.

I sidled up behind the crowd and peeked at the TV, the way I join onlookers calmly watching an accident aftermath. A Brezhnev clone with a bass voice read a proclamation, sitting uncomfortably in the midst of a horrendous purple-velvet set, his tie breaking over his belly. It took me awhile to shake off my daze and parse what he was saying. The people around me shuffled their feet as if rattling their shackles. They murmured and sighed: somebody I understood, took over the power, declared martial law, because of anarchy and disorder.

"Gorbachev is out," Will said, suddenly standing next to me. "There's been a coup."

"Oh, fuck!" I said.

"Exactly," Will said.

I must mention this: abruptly and against my will, as it were, I was close to Will — abruptly, he was someone I could trust. But I felt a cramping urge to locate Jozef and break the news to him, to produce wonder in his heart and excite him. So I flew upstairs, not caring about my ankles or my neck, followed by an echo of Natalyka's tormented gasp. I burst into the room without knocking, and Jozef was naked. I could not help noticing — and I was too excited to try — a hair vine crawling up from his sooty crotch to his navel, and curls spiraling around his nipples.

"There's been a coup!" I nearly hollered.

"What?"

"There's been a coup!" I hollered.

"What is coup?" It was rather annoying, his ignorant calm, his boxers sliding up his alabaster thighs.

"A coup, a violent takeover of power."

"Take over from where?"

"You know, a fucking revolution." What was wrong with him? He couldn't understand the basic information, let alone assuage my fears. What was I doing here?

"Revolution?" Jozef said, his eyebrows raised, the sun of comprehension rising from behind the dark mountain of his dimness. "Where is revolution? Who is organizing revolution?"

"God damn it, a putsch. Gorbachev's out." That was going to be my last attempt. He had no chest hair, and his navel had a birthmark satellite, shaped as a mouse.

"Putsch," he finally understood. "Maybe they want to arrest us."

Now, I have to confess that I hadn't thought of that — why would anyone want to arrest me?

"Trouble, trouble," he said.

I needed to talk to Will, so I left Jozef behind to wallow in his fake wisdom, muttering something in his weird language, and I ran downstairs. Down in the hall, there was no one but Natalyka, sitting in the same place, but no shoulder to support her, her hands dead in her lap, like hairless bloated hamsters, her round little body aweary of this great world. She was watching the Red Army choir, handsome men endowed with mandibular strength, thundering a victorious song.

I ran to the cafeteria, where there was a hopeful line of second-helpers, led by the indomitable Vladek, as if nothing had happened, but there was no Will. I ran to his room, leaping across stairs, rapidly running out of breath, and I found him there, with his ear pressed against his transistor radio.

"What's the news?" I asked in a series of pants that must have suggested frenzy.

"Haven't found any news yet," Will said. "I'm trying to find the Voice of America."

I had never been in Will's room — his clothes were neatly stacked in the closet, and he had tubular boxes full of fluorescent-green tennis balls positioned unrandomly around his room like little watchtowers. He had a family picture on the nightstand: there were five of them, Will in the center, flanked by his sisters, Mom and Dad standing behind them. They were sublimely beautiful, blond and suburbanly, all resembling one another as if they were a variation on the same person, a family procreated by fission rather than fucking.

"What are we going to do, Will?"

"Well, they can't arrest *us*. And even if they arrest us, they will exchange us. We don't leave anyone behind."

"I never thought of it that way."

"I mean if the American embassy knows we are here, they are going to get someone to get us. They might send a bunch of marines or something. We take care of our people, right?"

"Do they know we are here?" I imagined a herd of robust marines storming into the building, the sergeant bellowing: "Move! Move!" shooting to pieces whoever unwisely stood in their way, crawling along the walls, exchanging mysterious finger signs, patriotic paint smudged all over their endearingly familiar faces.

"I don't know," Will said. "I hope they do. I want to go home."

"But what are we going to do until they come?"

"We're gonna stay put. Get your stuff ready in case we have to leave soon. I'm gonna talk to other people. We oughtta have a meeting."

I ran back to my room, but Jozef was not there. All that running: maybe I didn't run at all, but now as I remember it, it all seems speeded up, with plenty of huffing and puffing and urgency. And I was tired and the running (if indeed there was any) seemed pointless. The bed beckoned me and I stretched on it, pulling the blanket over my head. Here is a confession: When the future is uncertain, when there are many events in the womb of time about to be delivered, I take a nap. I roll down the shades and creep under a blanket and cover my head, and I try to imagine a safe, warm place — a tip from my therapist. Usually, it is my tent. We are on a camping trip in Wisconsin, somewhere near a shimmering lake. The sides of the tent are throbbing slightly. I can hear the crickets on the fragrant pines, and I can hear my mother humming an Irish song. The shadows of the pine's branches are quivering above my head, and I can hear the splashing of the struggling fish my dad is pulling out of the lake.

◆ ◆ ◆

A cold hand on my forehead woke me up, and before I could see her face darkened and haloed by the background light, I recognized her smell: sweet sweat and coconut.

"Are you sleeping?"

"What do you think?"

"Have you heard?"

"Yup."

"How can you sleep?"

"How can you not sleep?"

"Can I come into bed with you?"

"Sure."

Vivian took off her sandals and her hairpins and weightlessly landed her body next to mine. She had on the flowery dress, which slid up to her thighs, and I could feel them against mine. She kissed my neck, and I curled her hair behind her ear. She put her hand on my stomach and then it edged toward my underwear.

Never mind the details: there was penetration, there was pain, and she was a virgin; there was guilt and avoiding each other's eyes afterward, yet there were touches that implied the required postcoital closeness; there was sweat mixing. And there was embarrassment with the rich assortment of bodily imperfections: a solitary red pimple gestating on my chest; her asymmetrical, cross-eyed breasts; my nose hair; the charcoal-dust hair on the fringe of her cheek. We exchanged susurrous, empty words, not quite lies, but certainly not truthful, while my body tensed and tightened, eager to get out of her hold. I imagined describing the whole haphazard event to Will, Mike, and Basil and the salvos of laughter I would get, knowing all along that I could not do it. And I kept fretting that Jozef might come in, trying to think of things I could say to dispel the accusatory, questioning gaze, and the only thing I could think of — eminently useless — was: "We're just friends." God help me. It was much easier to succumb to sleep than to expect Jozef, and succumb I did, again.

◇ ◇ ◇

Then the door of our room went down with a horrible crash and a bunch of KGB men with painted faces burst in, ripped us out of our beds, threw us on the floor. One of them stepped on my neck, pressing it with his boot viciously. The pain was intense, my neck stiffening up, but it was pleasurable and when the handcuffed us together, Jozef and me, I found myself wanting a second helping of that pain. They pushed us down the stairs and I twisted my ankle, but Jozef kept me from falling and breaking my neck. Then they ushered us with their rifle butts into a Black — very black — Maria. And when we entered it, I could not see anything, and I did not know whether it was because we were blindfolded or because the darkness was so thick that I could not see Jozef's face, even if our breaths embraced together. But I could feel his bleeding wrist fidgeting on the other end of the handcuffs that tied us. Then we escaped from the Black Marenyka, when they stopped to pick up more arrestees — I recognized Mike and Vivian and wondered where Will might be — Jozef head-butted a guard and barged forward. We heard shouts and shots and the gallop of boots, but we were hidden by the darkness. I just followed Jozef and we ran and ran, but it was as if we were skidding along the surface of a placid sea. I simply let myself go, gliding over water, and then we hid in the forests of Ukraine. We dug a hole in the ground, and woke up sheathed with frost. We bit off chicken heads and drank the blood straight out of the necks. We hopped on a train, where Jozef strangled a policeman, while my handcuffed hand shook like a rattle in front of the dying policeman's crooked eyes. We crossed borders and more borders, some of them were hedges, with watchtowers and sharpshooters strewn all over, waving at us, letting us through, so they could shoot us in the back. And they shot and I could feel their bullets going through me. Then we slept on a train car floor, like hobos, there was no one there, but as we slept, it filled with furniture and people sitting in armchairs and on sofas, and Jozef and I were sitting next to each other, and somehow our hips were handcuffed, and where the handcuff bit into my flesh there was a hole and I was leaking out, buckets of bile.

◇ ◇ ◇

It was Will who walked in on us. It was morning again, we slept with out backs turned to each other, Vivian's full frontal nudity facing the door.

"Jesus," Will said, and Vivian covered herself. Jozef still was not in the room. Will brandished a tennis racket, as if it were a sword. He leaned over us — we could see our distorted little heads in his glasses — and said: "Meeting. In my room. In fifteen minutes."

I may be this, and I may be that, but when I am told there is a meeting, I get up and attend the meeting.

"I need to go to my room," Vivian said, pale and in need of a carrot or something.

"Okay."

The meeting, ah, the meeting: Vivian and I, sitting on Will's bed next to each other. Mike and Basil on the other bed, and Will amidst us — his family benevolently beaming at all of us. Andrea was not there, probably stretching in her bed next to Jozef. Will told us what he knew: there had been a coup; Gorbachev was in the Crimea, under house arrest; hard-line Communists and generals took over; there were arrests everywhere, people disappearing; street fighting in Leningrad, tanks on the streets, bloodshed; large army contingent movements from western Ukraine and Belorussia toward Kiev. He had received a call at Igor's office from his father, who for some reason was in Munich. Will told us everything was good at home, and I may be misremembering a collective sigh of relief.

"We gotta get the hell out of here," Basil said.

"We gotta wait," Will said, "until we know what is going on. I think we are okay here."

He ordered us not to leave the school and to let him know at any given time where we were. Throughout this performance, he had a somber frown and kept pushing up his glasses, mindfully allotting his glances in equal numbers to all of us. He instructed Vivian to inform Andrea about our meeting and its conclusions, and he told Mike and Basil that he needed to talk to them after the meeting — I seemed to be out of the loop, though I didn't know what they were looping for.

Jozef was back in our room, radiant on his bed, not able to suppress his grin, his hand roaming under his shirt, as if marking the kiss traces, the tongue trails.

"It looks like you had some fun last night," I said.

"Love is beautiful thing," he said, pronouncing *thing* as *ting*.

"It is indeed," I said, for a moment entertaining the thought of telling him about my *ting*.

"They demonstrate on Khreshchatek," he said. "Many people, all night. Police is everywhere. I go now, again. You want to go?"

"Oh, I don't know. I have to talk to Will."

"Why?"

"Well, because we had a meeting this morning."

"Which meeting?"

"Meeting, you know. We organized ourselves. We have to know where every one of us is, in case of trouble."

He put his left foot on his right knee, the sole facing me, and then went on picking on corns, peeling off dead skin, sliver by sliver, his toes watching it like five retarded hick brothers.

"You are like child. You must tell your parents where are you."

"No, man. It's just common sense."

"When you don't tell parents, you are bad boy. Bad boy," he said, scowling at his heel.

"That's stupid," I groused. "I don't have to prove anything to you, you know."

"I know. I go now."

"Who the hell do you think you are?" I said, and threw a pillow at the other pillow on my bed.

"I go now," Jozef said. "You don't want to go?"

◇ ◇ ◇

I followed him. We walked: it was a long walk, through largely deserted streets, except for a sporadic pedestrian, ambling conspiratorially, or an ominous truck of soldiers, roaring by, under a roof of tree crowns touching one another above the street. We didn't talk much; we heard birds chirruping and ruffling the leaves above our heads; the concrete was warm, and the light was soft, diffused by the humid air and the tree shade; fall was near. We walked by open windows exuding boiled-dough steam; by basement doors giving off damp coal-dust scent; by shuddering lacy curtains, behind which a shadow of an old woman's face was recognizable for a moment. A cat crossed the street with her belly lowered, and her head ducked, and then stopped in the middle to look at us in affronted amazement. The sun twinkled from the tree crowns, for a whir of wind divided the leaves for an instant.

But then we turned the corner and there was Khreshchatek: giant ore-brown men looming over austere concrete steps, too big to be human, their gaze directed at the horizon of rooftops, over our heads. There was a large crowd at the bottom of the stairs, with a speaker elevated above it, thundering into the squealing microphone something I could not understand. We saw a line of policemen standing a little below the giants' feet, up on the stairs, solemnly lined up like a choir, their hands on their asses. And then another police line, behind the speaker, in the shadow of the trees. We joined the crowd — I followed Jozef, who moved closer to the speaker — and stood there, unsure what to do, other than applaud when everyone else did. The mustached guy standing next to me, with an unruly dandruffy lock poking his eyebrows, spoke to no one in particular about the police coming down and wiping the demonstrators out. I was taken aback, because he was the King of Midnight himself; even if I was not sure about his face, I recognized Antarctica. I don't know if he recognized me, but he pointed at the trucks behind the backs of the umbrous policemen, deeper in the shadow.

"We go closer. I want to listen that man," Jozef said, and started moving closer to the speaker.

"I don't think that is a good idea," I said, but Jozef was already pushing his way through the throng, so I followed him. We ended up practically in front of the speaker, only a few wide-shouldered security men in front of us, looking up at him. The speaker had tears in his eyes, and he clenched black-and-white photographs in his hand. He kept ranting about genocide and Russians and plague, flipping and showing the photographs: a wasteland recognizable as Chernobyl; crooked and cramped tree branches, with misshapen monster leaves; a two-headed mouse, with only two eyes, the two snouts pointing in different directions.

My mind was brilliantly clear, aware of everything around me: the screeching and buzzing of a transistor radio; the hairy rungs of fat on the neck of the man right in front of me; the lemony smell of Jozef's skin; the policemen's seal-skin batons, doubtless bloodied many a time; the striped shirts of the KGB men who stepped out of their trucks and smoked, staring at us; the rustle among the policemen, the shuffle of their feet; the crowd cringing and contracting, before the policemen stopped; the woman high up in the window of one of the buildings, leaning out and calmly smoking, watching the whole shebang without particular interest.

Jozef gently put his hand on my shoulder and whispered into my ear, his lips touching the lobe: "When police attack, we must run, and if we lost ourselves we must run this way" — he pointed toward a red kvass kiosk — "and meet there."

"Sure," I said, but did not really want to leave, for I knew that nothing could happen to us today, that even if they arrested us we would get away together, that this was our souls' wedding; a wave of euphoric tranquillity went over me. I did not want to move, cherishing Jozef's palm on my shoulder — I can feel its weight now, his breath brushing the side of my neck. There was nowhere to go beyond this moment. I knew I should try to live in it for as long as possible. There was nothing to lose and everything to gain by being as present as possible.

So I turned to him and grabbed his face with both of my hands, and pressed my lips against his, feeling the air coming out of his nostrils on my cheek. To the men around us, it could have seemed a typically Slavic outpouring of brotherly feelings, but Jozef knew what I was doing, for I tried to put my tongue into his mouth. He opened his mouth and let my tongue in, then kept it in. Then he kissed my neck, bit my shoulder gently, and slipped his hand under my shirt. I grabbed his shoulders and pulled him closer to me. We kissed for an eternity, could not separate.

◇ ◇ ◇

A bird slams into the window of my office and startles me — my heart is galloping in frantic circles. The bird — a comatose sparrow — lies on its back on the windowsill, its little claws grasping nuggets of nothingness. I stored that kiss in the cryogenic chamber of my soul for some future, whose prospects are diminishing daily, and sometimes I take it out and tempt myself with the thought of thawing it. Outside, I can hear the din of the waiting students: a few young women with their feminist paper proposals on *Midsummer Night's Dream;* a winsome young fellow who wants to write about Hamlet and Kurt Cobain. Around me, there are stacks of knowledgeable books, some of which I have flipped through impatiently in the past few years, looking for some kind of wisdom or, at least, references to my published articles. I loved Jozef Pronek because I thought that he was the simple me, the person I would have been had I known how to live a life, how to be accommodated in this world. Today, I garbled through the class, teaching *Lear,* soliciting ideas from my students about the ways in which Lear's power was *discreated,* and what it meant to him as a man. But it was routinely absurd — everyone had something to say, everyone had half-baked opinions based on how they felt about this and that — and I kept wanting to read them the passage when Lear and Cordelia are about to go to prison, and Lear says: "Come, let's away to prison." And he tells Cordelia about all the things they can do together in prison: they will live, and pray, and sing, and tell old tales, and laugh at gilded butterflies, and hear poor rogues talk of court news, and they'll talk with them too — who loses and who wins, who's in, who's out, and take upon themselves the mystery of things, as if they were God's spies. And Cordelia says nothing beyond that point, she does not utter a word, they take them to prison and she's killed, Lear dies. I wanted to read that with them, and then sit in silence, make them imagine all the things that Cordelia might have said, think of all the things I could have said, and let the uncomplicated sorrow settle in and stay with me, like a childhood friend.

◇ ◇ ◇

We stood there, his hand on my neck, and listened to exhilarated speeches about the greatness of this moment, about the future shining bright behind dark clouds that hid our horizons. People cheered, and applauded, and sang songs about freedom. Policemen did not move, the KGB did not move, the giants did not move, I never kissed Jozef. I pretended to be listening carefully to the speakers, while I was trying to make a decision, one moment after another, and then turn to him, grab his face, and press my lips against his, dizzyingly aware all along how impossible it was. Jozef stood next to me, oblivious to my desire, unsinged by the fires of my hell. My stomach quivered, and iron fists pressed against my temples, until my sinuses were throbbing. He might have said something, I might have responded. He might have touched me a few times, I might have shuddered. But I looked not at him, and I touched him not, and it all lasted for years. Finally, we walked back to the Party dorm. Jozef went to look for Andrea. I went back to my room and fell asleep.

When I woke up, Vivian was resting her face on her palm, curled next to me. I thought for a moment that I had dreamt it all: the putsch, the non-kiss, my life. Vivian stroked my cheek, and told me that Ukraine was independent now. I told her to go away, that I didn't want to see her anymore, that it was not her, it was me. "Why? Why?" she cried. The image of her arched back and her craning neck as she left the room still, often, makes me contemplate my cruelty, producing a sneeze of intense grief. But I take out a handkerchief and wipe my runny moral nose.

I crept out of bed in the days after freedom arrived only to call home. Exhilarated gangs of newly independent Ukrainians still roamed the streets with blue-and-yellow flags. I talked to my father, who vociferated, in an exhausted, coarse voice: *"Shche Ne Vmerla Ukraina!"* Ukraine hasn't died yet! But he was about to die, my mother outright told me, too fatigued to lie. Everything inside him, she said, had been eaten away by cancer — it was a matter of days.

I found Jozef in Andrea's room playing chess with her. Andrea's things: underwear and shirts and bras and crumpled tissues were strewn around, as if a hand grenade had exploded in her room. I kept it simple and poignant. I told Jozef that I had just found out that my father was dying, from belatedly discovered cancer. He hugged me, his breath sliding down my neck. Andrea hugged me too, kissed my cheek, her lips warm and sincere. I thought then I would look her up in Chicago, but I never did. I never saw her again, and I never saw Jozef. Although there have been passersby and strangers who cruelly wore his lovely face and sometimes I recognize him among the extras in a lame Hollywood movie. Once I saw his face on TV in the crowd of Greenpeace protesters chanting some nonsense in front of a nuclear facility. I am used to those fantasies now, as one gets used to the voices of the dead talking to him.

◇ ◇ ◇

I packed up, said good-bye to Will — there were actually tears in his eyes when he said: "I know your old man will be okay." I took the night train to Warsaw and flew to Chicago, via Frankfurt, all in dazed numb pain, my only entertainment nightmares full of remorse. The funeral was the day of my arrival — he perished while I was in the Frankfurt Airport duty-free shop, considerately buying a few bottles of Absolut vodka that would be consumed at his wake. Straight from the airport, I sat in the first row at the Muzyka funeral home, with my sobbing, shuddering mother, dressed in deep black, while my father lay in an open coffin, and his war comrades — old men in dun suits that had been growing bigger on them, exuding defunct-prostate stench — held on to Ukrainian flags, and delivered speeches about my father's loyalty and generosity, about his love for Ukraine, about his final moments of sublime joy as he lived to see his homeland free. *Pan* Bek wept as he read a Taras Shevchenko poem that had our wheat fields extending into eternity. Then they all sang *"Shche Ne Vmerla Ukraina"* looking up, as if freedom were hiding its misshapen face behind fire alarms and dim ceiling lights. Finally, my mother and I stood up and walked to kiss my father good-bye, before they closed the casket for good. His face was laminated and hardened, his eyelids stiff as bottlecaps. As I leaned over him, I could see the tips of his trimmed nose hair, peering out of the dark nostril holes, but not moving, no breath coming out to tickle them. I kissed my father gently: his lips were frigid and tight. I know now when one is dead and when one lives.

PAUL GREENBERG

The Subjunctive Mood

1. It was already December, just a week before their departure, when Peter Isaakson realized that he did not feel young enough to transfer to Paris. He realized this at the same time he realized he didn't quite know why Isabel had suggested the move in the first place.

"Well," she said over her shoulder as she boxed up the last of her closet, "I always thought I could explore another side of myself in Paris."

"Another side?"

She smiled a strange smile — stuck halfway, it seemed, between her actress smile and her real smile. She walked to the futon couch and kissed him. If he had turned his head only slightly he could have really kissed her and shifted the odd look in her eye back to the bedtime-familiar. But as they'd been together almost a year, and the radiator was blasting, and he hadn't showered, and she hadn't brushed her teeth, he let her young mouth slide off his face and continue its progress in this new direction.

"If I told you something," she said standing up and putting her hands on her hips, "something really hard for me to tell you. If I asked you to support me in what I'm going to tell you, would you support me, one hundred percent?"

Peter took an older man's pause before replying, "Yes. Of course."

She kissed him once more, reached for a stepladder and climbed into the upper reaches of her closet. She came down with a suitcase that was octagonal and purple, slightly larger than a hatbox.

"The truth is," she said, "I haven't exactly been upfront about Paris. But I missed you during that stupid . . . what was that dumb 1970s expression you used? That 'trial separation'? Well, whatever, I missed you, okay? And then when we ran into each other, well, I was just all caught up in being with you again and I didn't want to ruin things."

"But now it feels like you're looking at me differently. I feel like you're really looking for me. For *me,* exactly *me*. Not some picture of me you put together in your head. And I've been thinking about it and I realize that I was the one who was being selfish. How could you find me if I didn't show all of myself to you? I kept telling you about this space between us, but I never realized that I was the one making it. Well, I'm done hiding. I know what it's all about now. And I want to show it to you."

She reached into the suitcase and pulled out a bright red wig. "This is her hair," she said, putting on the wig, "these are her shoes," a pair of oversized, floppy shoes was produced, "and this is her nose."

She put on the red rubber nose and the shoes and waddled across the room to embrace him.

"A clown?"

"Yes, a clown," she said. "That's why I asked you to transfer to Paris. I want to study clowning."

◊ ◊ ◊

Peter offered no protest during their first weeks in Paris. He took a sleep aid to more quickly adjust to European time and after finalizing his working papers at the UNESCO offices, he went about installing Isabel in an apartment that would be noticeably clown-friendly. While she visited a list of prescribed stores on the Right Bank for school supplies (a horn, two small metric wheels, red pails) he searched for flats with large open tumbling spaces, high ceilings (for aerial gags) and smooth floors. And although he could feel his traveler's enthusiasm dipping dangerously close to expatriate impatience, he made an effort to overlook things — like the fact that French apartments came shorn of electrical outlets and light sockets and that there seemed to be more taxes than rent on the final *facteurs* the real estate agents presented to him in their rococo *bureaux*.

He did all this with great dedication, suspended in the same dream-flight that had characterized his first days with Isabel. In this new, unlikely setting he was reminded how improbable her appearance in his life had been — a last minute reprieve from what he'd long ago accepted would be a life sentence of loneliness.

Love had eluded Peter in New York. He had expected it to make its appearance around the time he turned thirty. But then thirty came and went, and then thirty-five. And gradually, almost imperceptibly, the soft part of his heart — the outside tenderness that invites love — grew as tough as gristle. He could no longer bear the hollow chatter of a blind date. In the space of three months his hairline receded to nothing. He could sense his friends reassessing him, transforming him in their minds from an eligible bachelor to a middle-aged crank.

And so when he agreed to attend a UNICEF benefit in a hall crowded with screaming children he bitterly assumed his new identity and scowled and arrived late and then was irked that he could only sit in the front row. And as he watched the musical being performed — an adaptation of a children's book that concerned a toy rabbit which had lost its whiskers — he could not believe that the story was keeping his attention. And when the actress playing the girl who so wanted to have the rabbit with the lost whiskers called for volunteers, he could not believe that this young woman with thick auburn hair and clear green eyes took him by the hand and pulled him on stage — literally pulled him up into youth itself. And as he turned around and around on stage with his hands in the air, singing "my whiskers, my whiskers, at last I've got my whiskers," he discovered that he possessed a small, but possibly expandable capacity for ridiculousness.

◇ ◇ ◇

So he did not mind the effort or the money it took to rent an apartment for Isabel on the rue Raspail, catty-corner from the Lampière School of Mime and Bodily Transmogrification. During the first evenings there he took pleasure in the fact that he could look across the street and see the end of the late sessions, the shadows playing on the ceiling as the students moved through the phases of theatrical evolution that de Lampière explained were necessary to metamorphose into *Homo sapiens clownus.*

They settled into a kind of routine. They would have coffee and eat croissants out of the dirty common basket at the bar of the downstairs *brasserie,* trying to ignore the vaguely hostile stares from the early wine crowd and the big-knuckled plumber humping away at the Captain America pinball machine. Isabel would chat hopefully about her exercises for the day. Then she would kiss him and go across the street to clown school and he would make his way through the seventh and ninth *arrondissements* to the Lego-land 1960s UNESCO building.

He sometimes caught himself as he walked down the broad boulevard toward the Eiffel Tower, silently remarking that most people back in New York didn't know that the Eiffel Tower was actually painted a very unfortunate brown. He would interrupt his thought and scold himself and try not to be so critical and to remember, for Chrissake, that this was the frigging Eiffel Tower he was staring at *on his way to work*. Amazing. Sort of.

Inside the UNESCO *Bureau de Planification* his secretary, Beatrice, would have laid out his dossiers in cleverly clasped binders that he found difficult to open. And there would usually be a note or two in her curly, European hand: "Almir has telephoned from Sarajevo and is angry" or "Brad from the New York is asking about your status." And he would gamely work his way through calls and dossiers and read budgets for small amounts of money to be given to small organizations that would change very little in the world.

His long-ago high school French with all its associated teenage yearning returned to his consciousness like a dream recalled in the fog of early morning. He weirdly and uselessly augmented it. He learned the French words for the different functions on a calculator. He came to say sentences like "We support independent, democratic organizations whose goal is the propagation of knowledge and information" without an accent or an error. But if over coffee he asked his secretary to pass the sugar, Beatrice (who bore an uncanny resemblance to his very mean ninth-grade French teacher) would note that he had mistaken the gender of sugar and that he had addressed her as *tu* instead of *vous*.

Heading home in the early darkness he would walk out through the lobby, past the photos of doomed African development projects and step out to glare at the chicken wire UN globe at the front of the pavilion. And with the last of the day's enthusiasm drained he would feel his heart contract as he looked back at the vast UNESCO campus. The buildings were made of blocky communist-style concrete that must have seemed passable when the place was first built; now it all looked like a neighborhood of gloomy, third-world tenements.

He would try to take different routes home, hoping to somehow penetrate the cold membrane of the city. "Paris is as a snail," Beatrice had explained in what sounded like a grammar book reading exercise. "Follow the *arrondissements* in a spiral and they take you to the center." But as much as he tried to spiral his way into the vision he'd had of the Latin Quarter, it seemed he could never escape the orbit of what he came to think of as the "Bureaucratic Quarter." Again and again he rounded the UNESCO compound, passing over and over *Aux Ministères,* the silent bistro where he ate his lunch. In the end he would give up and take the Métro. He would stare at the strange rabbit howling in pain in the cartoon pasted next to the train door. *Ne mets pas tes mains sur les portes,* warned the sticker, *tu risques de te faire pincer très fort!* —"Don't put your hands in the door. You risk a very strong pinch!" And when he would leave the Métro and walk to his corner he would feel ridiculed and diminished by the blue and white sign that lauded the accomplishments of the street's namesake: *Raspail,* the sign declared smugly, *Chimiste et Homme Politique 1794-1878.*

By the time he reached the landing of his apartment, he would find himself flummoxed and bizarrely exhausted. He would shove the weird, aggressive-looking key into the electric lock mechanism of his front door. Once inside, he would want to collapse on the Ikea sofa and explain to Isabel why it was all so hard, why he was so sad, why he felt so old and slow. But Isabel was suffering too.

"He didn't like our *cahier.* He hated the improvisation," she would cry as he took off his coat.

"What? Where?" Peter asked.

"De Lampière hated it. He didn't even let us get to the main part."

"What did he say?"

"He said, '*bien, bien*' and then he held up his stupid little froggy hand like a stop sign."

"Doesn't *bien* mean good?"

"Not the way *he* says it."

And he would take her in his arms and comfort her and hold her until his shoulder was wet and he would cry too and this would somehow whisk away his own misery. Then they would go to the Chinese restaurant around the corner because they'd both quickly gotten so sick of French food.

2. It was not stagnant. It was not boring. She seemed more and more necessary to him. He still felt the old space, but now it felt as if something strange yet somehow vital inhabited that space. Some evasive yet possibly graspable thing. And occasionally, at night beneath Isabel's purple comforter, or across from each other in the *brasserie,* one of them would put a hand to it, like a child groping for a frightened kitten underneath a bed.

And it seemed for a moment that this very thing might be the aspect of them that would grow and mature.

But then Isabel mastered the subjunctive.

It sneaked out once when they were ordering an Easter pheasant.

"Je préfère que vous mettiez les pattes comme ça . . ." she said to the butcher, apparently explaining to him that she wanted all the breast bones removed but the legs left in to give the carcass structure.

"Wah, wah, mademoiselle," said the butcher, barely looking at her. He didn't seem to notice Isabel's accent. He showed her none of the hostility he regularly aimed at Peter — it was just as if one Parisian were talking to another.

And soon he noticed that he no longer understood Isabel when she spoke French. If she had a friend from clown school over to dinner the conversation would proceed almost entirely in French with the occasional blob of inflected English thrown in to make the conversation contemporary. She would say things like, *"Moi, je déteste les imbéciles New Yorkais." New Yorkais?* he would think to himself. And he would sit in irritated silence, glumly shoveling in his food like, well, like an older French husband, while the students discussed the relationship of the body and the voice, about who had stumbled, who had broken, who would be leaving the clown school, and de Lampière's brilliant use of space.

At a certain point he started excusing himself from dinner early, claiming a forgotten dossier or a meeting with someone visiting from the Balkans. He would head out into the city, hoping desperately to get lost in a labyrinth of tiny streets, but always somehow finding himself on the same big avenues. And though he had come to know Paris well enough to actually find the attractive parts, its staggering beauty — its blue-gray slate roofs, its chic narrow neon, its organized charcuterie windows, ducks bound up like prisoners — seemed only to recede from his reach. He would walk to the Seine and stare into the brown, turbid water from the Pont Neuf while the *bateaux-mouches* circled the Île de la Cité, recorded tour guides droning out the same descriptions of the same beauty over their P.A. systems again and again in French, English, German, Italian, and Japanese. And when he came home Isabel and Marion, or Isabel and Pierre-Yves or Isabel and Jean-Jacques would be watching one of de Lampière's famous performances on the video *magnétophone.*

◇ ◇ ◇

De Lampière's lessons progressed and Isabel bore down on colors. There was a chance that in a month's time her class might advance to invertebrates and maybe by summertime they'd earn the right to move on to mammals. But for the moment they were stuck aping inanimate abstractions — color, sound, space. They had been a "terrible group" — "*un groupe affreux*" — the worst group de Lampière had seen in many years and his scolding had spread like a sickness through the school.

Isabel was assigned yellow. Peter was assigned Bosnia. The UNESCO head of mission in Sarajevo had been shot and Peter was given the job of closing out his accounts. The Sarajevo chief was a German called Stoltz and the bullet had passed through his eye, through the back of his skull, and finally into the safe's combination lock. Stoltz had neglected to turn in his year-end ledger and so that was the first order of business — get a blowtorch to Bosnia, open up the safe and transfer the records back to Paris.

Stoltz's sad, blasé assistant called from Sarajevo and they talked through the different problems with managing the office in Stoltz's absence. They kept returning to the same hitch — the documents stuck in the safe. Finally after all the possibilities had been explored and rejected, Peter suggested putting a picture of Stoltz on the safe and maybe the same sniper would shoot it enough times to blow the safe open. Stoltz's assistant laughed at this.

"You have the right attitude for this place," Almir said. "You would do well in Sarajevo. We need a new chief, you know."

"No, no," Peter said, brushing off the suggestion. "I couldn't do it. I live with someone."

"Bring her," Almir chortled, his laughter clipped into eerie chunks by the choppy satellite line. "She can help here too. Everyone is needed. What is her profession?"

"She's a . . . She wants to be . . . Believe me, Sarajevo's no place for her."

He spent the rest of the week working with Projects on the Sarajevo job search. A DHL package of résumés arrived from New York and he tried to keep a cold eye out for the proper experience as he helped vet them. But each time he pulled up a new C.V. with the summary of yet another life more daring than his own he found his mind drifting to his own hypothetical résumé: "Peter Isaakson, 1993–1995, UNESCO SARAJEVO HEAD OF MISSION. DUTIES INCLUDED . . ." What would the Sarajevo mission chief's duties include? Would he move papers back and forth between Europe and New York and strategize data systems and design office protocol just as he was doing now and had done for many years? Or maybe he would do something else? Maybe he would pass money from the UNESCO account into the hands of clever partisans posing as puppet organizations, which he himself would set up and name. There had to be a reason why Stoltz had been singled out by a sniper and shot through the eye. No random shot, that. Soon Peter started tracking Bosnia in the newspapers. He asked Beatrice to help him translate *Le Monde Diplomatique* and *Libération* for him. He applauded the few French politicians who took a stand and demanded intervention in the conflict. He grew furious when he saw one or another columnist talk about the historic duty Europe owed the Serbs.

He tried to tell Isabel about Almir, about the peppering of automatic weapon fire he heard in the distance when Almir called from Sarajevo. He wanted to tell her that he had been dreaming of Stoltz's shattered eye socket. She smiled at him distantly. She told him she was pro-Serb.

"The Serbs defended Europe against the Turks for 300 years," she informed him.

"That's true, but —" Peter began to argue.

"But nothing," she said. "We've already covered all this in

Théories des Clowns. What would have happened if the Turks had invaded Europe? What would they have done to European culture? There would be no rue Raspail, just some Mehmed Pasha Boulevard or something. And there'd be no human arts at all."

"'Human arts' is not English, Isabel."

"What*ever.* It's about life. There would be no living art. No art of emotion. Just abstractions."

"Oh, like colors?"

"Meaning?"

"Meaning that colors are pretty abstract, aren't they? That's what you're doing at clown school, colors, right?"

"It's not 'clown school'. It's about movement. It's about a deeper laughter. Clown is a label someone hung on our art 300 years ago."

"Was he a Turk?"

"Was who a Turk?"

"The one who hung the label."

She turned away. He kept his distance. Her shoulders started to tremble. He heard her soft moan, so close to a sexual moan but so much sadder. It tugged at him. He flushed. He took her hand. She tried to speak several times. It finally came out in a wail of despair. The pruned, Gaulish exterior she had been cultivating came apart. And then, rising up from underneath all that, came the woman who had first moved him. His Isabel, his smooth, pliant girl. Not "Eez-a-*belle,*" as she was called at clown school. He felt so badly for her all over again.

"I'm sorry, Isabel. I'm so sorry," he said.

"It's hard, you know."

"I know."

"I mean, they screw around with your head there. You can't believe it. It's so weird. I need some guidance here. You're supposed to be the mature one. I need somebody behind me. Are you behind me, Peter?"

"Yes, I'm behind you."

"One hundred percent?"

"Yes, one hundred percent."

She let out a long, trembling sigh and then sniffled. Her expression calmed. "Then will you . . . come to my *cahier* tomorrow?"

"Yes, yes, I'll come."

◇ ◇ ◇

Almir called the next day in his darkest mood yet. A Serb detachment was attempting to take a narrow ridge just above the UNESCO offices and the sound of automatic weapon fire, normally in the background, now drowned out Almir's voice. The office had to be moved, Almir explained, but there was too much of value in the safe to leave it behind — registration documents, account ledgers, and money. His voice was patient and cool, more cool than the situation would seem to advise. Peter said he was working on the blowtorch.

"Work on it, Peter," said Almir. "Work very hard."

In the evening Peter came to the main *salles des exercices* at the clown school. The room was full and cigarette smoke hung like a murky second ceiling beneath the house lights. Peter craned to look between two French heads and caught a glimpse of de Lampière. He sat stony-faced in the front row, his nose pressed up against his folded hands. He was not as he had appeared on the cassettes. Here, the unclowned man looked scrubbed and tight. Amused but somehow prepared to be profoundly disappointed.

De Lampière demanded that the lights be dimmed. A burst of 1920s French café music followed. And then, all at once, there was Isabel. Sheathed in a purple leotard, she rolled quickly across the stage in a motion that looked like a combination of the backstroke and the Australian crawl. Her lips were pressed together in intense concentration. Her arms shot out. She seemed a perfect, graceful tube. But just as she reached the end of her roll, de Lampière burst from his seat.

"*Arrête*!" he said, furious. "Stop, stop. What are you doing there? What?"

Isabel rose up on all fours and looked at him like a stunned filly.

"I . . . I'm . . . I'm doing yellow," she whispered.

"Yellow? YELLOW?" screamed de Lampière. "Yellow doesn't do that."

"No?" she asked. "But then wha . . . what does yellow do?"

"What does yellow do?" de Lampière said, his little face growing big and threatening. "Class, what does yellow do?" No one answered. He shook his head. "Yellow jumps!"

The music on the *magnétophone* was silenced and Isabel shuffled off the stage.

After blue and green had each had their turn Peter took Isabel by the arm and led her back home along the boulevard.

"What an ass," Peter said, softly stroking her coat. "You shouldn't pay any attention to that crap."

Isabel sniffled once and pulled away from him.

"He's not an ass," Isabel said. "He's right. That wasn't yellow at all."

3. Peter got his first glimpse of Sarajevo when the military transport plane banked left and dipped under the remains of a rain cloud. Through the airplane's dirty porthole it looked at first like a hill town in the south of France — terra-cotta roofs scalloping the ridgelines, church towers here and there, little winding roads. But as they descended he saw the broken minarets and the burnt scabs of ruined concrete and metal. Trams piled up as barricades. Valuable, useful things dismantled and redeployed for their bulk and weight alone. He was buckled to a bench just off the starboard engine and the propeller's throbbing had penetrated his inner ear. He saw tracer bullets and artillery shots arcing from the hillsides below and then all at once the plane dropped like a stone. He gripped the bench hard and prepared for the crash, but a journalist in a flak jacket across from him laughed and gave him the thumbs up. Apparently this was the way into Sarajevo.

They landed hurriedly, pulled to an abrupt stop and then idled on the runway for almost an hour. Peter's hearing stayed muted and fuzzy. White armored personnel carriers surrounded the plane and blocked off what little view he'd had through the porthole. Then a UN soldier opened the door and started shouting at them in German. Peter followed the soldier down the ladder onto the tarmac. The soldier ran and motioned for them all to do the same. As he sprinted toward the terminal he saw two figures — one large, one small — move past him in the opposite direction. He heard two faint cracks in the air, like the pleasant sound of a faraway batting practice. The figures crumpled on the runway and were still.

He was shunted directly from the terminal door into one of the armored personnel carriers and again it was all noise and darkness. There was a new overpowering sound, this time a high-pitched whine coming from the drive shaft churning below his feet. It picked up where the earlier propeller droning had left off and wiped out the remaining spectrum of his hearing. He looked through a different dirty porthole now and saw the city flash by at ground level — half-standing offices and apartment blocks that seemed to have vomited out piles of shredded metal, mashed sheetrock, and rotten clothes.

Propellers and driveshafts were still in Peter's ears when he met Almir at the UNESCO office. Almir mouthed some words at him.

"Nice to meet you too," Peter replied.

Almir shook his head, repeated what he was saying, and made a gesture. Peter at last understood that he was asking if he had a cigarette.

"No," Peter said, shaking his head and shouting over his own deafness, "I don't smoke."

Almir looked at him blankly. He took out some tobacco remnants from his pocket and rolled them up in what looked like brown butcher paper.

While Almir smoked Peter unpacked the blowtorch. He fumbled with the hose and knocked over the tank twice. He tried to wedge the wrong end of the ignition rod into the tank's gasket. Almir watched this in growing irritation until finally he snatched the thing away. He snapped the hose in quickly, loosened the valve on the acetylene, pressed the trigger, and lit the gas with his cigarette. He put on a pair of cracked Ray-Ban glasses and made a circle around the safe's lock with the little blue flame. Sparks flew out from both sides of the nozzle, but when they hit Almir's bare hands he only shook them off, not noticing the burn marks they left on his skin.

When he had completed the circle he touched the metal with his hand with three quick taps. It was still hot. Finally he cocked his elbow and punched it in. His arm disappeared inside the safe. Gingerly he extracted its only contents: Stoltz's German passport. He handed this to Peter and went into the next room to finish his cigarette.

◇ ◇ ◇

Another APC left Peter at the Holiday Inn. It pulled up diagonally to the entrance with the hatch facing the hotel steps. Only a narrow crack of the city was visible and exposed to sniper fire. He sprinted into the hotel all the same.

Inside he found it to be colder than on the street. A lone bulb in the lobby ceiling shuddered with inconsistent current. The walls were dark, streaked concrete, the same Communist concrete that made up the UNESCO building in Paris. Chunks of it had tumbled down into little gray landslides in the lobby. Journalists and hotel workers stepped over the debris without looking.

He was not surprised to find his room without electricity or water. Strangely, though, the phone line worked and even more surprisingly, there was someone in the kitchen when he called room service. Half an hour later he was given a hard buttered roll, a cup of tea, and two buckets of water.

When the waiter had gone Peter sat down on the bed and ate his roll. As he chewed, he stared out through the blue United Nations plastic that had replaced the blown-out glass. A piece of it had torn loose and he could make out the sweep of the northern edge of the city if he craned his head in an arc from right to left. The sun was just setting behind the mountains and he saw fires and the lights from portable generators flicker on in a ring around him, marking the Serb line.

His ears started to clear. First the higher registers came back and he made out the *pep-pep-pep* of rifle fire. Then the lower spectrum returned bringing with it the mean belches of artillery. It was impressive how much of it there was, how thorough the siege-makers were in their work. The noise and flashes peaked and ebbed like the different phases of a fireworks display. When the shelling grew particularly intense the sound of failing roofs joined in, and, after that, sharp squeaks and hollow moans that could have been either metal construction beams faltering or the last sounds of human lives.

He stood up and paced. He looked at the phone. He picked up the receiver and dialed Isabel. He got an empty beeping in response. He slammed it down.

What would they talk about anyway? Orange? Red? Would she dare to make pronouncements from the seventh *arrondissement* about Serbs and Turks and "the human arts"? Would she justify the actions of the people on the hills who were now pointing their rifles down into the homes of children? He tried her number one more time. And though the call did not go through he started the conversation anyway. She had said her piece and now he was really laying into her. "How can you even defend yourself?" he said. "How can we even *have* this conversation. How can I even discuss these things . . . with . . . with . . . with a *clown,* for Christ's sake!"

A sentence started to form. It fought its way clear of the chatter in his head, detaching itself from the memory of Isabel's deepest smell and from the tugging sound she made when she came or cried. It was a small sentence but it carried all the gloomy nights of Paris and the unwelcoming stares of the French butcher and the passport of a dead German he now carried in his pocket. The sentence grew in size and brightness, rising up like a neon sign against a dark, offending background.

"I hate clowns," he whispered into the phone.

He laughed. He felt tears form in his eyes. He put down the phone. He cleared his throat and stood. He looked out through the torn UN plastic. "I hate clowns," he said now in a normal voice. He laughed maniacally. He paced. He smiled. He cheered himself at the thought of the new space he would have when Isabel and all her assorted Eurotrash were expunged from his life. And finally he thrust his arms in the air and shouted through the window at the Serbs on the mountainside in front of him:

"I HATE CLOWNS!"

The rifle flash was very close. Something nearby snapped clean. *Ne mets pas tes mains sur les portes,* said the howling Métro rabbit in his brain. That was true, he thought. You shouldn't put your hands in the door. You risked a very strong pinch. A very strong pinch indeed. He thought this as he watched his fourth and fifth fingers come away from his left hand and drop into the hotel trash can.

4. *Le Beaujolais Nouveau Est Arrivé!* — The Beaujolais Noveau had arrived. The signs were everywhere, even at the baggage claim at Orly airport where he picked up the blowtorch and his suitcase. Even in the Arab perimeter of the city which the taxi now circled, where the people didn't go anywhere near Beaujolais wine, new or old.

Peter sensed his hand pulse and, underneath the pulsing, a permanent-feeling numbness. The surgeon had laughed at his wound and done a hasty job sewing up what was left of his hand before he and Almir had packed Peter aboard the morning flight. What the surgeon had not accomplished with stitches and bandages he had smoothed over with a large dose of morphine, for which Peter had paid dearly. Now as the drug receded he watched Paris glare up at him through the taxi window in raging Technicolor. The drug had calmed him, taken away the panic. He sensed it rising again like a tiger behind glass. Soon the glass would lower and the tiger would jump through and clench its jaws around his head.

"*Alors, on va où, eh*?" the taxi driver said over his shoulder.

"Hospital" Peter said. He could not bring himself to pronounce the French word.

"*Comment*? *Comment*?" the driver asked.

"Pain, pain," he had said, "The nearest hospital. Please."

"*Comment*?" said the driver, a glitter coming into his eye.

"The hospital. The nearest hospital!"

"*Comment*?" asked the driver, smiling now.

Peter held up his hand in its bandage. "You see, HOSPITAL!"

"Ah, l'hôpital! Quel hôpital, monsieur?"

Which hospital? How did *he* know which hospital? The good hospital. The hospital with the morphine. The hospital where the doctors presented several options and helped him make an informed choice about the rest of his hand.

"*Quel hôpital, monsieur*?" the driver repeated.

The hospital where they were nice.

"Which one, eh?" the driver said now in a mocking English.

Maybe there was no nice hospital? How could he know? He had a great need for the subjunctive mood. "Would you prefer if I were to amputate the remainder of the fingers?" the doctor might ask. "No," Peter would need to respond, also in the subjunctive, "I would prefer if you left the remainder of the fingers, and I would also appreciate it if you were to administer great quantities of morphine at this time."

"*Comment*?" demanded the taxi driver.

Yes, these were the sentences he needed. He needed the spry grammar skills of a younger mind. And he would need them more and more the older he became. Now, on the other side of forty, he realized that fifty would hit him fast and hard. Sixty would feel like an armed robbery.

"*Monsieur*!" the driver demanded again.

It wouldn't be just fingers. It would be whole limbs and organs and even the brain itself that would fail. Even in New York, with English spoken all around, it would grow too confusing. *Was* there a subjunctive mood in English? Who would express it for him?

"*Alors, on va où monsieur*?" the driver said, yelling now.

Peter's thoughts churned and swirled and intermarried and bred new and more horrible thoughts — an overload of inputs jammed down a tiny hole of reason until he could do nothing else but blurt out one word:

"Raspail."

"*Comment*?"

"Raspail," he shouted.

"Zere is no hospital called Raspail," the driver said.

"Raspail. Rue Raspail. Raspail, *chimiste et homme politique*!"

"Ah, Raspail!" the driver said. "Raspail, you do not say it correctly." The driver exited off the *Périphérique* and began a spiral down into the seventh *arrondissement*. Peter looked at his misshapen hand and saw the beads of blood from the bad suture work start to spot the bandage. He searched for the last Percocet pill he had been given by the surgeon, but it had slipped through a hole in his blazer pocket and was lost somewhere in the lining.

The driver informed Peter that a U-turn at his corner was illegal. He got out and bumped the blowtorch across the street to his building. The acetylene tank would not fit into his tiny European elevator. He turned to the staircase and started his ascent — *clink*, step, *clink*, step, round and round, until he paused for a rest on the landing just below his floor. He heard music. It grew louder as he started up again and drew near his door. His good hand trembled as he fit his key into the tricky lock. The door clicked open and he saw the banner hanging from the ceiling.

LES CLOWNS DE LAMPIÈRE ACCUEILLENT LE BEAUJOLAIS NOUVEAU! — THE DE LAMPIÈRE CLOWNS WELCOME THE NEW BEAUJOLAIS!

Inside a mass of clowns pulsed to a synthesized beat. They jumped up and down on the floor so hard Peter felt the pounding in his sutures. A girl from Isabel's class grabbed his bad hand and tried to pour a glass of wine down his throat. He screamed with pain and spat the wine out onto the floor.

He saw that the parquet was awash in Beaujolais. The clowns tromped around in it, leaving burgundy footprints on the Ikea area rug and the foldout sofa. He pushed into the bedroom. Clowns were rolling across his mattress and sprawled out on the window ledges. The girl who had played green had her mouth on the neck of the girl who had done blue and the supporting cast of colors worked themselves against the two while the techno pop raged on, the synthesized voice coming clear:

I want to rock,
Around the world.
Around the wor-ld,
Around the wor-ld.

The crowd thrust in the direction of the bathroom door, moving their hips and pumping their arms in synch, as if they were pulling the rhythm from the bottom of the bidet. They pointed at the door and clapped and cheered. Peter tugged on the bathroom doorknob. It wouldn't move. He tried the other direction and felt a force opposing him. Finally he let go and the door seemed to come open of its own accord. Isabel wobbled out, a smudge of white make-up on her cheek. Her frilly pink shirt was half buttoned and she was naked from the waist down.

"Where is the clown?" she mumbled and then vomited on the floor.

Peter reached out and grabbed her. She flopped over and seemed to break in two. She fell apart in a blister of giggles.

"Oh it's you. You my love. He rocked me around the world."

She reached up and pulled his head down and kissed him. He could taste the sour wine and the vomit on her tongue. She laughed and giggled and the giggles made her break out in laughter and flop over again.

"Stop laughing, Isabel," he said. "Please stop laughing."

And then, de Lampière burst from the bathroom, nude except for a pair of purple European briefs.

"*Mais, non*! Don't make her stop. It is beautiful. You see how she laughs, Peter. You see? Do you know why is that?"

"She's drunk."

"H-oui!" said de Lampière. "H-oui, she is drunk. But she is drunk on her *identité*. You hear that way she laughs. That is the laughter of a clown. But you cannot hear it, can you? You can only hear the empty space."

"I don't hear anything but a drunk girl."

"You are hearing not a drunk girl — you are hearing a full girl. I have filled her up."

"Listen you. . . you clown —"

"You say this word 'clown' as an insult. But it is the most extreme praise. You say 'listen clown' but I say to you 'shut up, non-clown.' Go! Go and turn on the floor as the dark colors do. All is done for you. Now she is full."

And with this de Lampière bounced onto the bed and out of the room. He grabbed Isabel's horn off the dining room table, honked it twice, and cartwheeled out into the night.

◇ ◇ ◇

The hangover never quite left Isabel. The hospital where she took Peter the next day made her sick and then three weeks later the hangover came back and she vomited nearly every day for a month.

She desperately wanted to return to clown school but she found she didn't have the stomach for it. All her spontaneous mirth needed to be conserved now — a precious balm saved for the tender tissues forming within her. And as the space in her gradually filled, Peter's wanderings in the Paris streets took on a smaller and smaller circumference. "Paris is like a snail" they had told him, "you find your way to the center in a spiral." He saw the truth in this now, as he watched Isabel watch the French doctor unwind his bandage and reveal a red, three-fingered instrument that resembled a chicken's foot. He found his mind turning in again and again on itself until she had walked him back to the rue Raspail, where the circle became no bigger than the circumference of his own apartment.

It was entirely possible that what had been conceived was theirs and theirs alone. Accidents happened all the time, as they both knew. And whatever the truth might be, they realized it would be preferable if the father were not a clown.

But the mother definitely was. What the child would be was yet to be determined.

MILJENKO JERGOVIĆ

TRANSLATED BY STELA TOMAŠEVIĆ

The Condor

Izet was what they call an *eglen-effendi,* or brilliant talker. He could talk non-stop from dusk to dawn. One story flowed into another, one event turned into the next. Often he'd use the day's events to begin a story that would range across whole centuries and finally return to the price of meat or some gossip about a chap called Hido who led a ram across Mount Jahorina just before the animal sacrifice of Bairam, right through the Serb positions, until he reached the Visegrad gate, where he was hit by a UN armored truck — I swear to God — and thrown into a ditch, while the ram was killed instantly. There was no end to Izet's stories, just as there's no end to time, the past or the future. But they were never dull and they usually had a message or a moral and were seldom erratic: a tiny narrative thread kept you tied to the story, and forced you to listen, even if it meant that you had to go hungry or without drink, or that your life as a whole became a tense silence in which things only mattered if they could be described by a storyteller.

At the outbreak of the war Izet was staying at Vraca. Before he could even blink, let alone run away, a gang of Serb Chetniks turned up outside his house. His neighbor Spasoje immediately began to point the finger at Izet. It was very sad. Until the day before the two of them were always drinking *rakija* together. Spasoje was good as gold and harmless as a water pistol. But on the day in question he dressed up in a black uniform, a knife flashing at his waist; his beard seemed to have grown overnight, as though he'd fertilized it with manure. Anyway, he was outside Izet's door yelling that he'd slit his throat if he didn't open up. Suddenly Izet lost his tongue, and his knees began to tremble. He didn't want to open the door. He didn't really want to keep it shut either. But since he couldn't say anything in reply, able to manage only a hiss in the back of his throat, he just made his way to the door and painstakingly fumbled with the key in the lock. He could smell the *rakija* on Spasoje's breath through the wooden door. As soon as he opened up the door he was hit in the face by a rifle butt. Izet fell to the ground like a stone. He was so light that Spasoje was able to pick him up by an arm and a leg, and carry him through Vraca. Blood was pouring down Izet's face, but he was still conscious. Even so, it was impossible for the *eglen-effendi* to utter a single word.

His neighbor didn't let go of Izet until he reached the Stara Rampa bar. He carried him inside the building, where pictures of King Petar and Draza Mihailovic had sprung up overnight. Yet there was no sign of any bar-room furniture. Instead, five men in uniform sat at three tables in the empty room. Spasoje dumped Izet on the floor in front of the soldiers, but the wounded man quickly got to his feet. A fair-haired captain wearing the uniform of the Yugoslav National Army pulled up a chair for Izet.

"Where are your weapons?" demanded one of the other soldiers, who had a beard down to his belly button.

Izet opened his mouth but only hissing came out. The bearded Serb repeated the question, and Spasoje delivered another blow with the rifle butt. Izet was feeling dizzy. He could see that his captors weren't fooling around, and so he began to make up plausible lies, except he couldn't give voice to any of the stories. As the question was repeated for a third time, the five soldiers jumped up, almost fighting one another for the privilege of hitting Izet. In the end he was pummeled from all sides. At one point he imagined that he heard an echo in his ears, as if the Chetniks were beating somebody else, or as if the neighborhood children were shaking apples from the tree. The lies slipped his mind, and he drifted first into indifference and then into a soft comfortable darkness from which he didn't emerge until the next day.

He woke up battered and broken, with his arms and legs tied, in the cellar of the bar. The first thing he saw when he opened his eyes was a pile of tables and chairs. On top of them lay Mijo Penava, also battered and tied up. He was the butcher from Lenin Street who'd cut off his left thumb six months ago. The two of them looked at each other for about ten minutes, Izet lying on the wet cellar floor and Mijo on the heap of furniture that was almost collapsing.

"Why did they put you up there, you poor thing?" said Izet, who had by now recovered his voice.

"Because they threw you down there, I guess," replied Mijo.

"What did they want to know so badly that they had to beat you to a pulp?"

Mijo was trying to put his head between two chairs. "The same thing they asked you, I guess."

"And what did you tell them?"

"I said whatever came to mind. But now they want me to take them to the place where the guns are hidden. Dammit! How will I show them what isn't there? If I tell them I was lying, they'll just beat the hell out of me. I have to think of something else. Blow me if I know what. And you? How did you butter them up?"

"I lost my voice so I couldn't tell them anything. I opened my mouth but the volume was off. Mind you, I'd have told them whatever they wanted to hear, just as long as they didn't reach for their knives. Except I couldn't, for the love of God. D'you think I'm being punished for having a tongue that's quicker than my brain? How unfair! Just when life depends on it, my tongue knots up."

"Tell me then," said Mijo, "what story I can make up so I don't have to take them to the weapons?"

Izet considered the question, licking his dry lips. He knitted his brow for a moment and then suddenly opened his eyes wide, as if he could see the story he was about to invent.

"Here's what you tell them, Mijo: all the guns you talked about were picked up by that guy Zvonko who worked as a bouncer at the nightclub. They won't be able to check the story, because Zvonko has escaped to town with his mother and wife, to stay with that small-time crook who owns the jewelry shop on Slatko corner. Then you tell them that the jeweler was always a saboteur, and that he more or less brainwashed Zvonko. You can say that he spent time as a political prisoner on the island of Goli, because it was alleged he had ties with the Russians, and that he sent his mother to an old-people's home, even though he owns three villas in Sarajevo and Split. Tell them it's easy to recognize the guns by the sound of the bang — it's kind of dull, as if you were using a silencer but it wasn't fitted correctly."

"And what's this dealer of Zvonko's called?"

"Make something up on the spot — a Muslim name, though, so they get the idea that Zvonko has links with both sides, and that's why he wouldn't have told an out-and-out Croat like you what they were planning to do with the weapons."

Soon afterwards the Chetniks came and took Mijo away for more questioning. Izet never saw him again. But when his turn came to be interrogated again — would you believe it? — his throat seized up again and he found that he was unable to speak a word. Three times the soldiers beat Izet until he was unconscious, only to revive him and start the questioning over. In the end they decided that Izet was a bigshot. "Well, he must know a lot if he hasn't talked yet," they reasoned. So they didn't sling him back into the cellar. Instead they put him in a room with a bed, fed him well and gave him enough to drink — and then took him to Lukavica. He was questioned there by several colonels, but they didn't bind his legs or his arms, and they even offered him coffee and cigarettes. After a while Izet got his voice back. Now he could tell the Serbs whatever he wanted, except they were no longer interested in guns: they wanted to know his rank and various troop formations. As Izet had never served in the army, he didn't know anything about the latter, but self-importantly he proclaimed that his rank was that of colonel in the Green Berets. As for military plans, he went on, they might as well kill him because he wasn't going to reveal any secrets. Of course, he wasn't lying about that — he couldn't invent things about a subject he didn't understand.

The officers smiled at Izet, almost out of a sense of camaraderie, but didn't press him any more about the troop formations. Instead they began a friendly conversation about other things. Izet talked knowingly about the political situation, though he was careful not to say anything to annoy his inquisitors or to give them any reason to suspect that he was trying to suck up to the enemy, or that he wasn't in fact a colonel who was prepared to give up his life to safeguard military secrets. Izet played with words and swayed like a pelican on a wire. He talked nonsense but it sounded ambiguous and therefore wise. You utter a word, you weave it backward and forward, and at the end of the sentence you stand it on its head. You're not making any sense, but you're the only one who knows that.

The next day a colonel came into his room and announced that Izet was going to be released in exchange for ten Serb prisoners of war. Everything was arranged with the Croats, who wanted to know the identity of the war hero held by the Serbs. It was merely a formality. The other side had to guard against swapping ten Chetniks for a nobody who was lying about being a colonel in the Green Berets.

Izet panicked. If he didn't come up with a meaningful lie to tell his own people, the Chetniks would take great pleasure in slitting his throat, whether he confessed to stringing along the interrogators or continued to protest his high military rank. Hundreds of stories flashed through his head, but each was as unconvincing and complicated as the next.

At last he blurted out, "Tell them you have captured the Condor from Treskavica."

The Serb colonel looked at him blankly, then took a pen and paper, wrote it down and went out. That night was the longest in the whole of Izet's life. All he wanted was to die without suffering, to fade away or disappear, so that he wouldn't have to face the morning and the knife of his neighbor Spasoje.

At dawn, three privates came to get him. One of them said, "Condor, it's time!"

Izet left the army camp at Lukavica with a heavy heart. His knees were trembling. Outside, the door of a yellow Golf was open, and as Izet huddled in the back seat, he realized that he'd lost his voice again. Only this time nobody was asking any questions. Instead of taking him all the way to Spasoje, they just drove him to the bridge, where he was released. Half-way across the bridge he passed a group of men whose lives had been exchanged for his own.

As soon as Izet came clean and admitted that he wasn't the Condor of Mount Treskavica, he was given a violent beating by his people. The soldiers kept him locked up for days and threatened to shoot him or give him back to the Chetniks. With each blow of the rifle butt they shouted out the names of all the prisoners whose freedom would have been negotiable in exchange for the ten Serbs. They could have liberated war heroes instead of ending up with a sad case like Izet, who was good only at talking nonsense. In the end they let him go — fuck it! — it was their own fault for watching too many movies and believing in stories about condors.

Sooner or later Izet recovered from the shock. He forgot about his episode in prison and went back to telling safer and more intelligent stories.

Having recovered from his wounds and his nightmares, the only painful memory that stayed with Izet concerned Mijo, the butcher, whose throat was slit by the Chetniks in Vraca. He couldn't help wondering if Mijo had been killed for spouting the lie that Izet invented for him, or if the poor man had simply lacked the ability to use the right words at the right time. Perhaps there really are occasions in life when it's best not to say anything.

JOHN BECKMAN

Babylon Revisited Redux

1. James Danforth Quayle was a natural-born diplomat, one of those rare and expansive human beings who light the lights wherever they go, who bring cheer to the room — draw folks together — and deliver their own native prosperity to the world. Thirteen years earlier, when he had risen from humble roots to become Vice President of the United States of America, he had been called on to bring diplomacy to the new nations of Eastern Europe. Of these new nations, Poland had had the most promising economy, and the Cabinet had declared Krakow the city of the future. Arriving there in 1990 to an overwhelming welcome, Dan did not doubt it. And what times! Air Force Two dropped in through the smog, and though the airport security was drunk and disorderly, the great crowd of Poles in that funny-smelling terminal — where the water-stained ceiling tiles sagged from their frames — sent up such a blast of confident applause that he knew in his heart he was delivering the goods. Flashbulbs sunned his face, his golden hair shone, and the hopeful masses basked in the glow of the New World.

Those were revolutionary days, when the people wrestled free from the clutches of the Far Left and took to the skies like birds. It had been called the Velvet Revolution, a beautiful choice of words, and right they were. Dan Quayle had participated in the Velvet Revolution.

Now, however, content though he was on those pearly Phoenix mornings when he trundled along the links, trailing a sliced golf ball like a will-o'-the-wisp, he still heard the call for his diplomatic gifts. The world, he knew, had more to gain from the youthful talents of Danforth Quayle. And then, what ordinarily hung about as a free-floating desire, not exactly anxiety, more like a wish, struck like lightning one morning in the pro shop when a distant song was playing on the radio. He ignored the snorts from the men in his party and was transported by a low, soulful whistle to a springtime moment in his life. He broke free from the others and went alone onto the fairway, and there he reconstructed that valuable memory. It was, yes, his one night in Krakow, and his encounter, yes! with two impressive young men. They were entrepreneurs, fresh from college, a new generation of DKEs from the old fraternity house at DePauw, and they had joined him at a dinner of American investors. The taller one resembled a young Steve McQueen, the shorter one, even more so, a young Marlon Brando.

"We are not ex-patriots," he recalled the shorter one having said, his eyes leveled with admirable force. "We are *re-patriots.* We are Polish Americans, the pride of our generation, and we are returning to rebuild this country in our image."

This youthful idea got the Vice President's attention — more precisely, it captured his imagination. They were not ex-patriots — for who *would* be? They were re-patriots. What an idea! These lads were anagrams of the American Dream — wealthy emigrants returning to the homeland! Bold Forty-niners on the wild frontier! That night they invited him out on the town, and having first phoned home to George for the go-ahead, he *went.* Followed by a phalanx of Secret Service agents, Dan Quayle and his Dekes did it up *right.* The night life in Krakow was strange and exciting. The bars and nightclubs were underground caverns, and the drinks were blue, green, yellow, and pink. Very colorful drinks! Everywhere there were young people speaking foreign languages, and though the Dekes protected his anonymity he was embraced by one or two well-meaning Americans who unfortunately were thrown to the ground by the Service. It was legal to gamble at the Casino Krakow, so they went there, too. The floors were marble, the ceilings were high, and the twinkling chandeliers gave it the look of a palace. He won more than forty dollars playing roulette. He clearly recalled a moment at the casino when the young Marlon Brando took him aside and asked him to look at the television.

"Do you watch MTV?"

He did not.

"You are watching it now. Euro MTV."

A male rock star with the hair of a female was crooning to a cheering stadium.

"This is the Scorpions. Do you like this song?"

He did not, though it stirred something in him. He gave a diplomatic response.

"It is called 'Wind of Change,' " Brando said, significantly. " 'Wind of Change.' Right now it is the most popular song in Europe."

That was all that was said about it, though they listened to the entire song, and when they went out into the chilly April night, and his entourage divided the crowds of the market square, the haunting ballad chimed in his mind as if it were ringing from the nearby cathedral. The Scorpions. "Wind of Change." Maybe he *did* like the song. At the end of the night, at a private party, the Dekes filled him in on their entrepreneurial scheme. Real estate was their game. They had gathered seed money from Polish-American magnates and were buying up the very best properties in Krakow. They were reopening the city in the name of freedom. What had enraged Dan Quayle, prompting him to drop a sausage canapé on the floor, was what he learned of the shifty Viennese, their stiffest competitors in the real estate market. He leaned in close, trying to ignore the canapé, and learned that the Viennese, hailing from Austria, went about their business like Pirates of Old, greasing palms and accepting bribes while his principled young Americans, kept honest by the Foreign Corrupt Practices Act, played fair in fear of being convicted of a felony. These young men were ambassadors of American Values, swept ever eastward on the Wind of Change, swept like pioneers in their prairie schooners, and he looked on them with fatherly — *brotherly* — approval. "Danforth the Manforth" he was called by Steve McQueen, with whom he shook hands before retiring to his hotel.

Who *were* those boys? What were their names? Gazing at the blue sunlight behind Mazatzal Peak, Dan Quayle simply couldn't remember. But they were extraordinary Dekes, and the recovery of their story now bothered him to distraction. Somehow he knew that he was returning to Krakow, and that, without question, he would go it alone. That morning he bogeyed the first seven holes and narrowly finished three over par. When the guys gave him heck at the end of the round, he retorted, mysteriously, "Go tell it to the Viennese."

◇ ◇ ◇

Marilyn Quayle, the former Second Lady, was co-author of three very popular novels. She was his best resource in tricky matters like these, though he knew better than to get her help in tracking down the Dekes — especially since he had never told her about his wild night in Krakow. When he returned from the club later that morning, he found her working in the sunny kitchen. Dan slipped past her into his office and set about the task after his own fashion. Near lunchtime, having checked the golf stats on the sports channel, he ventured out and watched her count aloud while stirring a yellow sauce.

"Honey?"

"I'm counting, Danny."

He waited for her to finish. "So I was wondering."

"Here," she said, putting the spoon into his mouth. The sauce was tart and smooth.

"What is it?"

She took the spoon. "Hollandaise."

"Ah." She stirred a fresh spoon into the bowl. "So I was wondering. If, let's say, you were writing a novel, and one of your characters had met a fraternity brother many years before, and he looked like a movie star, but he wasn't a movie star, and he couldn't remember the brother's name, what would you have him do?"

She turned around and glanced at his notepad. "I don't understand," she said. "Who looks like the movie star?"

"The fraternity brother."

"And my character wants to remember his name?"

"Precisely."

"Is this an intelligent character?"

"Of course!"

"Who's the movie star?"

Dan paused. He concentrated on the bright yellow sauce. "Tom Cruise."

"Where did he meet him?"

"He doesn't remember."

"But you said he was intelligent."

"New York, London, it doesn't matter."

"I guess the first thing he would do is consult the fraternity's composite photograph for the year in question."

"Ah."

"Then he'd look for the Tom Cruise look-alike." Marilyn gave him that funny look, as if she trusted him implicitly even though she knew he had something up his sleeve. He was used to getting that look.

He spent the afternoon in his office, assisted by his secretary, and it wasn't as easy as his wife had made it sound. To Dan's dismay, the DePauw chapter had closed its doors in the late 1990s, leaving a ghostly hole in the center of campus. What to do? It took hours of Internet research and unreturned phone calls before, at last, they reached a free-lance DKE archivist who, for an astronomical fee, could provide color reproductions of all the composites of the 1980s. His secretary arranged to have them flown in, next-day air, morning delivery, and Dan went home alive with new ideas.

The difficulty of this project only increased his resolve. He relished the challenge. He had encountered few obstacles in his fifty-six years, having crept like a cable car above the rocky slopes, and now that he had arrived at the pinnacle of existence and could look out over the thousands of miles beneath him, he envied, in secret, those red-cheeked climbers who hadn't had it quite so easy. The Dekes of Krakow had been just such adventurers. They had torn free from the bosom of Mother Indiana. They had followed their dreams into a barbaric land. They were explorers, entrepreneurs — patriots *par excellence*! Marilyn rolled over and told him to shush. (He must have been mumbling.) He pressed his face into the pillow. He too had caught the bug. It had been his duty and privilege since September 11 to secure the interests of Americans abroad. He was prepared to risk even personal safety to defend his young lions against those hyenas, the sleazy Viennese.

The next morning, it was fun sorting through the composites. All of these young men could have been his Dekes of 1967, with their sporting looks and mischievous smiles, as if they were all party to an April Fools' prank. Seeing the old house put a lump in his throat. Generations had passed under the shade of her yellow maples, legions had gathered around her TV — but then she'd been consumed, as if by fire, in the mayhem of the Clinton years. He had made such a mess of things! Dan set his mind to the task at hand. The faces were small, no larger than his pinky nail, just the job for his magnifying glass. Upon close inspection, many of the faces looked familiar — youthful versions of fellow golfers, a lifetime's worth of lawyers and politicians. He even found himself in the class of '83, a starry-eyed boy named Douglas Green who vanished in the years to follow. It was in the class of 1986 that Dan, with a start, got his first glimpse of McQueen and Brando — one tall, one short, both scrawny and gawky — and as he flipped ahead through the next four years, they remained side by side, gradually maturing, shoulders filling out, until, in 1990, they stood front and center, the Vice President and President of DKE. He let out his breath. Only then did he trace faces to names.

McQueen, he discovered, was Tommy Dziewiatkowski. Marlon Brando was Marek Bronek.

2. Drinking sweet coffee in the first-class cabin, looking down on the villages in their snowy blue hills where Europeans were starting their tiny blue days, he felt like a teenager sneaking out after midnight. His golfing buddies were at home, asleep. He had told his wife a little stretcher — that he had been called away on a diplomatic mission — and she had let him go too easily, almost trustingly. In truth he had made arrangements he didn't fully understand. Upon discovering the names of his junior Dekes, he had burst in on his secretary and set her to work. He had rejoiced with her news that the Dekes were still in Krakow, and he felt that old power when, later that day, she handed him the phone and Bronek greeted him with an enthusiastic invitation: "Danforth! Dekeforth! Where you been hiding? Don't you know we need you over here?" This was just what he had hoped to hear. Whereas in the past his diplomacy had been laid out well in advance, a subtle agenda drawn up in committee and carried out by his grace and finesse, here Dan himself was the hammering blacksmith, the Vulcan forging something from nothing, and as he took another look at the documents in his briefcase, a bunch of declassified real estate nonsense that his secretary had gathered at the request of Bronek, it chilled him to think, at 30,000 feet, that maybe he wasn't up to the task. He didn't understand a word! But surely it was only jetlag. Surely his talents would see him through. Jetlag had been the worst thing about being Vice President.

The month was February. This didn't mean much back in Phoenix, but here it smacked him in a blast off the tarmac. Forehead, nostrils, lips and cheeks — winter encircled his collar and cuffs and attacked the flimsy wool of his pants. He hugged the briefcase to his chest like a bomb and groped his way toward the warmth of the terminal. The heat felt cheap — hot and unregulated. The long wait in line gave him a tummy ache, and the customs agent, whose hands were inky, waved him past without noticing his name. Inside the gate, nothing had changed. Same funny smell, same water stains, though it felt small and lonesome without a cheering crowd. Marek Bronek was nowhere to be seen. The sleepy mob looked straight through him, searching the stream of new arrivals. He found a seat on a white-cushioned bench.

When he awoke the crowd was gone and two girls in fur coats were crouching before him. One was chubby with badly frosted hair. The other, a brunette, had her hand on his knee. She had a smoker's voice, but her breath was sweet. Presently he realized she was saying his name. A hand-written note from Marek Bronek apologized for not showing up in person but explained that the "young escorts," Beata and Danuta — his and Tommy's wives, respectively — would deliver him home to the "Krakow Chapter." Beata, Marek's wife, was the perky brunette.

The power nap had done him some good, and having lugged his bags across the sub-zero parking lot, it pleased him to ride shotgun in Beata's black Mercedes while the girls chatted back and forth in Polish. Even their smoking didn't bother him much; it gave the morning a bohemian feel. There had been road trips back in college to visit the other chapters — philanthropies at Notre Dame and once even Yale — and speeding with these girls along the frosty freeway had that old exhilaration. Beata reached over and unbuttoned his top coat, a polite way of telling him to make himself at home. Her expressive brown eyes included him in their gossipy conversation, almost as if he could understand. He tried to follow along, nodding at the bouncing notes of their language, and occasionally she laid her warm fingers against his cheek, surely a Polish gesture of friendship.

The quaintly partitioned stretches of farmland soon gave way to towering blocks, drab as housing projects on Chicago's South Side, connected by networks of cables and clotheslines. The traffic slowed up behind a filthy red bus and Beata needlessly leaned on the horn. Danuta shouted out the window, filling the car with freezing fresh air. A chorus of blaring horns joined the cause. Dan held his mouth and closed his eyes and succumbed to a hand massaging his neck.

◇ ◇ ◇

What Marek Bronek had called the "Krakow Chapter," a lavender mansion in the center of the Old Town, reminded Dan of a circus caravan — gypsy-like carvings encrusting tall windows, cheerily painted flowers splashing the arcades — but the feature that stopped him cold on the cobblestones was the bold white lettering high above the doors, lovingly jig-sawed: DKE. Two flags jutted out over the street, Old Glory and one he didn't recognize. Poland, maybe. The girls whisked him through the heavily furnished ballroom, as if to spare him the unclean air, which was rank with spilt beer and cigarette smoke, but smell it he did. Male voices argued behind a closed door. The girls led him up the turning marble staircase, guiding him through a maze of pale blue corridors, and the deeper he penetrated into the Krakow Chapter the more he felt the importance of his return; though as with anything that is profoundly felt, the feeling wasn't easy, and it wasn't certain. And those sacred white letters — tacked onto some shabby Polish house!

Danuta turned back, and Beata got him situated in the Presidential Suite, where a dark portrait of George hung above the sofa and a breakfast service steamed on the table, the universal smell of sausage and coffee. She removed her coat and hung it on her arm, the soft, spiky fur dwarfing her small figure. Delicate neck, fine shoulders. Her breasts pressed hard against the fuzzy black sweater — she faced him as if inviting him to look her over.

She performed an adorable pantomime, demonstrating for Dan how he would eat his breakfast, take a long nap, then portage his towels into the bathroom.

Once she had left, he did as he was told, eating little and napping long, comforted by the vague and dreamy awareness that someone kept checking in on him. It was after four o'clock when he finally got up. The breakfast service had been removed. The light coming in was wintry and dim. He locked the door. Passing into the bathroom wearing only his briefs, he caught a sober look from George.

It was humiliating bathing in the cramped tub — the soap not lathering, just a handheld showerhead for washing and rinsing — and the feeling stayed with him as he unpacked and got dressed. He couldn't get warm. He wanted to call Marilyn. He had no clue how to get the wrinkles from his shirt — but instead of fretting, he chose to rough it. He could do this! The knotting of his tie had a snappy finality, like an invocation of his diplomatic muse. The wool of his suit was soft and smooth. He gave George the thumbs up and went looking for the others.

Nobody was in the ballroom, though the air smelled clean and the furniture shone. The dark, carven ceiling and red leather chairs gave the room a masculine look; one corner was occupied by a fancy billiards table, the other by a wet bar and a gallery of dart boards. All that was missing was a television. He listened. Voices down the hallway on the far end of the ballroom called him forth like a distant trumpet, and he followed the sound without hesitation, not obediently, but eagerly, navigating between armchairs and jutting tables, ready to make his big appearance.

The walls of this smaller room, animated in the firelight, were rough with skins and big-game trophies. Every free space was filled with people talking softly, as if they were hiding. He half expected them to call out "Surprise!" but only a few of them reacted, scowling at the brightness when he pushed through the door and prepared to be introduced. The rest simply ignored him. As his eyes adjusted, he cast about for Beata, even Danuta, someone to lead him to Marek Bronek and get this crazy show on the road, but he recognized nobody. His ears adjusted, and he heard no English. Hesitant to exit through the bright door, he ventured farther into the gloom, edging around bodies and low-lying furniture until he had found a space by the warmth of the fire. He had to smile. What a wonderful secret! Wait till they discover who is standing in their midst!

But the faces glowing in the radiant heat looked so foreign as to be almost hostile. Three dowagers — one with severely short hair — hissed at each other through plumes of gray smoke that seemed to rise from their fur collars and boas. A group of gentlemen roughly his own age (though in much worse health and stiffly dressed) huddled around a thin young man in a DKE sweat shirt who spoke Polish to the air and ignored his listeners. Indeed, most of these folks looked like threadbare aristocrats, not sweet like Beata, not dumpy like Danuta, but cynically European in their black turtlenecks, making him think he should conceal his identity. Everyone, he noticed, was drinking vodka. He was twirling his wedding band around his finger when a serious young couple offered him a crystal-stem glass. No sooner had he accepted it than their three glasses were raised and he was drinking to something he hadn't quite caught. They warmed to him when they realized he didn't speak Polish, but this only meant more vodka, and faster. He was enough the ambassador not to turn it down.

◆ ◆ ◆

Some kind soul had thrown a coat over his shoulders. It was long in the sleeves, furry in the lapels, the lining smelling sharply of human protein, but it tucked him in from the cold night air as the pack of them herded across the marketplace. Thoughts of Beata kept dragging him back, the wish that she could see this too, for here were the steeples spangled in snow, here the palaces and dark arcades that harkened back to the Velvet Revolution. "Hello Krakow!" Many stories up, the trumpeter appeared in his tiny aperture and pierced the sky with his ancient song. Dan waved. "Hello Krakow!" Two of his new comrades clapped him on the back. "Hello Krakow!" the three of them called out and skipped a few steps over the slippery stones. The lot of them sang a song that Dan could only hum as they made their way to a cavernous bar where the ceiling was stone, the air was close, and purple candles lit the tables. Again there was vodka, and plenty of beer, and yet he kept his identity a secret. The dowagers were snuggling up to the gentlemen. The boy in the sweat shirt played the slots. Despite his suspicions about the Krakow Chapter, and his doubts that they were Dekes at all, he was sure something good held them together.

"Danforth the Manforth!"

He knew the man immediately, but even as he was warmly pumping his hand he struggled to make sense of the razor-burned jowls, the slicked back hair, the painful red eyelids and jittery eyes. "Steve," he said faintly, realizing his mistake.

"Tommy Dziewiatkowski," the man said, helping him out. "And you know my wife Danuta, and Marek's wife Beata."

She had changed into a tacky, but ravishing, red evening gown. She held out her hand but avoided Dan's eyes. He looked down at his coat and felt self-conscious.

"It's not my coat," he told her, then remembered she didn't speak English.

"Danforth," said Tommy, clasping him around the shoulder and leading him to the side. "How you been, old man?"

He detected a slight accent. He resented the familiar tone. He said nothing.

"Too bad we lost you. We thought you might have got caught up with these clowns, so we sent out an APB, as it were."

Dan waited for more information.

"And here you are." Tommy smiled and gritted his teeth.

"Where's Marek?"

He smiled more broadly, lifting some jowl. "He's coming."

Tommy hulked into the crowd and selected a few "clowns," who, Dan learned, would be joining them for dinner. The boy in the sweatshirt didn't need an invitation. The rest looked on as the group made their exit, Dan following Beata up the corkscrew stairs, close enough to smell her strawberry shampoo.

Seated in the dank restaurant, where huge iron weapons hung from the walls, he counted ten at table, with no place for Marek. There was no talking to Beata, who sat chain smoking to his right, so he divided his attention between the pickled herring and whatever it was that Tommy was saying. The silvery herring came in large fleshy strips that he was tempted to coil around his fork, but of course he cut it into bite-size pieces. The others did the same.

"These are bully people," Tommy was saying. "Bully good people. And you're a stand-up guy. It's a bully good thing you're doing here, Danforth, coming all this way on the spur of the moment to lend a good hand to these good, good people. A bully good thing. Look at it this way. This is your habitat for humanity. All across Europe and all over the world, the world's good people are going to look at this and say, that's Danforth Quayle's habitat for humanity."

Dan was listening. Angry though he was at Tommy's chummy tone, angrier still at the sprinkle of sweat appearing across Tommy's broad, ashen forehead, he was attracted to this phrase, "habitat for humanity." He thought it should be capitalized. Habitat for Humanity. He forked some herring. "Say more," he said.

"These are bully people, bully good people." Tommy indicated the others with a wave of his knife. "Imagine the feeling. Before the War, before the Red Scourge, these good people were the Hapsburgs of the East — the Hapsburgs of Poland, Latvia, Lithuania. Imagine how it must feel to be the Hapsburgs of the East, the veritable Rockefellers and Rothschilds of the East, only to be crowded into the fields like peasants. Your palaces taken, your jewelry stolen. Look at them, Danforth. Look at the Hapsburgs."

Suppressing his annoyance, Dan looked at the Hapsburgs. Straightening his tie, he felt a surge of diplomacy as he looked into the faces of these belated Rockefellers — an older lady with leopard-like eyes, a portly gentleman with a ruby pendant, all five of these aristocrats bearing a steely air of dignity that reflected both their pedigree and their lifetimes of hardship. Plus Dan had frolicked with them in the snow! Full of admiration, he raised his wine glass. "To the Hapsburgs!" Automatically, they raised their glasses. Then Tommy did something quick to his nose, something half-seen, like a magic trick. Dan looked. Tommy raised his glass. "To the Hapsburgs!"

He wasn't accustomed to drinking so much, for Marilyn kept him on a strict regime, but as the courses kept coming, generous servings of dumplings and potatoes and gorgeously seared cutlets of tender veal, Beata made a point of refilling his glass. It was their only means of communication. Occasionally she rested her hand on his leg. He wanted to know more about his Habitat for Humanity, though the more he drank, the freer he felt in his disgust for Tommy and his conviction that he could talk turkey only with Marek. It was true, he believed, that these good people were Hapsburgs, but he was under no illusion that the kid at the far end, smugly twirling his meat in the sauce, could even remotely be called a Deke. He broached the topic.

"I have my concerns about this Krakow Chapter."

Tommy patted his lips. "Oh?"

"You have the letters of Mother Deke right there on the house."

Tommy smiled at his plate, blinking sadly. "And were not those letters a welcoming sight to a Brother Deke who had traveled so far?"

"You listen here, Giacopuzzi —"

"Dziewiatkowski."

"You listen to me."

"Listening."

Dan collected his furious thoughts. He had dropped his diplomatic poise.

A bright stream of blood slipped from Tommy's nose. Dan recoiled into Beata's shoulder, thinking, for an instant, that he had struck the man. Tommy left the table with his head tilted back. Dan met the eyes of the kid and turned away. Across the table, Danuta stared. Under the table, with the utmost secrecy, Beata enlaced her fingers with his.

◇ ◇ ◇

When they returned to the Deke house a party was raging. It was in Dan's good nature to pump his fist in the air and cut a path through the rocking crowd. At first the partiers paid him no heed, and that was quite all right with Dan, but soon enough the buzz was spreading, a circle forming, and all around him Dekes were whooping and pumping their fists in appreciation. What a lark! What a gas! A shining pop song blared from the speakers and everyone cheered and shouted the words. Bruisers in track suits sang at each other's faces, women bumped their hips and snapped, a conga line snaked around the pool table and into the throng in the center of the room. Beata joined them and he slipped in behind her, placing his hands where her belly met her hips. They rocked and swayed to the jaunty tune. She turned and sang at Dan, improvising the English, and Dan sang back, making up words and holding her gaze until he reached the unmistakable chorus: "Losing my religion!" This he called out loud and clear. As the song fizzled out with a pretty little riff, Dziewiatkowski danced up next to him, nodding and affirming, "1990, baby. Nineteen-fucking-ninety."

Beata pulled Dan's arms across the front of her body, smuggling him deep into her strawberry warmth. He tried getting free, but she wouldn't let go.

"Nineteen-fucking-ninety," Dziewiatkowski repeated.

She pressed her head against his chest and he relaxed.

"Nothing's changed since 1990. Not one thing. It just keeps getting better."

Gradually undulating, the music traveling through her limber young body, her easy dance made him feel old and rigid. Once or twice he rolled his hips, letting Beata know he was there. Dziewiatkowski, still dancing, shouted over the smoke-filled rock music.

"That was the *year*. Hundreds of kids, straight out of college, nobody knowing what the fuck was what. You had all these college kids? You had all these *American* kids? I'm telling you, man, some of these kids were not fucking Americans. Get this. This stupid little shit from, like, San Francisco? He used to hang out at our bar on the square, skinny little Bolshevik in a Tootsie Roll cap. We never told you this. You're going to love this. He had all these pinko ideas about Desert Storm and shit, and we used to go at it all the time because, you know, who fucking cared? But then when we told him that you were coming to town, he started talking about causing you some trouble." He danced more purposefully, aggressively. "That's when it all got kind of messy."

Dan eased himself away from Beata. "What do you mean by messy?"

"He was no Deke, that's for sure. He learned *that* one the hard way."

Dziewiapuzzi was splitting in two, one face floating over the other. Beata disappeared somewhere to the left.

"Danforth, chill, it was *ages* ago. Nineteen-fucking-ninety."

"Ninety-one."

"Was it?"

"1991. Tell me what you mean by messy."

"Drop it, dude." His face still shifting, Giacopuzzi danced with his shoulders while lighting up a cigarette. "We were just sticking up for you."

Dan waited for the faces to reattach. "Was he a terrorist?"

The question caught Giacopuzzi off guard: the mass of him shook with belches of laughter bubbling up from his corpulent depths. "A terrorist!" he shouted, staggering backward, mowing into dancers. He pitched himself forward and landed against Dan, who, in turn, mowed into dancers. "He was a little fucking squirrel. We took him out back and fucked him up." He raised his hand for a high-five that never came and went off boogying toward the bar.

The music blared and Dan's knees ached. The heaving crowd was thinning out, leaving bare patches between the dancers. Beata returned with plastic cups of beer. Water was what he needed, but beer would have to do. She led him to a hazy corner of the ballroom where they squeezed onto a sofa among a group of Polish kids, none of them older than fifteen, all of them adoring Beata. The boys had patchy attempts at beards. The girls wore sweaters that showed their tummies. They listened with intent as she told them about Dan. A chubby young lady with a studded dog collar presented her dainty hand to be kissed. "Good evening, Mr. Vice President!" she said in good English. He passed his kiss through the air above her fingers. These kids, he knew, were the latest of the Hapsburgs. It was for them that he had traveled all this way. They were the beneficiaries of his Habitat for Humanity. They engaged Beata in a lively conversation as he slowly regained his strength and clarity.

She gave the sign for sleepy time, laying her face against the pillow of her hands. Dan did the same. They helped each other up and bowed to the children, though as she led him by the arm to the winding staircase, a low, soulful whistle rising from the speakers made him pause and turn around. Talking had stopped among the older members of the party. It was, he knew, the call of the Scorpions, a distant song drawing this generation together, linking them up in the center of the room, bringing them close as a football team. Feeling the spirit, Beata slid her arm around his waist, and as the drums kicked in and the ballad slowly rocked, the partiers swayed and softly sang, something about something and then "Down to Gorky Park . . . Listening to the wind of change." They mounted the stairs, followed by the triumphant guitar solo, and Dan regretted that he had been so cynical about the good people of the Krakow Chapter.

3. He did not have sexual relations with that woman. And while it was true that he had not had sexual relations with that woman, even as he woke up alone the next morning, decidedly alone, without even her strawberry scent on the pillow, those very words, *that he had not,* sounded almost like an admission of guilt. He couldn't shake that feeling of guilt, and the portrait of George made it all the worse. They had merely slept in the same warm bed, innocent as children, never even kissing.

Their only crime had been a mingling of heat.

Beata's young heat had radiated the sheets, seeking him out (though he had kept his distance) and drawing him close (though he hadn't drawn close). Her slight little frame had been hot as a hamster, smoldering, glowing, as though running a fever. It had been difficult to sleep, tired though he was, and it had bothered him to know that she had removed her gown, leaving but a slip of underwear between them. He had sat up once in a sleepless rage, unsettled by the utter absurdity of it all. Why was she there? What were they doing? But the heaving of her breathing eventually calmed him down, and he awoke alone, feeling all the more absurd — for he had somehow failed to have sexual relations with that woman.

Tommy Dziewiatkowski came to call around eleven, angry that they had forgotten to deliver Dan's breakfast. He smiled down at Dan, still groggy in bed, and made some asinine remark about a hangover.

"Jet lag," Dan said.

Tommy laid a clever finger on his nose. Dan had never understood that sign. Today, Tommy said, would be the big day, today they would pitch the properties, and they would appreciate Dan's presence in the ballroom at noon. He left a bottle of painkillers on the nightstand.

Showered and groomed with ten minutes to spare, Dan decided to have a look in his briefcase. Same nonsense. But if before he had been annoyed by the pages of legalese, now he was filled with a faint sense of terror — not on account of the tricky language, but at the thought of talking to Marek Bronek. Her husband. He seriously considered finding the back door.

It was the portrait of old George that brought him around, for it made him think of his Hapsburgs for Humanity. It reminded him that he had come to Poland with a purpose.

Only Tommy was waiting in the ballroom. He wore a floor-length leather coat made of varicolored patches. Embarrass him though it did to be seen with such a clown, Dan followed Tommy into the wintry streets to take a tour of the major properties. The further they escaped from the terrible Deke house, the more he felt like he was traveling again. Tiny cars. Clanging trams. Newsstands crammed with Polish papers. The mischievous snowflakes refused to fall, swirling back upward, homeward to the clouds, sticking to everything with infinitesimal hooks. Dan managed to catch one or two on his tongue. They turned from a boulevard onto a storybook street where neat clumps of snow capped the turrets and domes. Tommy spoke in a confessional tone.

"It was Marek's idea to come to Krakow. I didn't have any ideas of my own. I definitely didn't have any dreams. If it weren't for Marek I would have stayed in Indianapolis and joined the old man's securities firm, but I tell you, that kid lit a *fire* under my ass. Twenty-two years of age and Marek — that little fucker! — was spinning the globe like the Wheel of Fortune! He must have been some kind of prophet or magician because right when things were tanking back home, Marek saw the lights shining in the East! Twenty-two years old! I couldn't see them, not until he showed me. I only had eyes for beer and pussy, and my old man'd never had anything good to say about Poland. But Marek — he knew his history! He said there are hot spots all across the earth, just waiting for their moment. In the California hills, it was gold. In the Congo, it was ivory and mountains of diamonds. In Iraq, goddamn it, there's a world's worth of oil. Well, in this little city, buried under decades of soot and neglect, buried by the Nazis and those scheming fucking Commies, there was a veritable treasure chest of real estate gold. Now look at this one. This is one of ours. Or I mean, it's going to be."

It was a lime-green mansion, four stories high, and the alabaster carving around its doors and windows, softened by the piling snow, called to mind the music of Mozart. To hear Tommy describe its noble history, Dan had to agree that the building was a treasure. While its sturdy frame and spacious rooms were rare examples of Renaissance design, the grand façade, with its delicate emblems, represented the zenith of Austro-Hungarian neoclassicism. It had belonged for decades to the ——— family, though all had been lost in World War II. Since then it had been broken into shabby apartments for the pleasure of any Joe Six-pack. Tommy showed him the outsides of several such mansions, most of them rich with similar histories, and with each new stop Dan's sympathy deepened, for in his mind formed the image of a world in decay, a luxurious culture of pheasant and trout, abandoned to the rats during a pointless revolution. The specter of death was too much to bear. Though best not to forget — he had frolicked in the snow with these vigorous nobles! He had listened to the lively voices of their children! As he braved the headwind back to the Deke house, squinting into the prickly blizzard, he accepted his role with firm resolve. All was not lost for the Hapsburgs of Krakow.

They stopped inside on the winding staircase, both of their coats slumped on Tommy's arm. "One thing we need to establish before you see Marek."

Dan listened.

"All proper names are confidential." He looked at Dan, then spoke more explicitly. "At no point do we call either the properties or the families by name. And we never mention addresses or prices. At this stage we speak in very general terms."

"Obviously," said Dan, experiencing a rush of nerves and excitement.

Tommy guided him back through the house, and as they turned the corner toward the Presidential Suite, maniacal banjo clanged in the corridor — coming, astonishingly, from the door across from Dan's. When Tommy knocked it seemed to play louder, so he let Dan in and closed the door behind him. The antechamber was dark and musty, banging with sinister hillbilly sounds. The larger room, which he entered with caution, smelled overwhelmingly of a men's locker room, though by all appearances it was a well-appointed office. The curtains were drawn, the lamps were low, chains of smoke floated in the air. Rocked far back behind an antique desk, Marek Bronek attacked his banjo. He still resembled Marlon Brando, though now an older Marlon Brando. He was dressed for business with a loosened tie. Beata admired him from a heavy, leather chair, lounging in a purple track suit. If they had noticed Dan, they were ignoring him, devoting their attention to the hideous song that took several minutes to reach its conclusion. When it was over, Marek scowled into the air. "Sir Gowen!" he called out, cradling the banjo.

Dan kept his distance. He didn't offer his hand.

"Maybe I should spell that name out for you. It sounds like Gowen, but it is spelled G-A-W-A-I-N, like Guh-*wayne*." He plunked his thumb across the banjo strings. "Guh-*wayne*." He did it again. Beata laughed and drew her legs to her chest.

Dan wondered if they were drunk. He also wondered if Beata understood.

"How are your accommodations, Sir Gowen?"

"Why do you insist on calling me Sir Gowen?"

"I told you it is spelled G-A-W-A-I-N. Why do you insist on spelling it wrong?"

Dan muttered the letters under his breath.

Marek exploded in friendly laughter. Dan shook his hand, likewise passing a kiss over Beata's fingers before taking a seat in front of the desk.

Marek poured out three glasses of cognac. "I will tell you why I insist on calling you Sir Gawain, the noblest Knight of the Round Table." Dan relaxed. He rolled the pleasing cognac on his tongue. Marek's gravelly voice was strangely soothing. "It is possible that you know this story. This brave young knight, not unlike yourself, had traveled a long way to defend his beloved Camelot against that scurrilous bastard, the Green Knight. And it was on a snowy day, not unlike today, that he was lost on his quest and fell upon a strange but friendly castle. The king of the castle gave him his finest lodging, no doubt the Presidential Suite, and invited him to rest there as he went off on the hunt. Naturally the king had an enchanting young queen, and she befriended Sir Gawain and regaled him with stories and each night she tucked the lucky ducky into bed. And though each night he refused to kiss the queen, the last night his desire got the better of him, and he gave the queen exactly what she wanted. A kiss. In return she gave him an enchanted belt that would protect him from the axe of the Green Knight."

Dan held out his glass. Marek filled it.

"Long story short, Gawain goes to meet the Green Knight and he rises to the Knight's impossible challenge — to take three strokes of his axe on the neck. Brave Sir Gawain readies himself for the blows. The first two glance off, leaving him untouched. But the third stroke makes a bloody nick."

Dan shuddered. For some reason, he thought of the kid with the Tootsie Roll cap.

"Do you know why?"

"Why what?"

"Why the bloody nick?"

"Not a clue."

"Because the Green Knight is the king in disguise, and he is sparing Sir Gawain for his probity and honor. And he is punishing him for his small transgression."

Dan stiffened. He did not have sexual relations with that woman.

Beata glanced from one man to the other, no perceptible emotion on her face. She was puffy around the eyes, plainer than yesterday, though no less attractive.

"You, Danforth Quayle, are a man of probity and honor."

Dan nodded. He swallowed.

"Your virtues are in short supply these days. Especially in the East. Even in Poland. It's filthy work doing business in the East, everybody knows it, nobody touches it. The worthiest of schemes die an early death. Unfinished skyscrapers mar the landscape. Long-distance carriers, ISPs, imports — you name it. Either they're doomed by mismanagement and corruption or they're abandoned by fat-cat investors."

Marek sat up and took the meeting more seriously. Beata put her feet on the floor.

"That is why your visit is a true gift to Poland. You have come to us at a time when morale has fallen, when, God help us, even the Catholic Church sometimes looks like the Russian mafia. You have come to us in dark times, Dan, but you come to us as a symbol of confidence — consumer confidence, investor confidence — for you carry the Imprimatur of Probity and Honor, you wear the Seal of the First George Bush, you bear the Standard of an Upright Age when we were Innocent to Impeachment Trials and Jury-rigged Election Scandals. Yours was a Government *of* the People, *by* the People, and, Dan, *for* the People. You have come to us, Dan, at a Turning Point in History, when the Virtues of Old Europe have come under Siege, when the Madness of the Many threatens the Integrity of the Few, but like Sir Gawain, that Noblest of Knights, you inspire us to believe that you will Spirit us Onward — Onward to a New Golden Age."

He left it at that. He opened a drawer and produced a short stack of note cards. He slid them to Dan.

"You know the routine," he said. "You're the professional. We've got a conference room at the Grand Hotel, and there will be two investor expos, one at 4:30, one at 6:30, both identical. To maximize your star power, we'll sweep you into the room right before your speech, then sweep you out directly after." His theatrical sweeping motion made Beata laugh. Dan laughed, too. "You'll have a nice little room to hang out. A green room of sorts."

Dan flipped through the cards, a ten-minute speech. They looked at him expectantly, clearly signaling that the meeting was over.

He spent the next hour in the quiet of his suite, watching drifting snow on the roofs, listening to the wind and the muffled banjo song. He felt an uneasy sense of safety, as though he had gotten away with something.

◇ ◇ ◇

Applause massaged him in lapping waves, powerful rounds of clapping human hands, and it followed him from the door to the spacious blue podium, where he stood for a generous length of time, beaming over the appreciative crowd, sharing in the satisfaction of this public moment. He saw faces from the night before, but now it was his job to befriend the crowd. His note cards were there, simple and clear, and then his voice, his trusty voice, his bright and finely tuned instrument of democracy that could change the lifeless written word into energy, living history, the Battle Hymn of Republican Prosperity. He was so happy to be working that he nearly sang it out. His voice was measured in the interpreter's Polish, translated into a cheaper currency, and yet it raised the temperature in the room, established confidence, built faith, peaked in one strong and solemn thought that got them clapping more joyously than before.

Emotionally drained, he returned to the green room. He watched a dubbed episode of "Leave it to Beaver."

The applause was subdued the second time around — perfectly polite, though not as loud. It stopped the moment he reached the podium. This crowd was much smaller, full of middle-aged men, all of them expensively, if casually, dressed. Apart from the kid with the DKE sweat shirt, who was wearing a flashy blue suit this evening, Dan didn't recognize a soul. Tommy and Marek sat on the panel, but Beata, he noticed, was nowhere to be seen. His voice came out as clearly as before, but he had to pause and look to the right when he realized the interpreter was speaking in German. This little surprise dampened his attitude. He felt himself restraining the enthusiasm in his voice to match the interpreter's monotone. It was as if he were playing a muted trumpet. His crowning idea fell kind of flat, making the speech sound ineffectual. The applause was as polite as when he had entered. He was turning to leave when a hand shot up.

"One question," said Dan.

Marek gave him an unreadable look.

The questioner stood up. "Mr. Vice President." A charming accent. "What's your *personal* investment in Krakow's future?"

He said the first thing that popped into his mind. "I'm here for the Hapsburgs!"

Laughter and clapping seized the crowd.

This final note was just the thing.

◇ ◇ ◇

It was an easy walk back to the Deke house, and his satisfaction with a job well done shone in the snow that fell past the streetlamps. This marvelous town had survived the wars, outlived the tyrants, rung its bells throughout the ages, and yet it was ironic, and very exciting, that its oldest traditions had been preserved through a series of spectacular revolutions — bloody revolutions, Velvet Revolutions, good people fighting to keep things the same. Tonight, he whispered, it was a Snowy Revolution. This beautiful thought he would keep to himself.

Nothing could have prepared him for the shock. Seated in the ballroom beside Beata, who continued to lounge in her acetate track suit, was Dan's wife, Marilyn, tentatively perched on the edge of the divan. Dan started. Both women rose. His wife rushed up to him and engulfed him in her arms.

"But, honey," he said. "It's only been two days."

Her beautiful face studied his, a diamond-like glint in her smiling eyes. He knew his wife, and it seemed she didn't know about Beata, though he could tell there was something else. She, too, had come on business. She turned to Beata and asked to be excused.

"I shall excuse you," Beata said, her pronunciation impeccable. She smiled at Dan as she left them alone.

"Take me to your room," Marilyn said.

Their silent march through the now-familiar hallways told him that he had made some serious mistake. In the safety of his suite, facing his wife under the eyes of George, he was sick with nerves and unfocused shame. But what had he done? In a whisper she asked him to explain all he knew about Marek Bronek's real estate scheme. He did his best. When he was finished she commanded him to pack his bags. It would be foolish, she said, to stay a moment longer. "The Poles won't be a problem. They can't afford to be. Our biggest worry should be the Viennese."

"What Viennese?" said Dan, indignant.

"Pack your bags."

"What Viennese?"

"Dan, calm yourself. The big investors are obviously Viennese."

He took offense at her emphasis on "obviously."

Marilyn explained, in very clear terms, that he had pitched the same properties to two different groups. The first group comprised Poles and Jews hoping to reclaim their ancestral homes. The second group comprised wealthy Viennese, no doubt nostalgic for the Austro-Hungarian Empire, vying for their chunk of this charming little city.

"The second group spoke German!" he said.

She rolled her eyes. He could tell she had done her homework.

She refused to say another word on the subject until their plane was far from Poland, and even then was she stingy with information! In a whisper, she addressed his greatest fear:

"The Viennese aren't going to get those properties. Neither will your 'Hapsburgs,' nor the Jews, nor anyone. They're not even for sale."

He didn't follow.

She checked on the one other first-class passenger. He appeared to be sleeping. "Nobody's buying those houses," she said. "But there's plenty of cash changing hands, and the lion's share is going straight to your so-called Dekes."

She heard him mumbling about his Habitat for Humanity.

"Habitat for Humanity!" Her tone was cold. "Honey, it's a darn pyramid scheme. The Austrians at the top, the Poles at the bottom, your crooked friends scraping off the cream."

He wanted to say that they were not his friends, but this he could not easily do. What he felt was sheer indignation — these Americans! These Dekes! They had helped themselves to his rarest gift! They had used it like a garden tool. He eyed the Airfone, ready to call, but the sudden, icy recollection of his night with Beata forced him to reconsider.

◇ ◇ ◇

The sun was setting when they arrived home to Phoenix, the mountains black against the desert sky. A round of golf was out of the question, his heightened alertness notwithstanding, so he took a stroll in the dewy garden. On her way upstairs Marilyn had said that maybe the vacation had done him some good, thus putting the difficult subject to rest; though he had balked at the word "vacation," aware of its belittling connotations, now it was the thing that put his mind at ease. Maybe it was the succulent purple blossoms, maybe the clowny heads of hydrangea, but for some reason this fanciful word "vacation" saturated the colors of the past couple of days and arranged the contradictions into a delicate harmony. For a vacation, he decided, is not an escape, and no mere matter of ski slopes and beaches — it is your chance to risk that intensity of feeling, to plant your nose inside the flower and draw it in to your heart's content. James Danforth Quayle had taken a vacation, he had held his hand to the fiery light.

CHARLOTTE HOBSON

The Bottle: A Provincial Tale

At the edge of European Russia, in the steppe region that flows eastward, as featureless and uninterrupted as the sky, there is a medium-sized town called N. In the middle of N. there is a square, and in the middle of the square a statue. And although the statue's face is quite expressionless, we might be curious to follow its pointing finger across the square to the fifth-floor window of a large, nondescript building. Then again, you might not bother, for all you would see is an office on a typical Friday morning. A shabby desk, a few dirty glasses, a brimming ashtray, and an empty bottle of vodka. A high-pitched whine is coming from somewhere. It's not the central heating, as it's May, and it can't be the air conditioning, as that was never installed.

. . . Oy-oy-oy . . . my head, what a cracker of a headache! . . . I'm not well, I'm a fragile man. Wait, what the devil . . . No, Vova, keep calm. Let's think — I had a drink last night, that's clear. A couple. With Seryozha and Sasha, and . . . God! . . . I can't understand it. Am I hallucinating? Was that vodka poisoned? There's all this talk of impurities getting into the bottles. That crook of an inspector, I'll tie knots in his tonsils when I get hold of him . . .

Vladimir Ivanovich Vypivkin, Mayor of the town of N. and loyal servant of the former Soviet state, had good reason to be perplexed. His had always been a small, stout figure, short in the limbs, round and solid in the torso. But now . . . All he could feel, apart from his headache, was a smooth, glassy surface encasing him and a hollow sensation in his belly. Overnight, and against all precepts of logic, Mayor Vypivkin had turned into a vodka bottle — and an empty one at that. What an inconvenience to befall the mayor of a medium-sized town! And it was particularly upsetting just then, at the beginning of May, a few days before the privatization of the town's only profitable enterprise, the Kubanskaya Vodka Factory. Mayor Vypivkin had a reputation for driving a hard bargain, but, in such circumstances, even he might find his negotiating power diminished.

No, no, Vova, don't be a fool. It's just a hangover . . . I'd better lay off the booze for a while, though, this is too much. I'll just go back to sleep for a moment, and I'll be fine . . . Wait, here's someone coming in . . . Ah, it's my secretary. Good morning, Maria Ivanovna! I'm sorry to greet you like this. The thing is, we had a bit of a drink last night, so I'm not looking my best this morning . . . in fact, how do I look? You see, I had the most peculiar dream . . . Maria Ivanovna? She's not even listening. She doesn't have the intelligence to deal with a situation like this, that's the problem. Just a foolish woman. Maria Ivanovna, I order you! If you don't pay attention, I'll . . .

Maria Ivanovna flung open the windows of the Mayor's office, wedging them with a box file. "Foo, what a stink!" she muttered. "The drunken sot . . ." He'd said he was going on a business trip, but she knew he was lying in a hammock at his dacha right now, drinking beer and moaning about his hangover. She emptied the ashtray, swept the table free of crumbs and put the vodka bottle in her bag. It was worth four hundred rubles at the bottle bank. Not even money these days, of course, but her Nadya was saying she needed a new pair of shoes. Nadya was such a clever darling, thought

Maria Ivanovna. All that philosophy and such at University! That's a real Soviet education for you, the best in the world . . . I'll pop down and hand these bottles in straight away, as the Mayor isn't in. I did hear that Nadya's been spending time with his son, Kyril, at that kiosk of his. If he's anything like his father, I wouldn't trust him for a moment . . . Goodness, the heat today! It's not like May. And the sky as black as an Armenian's bottom, as my dear Slava used to say.

Maria Ivanovna joined the queue at the bottle bank, which curled out of the yard onto the street. "These reforms are turning us into a nation of beggars," she muttered to her neighbor.

Oh, so I'm a drunken sot, am I? Very nice! You didn't seem to mind when I fixed your nephew up with that job! Goodness, what a heap of bottles in this bag. Collecting bottles like a tramp, eh, Maria Ivanovna? Lord, what have I done to deserve this? Is it some kind of punishment, can I have offended someone in Moscow? I always helped people when I could, didn't I? If they brought me little presents out of gratitude, how could I refuse them? Oh, Maria Ivanovna! Masha! Don't leave me here! I order you . . . please . . .

◆ ◆ ◆

SUNDAY

Extract from the N. Gazette

The mysterious disappearance of our Mayor, Vladimir Ivanovich Vypivkin, is causing anxiety. Vladimir Ivanovich was last seen on Thursday evening by his colleagues, Deputy Mayor Sergei Vladimirovich Stopkin and Aleksandr Sergeevich Alkashov, director of the Kubanskaya Vodka Factory. They had met in the Mayor's office to discuss the privatization campaign, which is to be inaugurated at City Day next Saturday. Mr. Stopkin and Mr. Alkashov were transported to their homes by their drivers at around midnight, leaving Mr. Vypivkin with, as they called it, a little something to finish off. Oleg Vsegdapian, the Mayor's faithful driver for eleven years, reported that Mr. Vypivkin never emerged from his office; when pressed further by the police, however, he admitted he could vouch only for the earlier part of the evening. At around eleven, the hard-working Vsegdapian had been overcome by sleep.

Mr. Nazdorovsky, the Mayor's personal physician, suggested that the Mayor may have been taken ill by the extreme heat we have been experiencing lately. "There are cases when great heat, in combination with a certain exhaustion of the nerves, can cause a mild aberration. In this way, our Mayor may have suffered a temporary memory loss. We appeal for all citizens to come forward with any information they might have on the Mayor's whereabouts."

"The heat has been having a strange effect on all sorts of things," commented the Deputy Mayor, Sergei Vladimirovich Stopkin. "Just yesterday, a balcony fell clean off the wall on October Prospect, nearly crushing the Dean of the University's little dog. We are most anxious about our dear friend Vladimir Ivanovich."

In the Mayor's absence, Deputy Mayor Stopkin will fulfill Mr. Vypivkin's official duties.

◇ ◇ ◇

MONDAY

That feels better. They've put the label on crooked, but at least they've filled me up again. I suppose I'm at the factory, what old Stopkin calls "the stomach, heart and head of our city." Wouldn't you add the liver, Seryozha, my cucumber?! Heh heh. Hey, there is old Alkashov himself! Now, there's a piece of luck — surely he can help me! He's the Director, after all . . . It's to one's friends that one must turn in times of crisis, of course. I'm fortunate to have such friends, always have been — lots of them, and most of them in useful places. Hey, Aleksandr Sergeeich! Over here! There's something rather strange going on . . .

Director Alkashov mopped his forehead. It was cool in here, in the storerooms, but even at this time of evening the air outside was as wet and hot as a bath sponge. He hadn't really recovered yet from the night he'd spent with the Mayor and the Deputy Mayor. They could drink like boilermen, those two, great lard-pots that they were. He didn't have the constitution for it — the doctor had told him his liver was like a piece of lace, simply riddled with holes. He said he couldn't touch alcohol, or perhaps only a glass of beer here and there — now there was a joke! How is the Director of a vodka factory not to drink? Mrs. Alkashova nagged him, said she didn't want to be left on her own at the age of fifty-three, but Alkashov couldn't retire until this privatization matter was settled. And now the Mayor himself had vanished. It was a nasty business. Alkashov didn't trust Stopkin one inch . . .

Through the gloom of the warehouse, heavy, clipped footsteps were approaching. Stopkin appeared, throwing a fat-bellied shadow on the crates of bottles. "Ah, Sergei Vladimirovich! Thank you for coming to see me so promptly!" Alkashov called. "Not the most comfortable meeting place, but discretion . . ."

Stopkin smiled gravely. "Quite right, Aleksandr Sergeevich, quite right . . ."

"Terrible news, this, about our Mayor?"

Stopkin sighed. "Indeed. What a tragedy. He was a fine man. Fifteen years we worked together, and never a cross word between us."

Alkashov studied the other's melancholy expression. There seemed something utterly unconvincing about it. "Well, as his colleagues," he began, "I feel sure he would prefer that we did not allow the privatization campaign to stall on account of his absence. Don't you agree?"

"Indeed —"

"Well . . . in that case I suggest we alter the percentages to 50–50, don't you? Of course, when he returns, we can renegotiate with him . . ."

Stopkin's eyes sparkled for a moment. Then he recovered himself and reassumed his look of gloom. "That's a very practical suggestion, Aleksandr Sergeevich . . . I'm sure that Vladimir Ivanovich would do just the same himself. Can I leave the contracts to you? We'll meet on Saturday, as previously planned. We can sign the necessary papers after the unveiling of the Commemorative Object."

They shook hands, and soon Alkashov was again alone in the

warehouse. What a filthy old fox Stopkin was, he chuckled. To work with the mayor for fifteen years, and then toss him overboard just like that! Alkashov wasn't proud of his proposal, but at least he only drank with the man now and again. Well, perhaps he really would be able to retire at the end of this year, as Mrs. Alkashova wanted . . . Goodness, what was that rattling? He cocked his head and listened. There was something sinister about the warehouse at night, he didn't like it. Still, he'd better work on those contracts now, when no one was around. Sighing, he walked slowly back to his office on the first floor.

Now I understand who arranged this little caper! Those bastards Stopkin and Alkashov — they obviously poisoned me while we were drinking together, gave me some kind of drug . . . Stopkin has KGB contacts, I've always known it. And I thought they were my friends! The number of evenings Stopkin has taken advantage of my hospitality! God, I could strangle him. If I had any arms . . . Oh, this is ridiculous. I'll get even with him, the toad . . .

◇ ◇ ◇

TUESDAY

. . . Whoa! When was the last time this guy washed his clothes? Ow, easy with all the bottles in here! So this is the gap between production and distribution! Well, who doesn't like a nip of vodka? It's good for you, clears the chest. Wait, I recognize his voice — it's Sasha Stakanov, one of the foremen . . . Into his Zhiguli now, my God do they rattle. One forgets how lucky one is with the official cars . . .

"These bloody cars," fumed Sasha. It must be the electrics, they'd always been unreliable . . . He pushed one end of his tattered moustache into his mouth and began to chew. He'd planned to get home in good time today. Yesterday, he'd gotten home after midnight. He'd driven out of town to visit a collective farm manager he knew, had swapped several bottles of Kubanskaya for a couple of kilos of beef. It was the only currency available these days, it seemed; half the city received their wages in alcohol and bartered it with the other half, and not a single soul was sober . . . Tonight, he hoped for a little dinner with his wife, a couple of drinks, perhaps they'd go to bed early. Now she'd be irritated with him again for being late, and the bloody mother-in-law would be there too, nodding knowingly and saying, "I *told* you at the time not to jump the queue for cars. Oh, in my day your sort would be cooling your heels in Siberia, and quite right too — there's some people that have been waiting for a Zhiguli for ten years! Yes, it's behavior like yours that's got this country into such a mess. They're just selling the whole lot off, parceling up our homeland and selling it off to the first comer!"

He could hardly say that without this car they'd be starving, that it was only the taxiing and bartering things here and there that fed them, because then the old witch would start saying that *she* knew when she wasn't wanted, and then the wife would cry and make him sleep on the divan . . .

"Christ," Sasha swore. "That's all I need." In the distance, a police car was approaching, following an erratic path between the potholes.

Sasha switched off his lights and waited.

"Problems with your lights, then? Problems with your engine?" said a lean and mournful lieutenant of the traffic police when he pressed his face to the window. "It's illegal to park in Lenin Square, you know."

"Just a little overheated, sergeant," Sasha assured him. 'It's this hellish heat we've had all day."

The lieutenant sighed. "Have to charge you, unless . . ."

"Oh, surely not, lieutenant! It's the end of a long day, you won't want to hang around for a trifle like this! In a few minutes I'll be gone . . ." Sasha said soothingly. "Won't you accept a little token . . ." He took the bottle of vodka from under his seat and pressed it into the policeman's hands. "Kubanskaya, our very own product!"

The lieutenant looked at the bottle. "Well . . . Don't stand here long, then . . ." he said uncertainly, and disappeared into the darkness.

For several minutes, Sasha sat very still. Then he sighed, stepped out of the car and locked it. He'd have to move before tomorrow somehow — he'd broken down right in front of this idiotic statue they were putting up to the vodka factory. Sasha gazed at the vast lumpy block shrouded in tarpaulin, then sighed and turned towards home. Another night on the divan.

All right, this is Lenin Square, and there's Kyril's kiosk just opposite. Thank God. Kyril will rescue me, his old dad. You can only trust your own when things get unpleasant. In any case, us older folk don't understand anything about the world nowadays. I've always said the future of Russia lies with the young. Kyril will make sense of this craziness, I'm sure of it . . .

Kyril leaned back in his chair and flexed his biceps. His mustached, gleaming face was lit from beneath by a line of orange bulbs along the counter and surrounded by his massed, sparkling wares. He looked irritable, Lieutenant Zakuskin thought as he picked his way across the tramlines in the dark. Zakuskin regularly passed on to Kyril the little gifts he amassed during the day. Just as he was about to emerge from the shadows, Deputy Mayor Stopkin's BMW pulled up in front of the kiosk. Zakuskin paused under a poplar tree.

"Ah," Stopkin said solemnly. "Kyril. I just stopped to offer my condolences. Very sad news about your father, you know. Very, *very* sad. We have our best men working on the case . . ."

"Good evening, Sergei Vladimirovich!" Kyril was a broad man, and his padded leather jacket made him seem even broader. He was full of *bonhomie*. "I appreciate your concern. It is a terrible business, but I should tell you that my father would be relieved to know that you, of all people, are standing in for him. He had the greatest admiration for your abilities."

"Oh, you're too kind . . . I shall do my best, naturally.

". . . For your administrative abilities, as I say, and your dedication to local government. As a man of business, however, I know that he desired, quite naturally, that his family should receive their rightful inheritance." Kyril was smiling.

"But of course . . . the council has already discussed a generous pension for your mother."

"How admirable. But I'm not talking about pensions. I'm talking about the privatization of the Kubanskaya factory, which I believe you were discussing with my father on the night he disappeared."

"Oh . . . indeed. But you are mistaken, Kyril. That's not private business, it's undertaken according to Presidential decree."

"That, Sergei Vladimirovich, is something we disagree on." Kyril's smile was, if anything, wider than ever.

"However, I share my father's high opinion of you. I'm quite sure that on further consideration, the correctness — in the tragic circumstances — of my position on this matter will become apparent to you."

Stopkin's face was slowly turning red, from the chin upwards, like a sunset. "With all respect, Kyril, I see no reason . . ."

"I quite agree, there's no reason for us to fall out. I'm just suggesting you think about it as a friend, as someone who wouldn't like to come to any harm."

"Harm?"

"Nothing to worry about, so long as you are sensible. Well, good night, Sergei Vladimirovich. Thank you for dropping by." Kyril held open the car door for him. "Do keep in touch."

In the shadow behind them, Lieutenant Zakuskin almost dropped the bottle of Kubanskaya. His only wish was to vanish, and erase all memory of the conversation he had just heard. Instead, to his horror, he watched as Kyril tapped a cigarette from his packet of Camels, swiveled in his direction, and saw him.

"Ah, Lieutenant Zakuskin, brother!" he exclaimed.

"Come in and have a hundred grams with me, to cool the blood! This heat is inhuman!"

In the kiosk, Kyril poured out shots of vodka. He tossed his back and followed it with a long exhalation. Then he turned back to Zakuskin with a smile. "So you were listening to my little chat with Stopkin, eh?"

"No, no, I was just passing . . . I mean . . ."

"Shut up," said Kyril conversationally. "That Stopkin is quite a bastard, wouldn't you agree? I mean, I know my dad was a scoundrel, and stupid on occasion, but he knew when he had a good thing . . . I swear, Zakuskin, I'm not going to let Stopkin get away with Papa's share. I'll have to give him a scare. And you can help me . . ."

Zakuskin swallowed. "What can I do? A traffic policeman . . ."

"Don't whine, you fool!" hissed Kyril. "You'll do what I tell you, a family man like you. Anyway," his tone changed, "it's nothing. Won't you be in charge of the stage area for the City Day ceremony on Saturday? All I need is for you to let through a friend of mine just before Stopkin makes his speech, ok? He'll make himself known to you. You just make sure he gets what he wants, and everything will be fine. Understood?"

"U-understood."

Kyril watched him for a second, then began to laugh. He was so close that Zakuskin could see the glistening pores on his nostrils, the fleck of spittle at the corner of his mouth. With an effort, Zakuskin stopped himself from flinching and forced a laugh. "Well, I must be getting on . . . here's today's goods." He placed a bag on the counter containing two cartons of cigarettes, a gift from an old BMW with no brake lights earlier in the day, and next to it the faintly perspiring bottle of Kubanskaya.

"Oh, yes," Kyril reached into his inner pocket. "And here's something for your family." Still chuckling, he brought out two fifty-dollar bills. "Just be hospitable to my friend, eh?"

Kyril, my boy! Can it be? I can hardly think, my head is whirling. My little boy, talking about my affairs with some miserable traffic cop! I thought you'd be the one to save me from this mess, and instead you're planning something criminal. Not that I care if Stopkin gets a scare, it's just what he deserves, but . . . God, it's so humiliating! My own son, going on about me with such contempt . . . I suppose the whole town talks about me this way — all those people who were so oily to my face, and now not a single soul cares where I've disappeared to — they'd rather have a bottle of vodka, no doubt — while I . . . I'm so miserable . . .

◇ ◇ ◇

THURSDAY

Leader article in the N. Evening Chronicle
A Mystery on Lenin Square

The citizens of N. have been taking advantage of the balmy evenings to stroll along the pleasant avenues of our town, quench their thirst in one of our summer cafes, and, above all, to come and marvel at the mysterious construction being erected in our main square. It is, of course, the Commemorative Object in honor of the town's main industry, the Kubanskaya Vodka Factory. The first piece of municipal art to be commissioned for some years now, it is surely an object that will inspire many memories in all our hearts, both of hard work and leisure. But what form exactly will it take? Every passer-by has a theory. Some insist they can make out the shape of a gigantic still, made of stained glass and concrete. Others say it's an abstract representation of thirst, or a three-meter portrait of our Mayor — tragically missing — or a tumbler topped by a plate of sausage sandwiches, or a camel, hinting, perhaps, that the Vodka Factory is like the camel's hump for our town, a sole and welcome source of refreshment in the desert. All will be revealed on Saturday at three o'clock by Deputy Mayor Stopkin. Cut-rate vodka will be available.

◇ ◇ ◇

FRIDAY

Kyril's henchman Ptitsa had propped a little shaving mirror against the vodka bottle at the front of the kiosk and was looking into it menacingly. Kyril had told him that if he didn't start acting more like a hawk and less like a bloody sparrow, he didn't think their business arrangement had a future. If Ptitsa couldn't stop mooning around like the village idiot, Kyril promised he would take pleasure in beating the other half of his wits out of him. Then he and his other goon, Anatol, had gone off to see a friend, leaving Ptitsa in charge of the kiosk.

"As if I didn't know what they're doing," Ptitsa thought, snarling at the mirror. "Getting a gun for tomorrow, that's all. It's no big deal. I've used a gun before — Uncle Dima said I was a serious shot, he said. Rabbits beware, *he* said. He didn't say things like that lightly, my Uncle Dima, either . . . Oh!"

A long red fingernail flicked the mirror onto the counter, cracking it in two.

"Hi, Ptitsa," said a breathy, amused voice. "Why're you looking so angry, baby?"

"Oh, hello, Nadya," Ptitsa stammered. Nadya always made him nervous. The truth was that Kyril was fooling around with both Nadya and Albina, and Ptitsa could never quite remember what he was meant to tell each of them. And she was so . . . well, kind of *pressing*; Ptitsa found it hard to make sense in her presence. "You — you broke the mirror! It's bad luck."

"Well, I'm a bad girl, aren't I, my little dove?" Nadya, who was wearing a tight red top, leaned against the counter and Ptitsa watched, fascinated, as her milky breasts rose and rose — and stopped just short of boiling over. "So where's my bad boy?"

"He's . . . um . . . he'll be back soon, he's gone to see a friend."

"Oh? What friend is this?"

"Oh, this one's a man, a business acq —"

"*This* one? And what about the other?"

"No, she's — I mean they're — I mean, what other?"

"So there is another *she,* is there? I knew he'd been playing around, the scum. Who is she?"

"I — I don't know what you're talking about."

"Yes you do, darling. And you're going to tell me, or I just might have to complain to Kyril about the way you received me today. Everyone's seen the way you look at me, but this time, you've taken your insolence too far. I had to push you away, look, the mirror even got broken. Didn't it?"

Ptitsa fell silent. Finally he said, "Promise you won't tell him I told you?"

"You're safe with me, baby, you know that."

"Albina."

"The *bitch.*" Nadya turned her back on Ptitsa, and lit a cigarette. For a minute she surveyed the square, the drifts of litter, stray dogs. Then she turned back, blowing smoke into the kiosk. "Right, you little half-wit, give me a bottle of champagne — no, make it two. That kiwi fruit liqueur as well. The French chocolates, a carton of Marlboros, a packet of condoms. Oh, and I'll take that bottle of Kubanskaya as well. Yes, this one right here. Get a move on it."

So he's been cheating on his women as well. Not that I blame him, a tasty piece like this one. In my youth, I was the same way . . . Oh, it's no good remembering. Look at me now. What a fate! I'm helpless, dumb, just passed from hand to hand like . . . well, like a bottle of vodka. And all around there's nothing but filth and corruption, people living like pigs, cheating their friends . . . I'm the only one to see it all clearly, and yet I can't tell a soul! . . . Why? Oh Lord, why me? I'm starting to think . . . Yes, that must be it! . . . I have been chosen! I knew there had to be some kind of reason . . . They want me to speak out — tell the world that all this talk of democracy is a con. They wouldn't choose just anybody . . . And you know what — I'll do it! I'm a patriot, I'll sacrifice myself for my country! Because it will be a sacrifice, I'll lose everything, but I'm prepared for my destiny . . . Give me a chance and I'll prove it!

◇ ◇ ◇

SATURDAY (CITY DAY)

Sasha was driving nowhere in particular. The night before, he had lost his temper with his wife. "You send me to sleep on the stinking divan like a dog!" he'd yelled, storming out of the apartment. "I won't put up with it . . ." Early that morning, he'd woken in his car with a vague sense of despair that announced itself as a volcanic rumble in his belly. There'd been only one thing for it — head straight for the nearest *gastronom* and swallow one hundred and fifty grams of Stolichnaya. Since then he had circled the town, bumping to a stop outside every booze shop he found. He drove more and more carefully, creeping along the curb, and thought about what to do next. Clearly, he should have another drink, but he'd run out of money. He searched first his trouser pockets, then his jacket, then his trousers again for a few stray rubles. Suddenly a young woman with very red lips loomed up through the window.

"Are you going toward Lenin Square?" she asked.

Sasha noticed that the car did not seem to be moving. "No," he said reasonably. "I've stopped."

"Fu!" Nadya turned away from his breath. "You're drunk. Oh well, we're in a hurry. Will you take us to the City Day celebrations? We can give you a bottle as payment —"

"All right, then," said Sasha, taking the bottle of Kubanskaya. "I'm on my own now, I can do as I please . . ."

Nadya and her mother, Maria Ivanovna, slid into the back seat with a look of disgust.

"I'm on my own," Sasha repeated. "My wife's convinced I'm having an affair. 'Sasha,' she says, 'You're back late night after night, I know you're with another woman. Well, I'm sick of it. You can just stay with her for good . . .' What does she know? The only other woman I've got is this stinking Zhiguli, and she lets me down most days too. When I'm not fixing it, I'm carting people around to earn money for spare parts. I'm going out of my mind . . ."

"I'm sure your wife can understand that," said Maria Ivanovna, leaning forward. "Everyone knows these Zhigulis are unreliable."

Nadya lit a cigarette and gazed out the window. She was looking forward to seeing Kyril. There were women who didn't enjoy making a scene, but Nadya was not one of them.

"The fact is, she's too busy looking after her mother," said Sasha.

"It's always 'Mother, Mother!' The old hag's all right, but I love my wife and I want her to myself on occasion!"

"That's quite within your rights as a husband," approved Maria Ivanovna. "Why not invite your wife to a restaurant for a romantic dinner and tell her just that?" They had arrived at the edge of the main square, where the stage had been set up around the Commemorative Object. Sasha stopped the car and gesticulated with the bottle of Kubanskaya. "I'm gonna tell her . . ." His words ran together. "I'm gonna let 'em know what I think . . ."

"There's a policeman," interrupted Nadya. "Oh look, it's Lieutenant Zakuskin. Goodbye, Mama. I'll see you later." She pressed her glossy, scarlet lips together with a tiny smacking sound and slid out of the car.

◇ ◇ ◇

Ptitsa thrust his shoulders back in the car seat and tried to look happy. He was lucky, he was. Kyril had said so. If he proved himself now, he'd be promoted instantly and Kyril would give him a bonus in hard currency. Ptitsa had confessed to Kyril about Nadya right away; it was no good trying to keep secrets from him. For a second it had looked like Kyril was going to hit him, but he laughed instead and reached for the brandy.

"Women, who needs 'em?" he said, raising his glass, and Ptitsa laughed too, with relief. "There's been a mix-up with this job for tomorrow, Ptitsa," Kyril went on. "I think you're going to have to do it for me." He took a Makarov pistol out of his pocket and laid it on the table. "Stopkin, the Deputy Mayor. He'll be on stage tomorrow at three o'clock, something to do with this City Day nonsense. Go to the barriers by the platform and Lieutenant Zakuskin will let you through . . . It's your lucky break."

They drank together, although Ptitsa could barely swallow, he was feeling so strange. "D . . . dead?" he croaked at last.

"Either Stopkin, or you," Kyril confirmed. "You're a great chap, Ptitsa . . . I thought I might feel sorry for you, but what with this Nadya fiasco, there's no fear of that."

There was Lieutenant Zakuskin in the road ahead of him now, twirling his baton. Ptitsa stopped the car. Sweat was trickling behind the Makarov in its holster under his arm. Would it work if it got wet? Ptitsa didn't know.

◊ ◊ ◊

"So, Lieutenant Zakuskin," said Nadya, "you're the boss today, I see."

Zakuskin narrowed his eyes. "I'm in charge of the stage area, yes."

"I think Kyril would like it if I were there for him, don't you, Lieutenant Zakuskin?"

Zakuskin hesitated. "I was expecting a man . . ." The speeches were due to start in a few minutes; almost all the seats on the platform were already filled.

"Oh, really?" Nadya smiled at him, sidling past.

"Well, aren't you glad you've got me instead?"

Zakuskin gazed out at the crowd. "Go on then, quickly," he said. He watched her head for the stage, and a flush of nervous sweat prickled under his arms.

"Excuse me," said a boy's voice. "Lieutenant Zakuskin?"

Zakuskin turned. A scrawny runt was staring up at him expectantly. "Don't you recognize me?" the kid said after a moment.

"No . . ." The boy did seem faintly familiar; Zakuskin thought he might have stopped him a couple of times on traffic violations. Behind him the band had fallen silent and Alkashov, Director of the Kubanskaya Factory, was clearing his throat in front of the microphone. "Please welcome the Deputy Mayor, Sergei Vladimirovich Stopkin . . ."

"Oh . . . I'm Ptitsa, I work for Kyril? You're meant to let me through?"

"Lord!" hissed Zakuskin. "How many people does Kyril want back there! Is he planning a party?"

"Just . . . just me."

Zakuskin saw Stopkin stepping up to the microphone and clearing his throat. The people who were milling about in front of the stage gazed at him without much interest. "Dear citizens!" he began. "Dear comrades! . . ."

Sasha was pushing his way through the crowd, clutching the bottle of vodka.

". . . from the earliest days of the Russian state . . . the fiery health-giving spirit, the heaven-sent refreshment . . ." Stopkin expounded, puffing out his chest and opening his arms like an opera singer.

Kyril, sitting at the back of the stage, looked around. There was Nadya, what was she doing here? And where was Ptitsa? He didn't really expect him to succeed; the idea was really only to give old Stopkin a scare. But that idiot Ptitsa could at least show up.

Ptitsa was still at the barrier, speechless, his face flushed with adrenaline.

"It's not possible . . . I've already let one person through," hissed Zakuskin.

Suddenly there was a voice from the wings. "Kyril Vypivkin . . ."

Stopkin faltered. "This fine Commemorative Object . . ."

"Kyril," Nadya went on, walking calmly into the middle of the stage, "you are a cheat and a louse."

The crowd, which had been grumbling with boredom, cheered up and began to laugh.

"Now, now," Stopkin interjected, "Can't you see I'm in the middle of . . ."

"Are you passing me the microphone? How kind. I think the whole town should know: your widdler, Kyril, smells of month-old cottage cheese."

The crowd shouted with delight. Kyril let out a roar and tripped over the legs of the superintendent of police as he tried to get at Nadya. Ptitsa, seeing his chance, pushed past Zakuskin and ran towards the stage, fumbling for his gun.

"And it's a soft as cottage cheese, too!"

Kyril lunged at her.

"Now," quavered Stopkin, "let's all keep calm . . ."

Sasha, who had been trying drunkenly to climb onto the stage, finally succeeded. He lurched towards the microphone and began to shout: "Calm! What filth the lot of you are! Agree with me, good people, they're all crooks! Democrats or Communists, they suck our blood just the same!"

"He's right!" shouted a voice from the crowd.

"I'll tell you what democracy means in this shitty country . . ." Sasha yelled. "It means you can't even sleep with your wife without bribing a policeman! You can't have a piss without these bastards demanding a fee! Freedom . . . what does freedom mean to us? There's only two ways to be free: to be rich, or to be drunk . . ."

The crowd was laughing and clapping. "*Molodets*! Good bloke!"

"Let's drink to that . . ." Sasha raised his bottle of vodka to his lips.

A shot rang out. Something burst, a glittering explosion. Shards of glass sparkled in the air. In the wings, Ptitsa was clutching the Makarov, his eyes squeezed shut. Sasha, mouth gaping, stared at the broken bottle neck in his hand. There was shouting, jostling, panic among the spectators, and then, inexplicably, everything fell silent.

In the middle of the stage, in a puddle of vodka, lay the Mayor of N., as pink and naked as a piglet.

"My dear friends," he began to gibber, "how I've suffered, if only I could tell you . . ." He scrambled to his feet, panting and slipping about in the puddle. The crowd contemplated his quivering bum. "They are all crooks, yes, this man is telling the truth . . . evil forces are at work in our city . . . and my own son is the worst of them —" He burst into loud, ragged sobs, his arms hanging by his sides.

"Papa?" stammered Kyril.

"I heard your criminal plans, Kyril!" he blurted. "You should be in prison, I tell you, even if you think I'm an old fool!"

Stopkin suddenly found his voice. "Now, calm down, Vladimir Ivanovich," he began. "You are overwrought . . ."

"You traitor," spat the Mayor. "I know about you and Alkashov . . . After all the deals we've done together!"

The spectators were finding their voices. "He's a madman," said some. "No, no, it's a stage trick they're playing on us," others interrupted. "An entertainment!" But a clear voice from the back shouted out, "Tell us, Vladimir Ivanovich! Tell us what all these crooks are up to!"

"I will tell you, I will . . . I'll sacrifice myself," the Mayor proclaimed. "There'll be an investigation . . ."

At that moment Maria Ivanovna, the Mayor's secretary, hurried on from the wings.

"Lord have mercy," she said, exasperated. "You are all as bad as each other! Come on, Vladimir Ivanovich, come with me. We'll get you dressed . . . and home, in bed . . . You're drunk, that's all, just drunk again . . ."

She wrapped her coat around the weeping man and led him off the stage.

◇ ◇ ◇

Extracts from the N. Gazette
Events of the Day

Today we were delighted to find our Mayor, Vladimir Ivanovich Vypivkin, restored to his usual robust health. At a meeting called to announce the first stage of privatization of the Kubanskaya Vodka Factory, the Mayor joked merrily about his indisposition at the City Day celebrations with his new Deputy Mayor and the temporary Director of the Factory, appointed after Mr. Alkashov's early retirement. His illness had, he claimed, given him a new perspective on many things and he now felt ready to tackle the municipal agenda with renewed gusto. Once the privatization campaign is successfully completed, he plans to further the business interests of our city on a two-month tour of the Caribbean, where the Mayor says he has identified a number of possible investors. The Mayor explained that this unique opportunity means he'll have to postpone his much-anticipated investigation into misdoings associated with the privatization campaign, but he has assured the *Gazette* it will be the first order of business upon his return.

Sights of Our City

There is no doubt that N. has gained a most unique and technically innovative monument in the newly inaugurated Commemorative Object for the Kubanskaya Vodka Factory, which will raise the profile of our city and probably draw not a few visitors, to the benefit of the whole municipality. There has already been some interest in the national press, and the Object was featured on a well-known current affairs program on Channel 1. The choice of a human liver, sculpted in bronze, was visionary, and its internal light, which adds a reddish-brown, gently pulsating glow, was an inspired finishing touch. A piece of true Art, says *Sights of Our City!* It truly is a progressive region we live in.

THOMAS DE WAAL

The English House: A Story of Chechnya

I visited Grozny, the Chechen capital, for the first time in January 1994, eleven months before the Russian Army invaded to suppress the Chechen bid for independence. I was a young reporter for *The Moscow Times*. Like many Westerners venturing to post-Soviet Russia, I was drawn by my love of Russian literature and by curiosity about the country's exhilarating transformation and its attempts to come to terms with the legacy of Stalin. To be in Russia, it seemed, was to be in a place where, unlike the settled societies of the West, the ink on the pages of modern history was still wet, where big, Shakespearean truths about human nature were the stuff of each morning's newspapers: What motivates such evil? Why didn't its victims resist? What would I have done in the places of both? Chechnya, in particular, seemed to be fertile ground for some of these inquiries. Besides, two months of a drab, slush-soaked Moscow winter had left me stirring for the south. So I lobbied my editor to send me to write about the fiftieth anniversary of Stalin's mass deportation of the Chechens to the steppes of Central Asia thousands of miles away.

I went to Chechnya to learn about what had happened in 1944, and understood that little had improved in fifty years. I became attached to the place and its people just as the region was about to slide into chaos, in particular to one family whose patriarch became my link to the Chechen deportation. They remain one of the several threads that bind me to Chechnya ten years on, and it is their story that I want to tell here.

These days, for most people, the word "Chechnya" conjures only war, indiscriminate destruction, savage primitivism. Grozny — named with Ivan the Terrible (Ivan Grozny in Russian) in mind by Russian generals in the 19th century to cow the natives — summons images of a ravaged wasteland where the piles of rubble rise higher than the buildings that remain. But I got to see it as it was before all this. My hotel, nicknamed the French House for its Gallic-style apartment-like rooms, stood just off Victory Prospect, the main thoroughfare. From there, I ventured into a city of broad boulevards and squares that was still heir to a handsome nineteenth-century garrison town. I visited the university, where a brilliant young professor quizzed me about English verbs and Nietzsche. I wandered down Victory Prospect, sharing the pavement with elegant Chechen women, their lips scarlet and their eyes black as ink, strolling arm in arm. At the end of the street stood Freedom Square, where Jokhar Dudayev, the leader of the Chechen rebels, held court in an ugly nine-story rectangle of concrete that was optimistically known as the "Presidential Palace."

Dudayev wished to wrest Chechnya from Russian control, but his vision of an independent state didn't seem to differ much from the conspicuous corruption I'd left behind in Moscow. Dozens of glossy Mercedes sedans overran sputtering Ladas and Moskviches in Grozny as well, but they seemed to me far more incongruous in its shabby districts than amid the opulence of central Moscow. Sometimes, they sported Hungarian or Lithuanian license plates, sometimes none at all — evidence of theft. Sometimes, a Lincoln Continental would make its way pompously among them, baronial and languid, floating past disapproving matrons and unimpressed teenagers, quickly accustomed to post-Soviet excess.

◇ ◇ ◇

Jokhar Dudayev's putative presidency was like this: a triumph of style over content. Dudayev appeared on television and in town squares in handsome three-piece suits, a 1920s-style fedora perched above his dense black eyebrows and immaculately trimmed mustache. He looked like a Chicago gangster. Every night, in a lilting voice tremulous with emotion, Dudayev harangued Chechens with monologues about Russian imperialism and genocide. "We have been at war for two hundred years!" he said again and again. All that time, the Chechens had endured privation and insult. No more; the time had come to revolt. For those who were reluctant, he invoked an implacable verdict: "A slave who has reconciled himself to his slavery deserves to be a slave twice over." All this he delivered in accented but eloquent Russian, to make sure Moscow knew what was coming.

It was only two years before, in the autumn of 1991, as the Soviet Union was falling apart, that militant Chechens led by Dudayev, the USSR's first Chechen general, had, quite literally, thrown Communist Party officials out of their offices onto the street, taken down the red flags, and declared Chechnya an independent state. Now, many of the same fighters patrolled the echoing halls of the Presidential Palace, unshaven and eternally displeased, Kalashnikovs peering out from under their jackets like new limbs. They were also practically the only people who received a salary in the new Chechnya. Ordinary Chechens scraped by, traveling to places like China and Dubai to buy televisions and clothes on the cheap, which they would resell on the flourishing black market at home. In retaliation for the de facto coup, Moscow had gradually cut off the gas supply, and the approaching winter infiltrated homes, cooling ardor for Dudayev's revolution.

A novelist in his forties named Said-Khamzat Nunuyev explained to me that the Dudayev regime had squandered the support of the educated classes and most urban dwellers. It existed thanks only to the threat of Russian attack. We spoke in his unheated office at the Chechen Writers' Union, sipping hot black tea to keep warm. Nunuyev could afford to be candid with me, as, like most well-to-do Chechens in "independent" Chechnya, he spent most of his time in Moscow. Chechens were stranded between two equally unattractive options, he said: an authoritarian state bearing down from the north and a bandit tyranny stealing everything in sight at home. Why was Dudayev's regime holding up, I asked. Nunuyev said that in the villages there was a whole generation of older people who had known nothing but poverty and harassment their entire lives. Dudayev's talk exalted their suffering, allowed them to stand tall for a change. And the gas shortages didn't bother them; gas stoves had never appeared in their corner of the world, and they burned wood as they had for centuries.

As in any other Soviet city, Grozny's streets carried the names of Communist icons, and two near the French Hotel were named, bizarrely, after the German Communists Rosa Luxemburg and Karl Liebknecht. But the uneasy atmosphere in Grozny actually reminded me of another German Communist, Bertolt Brecht, that great connoisseur of failed revolutions, who had said, "Food comes first, then morals." And wasn't it he who had cynically advised a disappointed government "to dissolve the people and elect another one"? After a century of betrayals, it seemed the people of Grozny were about to endure yet another.

The twentieth century was unkind to the Chechens, but none of its trials compared to the tragedy that befell them in 1944, when they were forcibly deported en masse from their ancestral lands in Chechnya. Many died along the way, others in the inhospitable terrain of the Kazakh desert, where they lived in makeshift dugouts and labored on local collective farms. Food was scarce, and people often ate grass, until their bodies swelled beyond repair. The survivors did not return to Chechnya for thirteen years, until Nikita Khrushchev, emboldened by his denunciation of Stalin's cult of personality at the XX Party Congress in 1956, reversed Stalin's mandate. In time, I would learn that this wasn't the only factor in his decision.

◇ ◇ ◇

I wondered if any records of the deportation existed at the historical archive on Freedom Square. I found Chechnya's chief archivist, Magomed Muzayev, shivering in an overcoat next to a tiny electric heater in a spare room with a cheap plywood table in the corner. Jokhar Dudayev looked down from a photo on the wall, next to a drawing of a wolf baying at the moon — a depiction of the Chechens' foundation myth — and a frame containing Dudayev's words about reconciled slaves being slaves twice over. Several assistants sat nearby. No one seemed to be doing any work. Certainly no one wished to discuss politics. Stalin's crimes were another matter altogether. One of the archivists mentioned a man named Dziyaudin Malsagov. Malsagov had witnessed the most harrowing atrocity of the 1944 deportation in a mountain village called Khaibakh, and had then spent the remainder of his life making sure the event was never forgotten. Malsagov was very old, but still alive, and I asked Muzayev if he could arrange a meeting.

The next afternoon, the archivist walked me down Victory Prospect to a red-brick apartment building I had already admired on my way from my hotel. It was called the "English House," as it had been built for British workers who lived in Grozny in the 1920s while working on the surrounding oil fields. It was an oriental confection created for the pleasure of visitors from abroad: a kind of toy desert fortress of plum-red brick built around a courtyard and adorned with turrets and pinnacles.

"It's your house!" Muzayev joked. "You're from London, aren't you?"

Valentina Malsagova, Dziyaudin's wife, answered the door and welcomed us into a bustling apartment, filled with what seemed like a dozen people, the Malsagovs' large extended family. She was broad and motherly, and immediately ushered us into the kitchen, chasing the cold away with cups of steaming tea. Twice she pried the unfinished cup from my hands, emptied it into the sink, and poured me another. Eventually, it was explained that the fanatically hospitable Chechens think it discourteous for their guests to drink tea that isn't piping hot.

Valentina agreed to introduce me to Dziyaudin, but warned that he was eighty and had just suffered a stroke. He was sunk in a narrow bed, wearing pajamas. There was a shock of white hair, vacant, staring eyes, and a barely audible rasp. He tried to sit up and speak, but the words came out haltingly, or none at all. But he reached for my hand, and shook it firmly. His hands were warm. Dziyaudin was too frail that day to tell me in detail what he had seen, but that strong, bony handshake passed it on by other means, made this foreigner one of the heirs to his remembrance. Go on, it seemed to bid me.

I left the Malsagovs' with a bundle of papers and a hardcover book about what had happened in Khaibakh. The French Hotel wasn't far away, but Muzayev, the archivist, insisted on escorting me through the unsafe streets. When I got home, the women on duty began to remonstrate that I had been out past dark. I had dinner with the hotel's only other guest and the city's only other Westerner, an old Etonian who split his time between Greece and South Africa and intended to install a new telecommunications system in Grozny.

That night, the temperature in my bedroom sank, and I lit all the gas rings on the kitchen stove, sat on a stool, and, keeping warm by the blue flame, laid out two books on the kitchen table — the account of the Khaibakh massacre and Gabriel Garciá Márquez's *One Hundred Years of Solitude,* which I had brought from home. The latter book summed up how I felt. Not a single car passed; the streets were deserted. Once or twice, there was the crackle of gunshots (a wedding, I hoped, or a robbery?) — tarrarat-tarrarat — in the darkness. A dog started baying, and then another yowled, as if in competition, or, perhaps, sympathy, and then a third, further away. The foreboding in the air was almost palpable.

◇ ◇ ◇

What I read in the Malsagovs' book about the events in Khaibakh appalled me. In 1944, Stalin decided to abolish Chechnya — destroy its books and graveyards, excise it from Soviet encyclopedias, parcel its territory among neighboring regions, and deport its entire population to the faceless plains of Kazakhstan.

◇ ◇ ◇

Stalin wanted to break the will of the most rebellious people of the North Caucasus, a distinction the Chechens worked hard to maintain for nearly two hundred years. Imperial Russian officers who survived skirmishes with Chechen tribesmen in the nineteenth century reported on them with a mixture of dread and admiration, and earned the eternal envy of their comrades. Mikhail Lermontov had written ballads about the "wicked Chechen" crawling with his dagger toward Russian encampments, and in the 1840s, while serving on the front-lines of a campaign against Imam Shamil, the most famous Caucasian rebel of the time, Leo Tolstoy had felt a grudging respect for Chechen resistance to imperial expansion, which he chronicled in *The Cossacks* and *Hadji Murad*.

The area was slow to modernize in the twentieth century. The Chechens of the plains and the residents of Grozny had accepted Russian rule and the benefits of colonialism, but highland Chechens continued to rebel, resisting the Whites and the Cossacks in the Civil War, the Bolsheviks in the twenties, and collectivization soon after.

Stalin struck in February 1944, at the height of the war with Hitler. As the Red Army pushed the Germans back in Ukraine, about 100,000 soldiers and 12,000 train carriages were diverted from the front to Chechnya and Ingushetia, a neighboring region populated by the Ingush, ethnic cousins to the Chechens. Studebaker trucks, lend-leased to the Soviet Union by the United States, were sent into the mountains. Over the course of a week, the army and the NKVD, the secret police, packed the entire population of Checheno-Ingushetia — 480,000 people — into cattle trucks and shipped them off to Central Asia. No one — infants, pensioners, Communist Party members, soldiers on rest from frontline duty — was exempt. Several hundred resisters fled into the mountains, but were hunted down by soldiers.

Tens of thousands died in the typhoid-ridden railway carriages en route to Central Asia and tens of thousands more from the glacial winters in Kazakhstan. A special 1949 report on the deportees declared that of the 608,749 Chechens, Ingush, and other regional ethnicities who were deported, only 450,034 had been counted by a recent survey. 144,704 had perished by July 1, 1948, the report noted dryly in a right-hand column titled "Notes."

A year after the end of the Second World War, Stalin finally offered an official explanation for the deportation. He said the Chechens and their neighbors planned to collaborate with the German Army, and were exiled as saboteurs. This was a fabrication. The Germans were nowhere near Checheno-Ingushetia when the deportation took place, and were actually beginning to retreat.

Dziyaudin Malsagov was a believer. He was one of the first Chechens to study to become a lawyer in the 1930s, and he joined the Communist Party, believing it would pull Chechnya out of backwardness and poverty. In the British Raj, he would have been an Anglo-Indian, allowed, thanks to his talent and keenness, to serve the colonial power and reap all the privileges that entailed, but also isolated from fellow natives, and constantly insecure about where his loyalties lay.

The Communists certainly believed in Dziyaudin Malsagov. At twenty-eight, he was made a "people's commissar" in the local department of justice and was attached to a special unit that combed the mountains for Chechen rebels holding out against Soviet rule.

In February 1944, Malsagov was invited to a meeting in Grozny and told in confidence about the NKVD's plans for deportation. Three senior NKVD men would direct the operation: Lavrenty Beria, Sergei Kruglov, and Ivan Serov. Malsagov asked why the entire population was being deported without exception. He had five brothers fighting at the front, he said, another who had just returned with a serious concussion. Why couldn't they continue serving their country? Serov answered only that the deportation was a "temporary measure" required by the war effort and that most of the Chechens would return shortly. There is no record in the family archive of Malsagov's reaction to Serov's promise. I'd like to believe Malsagov, the young, loyal party member, sincerely believed it, but I wonder if he ever entertained the possibility that his superiors acted on ulterior motives, if he suppressed his apprehension for fear of jeopardizing his status. I never got the chance to ask him.

On February twenty-fourth, the second day of the deportation campaign, Malsagov was sent high into the mountains of southwest Chechnya. The expulsion of the villagers here had been postponed because of bad weather. Sleet was falling, there was a cold wind, and the mountain roads were blocked by snow.

More than a thousand Chechens from the area had been gathered in Khaibakh, an ancient village overlooked by a famous sixteenth-century fortified stone tower, for transport to Central Asia. As the convoy waited for the weather to clear, the NKVD, copying what was happening at Auschwitz perhaps at the same moment, declared several hundred villagers — old people, pregnant women, children — unfit for transit. When the weather improved on the twenty-sixth, the convoy left them behind. They were led into a large barn in the shadow of the famous stone tower. As Malsagov tried to figure out what was happening, someone nailed the barn doors closed. There was a shout of "Fire!" and Malsagov saw pink-orange flames envelop the barn. Soldiers and NKVD agents had stuffed the windows full of straw and poured gasoline all over it.

Malsagov was paralyzed by shock. When he came to his senses, he ran up to Mikhail Gveshiani, the NKVD general in charge of the operation. Gveshiani said that he was acting on the authority of Stalin and Beria, and threatened to execute Malsagov if he interfered. The fire was beginning to consume the rickety building, and some of the captives managed to push their way out through the flames. "Shoot!" Gveshiani barked, and the dispersing women and children were cut down by machine guns.

As I read Malsagov's account of the massacre and what he witnessed after being sent, under guard, down the mountain to the nearby village of Malkhesty — corpses in every house, a mother dead in one front-room, her two children dead on her lap — I was astonished by his restrained — muted, even — tone. All the facts were there, but the intense emotions he must have felt were not. His was the same evenly pitched, matter-of-fact voice I had heard from some of the people I'd interviewed in previous days as they discussed the possibility of war and collapse in Chechnya. In another context, I reflected, their restraint would have seemed rather English, though I wasn't sure the modern-day English any longer displayed this kind of self-control. The Chechen version was sustained by a clear-eyed realism: talking things up here wouldn't make them any more tolerable.

With Malsagov, it was something else as well. In the twenty-first-century West, the Stalin era is a synonym for terror, but sixty years ago, amid rapid industrialization and increasing literacy, this must have been difficult to make out for a loyal Soviet apparatchik. For a long time, it seemed, Malsagov couldn't imagine that the massacre at Khaibakh had been perpetrated not by rogue officers, but at the behest of the political order he venerated. Like that other tenacious witness, Aleksandr Solzhenitsyn, Malsagov was a faithful Communist — faithful to the political theory and its promises — and when he sought justice, he did so through the instruments of the state. This was typical of Soviet dissenters, but Malsagov's was also a uniquely tragic case of bearing witness. As the custodian of the massacre's memory but also an inadvertent hand in its taking place, Malsagov's remembrance was by definition an act of self-incrimination, and also of expiation.

The massacre at Khaibakh would shape another man's life as well. Among the victims that day were four people from the nearby village of Yalkhoroi — an old woman, her daughter, and her two children, aged eight and eleven. A month before, there had been a birth in the family, a boy, to another daughter of the old woman. During the deportation, that part of the family had been sent down into the valley and shipped off to the Kazakh city of Pavlodar. Though Khrushchev would revoke the deportation order in 1957, except for several brief visits, the boy wouldn't return to

Chechnya until 1991, when he returned as president. His name was Jokhar Dudayev.

As for Malsagov, he believed that Gveshiani was exceeding his orders that day at Khaibakh, and, defying Gveshiani's warning, complained to a string of NKVD officers. He was shrugged off and admonished not to talk about what he had witnessed. In Grozny, General Serov himself reprimanded Malsagov.

Six weeks later, Malsagov was ordered into exile in Kazakhstan. From there, he wrote a letter to Stalin, describing what he had seen at Khaibakh, and was warned by the secret police — by now renamed the MGB — that he would "lose his head" if he continued to attract attention. Malsagov found work as a lawyer. In 1952, he married a young ethnic Russian woman named Valentina in Alma-Ata, the capital of Kazakhstan. "I was only nineteen!" she would tell me when we met. (And evidently a bit of a rebel to marry an older man, and from a "punished nation" to boot.)

Malsagov's fortune changed in 1953, when Stalin died and succession quarrels broke out between his would-be successors. When Lavrenty Beria, the head of the secret police, was arrested, Malsagov was summoned to Moscow to give evidence against him. Malsagov noticed that while his statements about Beria were fastidiously noted, nothing he said about Serov, now the head of the secret police, or Kruglov, now the Soviet Union's Interior Minister, was recorded. Beria was shot and the case was closed.

Malsagov waited for his moment. It came in July 1956, when Nikita Khrushchev visited Kazakhstan, five months after the "secret speech" in which he first denounced Stalin. He and Valentina conceived a plan: they would put a letter to Khrushchev in the fist of their eighteen-month-old son Zambek, and the boy would "accidentally" drop it near Khrushchev during the welcoming ceremonies outside Communist Party headquarters. It failed: Khrushchev's bodyguards would not let them close. But Malsagov got another chance. As a respected member of the local community — he was now a deputy judge — Malsagov was invited to hear Khrushchev speak at the local opera house. The regional

KGB — the new incarnation of the secret police — answered for the leader's security at the event, and Malsagov knew the man in charge of the detail. Malsagov's friend passed on the letter to Khrushchev.

Khrushchev invited Malsagov for a private conversation. "He received me well," Malsagov told me when we spoke in 1994. Khruschev questioned Malsagov about his claims and asked his guest over and over whether he realized the gravity of the accusations he was making.

Whether Khrushchev was motivated by a search for justice or merely wished to move against Stalin's heirs in the apparat, he organized a secret commission to investigate the Khaibakh killings, and Malsagov was invited on a research trip into the mountains of Chechnya. Based on extensive interviews and excavation near the burned barn, the investigators confirmed Malsagov's story. Both Serov and Kruglov were ousted from their positions.

Six months later, in January 1957, Malsagov opened a telegram and shouted to his wife: "We're going home!" The letter was an invitation to join a "return committee" organizing the repatriation of the Chechens and the Ingush. The privilege included a new apartment in the English House on Victory Prospect. That year, tens of thousands of Chechens rushed home by train, rattling boxes filled with the bones of their deceased relatives, whom they wanted to re-bury in their ancestral graveyards. They begged, bought, and argued their way back into their old houses, some falling apart in disrepair, others occupied by ethnic Russians or North Caucasians who had settled in the region while the Chechens were gone.

A year later, a large crowd of ethnic Russians staged a rally in the center of Grozny, calling for the return of the "bandit" Chechens to Central Asia. Dziyaudin and Valentina unwisely got involved, going into the street and arguing back. Dziyaudin would pay for his rash behavior. When Valentina went to Grozny airport one spring day in 1959 to meet her husband, who was studying for a new law degree in Moscow, she was greeted by three gray-suited KGB officers, who drove her back home and began to rummage through the apartment. Eventually, they informed her that her husband had been arrested on a charge of "anti-Soviet agitation and propaganda." Malsagov would spend the next four and a half years in prison camps. Valentina would lose her job, return to school, and struggle to bring up their two young sons alone.

One day, as she was about to take the entrance exam in history at the University of Grozny, Valentina received a letter from her husband. He wrote that he had been forcibly admitted to a psychiatric hospital in Leningrad, where political dissidents were often declared insane and suppressed. Valentina placed the letter in her pocket, went to the university, and wrote her entrance exam essay about Mikhail Sholokhov's "The Fate of Man," a standard Soviet text, the implications of whose title suddenly no longer seemed so banal to her.

◇ ◇ ◇

Malsagov was released on New Year's Eve, 1963. The years of stagnation followed: Soviet citizens got their own apartments, complained about queues, took their annual holiday to the Black Sea. Writers wrote for the "top drawer," knowing they couldn't publish, but that no one would arrest them either. Few protested. Malsagov was one of them, calling for a public reckoning with what had happened at Khaibakh. He wrote letter after letter, but to little avail. The official line during the Brezhnev era was that exile had been beneficial for the Chechens, as time in another part of the country had supposedly helped them modernize. When I visited the Malsagovs in 1994, Valentina had passed me a bundle of letters tied with string: copies of all the letters Dziyaudin had ever written about Khaibakh. There must have been thirty letters there.

By 1990, the decaying monolith was finally beginning to expire. The executioners were dying out: that year, Ivan Serov died peacefully, forty six years later than the people he had ordered killed in Khaibakh. People began to declaim about Stalin's crimes. The new human rights organization Memorial started to dig up mass graves. The Soviet Union began to fly apart centrifugally: Chechnya declared sovereignty, and Jokhar Dudayev stepped down from the Soviet Air Force to be elected Chairman of the new Congress of the Chechen People. A year later he was president declaring independence for a would-be republic.

What the increased openness also meant was that the Chechen deportation was discussed publicly for the first time, Malsagov's goal for so long. For several years, he was feted and interviewed. Newspapers ran long exposés about Khaibakh, there was a documentary, and journalists tried to track down Mikhail Gveshiani, only to discover that he had died in the 1960s. In the summer of 1990, Malsagov was invited to participate in a new investigation of the Khaibakh killings. Near the ruined barn, Malsagov and the others dug up charred bones, spent bullets, and skulls pierced with neat circular holes.

Soon enough, Khaibakh became a rallying point for Jokhar Dudayev, who seemed to have little trouble summoning the emotion that Malsagov did not. The Dudayevs and Malsagovs came from the same ancestral village, Stary Achkhoi. Surely Dudayev realized the value of an endorsement from a man like Dziyaudin Malsagov, and one day, after learning that the elders of the Malsagov family, including Dziyaudin, had gathered for a *movlid,* a get-together for a clan's patriarchs, in the village, Dudayev paid his respects, slaughtering for them a sheep he had bought along the way.

I sensed that the gesture had done little to impress the Malsagovs. It seemed they viewed Dudayev's rise to power with distaste, his defiance of Russia a reckless stunt. Dziyaudin was too infirm to tell me what he thought about Dudayev when I visited him, and his family members were noticeably reluctant to criticize a man rapidly turning into a dictator. But something one of Malsagov's daughters-in-law said made it clear to me that there was little love in that household either for the Russian authorities or Dudayev. As I was leaving, she complained about the cost of medicine for her father-in-law, and I naively expressed surprise that the government — some government — wasn't funding the treatment for this man, the conscience of an entire nation.

"No one cares about us," she said. "They worry about other things."

◇ ◇ ◇

I kept coming back to Chechnya. Eventually, I would make ten trips in just over four years. Every time, things seemed to be getting worse. Too close to what was happening, I disbelieved the evidence around me. In early December, 1994, I watched Chechen fighters in Freedom Square hoist their guns in the air and fire at Russian jets, but still I clung to the idea that it was all an elaborate bluff, that war couldn't possibly start.

But start it did, only a week later, with tens of thousands of Russian troops arriving in Chechnya. At least a thousand of them, ambushed in the unfamiliar streets and squares, perished in a battle that began on New Year's Eve, 1994. By the time of my fourth visit to Chechnya, in February 1995, I was a war reporter. (The war dashed hopes large and small. My old South African-Greek acquaintance from the French House, with whom I'd stayed in touch, had actually won approval for his telecom project from the Russian and Chechen bureaucracies, but his contract, slated to go into effect in mid-December, was pre-empted by war.) The disorganized attack and arbitrary slaughter sanctioned by Russian president Boris Yeltsin had turned the faltering Dudayev into a national hero, especially after a force of no more than several hundred Chechen fighters repulsed the New Year's Eve offensive.

I visited again in the summer of 1995, just a month after Chechen fighters led by the commander Shamil Basaev took hundreds of Russians hostage in the town of Budyonnovsk a hundred miles inside Russian territory, embarrassing Russian authorities and taking the war deep into Russia. In Chechnya proper, the Russians had won full control of Grozny, and the Chechen fighters had retreated to the mountains.

The capital was in ruins, and much of the center simply no longer existed. On Victory Prospect, only the facades remained, the buildings behind them scooped out by bombs. The great Soviet apartment blocks across the river from Freedom Square had become mounds of rubble. The air smelled of brick dust and upturned earth. Walking around town, I had an inkling of what Malsagov must have felt at Khaibakh: speechlessness, and the strongest urge to record what I was witnessing.

I had not seen the Malsagovs since my first visit. The poplars in the courtyard of the English House were rippling and green. It was summer, after all. For all its cruelty, war, I learned, was never permanent or total. Shrubbery was pushing its way through the shattered facades of Victory Prospect, and merchants were re-grouping on the sidewalks, selling Fanta or kebabs. Survivors did not pause for reflection, they carried on.

Valentina had survived, and her apartment had been spared during the bombing. She was watching *Santa Barbara* with a neighbor when I appeared. I asked her about Dziyaudin. Malsagov had seen out the fiftieth anniversary of Khaibakh, she said, and died three months after my visit with him, before the war had begun.

"Thank God he did not see all this," Valentina said. "It would have broken his heart."

Valentina's mother, who lived on the other side of the Sunzha river, which divided Grozny, had not been as lucky. The Malsagovs had not managed to reach her before the bombing, and she was dead, not from Russian bombs, but of hunger, cold, and fear. Of the thousands killed by the Russian Army in its advance that year, many were Russian pensioners.

I made another trip a year later, in the autumn of 1996, after, defying all expectations, Dudayev's rebels had routed the Russian Army, retaking the city of Grozny in a fierce offensive that began during the ceremony marking the inauguration of Yeltsin's second term and lasted less than twenty-four hours. Chechen gunmen, rocket-propelled grenades slung over their shoulders, were now moving back into town. Jokhar Dudayev was not leading their triumphant return — he had been killed by a Russian missile a few months before. He had become a martyr, and the returning fighters made a bid to rename the capital Jokhar.

Valentina lived out the battle for Grozny outside the city, with friends. Now she decided to return home. (No retaliation by ethnic Chechens against ethnic Russians took place in Grozny at the end of the war, as there had been no animosity between them before it. This was a political, not an ethnic conflict.) Her apartment was mostly intact, though it had been looted. One wing of the English House had been demolished, and bombs had also destroyed the Malsagovs' ancestral home in Stary Achkhoi, where Dudayev had barbecued lamb for the family elders, as well as the adjoining apple orchard.

So many people had died in the conflict that the 1944 Khaibakh massacre no longer seemed such an exceptional crime. Preoccupied by the daily horrors of the war, I had barely thought of the massacre at the village. But the end of the fighting restored the luxury of reflection, and I recalled that fateful place high in the mountains. Two colleagues and I found a couple of guides and someone who had a truck that could manage the mountain roads.

The beeches were already gilding with the colors of autumn on the day we set out; it was probably one of the last days of the year we could make a trip into the mountains, which become impassable in mid-October. We set off from the plains at dawn and traveled for three hours up a road bruised by rubble and ruts. We all stood at the back of the truck, holding onto its sides for balance as we bounced up steep inclines, half-expecting to have to turn back at any moment. Once, we had to squeeze between a boulder that barred the road and a sheer drop down a ravine. Finally, the woods thinned out, the road ended, and we walked another two hours up a chilly path into the hills.

We saw no one all day. The medieval tower, a masterwork of masonry, soared forty feet above the abandoned village. Apples were clogging the branches of the trees in the graveyard with its tall, pointed tombstones, in the Chechen style. I have never been anywhere so remote or so tranquil.

In January 1997, I came back to Grozny for the presidential election that would bring the moderate rebel commander Aslan

Maskhadov to power. In the intervening months, the concluding war had struck one last time at the Malsagov household. Valentina's younger son, Oleg, disappeared one day and went missing for a week. His body was discovered by the side of the road in western Chechnya. No one knew who had killed him. Valentina supposed it had been departing Russian soldiers.

When I visited her, Valentina was in the courtyard, feeding a dusty kitten. She was impassive, her grief suppressed somewhere very far within. It was almost forty years to the day that she and Dziyaudin had moved into the apartment in the English House. Back then, she said, her husband had been virtually the only Chechen, surrounded as they were by ethnic Russians who had moved in while the Chechens were in Central Asia. "Now," she said flatly, "I am the only Russian left."

◇ ◇ ◇

Five years passed before I saw any of the Malsagovs again, and I worried about the place and people that had become so dear to me. There was no good news out of Chechnya. The rebel commanders in charge fell out amongst themselves, turning to crime and kidnapping. In some ways, it was more dangerous than during the war. When I visited Grozny in the summer of 1998 — my last visit, to report on the abduction of two British aid workers — I was allowed to stay for only two days, and was required to travel with four government-supplied bodyguards, who became very anxious any time I wished to stop. I saw almost no one and felt like a thief, stealing through Grozny in the back of a car. I passed close to Valentina's house, but could not persuade my guardians to let me go in.

In 1999, war started again. The last surviving parts of Grozny collapsed, and Victory Prospect mostly ceased to exist. In 2002, Zambek, the older Malsagov son, who had moved to Russia, tracked me down and e-mailed me. He said his mother was in a Moscow hospital, having an operation on her legs.

We met outside a Moscow metro station. Zambek was limping, and his words were disjointed. He had been detained after a traffic policeman who had stopped his car saw in his internal passport that he was from Grozny. He was arrested and jailed in the town of Tula, about seventy miles south of Moscow. Almost a year would pass before the charges were dropped and he was released. His only offense was being a Chechen male.

The hospital's corridors gave off that uniquely Russian scent of disinfectant and sour cabbage soup. I couldn't see any doctors, and patients on metal gurneys lay like beached fish in corridors and foyers. Valentina wore a flowery housedress and embraced me. Her legs had almost given up, she said, and her heart was weak. She had aged, and spoke more quietly than before.

"I don't know how we survived under Maskhadov," she said. "But the second war is even worse than the first." The English House was now entirely in ruins; Valentina's apartment had gone up in flames. Russian soldiers appeared on frequent "clean-up" raids, supposedly looking for rebels, turning everything upside down and looting. But, she said, she had managed to hide from them my book about Chechnya, which had mentioned her husband's heroic exploits.

In the gray-blanketed hospital bed next to Valentina lay a pretty, pale-faced Russian girl with her leg in plaster. Her mother and friends were camped out around her, unwrapping food and drink from shopping bags. One of them poured a measure of Bailey's Irish Cream into a transparent beaker and insisted I drink it with some cake — it was the mother's birthday. Four months before, coming home one evening, Marina became another inadvertent victim of Russia's culture of perpetual, indiscriminate violence — a gang shootout. One stray bullet caught her in the breast, another in the leg. She was lucky to have survived, the doctors said, and would make a full recovery within six months. Her family visited her every day and had relocated all their celebrations and domestic gatherings to her bedside.

The matter-of-fact way in which Marina related her story reminded me of how Valentina spoke of the tragedies that had struck her, and of the way Dziyaudin had written about Khaibakh. The memory of violence was too fresh to allow it to rise to the surface. In Chechnya, they long for normality, at all costs, even denial. After years in Chechnya, I had noticed this even in myself. I became irritable and evasive when people asked about what I had seen. Usually, the person asking the questions expressed more emotion than I could afford to.

The difference between Marina and Valentina, I suppose, was that Marina could return to a normal life. Nothing like that awaited Valentina. But she wouldn't hear of remaining in Moscow. "Of course, I'll go back. Where else would I go?" she said to Zambek when he tried to persuade her.

Valentina Malsagova is the widow not only of the remarkable man who had been her husband, but an entire generation of Chechens scythed down by war, poverty, and daily brutality. There is no end in sight to any of this, no "normal" life to look forward to, and yet, she decided to go back. Like her, the Chechens go on, that great grief still trapped inside them.

VLADIMIR SOROKIN

Translated by Jamey Gambrell

Hiroshima

11:48 P.M.
The Yar Restaurant

Lukashevich, the vice president of a modest but stable bank, and Zeldin, the owner of four supermarkets, were sitting at a table set for three. A gypsy choir sang onstage. Next to the table a birch tree grew in a tub. On the table, a carafe of vodka sparkled, and a platter of salmon glowed red.

The two friends were drunk. They had begun at the Pushkin restaurant: 850 milliliters of Russian Standard vodka, cranberry juice, beer, marinated white mushrooms, stuffed pike, veal pâté, Caesar salad, lamb à la Hussar, sterlet in champagne sauce, crème brûlée, crepes with crème caramel, coffee, cognac, Calvados.

They continued at the Biscuit: 380 ml of tequila, green tea, fruit salad.

"No way, Borya," Lukashevich carelessly lit a cigarette. "These gypsies don't rock."

"You don't like them?" Zeldin filled the shot glasses, spilling vodka on the tablecloth. "I love it when they wail."

"Come on . . . it's so depressing," Lukashevich lifted a shot glass. He splashed the contents onto the birch tree. "Bunch of shit!"

"What, the vodka?" Zeldin didn't understand.

"Everything."

"What everything?"

"I don't like places like this. Let's go to the Bridge. Dance with the girls."

"Right now? Come on, let's have a drink! What's with you, Sasha?" Zeldin embraced Lukashevich. "Everything's great. Hey, wait a minute," he suddenly remembered, "I didn't finish telling you!"

"Telling me what?" Lukashevich stared gloomily.

"About the bell."

"What bell?" Lukashevich was bored.

"The one in Christ the Savior Cathedral! The bass bell! The G note! Thirty-two tons. It's in the southwest wing, I think. Right. Well, that Gazprom broad, you know, the one with lung cancer, she heard that low frequencies destroy cancer cells. She paid them a bundle. So every evening they lifted her up along with the bell ringer, and there she was, naked. . . . Sasha, you bastard! I still can't believe you came. Goddammit! You're really here. You're here, you sweaty old asshole!"

Knocking over the carafe of vodka, Zeldin threw himself at Lukashevich and hugged him with all his might. The table teetered. Zeldin's striped jacket split. Lukashevich snarled, and his large, doughy fingers squeezed Zeldin's swarthy neck. Zeldin clenched Lukashevich's white neck.

"You Moscow scumbag!" Lukashevich growled, and they started choking each other.

◇ ◇ ◇

11:48 P.M.
Condemned Five-Story Building on Innovator Street

Two homeless men, Valera and Rooster, were sitting on a pile of damp rags in the corner of a gutted apartment. A slim crescent moon shone through the broken window. The men were drunk.

And polishing off a bottle of Russkaya vodka. They'd started drinking early that morning at the Yaroslav train station: a quarter liter of Istok, half a loaf of white bread, chicken scraps from the grill bar. Then they rode to Sokolniki Park, collected some empty bottles, turned them in and continued: three bottles of Ochakov beer and two poppy seed danishes. Then they had a nap on a bench and rode to Novodevichy Convent, where they begged for alms until evening. They got enough for a bottle of Russkaya.

"That's it," Valera drank down the last drop in the dark.

"You finished it?" Rooster croaked. "Fucking shit . . ."

"What?"

"I've got the shakes, goddammit. Like I didn't have a drop. I could use another swig."

"We'll go to Izmailovo tomorrow. We'll load up hard-core! Tomorrow! Tomorrow!" Valera began to laugh loudly and sing something incomprehensible.

"What do you mean, tomorrow?" said Rooster, slugging him.

"Shit! I'm pissing my pants, brother! Again! Holy fuck!" laughed Valera.

"You dick-face . . . asshole . . ." Rooster punched him lamely.

"What're you . . . Oh, go fuck yourself!" Valera hit him back.

They were quiet for a moment. A fire truck passed by noisily outside the window.

"A gangstermobile?" Rooster yawned.

"A cement crusher," Valera objected authoritatively.

They sat quietly.

"Tomorrow! To — moooooorrrrow! Fuuuuuccccccckkkkking tomooorrrrroooow!" Valera started singing and laughing again, opening his mouth of rotten teeth wide in the dark.

"Just shut the fuck up, you piece of shit!" shouted Rooster and grabbed him by the throat.

Valera wheezed and grabbed back.

They began choking each other.

◊ ◊ ◊

11:48 P.M.
An Apartment on Sivtsev Vrazhek

Alex, a dancer, and Nikola, a web designer, were lying in bed naked. Mozart's Fortieth Symphony played quietly in the background. Nikola was smoking while Alex cut cocaine on a compact disk of Alexander Laertsky's *Udder*. They had begun twenty four hours earlier at the birthday party of a makeup-artist friend (0.5 grams + orange juice), then continued at Tabula Rasa (0.3 grams + mineral water, flat) and Niagara (0.8 grams + mineral water, flat + two cigars). After that, having had some green tea at Shot Glass, they went to a morning showing of *Attack of the Clones*. Then they went out to the dacha of a woman designer they didn't know very well (1.3 grams + sparkling mineral water + fruit tea + 150 ml whiskey + apple juice + strawberry tart + grapes + candy + 150 ml of apricot liqueur + strawberries + green tea + strawberries with whipped cream). In the evening they returned to Nikola's place (0.4 grams).

"Just a tiny bit, Kol. We'll finish it off," said Alex, who was making two puny lines with a discount card from a "Party" store.

"Is that all there is?" Nikola squinted his beautiful glazed eyes.

"That's it, now — all gone."

They silently snorted the cocaine through a plastic straw. Alex wiped up the cocaine dust with his thin finger and gently touched it to the head of Nikola's member. Nikola looked at his member.

"You want to?"

"I always want to."

"Listen, do we have any whiskey left?"

"We never had any to start."

"Really?" Nikola tensed with surprise. "Well, what do we have?"

"Only vodka." Alex gently took Nikola's balls in his palm.

"I'm kinda out of it . . ." Nikola stretched.

"I'll get it."

Alex sprang up and glided to the kitchen. Nikola stubbed out his cigarette in a steel ashtray. Alex returned soundlessly with vodka and a shot glass. He poured. Nikola drank. Alex kneeled down in front of him and slowly ran his tongue around the lilac-colored head of Nikola's member.

"But first do it like velvet, hedgehog," said Nikola, licking his dry lips.

"Yep, massah," said Alex in English, taking two velvet women's belts — one black, one purple — off the chair.

They lay on the bed, pressed their bodies together, and wrapped their legs around each other. Alex looped the purple belt around Nikola's neck; Nikola wound the black one around Alex's. Their lips came together, opened, and their tongues touched. They began choking each other.

◆ ◆ ◆

11:48 P.M.
A Hut in the Village of Kolchino

Two old women, Niura and Matryona, were kneeling and praying before a dark icon case. The blue flame of the icon lamp barely illuminated the faces of Saint Nikola, the Savior, and the Virgin Mother. It was dim and damp in the hut.

"To you we pray Lord Jesus Christ, Son of God, and to Your Immaculate Mother and our Lord in Heaven and all the Holy Saints, hear our prayers and have mercy upon us."

"Amen," the old women murmured separately. They crossed themselves, bowed, touched their foreheads to the uneven floor, and with a creak began to stand up.

Matryona got up first. She helped Niura up by her bony elbow.

"Oof, God almighty . . ." Niura straightened up with great difficulty, took a step toward the bench, sat down.

"Maybe you'll write to Vasily after all?" asked Matryona, walking over to the table.

"No. No strength left," Niura started breathing hard.

"Well, I wrote a note to my people. Let them come."

"Mine hasn't been by for eight months. Oy, everything aches," moaned Niura. "On with it then, no point. . . ."

Matryona lifted the tablecloth. Underneath, beside the bread and salt, was a plate with one pancake. Matryona took the pancake, sat down next to Niura, and split it in half.

"Here, eat. I made it this morning."

"Just one?" Niura took the half-pancake with her thin, shaking hands.

"So what . . . Just one. With cow's butter. Eat."

"I'll eat."

They ate in silence, chewing with their toothless mouths. Matryona finished, wiped her mouth with her brown hand, got up, took Niura by the elbow.

"Let's go, praise God."

"Let's go . . . Lord Almighty . . ." The old woman rose with difficulty as she finished chewing.

They went out to the dark mudroom with the rotten floor. Moonlight broke through holes in the roof. A hemp rope with two nooses had been thrown over the ceiling beam. Matryona led Niura to the nooses. She helped her put one of them around her neck. Then she put on her own. Niura wore her new white scarf with blue polka dots. Matryona had put on her old black one, with the white speckles. Matryona clasped Niura by her bony shoulders and hung on her. Niura let out a sob, and hiccuped. The nooses tightened and the old women's legs gave way.

◇ ◇ ◇

11:48 P.M.
Boarding School No. 7, Kindergarten Dormitory

Five-year-old Rita and Masha were lying in their beds, side by side, their eyes open, and staring at the ceiling. The other sixteen children were asleep. On the opposite side of the wall, the nanny and the night guard were making love.

A car drove by outside the window. Strips of light slid across the ceiling.

"A dragon," said Masha.

"Nooo. A giraffe," Rita sniffed.

The nanny made muffled grunts on the other side of the wall.

"What is Nina Petrovna doing in there?" asked Masha.

"She and Uncle Misha are choking each other."

"What does that mean?"

"They lie in bed naked and choke each other. With their hands."

"What for?"

"It's how babies happen. And 'cause it feels good. My mama and papa do it all the time. They undress all the way and just do it. Do yours?"

"I don't have a papa."

They were quiet for a while. Another car drove by. And another.

"Oy, oh my, oy, Mish . . . Not that way. . ." the nanny muttered on the other side of the wall.

Masha raised her head:

"Rita. You wanna choke each other?"

"But we'll have babies."

They were quiet for a while. Rita thought about it:

"No we won't."

"Why not?"

"We aren't a man and a lady."

"Oh . . . then let's do it, okay?"

"Okay. Only we have to take our clothes off."

"Noooo! It's cold. Let's do it like this."

"If we're not naked it won't work."

"Really?"

"Uh-huh."

"All right."

They spent a long time taking off their pajamas. They got into Masha's bed. They grabbed each other by the neck. And began choking each other.

◇ ◇ ◇

The aforementioned Lukashevich, Valera, Alex, Matryona, and Rita didn't see anything in particular during the process of choking.

But Zeldin, Rooster, Nikola, Niura, and Masha observed a series of orange and crimson flashes, which gradually turned into a threatening purple glow. Then the purple light began to dim, changing to dark blue, and suddenly opened up into a huge, endless expanse. There was an unbelievably spacious, ash-gray landscape, lit from the dark-purple sky by a huge full moon. Despite the night, it was bright as day. The moon illuminated the low ruins of a burned-out city in minute detail. A scattering of stars glittered in the sky. A naked woman walked among the ruins. Her white, moonlit body radiated a mesmerizing sense of calm. She did not belong to the world on whose ashes she walked. In those ashes and ruins lay people injured by the blast. Some moaned, some were already dead. But their moans did not disturb the woman's calm. She moved serenely, stepping over the dead and the moaning. She was looking for something else. Finally, she stopped. Among the melted bricks lay a pregnant bitch, mortally wounded. A large part of her body was burned, and her rib bones protruded through clumps of skin and fur. Breathing heavily and whining, she was trying to give birth. But she no longer had the strength for birthing. The dog was dying; her entire disfigured body shuddered, tensing powerlessly. Bloody spittle drooled from her crimson mouth, and her pink tongue hung out.

The woman lowered herself onto the ashes next to the dog. She placed her white hands on the bitch's singed belly. She pressed down. The dog's dirty, blood-spattered legs spread slightly. She squealed weakly. Puppies began to squeeze out of her womb: one, another, a third, a fourth, and a fifth. A spasm convulsed the bitch's body. She glanced at the woman with a mad, wet eye, yawned, and died. The wet black puppies stirred sluggishly, poking their muzzles into the gray ash. The woman picked them up and held them to her breasts. And the blind puppies drank her milk.

Contributors' Notes

GARY SHTEYNGART was born in Leningrad in 1972, and came to the United States seven years later. His novel, *The Russian Debutante's Handbook,* won the Stephen Crane Award for First Fiction, was named a *New York Times* Notable Book, and was chosen a Best Book of the Year by the *Washington Post Book World* and *Entertainment Weekly.* His work has appeared in *The New Yorker, Granta,* and many other publications. He lives in New York City.

TOM BISSELL was born in 1974 in Escanaba, Michigan. He has traveled within Uzbekistan, Kyrgyzstan, and Afghanistan, both as a (short-lived) Peace Corps volunteer and as a journalist. His first book, *Chasing the Sea,* an account of his journey to the Aral Sea in Uzbekistan, the world's largest man-made ecological catastrophe, was published by Pantheon in September 2003. Pantheon will publish his short-story collection *Death Defier and Other Stories from Central Asia* in August 2004. A former book editor, Bissell has published work in many magazines, including *Harper's, Men's Journal, McSweeney's, Alaska Quarterly Review,* and *BOMB.* He lives in New York City.

ARTHUR PHILLIPS was born in Minneapolis and educated at Harvard. He lived in Budapest from 1990 to 1992. He is the author of the novel *Prague* and has been a child actor, a jazz musician, a speech-writer, a dismally failed entrepreneur, and a five-time *Jeopardy!* champion. He now lives in South Carolina with his wife and two sons.

WENDELL STEAVENSON was born in New York in 1970 and grew up in London. She wrote for *Time* magazine before moving to Georgia, where she spent two years living in Tbilisi. She now lives in Iran, where she reports for various newspapers. Her book *Stories I Stole* is published by Grove/Atlantic.

JOSIP NOVAKOVICH emigrated to the U.S. from Croatia at the age of twenty. He writes in English and doesn't miss his mother tongue (Croatian). Josip's collection of stories, *Salvation and Other Disasters,* won a Whiting Award, an American Book Award from the Before Columbus Foundation, and was a *New York Times* Notable Book. The story appearing in this anthology will appear in his new collection, *Infidelities: Stories of Lust and War,* to be published by HarperCollins next year. He lives in Warriors Mark, PA, and teaches at Penn State.

ALEKSANDAR HEMON was born in 1964, in Sarajevo, Bosnia-Herzegovina. He came to the U.S. as part of a monthlong cultural exchange program of journalists and was supposed to return to Sarajevo on May 1, 1992, the same day that Sarajevo came under siege. Instead he was granted political asylum and has lived in Chicago ever since. He is the author of *The Question of Bruno* and *Nowhere Man.* His fiction has also been published in *The New Yorker, Granta, TriQuarterly, Ploughshares, Luisitania, The Paris Review, McSweeney's,* and *Chicago Review.* He received a Guggenheim Fellowship in 2003.

PAUL GREENBERG is a writer based in New York City. His debut novel, a post-Soviet love story called *Leaving Katya,* was selected for the spring 2002 Barnes and Noble Discover Great New Writers series and excerpted in the *New York Times.* His essays, commentaries, and humor have appeared in *The Boston Globe, Forward,* and on NPR's *All Things Considered.* For much of the 1990s Greenberg lived and worked in the former Soviet Union and the Balkans, where he trained journalists and produced the first post-war satellite bridge between Belgrade and Sarajevo.

MILJENKO JERGOVIĆ was born in Sarajevo in 1966. A poet and journalist, he writes for the daily newspaper *Oslobodjenje*. He is the author of the collection *Sarajevo Marlboro* and the novels *Mama Leone* and *Buick Riviera*.

JOHN BECKMAN, a native Iowan, has taught literature at universities in Poland and France, and he is currently an assistant professor of English at the U.S. Naval Academy in Annapolis, Maryland. He has creative writing degrees from the Iowa Writers' Workshop and the University of California, Davis, where he also received a Ph.D. in English literature on the topic of American Fun. His first novel, *The Winter Zoo,* was a *New York Times* Notable Book of 2002.

CHARLOTTE HOBSON was born in Wiltshire, England, in 1970. She read Russian at Edinburgh University and went on to spend much of the 1990s living, working, and travelling in Russia. Her book *Black Earth City* won the Somerset Maugham Award and was short-listed for the Duff Cooper Prize and the Thomas Cook Travel Book Award in 2002. She lives in St. Mawes, Cornwall, and divides her time between writing and translation.

THOMAS DE WAAL has spent much of his adult life with, in, and around Russia and the Caucasus region to its south. He studied Russian and Modern Greek at Oxford and has worked as a reporter for the BBC World Service, *The Moscow Times, The Times* of London and *The Economist.* He currently edits a newsletter on the Caucasus and runs a program for Armenian, Azerbaijani, Georgian, and Russian print journalists with the Institute for War and Peace Reporting (IWPR) in London. He and co-author Carlotta Gall were widely praised for their book *Chechnya: Calamity in the Caucasus* (1998) and in 2003, as sole author, he published *Black Garden: Armenia and Azerbaijan Through Peace and War* (both New York University Press).

VLADIMIR GEORGIEVICH SOROKIN was born August 7, 1955 in the Moscow region. In 1977 he graduated from the Oil and Gas Institute with a degree in mechanical engineering, though he never worked as an engineer. In the West his novels have been published by Gallimard, S. Fischer Verlag, DuMont, and others. Sorokin is currently writing the libretto for an opera commissioned from composer Leonid Desiatnikov by the Bolshoi Theater.